BRIAR HEART

By MERCEDES LACKEY

HUNTER

Hunter

Elite

Apex

Briarheart

MERCEDES LACKEY

LITTLE, BROWN AND COMPANY
New York Boston

Copyright © 2021 by Mercedes Lackey

Image credits: Title page (shield): © Andrey_Kuzmin/Shutterstock.com; chapter openers (branch): © RachenStocker/Shutterstock.com; chapter openers (butterfly): © Vladimirkarp/Shutterstock.com

Cover art by Sammy Yuen. Cover design by Sammy Yuen.
Cover copyright © 2021 by Hachette Book Group, Inc.

Little, Brown and Company
Hachette Book Group
1290 Avenue of the Americas, New York, NY 10104
Visit us at LBYR.com

First Edition: October 2021

Little, Brown and Company is a division of Hachette Book Group, Inc. The Little, Brown name and logo are trademarks of Hachette Book Group, Inc.

The publisher is not responsible for websites (or their content) that are not owned by the publisher.

Library of Congress Cataloging-in-Publication Data
Names: Lackey, Mercedes, author.
Title: Briarheart / Mercedes Lackey.
Description: First edition. | New York : Little, Brown and Company, 2021. |
Audience: Ages 12 & up. | Summary: "When Miriam's younger sister, Princess Aurora, is born, she must learn to harness her new magical powers to protect her sister and the kingdom." —Provided by publisher.
Identifiers: LCCN 2020048431 | ISBN 9780759557451 (hardcover) | ISBN 9780759557864 (ebook) | ISBN 9780759557468 (ebook other)
Subjects: CYAC: Sisters—Fiction. | Princesses—Fiction. | Magic—Fiction. | Fairy tales.
Classification: LCC PZ7.L13543 Br 2021 | DDC [Fic]—dc23
LC record available at https://lccn.loc.gov/2020048431

ISBNs: 978-0-7595-5745-1 (hardcover), 978-0-7595-5786-4 (ebook)

Printed in the United States of America

LSC-C

Printing 1, 2021

DEDICATED TO THE MEMORY OF CHLOE
MARCELLA MEDHURST.
SLEEP IN PEACE, TINY TANK.

PROLOGUE

THIS IS A KIND OF FAE TALE. SO I'LL BEGIN IT THE WAY ALL good Fae tales should.

Once upon a time...

Once upon a time, there was a handsome, strong, gentle knight, the King's Champion, Sir Geniver. He was married to a beautiful lady, Alethia, and they had a daughter they loved very much who loved them with all her heart.

(That would be me.)

Because he was the King's Champion, Sir Geniver could have had whatever he wanted, but his wants were modest, so the family lived in a small but comfortable manor on the edge of the Veridian Forest, thanks to the stipend the King provided.

They had everything they needed. A staff of eight, exactly enough to make life pleasant and easy even though one of those eight was Lady Alethia's old governess, who simply could not grasp that the daughter would never be the sort of lady she was expected to be. They were near enough to the palace to be called on at need but far enough that neither Lady Alethia nor their daughter, Miriam, needed to be troubled by the pomp and politics of the Court. As the King's Champion, Geniver was not involved with the Court itself since he didn't rank high enough—by his own choice—to get tangled up in politics and policy. There was no Queen, so Lady Alethia did not need to join the other married ladies at the Court as one of the Queen's ladies-in-waiting. This is how courts work. The King's Court handles the "business of the realm," the Queen's Court handles the "business of the palace," and if there is a Crown Prince or Princess with a court of their own, they handle the "business of learning to rule." And not being part of the Court meant Miriam didn't have to navigate the potentially dangerous waters of a palace full of *other* daughters.

Sir Geniver understood his daughter even if her governess did not. So he taught her to climb trees (and not to do it in her good gowns) and took her on breakneck rides, first tucked before him on his gigantic black warhorse and later following after him on her own little pony. He gave her books her governess would never have approved of, books on battles and swordsmanship. And he taught her how to defend herself with the dagger he gave her that never left her side.

This is not to say that her mother didn't understand Miriam too—her mother also knew her daughter very well. And though sometimes she might have sighed because Miriam did not revel in pretty things, she was proud of her daughter's intelligence and willingness to learn almost anything, and said so, much to the exasperation of the governess.

Sir Geniver was the King's best friend. He and the King were together nearly every day since the manor was close enough to the palace to ride there in an hour, and sometimes the King came to visit—quietly. When he did, it was without his crown, and he would stand on no ceremony, even descending to play silly games that had everyone laughing hysterically (except Belinda the governess, who was scandalized). "You have a treasure in your keeping, and that is your family, Gen," he'd say as he slipped back to the palace. "Never lose it."

And everything was wonderful until the terrible day when war came to Tirendell, and the King's Champion rode off to command the army in the King's name and never came home again.

With his death, Sir Geniver brought victory, but that wasn't much consolation for Lady Alethia even though the King made her a Court Princess and did his best to make sure she and her daughter would never want for anything.

In retrospect, I think Mama and I were too caught up in our grief to notice for a long time just how *very* attentive the King was—but it certainly didn't escape the notice of most of the Court. People began paying a lot more attention to us, and people who wouldn't have paid much heed to the widow of a mere knight with only the land of the manor garden—even if her former husband had been the King's Champion—started hanging about, maneuvering to get themselves into an advantageous position with us.

I'll admit I thought it was because of Mama's new title; I was only thirteen, and I had no idea that a Court Princess had no real position and that all the title did was confer nobility on her line. For a while, Mama was oblivious too. I *stayed* oblivious, to the fact that she seemed to be feeling better and that I didn't have to work so hard at keeping her spirits up every time something reminded her of Father. So that meant I didn't have to keep bottling things myself, though I'd never let Mama or Belinda see it.

Of course, conferring nobility on Mama was the whole point of making her something other than a simple knight's daughter and knight's widow. Because exactly a year and a day later, during the anniversary of our victory, King Karlson proposed to Mama.

On the State Balcony.

In front of *everyone*.

It was ridiculously romantic.

It was also carefully staged so not a single one of his councilors got a chance to object or suggest someone that would bring Tirendell political advantage. In fact, by the time they all realized what he was about to do, it was too late to do anything about it.

There was a very long speech about how he had loved Mama for years, but she had chosen his best friend, and he was determined not to destroy their happiness by being selfish, but now that she was free, would she consider him? And he knew he could never replace Geniver, but would she—

Well, he never got a chance to finish the speech, because Mama got this expression of wonder on her face and maybe a little relief and just a flash of grief, and then all that turned into the most radiant joy I've ever seen anyone display, and she fell into his arms, and it was all like the ending of a Fae tale.

Except, of course, it wasn't the end. It was the beginning.

And where *my* story properly begins.

CHAPTER ONE

I HAD JUST STOLEN A MOMENT AWAY FROM THE DRESSMAKERS and my fitting to check on my sister. With sun streaming in through the window of the Royal Nursery, I stared down into the cradle at the face of my baby sister and fell in love all over again. It happened every single time I saw her, just as it had the moment she was born. Little Aurora was the most beautiful, perfect rosebud of a baby princess ever.

Of course, I might have been just a little bit prejudiced because we're sisters, but on the other hand, most babies seem to be—how do I put this nicely?—creatures only a mother could love. Some of them look like disagreeable old men even when they're little girls. Some of them look like unbaked bread loaves. Or wizened little Goblin changelings. Most of them are blotchy, red-faced things that emit noise at one end and terrible substances at the other.

But Aurora wasn't like any of those babies. She stared up at me with enormous blue eyes under a head full of delicate golden curls exactly like her papa's; her skin was identical in color and texture to a pink rose petal, her little flower bud of a mouth pursed in an O of surprise. And then, without any warning, her eyes got bigger, and she gurgled with laughter and held up two miniature chubby hands to me, begging to be picked up. She'd just started recognizing people a few days before, and having her realize the big person looming over her cradle was *me* made me warm all over every time.

I wasn't supposed to do anything to muss my christening dress, but what choice did I have? Her Highness commanded, and I must obey. I reached down past the dawn-colored silk curtains into the nest of creamy lambswool-and-linen bedding and took her into my arms.

I hoisted her up onto my shoulder, breathing in that sweet baby scent, part her and part the lavender that all her bedding and clothing were scented with, and jounced her as she cooed and giggled.

"*Who's* the fairest in the land, then?" I asked her, gazing into her beautiful eyes. "*You* are! Yes, yes, yes! Yes, *you* are!"

And of course, at just that moment, my governess and Aurora's nurse, Melalee, came bursting into the nursery, spoiling the moment. "Lady Miriam!" Belinda exclaimed in that fussy tone of voice that made me want to do something hoydenish, like climbing the tower—on the *outside*. "Your gown!"

And Melalee bustled up to me and took Aurora away from me with a suspicious look and a *tsk* that I'd have deserved if I'd been letting her suck on the pommel of a dagger or been caught feeding her honey water but certainly wasn't warranted by a little bouncing and cooing.

Belinda, of course, was concerned about the very expensive

gown—which I suppose was her job since she is my governess, but did she have to act as if Aurora were covered in filth? It wasn't as if Aurora was going to do anything to it that couldn't be undone. And Melalee didn't like anyone touching Aurora who wasn't her, Mama, or Papa.

"My gown is going to withstand a few minutes of baby cuddling, Belinda," I said as Melalee put the little darling back in her nest. And it would; it might be the best gown I'd ever owned, but Mama is very practical about what she has the seamstresses make for us. In fact, we were going to be wearing matching gowns of a green twilled silk that didn't show wrinkles like satin would, that was stronger than gauze, and that was dark enough it wouldn't get dirty by merely looking at it the way a lot of the pale gowns worn by Mama's ladies did. The trim of wide gold braid and our matching belts of the same material were practically as strong as armor, and that trim would probably outlast *me* and be handed down to some great-great descendant.

But the way Belinda fussed, you'd think Aurora was about to spew poisonous yellow ichor all over me like some demon-possessed thing, and this time it was just easier to let her hustle me out. No point in getting her knickers in a twist this close to the christening. I wanted to enjoy it, not be forced to sit in the solar, the room where Mama and her ladies did their fancywork in winter when they couldn't go out. And that's not me being rude; the moment Mama married Papa, I got a whole new set of lessons and duties, and none of them involved sitting in the solar and sewing for hours on end the way Belinda wanted me to do. I was supposed to be learning other languages, dancing, the lute, and history, and I was supposed to be tending the business of my new lands. I'm neither noble enough to be one of Mama's ladies nor old enough to just go and do what I want—like spend half my time exploring on my pony and the other half in the library and maybe getting to know the couple of girls who come there regularly. Belinda's idea of how I should fill the hours involved nothing useful.

The dressmakers had left me unattended for a moment while they looked for the three sets of oversleeves they'd made up so they could decide which set was most appropriate for a christening. Oversleeves, of course, are separate from the gown, and you can have as many of those as you have matching material to make. More practicality on Mama's part; by changing the oversleeves, which were the fanciest part of the gowns, and maybe the belts, we'd have what looked like three entirely different gowns for little more than the price of one. She might be Queen, but Mama still thought about how much things cost as if she were just a lady. She may not have to weigh the cost of roasts against the costs of new gowns, but she said it was up to us to provide good examples of not being extravagant.

The dressmakers were waiting for me in my room, wearing identical expressions of anxiety because I wasn't where they'd left me, as if they were afraid I'd run off to the woods or had done something else inappropriate in my gown.

They were probably so worried about the gown, they'd forgotten I wasn't as flibbertigibbet as Belinda seemed to think I was. They should have known that if I'd decided impulsively to do something *really* inappropriate (as opposed to baby cuddling), I wouldn't be doing it in a silk gown. I'd change into something a whole lot sturdier first. I'd been five or six when Father caught me ruining a new gown by playing mud pies in the garden in it, and I'd never forgotten the gentle but stern lecture he'd given me. And right after that, he'd made sure that I had some clothing suitable for doing the kinds of things I *wanted* to do—things like climbing trees and walls or learning to muck out a horse stall. My "hoyden" clothing wouldn't leave Mama wondering how to get a second dress out of the rags of the first and the remains of the one she'd cut down to fit me.

Besides, I didn't run off impulsively anymore. At least not much.

It wasn't an ordeal to stand quietly in my bedroom while the two women tried on sleeves and twittered at each other. They had the highest voices of any women I had ever heard. I couldn't make up my mind if those were their natural voices or some kind of affectation.

When Papa wed Mama, he surprised me with a bedroom of my own that so answered every one of my wishes, I suspected him of being able to read my thoughts. The ceiling was covered in a painting of the moon and stars. I had an entire *bookshelf* of books—and books are expensive! Every single one of them cost more than Mama's coronation gown, and the only other people who had ever considered a book to be a suitable present for me had been Father and Mama. People who had wanted to curry favor with the King had been giving me silk scarves, small pieces of jewelry, and enough candy to make me sick for weeks. There was a little desk of my own under the bookshelf and a huge bed with a wooden canopy and embroidered green velvet curtains to keep out the cold drafts in the winter. The walls were covered with precious tapestries of forest scenes and the Fae—those were expensive too and made a huge difference in keeping the room warm in cold weather. So while the seamstresses whispered about gussets and tucks and things that evidently made sense to them but not to me, I could stare at the tapestries and find new things I hadn't noticed before.

It wasn't a big room. There was just enough room for several essential pieces of furniture such as a bed and a wardrobe, along with a bookshelf and a dressing table. There wasn't even enough room in here for a bed for Belinda, and I *refused* to let her sleep with me the way she used to when I was younger. And I know it's not kind...but I never liked sleeping with someone else in my room. When I had finally gotten old enough to insist that she not sleep with me, she got the taller bed and I had to sleep on the truckle bed that slid under it during the daytime, which was nothing near as comfortable. But in this room, there wasn't space for a truckle bed, which suited me very well. Now Belinda had to sleep with Mama's ladies and I had the room all to myself.

My room was at a corner, so I had two windows too—and that meant no one else had to go through my room to get to theirs. The palace had been built so long ago that it didn't actually have corridors; people back then thought that they had to use every single inch of space within four walls for a purpose rather than waste it on corridors. And I had my own small fireplace, a great luxury. Since I hadn't seen it until Mama married the King and we moved here, it was hard to tell what the room had been used for before Papa had it made over for me; there were no clues on the walls behind the tapestries. A mystery. I liked to think that it had been for someone like me, someone not a princess but who was clearly loved, someone who had care taken for her comfort.

The seamstresses made up their minds that I was going to have the tightly laced two-part oversleeves that would let the silk chemise show through the lacings. Mama would probably have the big dagged oversleeves that looked like angel wings; they wouldn't want us to look *too* much alike. They finally decided that the fitting was over and let me slip out of the gown into something a lot more robust because today was my day to work in the kitchen. As the seamstresses sped away with drifts of fabric over their arms, I pulled my tough canvas skirt on over my linen chemise, tied my fustian apron over both, and slipped my feet into wooden clogs. Then I ran out through the solar and down the servants' stair to the bottom floor, where all the things that kept the palace going got done. The first room off the stairs was the laundry—which was lovely because when the big outer doors were closed in winter, the steam came up the stairs, carrying with it the scents of clean linen, lavender, and rose water. Then came the drying room, then the ironing room, and then the first of the kitchen rooms, the scullery, where all the pots and pans and dishes were washed. The next room was my goal, the bakery.

"About time, girl!" the chief baker shouted at me. "You're doing manchet bread today! Hop to it!" When I was in the kitchen, I (mostly) got treated like everyone else down here. This was on Papa's orders so I would get used to how servants were treated. Papa had very strong beliefs about how those who ruled should know exactly how those who served were treated and felt.

You might think it strange that here I was, the Queen's daughter, learning to work in a kitchen. You see, we are a very small kingdom. You can stand on the top of Mount Snowdown on the northern border and see all the way to the southern border, and if there had been a mountain on the eastern border, you could have seen all the way to the west. We're at peace with everyone around us *now*, but my father died in the last war only a couple of years ago, so the possibility that war could come again is always on everyone's mind. And though the last war was just between human armies, there was always the chance for something or someone magical and big and powerful to decide that little Tirendell would be a good morsel to gobble up. There is magic of all kinds in this world, and even little Tirendell has its very own wizard. So Papa insisted that I choose something useful to learn in case the kingdom was ever defeated and I might have to hide among the people. "A boy can always make his way as a common fighter," he'd said, and put a finger under my chin to tilt up my face so I could see that he was serious. "I want to be sure my darling Miriam will never go hungry—or find herself exposed and at the mercy of our enemies. No one will look for you up to your arms in flour or tending a stable."

So I decided to learn baking. And the chief baker—Odo— was told to treat me like any other apprentice.

I ran over to my station, where everything was ready, right next to my good friend Giles, who was doing trencher bread today. Trencher bread is a loaf that's sliced in half from end to end and given to servants to eat off of instead of plates. That saves on plate washing. Then, if they're really hungry, they can take it away to eat later, although I never saw any of Papa's servants doing that because Papa makes sure every single person in the palace down to the lowest scullion has plenty to eat. And even if it's not eaten, it's not wasted; the monks come every night and collect everything that isn't eaten and isn't being saved for the next day to give to the poor.

"You're late," Giles said, vigorously kneading his dough. Trencher bread is made of coarser flour than manchet bread, part barley or rye flour or both, as well as unsifted wheat flour. Manchet bread is made only of wheat flour that's been sifted through three sets of cloths. Only the flour used for cake is finer and whiter.

The bakery is a wonderful place to be except in hot weather. If there's anything better than the heavenly smell of baking bread, I don't know what it is, except maybe the smell of baking cakes. And today the air was full of both. There were a lot of conversations going on all over the bakery—the chief baker is strict but fair, and as long as the work is done, he doesn't shout about chattering. And with the christening coming, there certainly was a lot to chatter about.

I rolled up my sleeves, not just because I needed to get them out of the way but because it was good and warm down here. I picked up where the last person at my station had left off, peeking under the cloths over the bowls of second-rise dough first. Sure enough, they were ready, great mounds of creamy-white dough with a tight skin on them, so I carried them over to the bakers. Then I tilted out the bowls of dough on their first rise, punched them back, and covered them with the second-rise cloths. Then I set about making more dough.

I'd already mastered flatbreads, quick breads, and trencher bread. Now I was being given manchet to do, the "king" of the breads. Next I would learn pies, then cakes. But probably not the decorating of the presentation pieces and fancy subtleties; that took years to learn. Odo's brother had a bakery in the town, and if anything terrible happened, I was to run for my life to one of the secret doors out of the palace and go straight to that bakery. There were five of those doors, all hidden in places that were very hard to get into, all built so they couldn't be opened from the outside, and all guarded by Wizard Gerrold's magic so only a few people could use them.

We were making a *lot* of manchet bread; the christening was going to be in three days, and not only was every important person in the kingdom invited, so were a lot of eminent people from the kingdoms on our borders. There would still be cooking going on the days of the christening and celebration, but everything that could be prepared in advance would be. We had a special pantry with a spell on it that ensured whatever was stored in it wouldn't go stale or get moldy, and we intended to stuff it full.

Giles plopped his dough into a bowl and covered it, then measured out flour onto his board and began a new round of dough. I did the same, although my bread got milk instead of water and my dough was going to end up a little stickier than his was. But it would be easier to knead.

"You're soon going to have enough muscle to join the squires," I said, teasing him.

He grinned back. Giles wasn't exactly handsome, but he had dark brown eyes that generally danced with mischief and a mouth made for smiling, and he could always manage to make us laugh. "What makes you think I don't now?" he countered.

"Mostly because you're here in the kitchen instead of out in the yard rolling the barrels to shine the knights' chain mail," I replied.

"*Pish*. This is a better job," he retorted with a toss of his head. "Half of what a squire does is wait on some arrogant, empty-pated bully who swaggers around because someone tapped him on the shoulders with a sword. I'd rather do honest work."

"Not all knights are arrogant, empty-pated bullies," I said, and then, unexpectedly, I choked a little as a vision of my father suddenly sprang up in my mind and I was ambushed out of nowhere by how much I missed him.

I must have sniffed or something, because Giles stopped his mixing and shoved a clean square of cloth at me that he'd taken from the piles of bleached linen rags we used to cover the bread bowls. "Hey now," he said, patting my back. "I didn't mean—I mean, I'm sorry. Sir Geniver was…amazing. *Nobody* would ever have called him arrogant or empty-pated or…Miri, I'm sorry!"

"It's all right," I said, wiping my eyes, blowing my nose, and looking up into his concerned face with a watery smile. "I know you didn't." I choked up again, and he held my head against his shoulder and patted my back until I got control of myself, and Odo left us alone without yelling at us until I did. This wasn't the first time I'd fallen apart in the bakery because something had reminded me of Father, after all; and Odo was probably one of the nicest people you could ever have in charge of you if you were working in a kitchen. When Liss, the girl in charge of cleaning vegetables, got her heart broken by a flirtatious stone carver's apprentice, Odo had someone leave a big pile of clean rags next to her so she could stop and cry whenever she needed to, and he wouldn't let anyone tease her, either.

When I stopped feeling like my throat was too tight to breathe through, I pulled away from Giles, and he let me go with a last pat, and we got back to work.

When Odo dismissed me for the day, my arms were good and tired, but my day wasn't *nearly* done yet. There was still christening business to attend to, and as one of the people who could read and write, I was needed to help with that. If there hadn't been christening business to do, I'd have been going over the accounts from my manor with Papa's seneschal. One of the things Papa had done for me when he married Mama was to give me an estate of my own, which would give me my own income. Which was lovely, but that meant I *also* had to learn how to take charge of it, which involved...well, an awful lot of work. Things like finalizing orders for the work on my property (even though all I was doing was signing off on them, it was important to keep track of what was being done). If I were living there instead of here, I'd be doing even more work—keeping track of the household by taking reports from my chamberlain, my gardener, and my stable master, as well as taking care of the business of the manor properties with my steward or reeve. I'd have to know when the food budget didn't match the food accounted for and be able to inspect stock and crops to know they were healthy and prospering and what to suggest if they were not. For now, Papa had assigned a trusted man as bailiff to tend to all that for me, but if I ever went there to live, I had to know how to do all of that for myself.

But christening business took precedence over everything else right now. Today, it was checking off replies to the invitations on the master list. I was just one of a small army of people doing that, an army that included some of Mama's ladies and several borrowed secretaries, while Mama and the rest of her ladies greeted the incoming guests, saw that they were settled, made sure that they had everything they needed, and oversaw the rest of the arrangements. Of course, not everyone who was invited and intended to come would send a reply, but most would. And there was another reason for sending out invitations.

The Dark Fae.

Every kingdom has Fae, Light and Dark. The Light ones are said to live on human joy, the Dark on human sorrow. Obviously, the more of that sorrow there is, the happier the Dark ones are—which is why they seldom actually *kill* humans. They do things to make us as miserable as possible when we are alive. Fortunately, all the Fae have to obey the Rules, and one of the big ones is that they cannot act against humans unless the humans have harmed or offended them or are experiencing certain very specific times of vulnerability, times that usually correspond either to their ages or to rites of passage like—say—getting married. It's as if there is some sort of protection around us humans for most of our lives, but during those moments, those protections get weaker. For most people, those times don't matter. It's not as if the Dark Fae are keeping track of every single farmer's birthday. But for anyone with rank—people whose misery could impact the lives of dozens to thousands—you have to be mindful of those vulnerable dates because that is when the Dark Fae will jump at the chance to do some harm. Birth, christening, thirteenth birthday, sixteenth birthday, and wedding. And although it is rare for them to go that far, *your entire first year of life* can be a vulnerable time, as can your third and twenty-first birthdays. The more important you are, the more likely it is that you'll have a lot of vulnerable periods. Wizard Gerrold has a theory that this is because the *expectations* around you thin out whatever protection you have. The seneschals have a theory that it has to do with prime numbers. They often get into long congenial arguments about it during state dinners, enlisting whichever guest is nearest if they can.

And there are the Rules. We know that a long time ago, there were no Rules, that the Dark and Light Fae fought with one another indiscriminately and that the Dark Fae could pretty much do what they wanted to humans. That is, until the Light Fae allied with humans, and together we fought the Dark Fae into a corner. And for a while, it seemed that they were perfectly willing to destroy everything rather than surrender, but they finally agreed to a permanent truce. That was the Fae Compact. It was bound in place on all of us by the most powerful of magic, and it laid out a lot of Rules about interactions between Light and Dark Fae and humans. Some of them are simple: Dark Fae can't attack humans or Light Fae unless they have been attacked or offended. Light Fae can't attack Dark Fae (or their human allies, because there are some) unless attacked first. There are more Rules: Unless also attacked, a Light Fae cannot directly aid a human against the Dark Fae, but indirect help is allowed. Those are the main Rules that affect us. There are more, because the Light Fae wanted to give the Dark Fae no loopholes (they find loopholes anyway), but humans don't know most of those Rules and aren't directly affected by them. Breaking the Rules destroys the offender's magic. *All* of it. Which means that if a Fae breaks the Rules, he or she can end up with their home turned into dust and with every curse and spell they have ever cast broken—and there will be a long list of people and Fae they've hurt who will now find them fair game. That's the force of the Fae Compact.

Obviously, you would offend one of the Dark Fae terribly if you were inviting all the important people in the kingdom to a celebration and didn't invite her. Or him, though the worst Dark Fae, insofar as holding grudges goes, seem to be female. The female Dark Fae tends to attack individuals—the male tends to ally himself with really terrible humans and get involved in tyrannies and warfare. No one knows why that is, although Wizard Gerrold once told me that it's because men don't like to hunt alone.

But, of course, they are *Fae*, which means that the next day they could decide to do the opposite. Or both—back up a tyrant and act as his personal assassin, taking out his enemies one by one.

So before you held some great celebration or event, you first had to scour the kingdom for all the Dark Fae and be sure to invite them. Since Dark Fae can't resist announcing themselves by erecting lightning-shrouded towers and gloomy castles, it's not that hard to find them if you go looking for them.

But you could *still* offend them by only inviting them by themselves. So if you were smart, you invited the "Fae Sinistressa and guest(s)." That almost always guaranteed they wouldn't come because the Dark Fae were generally quarreling with one another as well as preying on humanity. You really did not want to live anywhere near one of the Dark Fae, given that they were prone to sending storms and plagues of insects and poisonous miasmas at one another—or calling one another out in mage duels, and you definitely did not want to be within a mile of one of those.

And even if the Dark Fae *did* come, partly because each of them would be very busy looking for any possible chink in the armor of his or her rival and partly because the Rules had been obeyed, there would be nothing they could do unless they were somehow offended by someone doing something they could take as an insult or a challenge. But the odds were that they'd be too busy glaring at one another, making brief alliances, or finding a new nemesis to take any notice of the humans around them.

It would make for a somewhat uneasy event... but that was better than the alternative, which would be for every Dark Fae in the kingdom to take offense. Which they would no matter what you did, because if you thought to escape retribution by simply not having the event in the first place, they'd take offense at *that*.

I ran up to my room and changed for a third time, back into my everyday gown, a lovely soft thing the color of bark. I sat on a stool for a few minutes and let Belinda take down the braids I had wound around my head to work in the bakery and wrap them in matching bark-colored cloth and embroidered ribbons. Then before I went to the library, where the replies to the invitations were sent as they arrived, I ducked into the nursery, gave my baby sister a kiss under Melalee's disapproving glare, and hurried off.

The library, which was where virtually all of the kingdom's paperwork was done, was the brightest room in the palace, with floor-to-ceiling windows and additional lanterns in case of bad weather. I got a fat handful of envelopes; joined the group of ladies-in-waiting, clerks, secretaries, and a couple of novices at the big table; and began my work. And even with all of us, if there were others who could have been spared, they'd have been crowded in here too.

It was pretty boring except when I got a reply from one of the Fae. They had this habit of embellishing their replies. When you opened the envelope from one of the Light Fae, illusory birds might fly out and sing, or vines covered in flowers would grow out of it and vanish, or miniature fireworks could shoot all the way to the ceiling. And as you might imagine, the replies from the Dark Fae needed someone who wasn't easily frightened—spiders would pop out and run over your hands, or the envelope would drip blood on the table, or you'd open the seal and be treated to several minutes of nerve-racking screams. I suppose that every time we opened one of those, the corresponding Fae got a little pinch of extra power, but it seemed to me that it could hardly be enough to make up for the effort that was put into the reply in the first place.

But maybe I was just thinking too logically.

None of these scare tactics counted as "harming" us because the effect was purely emotional and temporary. The Dark Fae were masters at skirting as close as they could to the edge of the Rules without violating them. They lurked in their creepy cottages or lonely swamp towers or fog-shrouded castles or arcane manors under a perpetual night, and I suppose that they fed off the fear of those living nearby. And when they were forgotten, they'd make village appearances, complete with dramatic entrances, to dispense vague threats and remind everyone of their presence. All things considered, if you were a peasant and didn't have the money to move and knew there was a Dark Fae living nearby...you'd be terrified most of the time too, and maybe that sated their appetites.

But, oh, big events like a royal christening would bring them *all* out if only to remind everyone in the entire kingdom that we were never really safe. You never knew, you see, if they'd found another loophole to exploit. The last time that had happened, a piper was going to lure an entire village full of children into a swamp until a heroic goose girl pointed out that the Dark Fae in question had arranged for the piper to be paid in counterfeit coin.

And, of course, the Dark Fae enjoyed reminding us of just that because it kept the unease going even during the happiest of days.

We worked away diligently, underlining the corresponding name on the list of invitees, with a check on the left for "not coming" and one on the right for "coming." And there was a pair of clerks going through the replies we had already opened, making sure we had ticked off the correct side. Then a set of ladies-in-waiting made several lists of "coming" and "not coming" to be distributed to the heralds who could read, so we'd have yet another check at the gates of the castle, at the front door, and at the door of the Great Hall. Because, when it comes to Fae, there is no such thing as too much caution. It was nearly supper-time when we finished the last of the replies, and I was glad of it. Being reminded of Father had put a shadow on my day that not even Aurora could lift, and having illusory blood dripping over my hands twice hadn't helped.

In the hour or so I had before suppertime, I needed to purge my melancholy. Before we moved to the palace, the place where I could do that had always been the woods on the doorstep of our manor. On the rare occasions when I wasn't happy, the peace and solitude of the forest had always put my heart at ease again.

Now that I was living in the palace, I couldn't get to the woods, but we had the next-best thing: a woodland garden, a piece of actual wild land that had been left to itself. According to Mama's ladies, you almost never saw that sort of thing in a formal garden like the palace had, and I think that someone in the past, a king or a queen, must have shared my love of wild spaces. The gardeners were forbidden to tend it, and at the heart of it was a tree older than any other I had ever seen. While the others hurried away to take care of personal tasks before dinner, I took the stairs down to the garden door, and since no one was there, I threw dignity to the winds and ran. Soon, I was winding my way through the tangle of vines and bushes on a little path I had found until I reached the ancient forest giant.

From here, I could neither see nor hear the palace and all the people in it. I might have been alone. I sat on one of the enormous roots that stuck up out of the soil and leaned against the trunk. I then pulled my handkerchief out of my sleeve and let go.

I never cried where Mama and Papa could see me if I could help it. It wasn't fair to them. Papa had made me a Court Baroness, given me our old manor and a separate country estate with enough land to make certain that I had my own independent income—even though he already supplied me with everything I could possibly want. I could be cynical and say that this made me an attractive marriage prospect, but I don't think he really had that in mind. It would have been unspeakably ungrateful to go about with a sad face, as if I didn't approve of his marrying Mama. So whenever missing Father got to be too much for me, I'd go to the one place almost no one else ever came to so Papa wouldn't be told about it. I never wanted him to think that crying for Father meant I hadn't come to love him.

So here, or with Giles, I could let down the walls and allow the tears to come.

I was so immersed in my own crying that I didn't hear Papa; I didn't even know he was there until he sat down beside me, took my shoulders, and turned me so I was crying into his chest instead of the tree trunk. By then, of course, it was too late to stop crying and pretend I hadn't been drowning in tears.

He didn't say anything at first, just let me sob. Then he pulled out a handkerchief of his own, took my soggy one away from me, and pushed his into my hands. "I miss him too, Miri," he said, one arm around my shoulders, as he began to stroke my hair with his free hand. "Every day. He was my best friend. We were squires together, did you know that? We both served Sir Delacar, the fattest knight in the kingdom. All Delacar wanted out of us was to serve him at meals and run errands for him. But Geniver used all the spare time he had to train; he probably did more work than any two of the other squires put together. He was determined to prove that he *deserved* to be among the squires and that he would grow up to be as good a knight as any of them. He used to tell me that when I was King, he'd be my Champion. And I used to laugh at him because, of course, my brother, Aethan, was going to be King, and who would ever make a landless boy whose mother had wheedled him into the squires a knight much less the King's Champion? But Delacar did make him a knight, and Aethan died in the wars, and I was made King, and..." He sighed and hugged me. "And now, every time I look at you, it's as if I were looking at him, my fellow squire. You have his black hair, his green eyes, and his way of sticking your chin out when you are about to be stubborn about something."

No one had ever told me that before. Maybe because there

weren't too many people in the palace who had known Father as a boy. "I...do?" I said haltingly.

"You absolutely do," he said firmly. "It wasn't until he turned sixteen that he developed into the stalwart warrior everyone else remembers—not even your mother knows what he looked like as a boy since they didn't meet until he was seventeen. But I look at you—and there he is. I see other attributes of his in you, Miri. His bravery, his intelligence, his honesty—it makes me proud and breaks my heart all at the same time."

I felt the tears slowing as my cheeks got hot. I wasn't used to being praised for things besides the stuff girls are usually praised for—being obedient, dutiful, pretty. I blotted my eyes. "I didn't want to make you or Mama unhappy, Papa," I said.

"And that's why you came out here by yourself and why you don't let us know when you need to cry, I understand." He continued to stroke my hair. "I noticed you weren't in your room reading and studying before dinner the way you usually are. I wanted you to know that you're not alone in missing him, so I came to find you. This is where Geniver always used to come when he was frustrated or angry or sad."

This was a whole new side of Father I had never heard about before, and I was hungry to hear more.

Papa took my chin and tilted my head up so he could look down into my eyes. "It's been a very upsetting time for you, and you've been a little star about it all. No sulking because I couldn't make you a princess, no jealousy over your baby sister, and no objections to my taking Geniver's place with your mother. So I am going to promise you something right now. When the christening is over, you and I are going to spend more time together, and I am going to tell you what Geniver was like when he was your age. I'll tell you everything I know and remember. And I'm going to promise you something else. Whatever you want or need to learn, I will find you the tutors for it. I want you to blossom. Be like Geniver, Miriam. Be everything you can even if it takes you into situations that may be strange to you or makes you try things that frighten you."

Maybe those last words should have scared me. But...they didn't. They lifted my heart and made me feel...exalted. And excited. A whole new part of Father's life had just been unveiled to me, with a promise of more to come. *And* the promise that Papa would stand behind me no matter what I wanted to do. Most girls never hear that from their blood fathers much less a stepfather.

"Feel better?" he asked. I nodded. "All right then. We'll stop at the fountain so you can splash some water on your face so no one will know you were crying. And then we'll get your mother and we'll all go in to supper together so everyone can see that no matter what your title is, you are still my daughter."

CHAPTER TWO

HAVING LIGHT FAE IN THE KINGDOM MEANT THAT ANYTIME there was going to be a big event, you could count on the weather being perfect. Actually, not even *Dark* Fae would allow bad weather for a big event they were invited to—sure, they loved to make a terrifying entrance with thunder and lightning, but they didn't want to get soaked by the corresponding downpour any more than ordinary people did. And, yes, they could have avoided that by simply not coming and sending the bad weather anyway, but that would mean that all their rivals would be there—and getting rained on—and then they'd begin gossiping or starting feuds.

Fae politics are worse than human politics, because Fae live so long and can hold grudges for centuries. Papa had a separate clerk of the court and two underclerks just to keep track of all the gossip and who was feuding with whom. Or at least as much of it as we were allowed to know. It isn't so bad for the common folk, but if anyone above the rank of a knight doesn't know about the feuds among any Dark Fae he might encounter, he runs the risk of offending them, and that opens the door for them to go after him and anyone else within a degree or so of relationship to him.

But the result of all that was that we were guaranteed to have excellent weather not only for the christening itself but also for a few days before and after. And what *that* meant was that we could invite a great many more people than we had space for in the palace because they could camp in their fancy pavilions in the great meadow in front of the main gate without any fear that horrible weather would spoil their stay.

I could already see some of those fancy pavilions from my room. I'd had a stroll down there yesterday, and believe me, those pavilions were the height of luxury. Carpets on the ground, clever folding furniture, cushions everywhere, masses of servants, anything you could ask for, really. To be honest, they had more room and were probably more comfortable than the guests who'd had the privilege of being squeezed into the small chambers in the palace. At least those out there had as much room as they cared to enclose under canvas. From here, it looked like a field of mushrooms, since all I could see from five stories up were the plain canvas tops and not all the pennons and hangings festooning the sides.

"My lady," said Belinda in that icy tone of voice that meant she was getting *really* annoyed with me. "You are not dressed. You are not one of the Fae. You cannot lark about in nothing but gauze."

"I have everything on but the overdress, and I was waiting for the maids," I replied truthfully, and I stepped away from the window with regret. Belinda didn't approve of my hanging out the window in my chemise. Not that anyone could see me; the window was narrow and no one would be able to tell if I was male or female, much less that I was in only my chemise.

Belinda was in a *mood*. And she had the overdress draped over both arms. I knew that there are times to talk back and that this wasn't one of them. Meekly, I held up my arms and she pulled the overdress on with impatient tugs. When she got it in place, she pulled the back lacings tight and picked up the upper oversleeves.

I was fortunate that the maids appeared, plucked them out of her hands, and got on with the job before she could try to wrestle those in place. I'd long ago learned the trick of taking in the biggest breath I could and holding it if Belinda took it on herself to dress me so the back lacings weren't nearly as tight as she wanted them to be. If they had been, I probably wouldn't have been able to breathe. If Belinda had put on the oversleeves, she'd have laced them as tightly as she could, and that would make it impossible to flex my arms properly.

With the oversleeves in place, the chemise nicely pulled through the openings at the shoulders and the elbows so it showed properly, and the gold belt fastened around my hips, it was time for the hair.

My hair was so straight and fine that there wasn't a lot that could be done with it. If you'd tried to put it into ringlets, they'd have disappeared by the time I got to the Great Hall. So, despite Belinda's disappointment, all the maids did was put it in a single long braid with green ribbons, then they took the gold chaplet that matched my belt and tied it around my head. And that was that. I looked into the little mirror at the side of my chamber, placed where it would reflect the most light from the window, and was happy to see that I still recognized the person in it.

"No necklaces? Earrings? No bracelets?" Belinda asked mournfully.

"No time," one of the maids replied, and hustled me out. She winked at me as we got outside the door. There was still plenty of time, but she knew how much I disliked being laden down with trinkets. If Belinda had had her way, I'd have been wearing two necklaces and an (aptly named) choker, huge earrings that would leave my ears sore for the next two days, and so many bracelets on either wrist that I'd jingle every time I raised my hand. Wearing that much heavy jewelry makes me look like I'm trying to attract attention when, in fact, I'd prefer to do the opposite. The only jewelry I ever really wore regularly was a plain silver locket on a silver chain that held three locks of hair—Mama's gilded chestnut, Father's night black, and now Aurora's golden curl, each one bound up with a bit of silk thread.

At this point, I really envied the servants who had dressed me. You never saw *them* laced into tight gowns until their cheeks were red. You never saw *them* wearing the sorts of things Belinda thought "appropriate," which generally meant "impossible to move in."

I *kind of* understood why Belinda thought that this was necessary. Servants had jobs to do. People like me were supposed to look as if we never had to raise a finger for anything because everything was done for us. But, in the first place, I'm not like that because I would always rather be doing things than having them done for me, and in the second place, that's always seemed very precious and pretentious to me.

The maids rushed off to some other task—probably to help one of the visiting ladies get into her gown—leaving me to make my own route to the chapel. Normally, I'd have taken the servants' stair rather than the long path to the main stair, but today there would be so many servants running up and down that I'd be seriously in the way. So I continued through the maze of interlocking rooms to the front of the palace.

Our little manor had actual corridors, so when I'd first come to live in the palace, all this running through other people's private spaces had just felt *wrong*. Actually, it still felt wrong, but according to Mama, the polite thing to do was to pretend that you were a ghost and saw nothing, so that was what I did.

I finally got to the front of the palace; the main stair was there, and it took up a lot of space. There was a walkway around it, and it went down to the fourth floor, where it split and went down to the third floor, where it joined up again into a much wider "presentation" staircase down to the second floor that ended in the anteroom to the Great Hall. The last part of it actually spread out with each step so everyone could make an impressive entrance.

I wasn't the only one on the stairs; I hadn't gotten far before I was joined by a growing stream of guests. I was extremely grateful not to be laden with jewelry at this point; most of these people didn't recognize me, but they assumed that I was probably their equal in rank, so there wasn't the constant interruption that there was anytime Mama and Papa went anywhere, with people stopping and bowing as they passed. When I reached the stairs down to the second floor, I stuck way over to the side next to the rail. Let other people make their impressive entrances; I was happy to stay unnoticed for the moment. Mama and Papa were finishing their own preparations and easing their nerves right now, and the best thing I could do would be to get to them as quickly as I could, which was something I wouldn't be able to do if people recognized me and stopped me for an obsequious little chat.

Everyone but me was filing into the Great Hall, which took up the entire width of the building on this floor. I, however, slipped over to the side and opened an inconspicuous door to another stair that took me down to the first floor, which was where all the business of the palace took place. From there, I could go through all the offices and workrooms—which were empty right now—to another stair that took me up to the pantry at the head of the Great Hall. This was where the food was brought when the Hall was being used to eat in. Papa, in a splendid indigo uniform, and baby Aurora, in a waterfall of white silk lace and cradled in her nurse's arms, were already there, and just as I entered, Mama came down the last few steps of the privy stair, which comes off their bedroom and goes straight down to the pantry. She looked amazing; the enormous dagged sleeves of her gown were lined in gold silk, and she wore her Crown of State, a more delicate match to the one Papa wore.

The Great Hall was used for every function where lots of people had to be housed, everything from meals to great ceremonies. There was a peephole in the door of the pantry that looked into the Hall, and I used it. The Hall was absolutely full.

At the front of the right-hand side were all the Light Fae. This was the first time I had seen more than two Light Fae at any one time, and I was a little startled by their variety. Some were wearing so little that they were almost nude; some wore clothing in styles like ours but made with much finer materials than anything I had ever seen; and some were wearing elaborate outfits that were so absolutely impossible, there was no way someone could actually have *sewn* them. Like the clothing that looked as if it was made of leaves or flower petals or snow or water. They all had long hair, often done up in equally impossible styles that came in every possible color. There were jeweled hair ornaments, and necklaces, and belts and bracelets on all of them, even—or maybe especially—on the ones who had very little actual clothing. One couple looked as if their clothing *was* jewelry.

And, of course, they all had wings. Tiny wings that seemed like an afterthought, huge sweeping wings that rose several feet above their heads, velvety bat wings, transparent metallic-veined insect wings, bird wings, moth wings, butterfly wings. The one thing that they all had in common was that they were studiously ignoring the group on the opposite side of the center aisle from them. If there were the kinds of infighting among them that we see in the Dark Fae, we humans would never know. We see only a tiny fraction of their lives and habits, and they like to keep it that way.

Living up to their name, the Dark Fae had similarly fantastic costumes that were almost all in shades of midnight blue or black, although a few wore white outfits that looked like spiderwebs or shrouds. Most of them were raven-haired, though a few ran counter to that trend with bone- or ice-white tresses. They too had wings: crow wings, the wings of death's-head moths, tattered bat wings, sable insect wings, carrion-fly wings, dragon wings, even a few bone wings. Some had impressive staffs, some carried wands, some were empty-handed. All of them were so pale that they looked bloodless in contrast to the complexions of the Light Fae, which ranged from pale pink to deepest brown with a few blue and green ones thrown in just for variety. They glared at the Light Fae with such rage that I almost expected the Light Fae to burst into flames. But, of course, they were powerless against the Rules. They were here mostly to show their contempt for us mere mortals, although there were a few who were here in the hopes of frightening enough of the guests to make a meal of their terror, which *was* permitted by the Rules.

One of the clerks of the court came in by way of the stairs I had used and carried a sheaf of papers in his hand. "All of the Dark Fae are present, Majesty," he said. He was one of the older clerks who had probably started service under Papa's father. He looked very calm for someone who had probably stood at the side of the Hall, papers in hand, counting Dark Fae off his list at least three times to make sure he hadn't missed anyone, because if we started before one of the Dark Fae arrived—and they were known to arrive late on purpose—well, there's another Dark Fae offended. The Dark Fae were the ones who mattered, of course. If any of the Light Fae came late, they'd laugh and be charming about it, but we didn't dare start anything until all the Dark Fae had arrived.

Papa nodded, and the clerk left to signal that the christening was to begin.

Just above us, the minstrels in the gallery at this end of the Hall struck up a lively, playful tune; this was to signal to anyone milling about in the antechamber that they needed to take their places. When that tune was over, the musicians began a stately march. That signaled the entrance of Archbishop Thomas, who would be performing the ceremony. This wasn't actually a religious ceremony, since that would be an affront to the Dark Fae, so although the Archbishop was accompanied by six of his acolytes, they weren't carrying holy symbols or swinging censers of incense. Instead of the aroma of frankincense, the air in the Great Hall was alive with the scent of the thousands of flowers that adorned every possible part of the room. The Archbishop looked very splendid in his scarlet robes with bands of gold embroidery and his matching ceremonial headgear. Wearing robes that matched his, the acolytes ranged in age from nine to twelve and were arranged according to height.

After the Archbishop came the choir in snowy gowns, mixed in both ages and sexes, who arranged themselves against the wall at the head of the Great Hall. When the march was over and the choir all in place, it was the choir's turn to perform, and they broke into an old song, the words of which were mostly "hail to the King, hail to the Queen, hail to the Princess." It might have been traditional, but the lyrics weren't exactly brilliant, and when I looked through the peephole again, I saw the Dark Fae smirking.

As if you could do better, I thought resentfully. The Dark Fae are horrible at music and usually have to resort to kidnapping and bespelling human musicians to get anything decent performed in their courts and manors, and before they can do that, they have to trick the musicians into offending them. Then I squashed my thoughts. Best not to think *anything* about the Dark Fae.

The end of the song was our cue to enter. First Papa, then Mama with Aurora, then Melalee all done up in a white coif, veils, and a dress that seemed to be made of about eight hundred yards of amber-colored fine linen. Melalee looked as if she was not entirely certain that Aurora was safe in Mama's arms. Her hands kept twitching as if she longed to snatch Aurora back.

Then Mama and Papa and I went to stand behind the traditional Christening Vessel, a very fancy waist-high pedestal terminating in a bowl, all made of carved alabaster, and we faced the Archbishop and the guests. Melalee stood at Mama's left, and I stood at Papa's right.

The Archbishop made a speech about the duty of parents toward a child and the duty of a child toward her parents. Then he turned toward the gathering.

"You are gathered here to witness that this infant is the right-born child of King Karlson and Queen Alethia. That she is the heir apparent to the Kingdom of Tirendell. Do you acknowledge and hold by these things?"

"*We do,*" said the crowd. Well, I couldn't tell if the Dark Fae did, but it didn't matter. This was purely human business, and they didn't have any say in it.

"Will the godmothers for this child please step forward?" the Archbishop asked.

Now, none of us had any idea which of the Light Fae who'd been invited had decided to be Aurora's godmothers. We knew there would be at least one but not more than three. I have no idea if there is some competition among the Light Fae over who will be a godmother, or if there's a meeting that chooses them, or how that happens, and neither does anyone else as far as I know. Of course, any of them would have been fine, but some were more powerful, and thus better protectors, than others. And should anything happen to Papa and Mama, that protection would be vital, since it would be their duty to whisk Aurora off to somewhere safe and train her so she could grow up and rule the kingdom wisely and well.

There was a reason for that. Those humans who were appointed Royal Protectors of infant kings and queens had a bit of a history of turning bad. Every kingdom that *I* knew of had had at least one who had let the power go to his or her head and decided that he or she would make a better ruler than the hereditary one. In the case of Tirendell, if it hadn't been for one of Prince Lionel's godmothers deciding to take matters into her own hands about three hundred years ago and kidnapping the boy just as his uncle's assassin had been about to push him over the edge of the North Tower, Papa wouldn't be here today.

So, obviously, we wanted *really effective* Fae for godmothers.

The first to step forward was a tall, dignified, green-haired Fae whose costume was a cross between a shimmering silvery gown and ornamental armor. That seemed promising. Her insect wings were protected by a shining green carapace that made it look as if she were carrying a shield made of emerald enamel on her back. "I am Bianca Stronghelm, and I shall stand godmother to this child," she said in ringing tones that echoed around the Hall.

"Welcome, and well come, Bianca Stronghelm," Papa said with a bow. "We are indebted to you for your favor."

The Fae bowed back to him and came to stand at my right.

The second Fae came forward. This was a slightly shorter Fae with snow-white hair who wore long jeweled robes. When I saw that her dragonfly wings were veined with the silver the Fae used to reinforce wings that were weakening from use and that her face showed the very faintest of lines, I realized with a start that her hair wasn't white from artifice, it was white with *age*. This, then, would be one of the oldest and wisest of the Light Fae of Tirendell. I nearly squealed with glee but managed to restrain myself.

"I am Domna Silvertree, and I shall stand godmother to this child," she said quietly, and yet her voice echoed in the hall.

Papa welcomed her as he had Bianca, and she came to stand at Bianca's right.

The third Fae looked as if she was barely older than I was. She had scarlet hair, scarlet bird wings to match, and a gown that looked as if it were made of flames. She also had the most infectious smile I had ever seen in my life, and I found myself smiling back at her. "I am Brianna Firehawk," she said, and her smile increased just a little as nearly everyone but the Fae gasped. "And I will stand godmother to this child."

Everyone in Tirendell knows who Brianna Firehawk is. She is the Fae who caught Prince Lionel up off the top of the tower and carried him to safety three hundred years ago. Papa bowed and repeated his welcome with not one jot of difference in how he had welcomed and thanked the other two. Which, of course, was proper. But I knew he must be nearly jelly inside. Mama's eyes were certainly like a pair of saucers.

The Archbishop didn't let any of this disturb him. Instead, he held out his arms for Aurora, and Mama placed her in his embrace. Despite Melalee's tightened jaw, he held Aurora like a man who knows his way around babies. He bounced just a tiny bit on his toes, and Aurora's delighted giggle rang out, making everyone but the Dark Fae smile.

He dipped his fingers in the water in the vessel and dabbed Aurora in the middle of the forehead. "Beloved child, the name that has been chosen for you is Aurora Chloe Serafina. Take this name upon you and grow in the light and love of your family and your friends. I give to you the protection and blessing of the Church and all her servants."

Now came the time when the godmothers gave their gifts. These wouldn't be tangible gifts like the ones piled up on the table at the back of the Hall. These would be...well...more important than that.

The Archbishop handed Aurora to Bianca. Bianca also took her with the confidence of someone who has handled a lot of babies, cradled her in her left arm, and dipped the fingers of her right in the vessel. She dabbed Aurora in the same place, and for a moment, the baby glowed with a clear white light. "Aurora Chloe Serafina, I give thee the gift of love. You shall give and receive love in equal measure and be beloved and loving for all the days of your life."

Mama smiled, and there were tears of joy in her eyes. I knew exactly how she felt. This was a *powerful* gift. No ruler who loves her people will ever mistreat them; any ruler beloved by her people will be protected by them.

Bianca handed Aurora to Domna. The ancient Fae whispered something to Aurora, who cooed with delight, before she dipped her fingers in the water. "Aurora Chloe Serafina, I give thee the gift of wisdom. You shall dispense wisdom, learn it in equal measure, and be heard and willing to hear for all the days of your life." And once again, Aurora glowed with a soft radiance for a moment as the magic settled about her.

Now it was Brianna's turn, and I held my breath, wondering what the legendary Fae would bestow. Brianna's fingertips left a drop of water on Aurora's forehead. "Aurora Chloe Serafina,

I give thee the gift of fortune's favor. When all seems darkest, the Infinite Light shall always find thee, friends will appear unlooked for, and—"

And at that moment, Brianna was interrupted by a terrible crash of thunder. Darkness enveloped the Hall in a shroud of inky blackness. Out in the crowd, people screamed as the Light Fae reacted by conjuring sources of illumination—floating orbs, flaming staffs, even lighting themselves up and flying a few feet above the crowd. Brianna instinctively gathered Aurora closer to her, Domna had produced a staff with a glowing gem on the top of it from out of nowhere, and Bianca held a glowing sword in her right hand and a shield of light in her left.

My eyes instinctively went to the Dark Fae, but they seemed just as startled and confused as the humans. They had crowded up against the wall in a series of defensive postures.

And then the thunder cracked again, there were more screams from the rear of the gathering as people tried to crowd away from the center aisle—and the eyes of all the Dark Fae literally glowed with pleasure and increased power.

And a Dark Fae and her entourage came marching toward us through the parting crowd.

Scampering along in front of her and behind her were ugly skeletal creatures dressed in stained rags. They were taller than humans, but there was something wrong about the way they moved, as if they had more joints than humans did. Their skin was stretched over toothless skulls, pale green eyes filled up their entire eye sockets, and they had no hair at all. The Dark Fae, stunningly beautiful, raven-haired, and wearing a headdress made of bejeweled sheep's horns, was clad in a red gown the

color of spilled blood. Black gems set in tarnished silver orna-
mented her gown and circled her waist.

I felt as if all the blood in my veins had turned to ice. At that
moment, I was surely a feast of fear for any of the Dark Fae who
were near me.

A slight movement to my left caught my attention as the Dark
Fae stalked up the aisle. Papa was looking frantically at the Clerk
of the Court, who was shaking his head. I looked to my right. Brianna, Bianca, and Domna stared at the apparition dumbfounded,
but strangest of all, every single one of the Dark Fae either stood
in shocked, stunned amazement or exchanged baffled glances
with one another, momentarily allied in puzzlement. And that
was when I realized that *no one knew who she was*. Not the Clerk
of the Court. Not the Light Fae and not the Dark.

Which meant she hadn't been invited, and she had been
offended. The Rules were clear. She could do what she wanted—
and Brianna had already given her gift, so there would be no
Fae gifts to counter whatever curse this uninvited guest cared to
deliver. And from the looks of her, she intended it to be something awful. Something lingering and painful to extract the max-
imum amount of sorrow out of not just our family but the entire
kingdom.

I felt paralyzed, feet rooted in place, hands clasped hard on
nothing, sick with fear and helplessness.

"So," she said, stopping with her entourage of monsters
crowding close around her. She had a voice like velvet, and she
was horrifyingly beautiful, a creature of icy perfection, with
green eyes that glittered like a pair of baleful emeralds. "I did
not receive my invitation to this festal occasion. I am *hurt*. Truly,

I am *crushed*." Her eyes swept across all of us, and it was clear she savored our fear. "What is it? A wedding? A sixteenth birthday?" She pretended to see Aurora in Brianna's arms for the first time as Bianca impotently clutched the hilt of her sword. "Oh, no, I see it is a christening! Well, *I* have a gift for the dear, sweet little child—"

Papa reached for the sword he wasn't wearing; from the look on his face, he was considering flinging himself empty-handed at the Dark Fae, but he had to know all those minions would tear him to bits before he could get within five feet of her. Mama was so white, she was transparent, but she held on to Papa's arm as if trying to hold him back.

The Archbishop's face looked like a thundercloud—but he was surrounded by his acolytes, who pressed close to him in terror and kept him from moving at all.

As for the humans in the audience, *they* had huddled as far away from the Dark Fae as they could get, inadvertently trapping the knights and the Royal Guard in their midst. They wouldn't be able to fight their way out without hurting someone.

The expressions on the faces of the Light Fae were variations on pure, helpless horror. *They* weren't the ones in peril. So they couldn't act. We had opened the door to whatever this Dark Fae wanted to do because we hadn't invited her. Brianna couldn't even flee with Aurora—the curse magic was specific and would find Aurora no matter where she was.

Meanwhile, the interloper drew herself up and raised her right hand, and the black crystal embedded in the top of her staff flooded the Hall with a sickly green light. "Aurora Chloe Serafina," she cried out. "I give you the gift—"

"*No!*" I screamed. "*Leave her alone!*" And I threw myself between Brianna and the Dark Fae, spreading my arms wide to absorb as much of the impact of the curse as I could. At least that was my plan, such as it was—which was *stupid*, of course, since it was a curse that had already been cast in Aurora's name, and I couldn't possibly intercept it.

But when the terrible magic of the curse, visible as a bolt of that green light lancing out from the Dark Fae's staff, struck me—it shattered. It fragmented into a million pieces that landed at my feet, sizzled on the floor, and vanished.

The Dark Fae stared at me. Her expression turned from gloating to one of rage. I had barely a breath of respite—I saw in her eyes that she was going to try to blast me into powder with the power of her staff, as opposed to cursing me—and I flung my hands forward, palms facing her, just as she let loose. The burst struck my palms and splashed off.

By now there were people screaming and trying to escape. The Dark and Light Fae faced one another across the aisle, everyone daring the others to make a move. One move, one slip, would be all it would take to spark open warfare in the Hall, and the Dark Fae would target us humans first. Behind me, I sensed my family escaping. *Now* Brianna could run; Aurora was safe. Specific curses like that take a long time to prepare—days, in fact. And by the time the Dark Fae had another one ready, the Archbishop would have given Aurora a new name and she'd be in hiding with Brianna.

And besides, the Dark Fae didn't care about Aurora right now. She had another target.

Me.

She narrowed her eyes. I expected her to say something, but she didn't. Where was our wizard, Gerrold? Trapped in the press behind the tightly packed Light and Dark Fae?

She raised her staff. I raised my hands again, spreading them like a shield.

The bolt of sickly green light struck my hands. And...I braced myself against the force of the interloper's power as if I were trying to hold a door shut, the magic reflecting off my palms. I had no idea what I was doing or even how I was doing it, but I felt my feet sliding on the floor and I knew I couldn't keep this up forever—or even for more than a few moments.

I wasn't afraid anymore and I wasn't angry. All I could feel was determination. I just reacted with pure instinct. I gathered my own strength, pressing hard against that force. I took a deep breath, squinted against the green glare, and screamed *"You! Leave! Her! ALONE!"* at the top of my lungs, and I gave a huge mental and physical push back.

With a *boom* that drove me backward so I sprawled on the floor, the dark magic reflected from my hands back to its caster. She screamed when it hit her with another *boom*.

There was a blinding flash. And when I could see again, she and all her creatures were...gone. There were just a few tiny black rags fluttering down from the ceiling and a scorched place on the floor where she had stood.

The Dark Fae were the first to react—and with faces now distorted by fear, they fled. Some opened portals right in the Hall and stepped through them; some took to the air and crashed through the windows to escape. A few ran for the door behind them, eliciting more screams from the guests they ran into or over on their way out. In an instant, the Light Fae set out in hot pursuit except for the first four or five from the front row who rushed to my side. I watched the pursuers for a moment; they weren't in pursuit to *catch*, they were merely making sure none of the Dark Fae returned. They still couldn't attack the Dark Fae—the one who'd started this was very dead, and if anyone here had been thinking of allying with this stranger, that thought had probably been blown out of their heads when I turned the tables on her.

A purple-haired fellow dressed mostly in scarves took my right hand while a dignified blond with blue-and-yellow bird wings got my left elbow, and between them, they helped me to my feet. I gazed into the Fae faces around me, my head still not working very well. "What happened?" I asked, dazed, as Domna returned through the pantry door.

Domna placed her hand on the bird-winged Fae's shoulder and gently moved him aside. "That, my dear young mortal," she said, "is what *we* would like to know!"

My knees more or less buckled at that point, and the purple-haired Fae caught me and lifted me in his arms as if I weighed nothing. "Up," Domna ordered. "We must gather in the King's private chambers." She looked around at the other Fae and nodded. "I see all the Council are here, save Bianca and Brianna, and they are already upstairs. Let us go. Take young Miriam up, Ealsfird."

Most of them flew out the smashed windows. I was too dizzy to think clearly, but it was fortunate that my purple-haired res-cuer was thinking for both of us and carried me into the pantry and up the privy stair, probably guessing that this was where everyone else had gone.

He located where everyone was by following the buzzing of voices in Mama's solar. He was still carrying me when we entered the door.

"Oh, my god—*Miri!*" gasped Mama, after seeing me being carried this way. My rescuer put me down, and I managed to stagger toward her. Mama was holding Aurora in one arm as she embraced me with the other, and that gave *me* a chance to reassure myself that *Aurora* was all right.

She looked up at me and cooed and burbled, and I nearly wept with relief. "I'm fine, Mama," I repeated over and over until she finally believed me and let me go. I wobbled over to one of the couches and thumped into it heavily.

Bianca sat down next to me while just about everyone else was doing their best to make sure Mama and Papa got calmed down. "I know your brain is most probably swimming," she said, and patted the hand I had resting on the couch between us. "But I need you to answer some questions now before your memory fades."

"I'll try," I said, with uncertainty, as Domna separated herself from the rest and came to sit nearby and listen.

I was feeling dizzy and light-headed, so I didn't think about what I was saying before I blurted it out. Normally—especially with Fae—I'd have thought twice about *anything* I was going to say. Belinda had trained me pretty strictly that way.

Bianca asked me a lot of questions: Had I done anything like this before? (Of course not.) Had I ever played about with magic even a little? (It never even crossed my mind.) Did I ever sense that something was going to happen before it did? (No.) Had Papa's wizard asked me questions about magic? (Never!) And a lot of other questions about how it had felt when I stopped the curse and how it had felt when I deflected the interloper's magical attack back on her. Really *detailed* questions. Bianca even suggested words when I hesitated so I could put a finger on what I'd been doing, and say, "Yes—like that." Words like "bastion," for instance, when she asked what I had been trying to make myself into.

Then Domna asked me how I was feeling *now*. "A little sick," I said. "My head is still spinning. And I don't think I can stand up right now."

She *tsk*ed, twirled a finger over her left hand, and created a whirlpool of sparkling motes of light; and a tiny sapphire-colored bottle coalesced out of them. She picked it up with two fingers and handed it to me. "Drink this," she commanded. "All of it down at once or you'll choke on it."

With a grimace, I unstoppered the bottle and did as I was told, and I nearly came out of my skin. It was like drinking *fire*! But the burning vanished quickly, leaving behind a lovely warmth that spread all through me; my head stopped spinning; and I began to feel normal again.

Now Brianna joined us. Looking past her, I saw that the rest of the Fae were in conference with Mama and Papa and that Aurora was in the cradle that had somehow been brought from the nursery, with Melalee standing over it like a brooding dragon and brandishing a candlestick as if it were a weapon. And while I absolutely sympathized with her instinct to protect Aurora, she did look kind of absurd. Then again, maybe her instinct was right; some Fae were susceptible to silver.

"Well," said the third one of the godmothers. "I certainly

didn't expect my gift to be exercised quite *this* soon." She tilted her head to the side and lookcd at me. "And what are we to make of you?"

Domna snorted. "She's Fae-blooded, that's what we make of her. How much and from where, I have no idea. We'll have to research her family tree."

Those words evidently caught the ear of the Clerk of the Court. Like the Light Fae, he had somehow weathered all this with his wits and aplomb still intact. He sidled over to her. "It has to be on her father's side," he said, talking as if I weren't there. Which, truth to tell, I was used to from the clerks and older courtiers. I didn't *like* it, but I was used to it. It's just the way some people are when they get old; they act like anyone younger than they are is invisible. "When His Highness proposed to the Queen, I traced her mother's lineage back so far that if she had any Fae blood, it couldn't be more than a fraction of a droplet."

"What about her father?" Brianna demanded.

Now the old man looked at me out of the corner of his eye and shrugged. "Not Court business," he replied. "*She* wasn't marrying the King, her mother was. The only importance she has is that she owns a baronial farm and manor and a knight's manor, and both of those are gifts of the Crown." Having tendered these pearls of wisdom, he sidled back to the other discussion.

Domna snorted. "What an irritating little man."

"He's saved us a lot of work," Bianca pointed out. "Now we only have to concentrate on..." She raised an eyebrow at me. I licked my dry lips.

Mama wasn't paying attention to any of this; she was deeply

involved with whatever Papa and the Archbishop and a growing gaggle of other important people from Papa's Privy Council were talking about.

"If I have living grandparents, Father never told me about them or...anything," I said lamely. "There's nothing about his parents anywhere that I know of—oh, wait—I remember one thing." The three godmothers hung on my every word, and I flushed with embarrassment that what I remembered was so trivial. "I was told once by one of the other knights that a beautiful woman came to the Knights' Hall with my father when he was six or seven. She asked to see Sir Delacar. She said a word or two to him, and he took her and my father to a private room, and when they came out, he told everyone that Father was now his page and that if anyone bullied him, Delacar would beat the blackguard three times around the courtyard with his sheathed sword. The lady disappeared, and Father went into Delacar's service, and everyone assumed that Father was one of Delacar's..." I blushed.

"By-blows," said Bianca briskly. "Well, I think it's clear that he *wasn't*."

"In fact, I think it's clear that he was fully Fae or at least half," Domna opined. "The question is, why would a Fae woman entrust her precious child to a mortal—and a mere knight at that?"

"Maybe she wasn't Fae at all. Perhaps she was mortal, and the child was her half-Fae son with a Fae lover?" Brianna asked. "That makes more sense, doesn't it?"

Domna pinched the bridge of her nose between her thumb and forefinger. "At the moment, the only thing that makes *sense* is that we need to get this child trained, and the sooner the better."

The other two nodded, but my mouth dropped open. "Wait—me? But—"

"Your sister is in grave peril," Domna said ominously. "Think about it. A powerful Dark Fae from *outside* this kingdom spirited herself here secretly and established a home so hidden that not even the native Dark Fae knew about her—and why? Was it all so she could attack Aurora on her christening day? And why would that be? She played very cleverly within the Rules, but what is so important about this particular child and this particular kingdom that she would do this?"

"That is a great deal of work," said the purple-haired Fae. "And yet, there is no sign she intended anything else. She brought with her no army, no allies, so she did not intend to harm anyone but the child—"

"Exactly!" Domna said grimly. "Surely you see what that means?"

Bianca rushed to answer. "It means that something about Aurora is portentous and that either the Dark Fae of some other realm know it or some mortal, king, or wizard knows it and hired a powerful Dark Fae to eliminate her, one clever enough to calculate a way to get the task completed without breaking the Rules. And it is something no Dark Fae resident in this kingdom is aware of."

"We can't protect her," Brianna said grimly.

"The wizard could do that now," said Domna. "Simply take her away, hide her until we can think of a way we can keep her protected."

"Oh, because *that* has always gone so well in the past."
Bianca snorted. "Or need I remind you of all the times it hasn't?
She needs an actual protector with powerful magic! I do respect
Gerrold, but he is old and hasn't the stamina to ward off an
attack like the one we just saw."

But I have Fae magic....

"Am I bound by the Compact, the Rules, and the Strictures?"
I asked aloud.

"No, of course not, dear," Domna said absently. "You're at
least half human. You are outside the Rules."

I still hesitated. Because this was terrifying. Just because I'd
managed to prevail by sheer force of will the first time, it didn't
mean I could do it again. I sure wasn't expert enough to be a
knight. And a knight—a magic knight—was what she needed.

But then Aurora giggled, and my panic fled before determination. I was *not* going to let anyone harm my sweet baby sister!
And boys younger than I was were made knights all the time. If
they could go to war, surely I could find the courage to defend her!

"All right," I said, my voice shaking but my fist clenched.
"I'll do it. I don't know how, but I'll do it."

"Do you think she can?" asked Bianca.

"We could train her ourselves," Domna pointed out. "She's
not the first half-Fae to appear and need training. We'd have to
train her *anyway*, so why not focus that training on how to protect the baby?"

"Well, we'll have to do something given what just happened."
Brianna looked into the middle distance. "No one has tested the
Rules and the Compact this blatantly for three hundred years. I
don't think we have any choice in the matter."

Papa and Mama had caught wind of the tail end of this conversation and turned to us with looks of horror on their pale faces.

"She's only fifteen!" Mama cried.

"I'll not have you risking a *child*!" blustered Papa, and I was more or less shoved unceremoniously aside and talked over, under, and around by Fae and humans all at once. It went on for long enough that the potion started to wear off, and I felt a headache start between my eyebrows.

"*Stop!*" I finally shouted. And amazingly enough, they all did and stared at me.

"Look," I said into the sudden silence. "The godmothers all say that I'm Fae-blooded, but since I'm *not* Fae, the Rules don't apply to me, and I can do whatever I want to any Dark Fae who sticks its nose into our business."

Well, that wasn't exactly what they'd said, but I supposed it was close enough.

"They said they'll train me so I can protect Aurora." Mama's lips started to move in protest, but I turned to Papa. "The christening's over. Aurora should be fine until she's thirteen, right? That's the next time she should be vulnerable. Papa, that's *thirteen years* for me to learn Fae magic. That's three more than it took for you to go from page to knight!"

"That's true," he admitted as Mama's face took on an expression of dismay.

And now I turned to her. "You always say how much like Father I am—well, what would Father have done, even at fifteen? He'd have said the same! Mama, I have *Fae magic*. What's going to protect Aurora better? A knight with a sword or a knight with magic?"

But it was Papa who answered, his brow clearing. "Someone with both," he said softly, looking at me as if he saw not me but his old friend, his fellow squire, Geniver. He turned to Bianca. "Is there any reason why she can't learn weapons along with magic?"

She smiled and held out her hand. Another one of those streams of sparkling motes of light appeared vaguely in the shape of a sword, then mostly in the shape of a sword—and then a sword manifested out of them before vanishing in a little *poof.* "None whatsoever," Bianca replied. "I've been known to prefer the sword to the wand many times."

"I'd really like that," I said fervently. There *were* female knights—not many of them, and there were none in our Court at the moment, but they did exist. It wasn't as if I was going to be something entirely unheard of. And, to be honest, that had been one of the things I was going to ask Papa about—to let me train with the squires.

And it looked as if Papa had made up his mind.

"Very well then," Papa said, with a firm nod. "We'll give her every weapon to defend herself and her sister that the mortals *or* the Fae can muster. Mornings, Miri, you'll train with the squires. Afternoons with the godmothers. Let this be my official decree, and let *no one* interfere on pain of punishment."

Mama clutched his arm but didn't object. The Clerk of the Court scribbled it all down. The godmothers looked pleased, the other Fae on the Council a little dubious but not so much that they were going to disagree.

Only the Archbishop looked unperturbed. He placed one hand on my head. "You have a brave soul, a kind heart, and a good mind, Miri. You have my blessing."

Somehow that settled things for me, and I felt the decision drop into place inside me. I was still scared of all of this, but it felt right. I sighed.

CHAPTER THREE

A FEW DAYS LATER, I WAS JOLTED OUT OF SLEEP BY THE SOUND of my curtains being yanked unceremoniously open. Sunlight streamed in my window, smacking me in the face and making quite sure that I was thoroughly awake. "Time to get up," Belinda said sourly, staring down at me with a scowl. "Your *knight training* starts in an hour."

I jumped out of bed and quickly put on the garments she laid out grudgingly, handling each one as if it were poisoned—slightly baggier breeches than the boys wore made of brown moleskin, a loose cream linen shirt not unlike a farmer's smock, brown boots, and a matching wide belt. Then, at Belinda's abrupt gesture to *sit*, I took a seat on the little stool from my dressing table, and she pulled all my hair up onto the top of my head and coiled it into a bun and pinned it in place. And she didn't do it gently, either. Every inch of her radiated how much she disapproved of what I was doing, and I did not care. As soon as she was done with me, I bolted out of my room to the stairs. She could work out her bad temper on something else.

I ran down to the kitchen; had a quick breakfast there of warm bread and butter, milk, and an egg; and pelted for the Knights' Yard as fast as my legs would carry me, reveling in the freedom of my new clothing. *I wonder how much of a fit Belinda would throw if I decided to wear this instead of gowns except when I really had to?* But I knew the answer, of course. It probably wouldn't be worth the way she'd loom over me every chance she got like a disapproving storm cloud. *I wish Aurora were old enough to do without a nurse and get Belinda for her governess.* Belinda and I were like fire and tinder. We would never agree, and we'd always be in conflict. But Mama would never turn her out because where would she go? She was too set in her ways to go to a new household.

When I got to the yard, there were five people there already. Giles, two boys I didn't know about his age and height, and two of the younger maids of honor, Susanna and Raquelle, who were about *my* age and height, and whom most of us called Anna and Elle. They were all wearing pretty much what I was wearing.

I didn't know most of the maids of honor, but I did know Anna and Elle. I liked them; I'd wished over the year that I'd been here that we didn't keep going in opposite directions all the time. But they had their duties to their mothers; when a lady was living at Court, she couldn't have all the personal servants she'd have in her own manor, so daughters were expected to serve as their mothers' personal maids. And if you had a surfeit of girls, you loaned out your eldest to ladies who didn't have daughters. That built alliances between families, got girls at least familiar in passing with eligible boys, and was *supposed* to help keep Court politics from getting out of hand.

I'd had what I thought was a good idea after the godmothers

had left. I was going to need someone to train with, someone on my level, which would ordinarily mean the humiliating fate of training with the little pages. But if I could get four or five others from the Court who were about my age and lacked experience— that would be different. Plus, they'd be a *lot* of help. We'd be Aurora's special bodyguards. Maybe I could even get them weapons and armor that were good against magic.

Papa had agreed and said that he'd make sure it happened before I started training. And, as always, Papa kept his promise.

Just then Sir Delacar came strolling out of the Knights' Tower toward us. *He* was going to be my trainer? My heart fell. He was the fattest knight we had, and as far as I knew, he didn't do much or ask much of his squires. Even Belinda looks more like a knight than he does.

But then he opened his mouth, and when he spoke, the authority in his voice startled me so much that I found myself obeying him automatically.

"Squires!" he barked. "Form up!"

And we all jumped and arranged ourselves in a straight line. He nodded with approval.

"You cubs are too young to remember," he said. "But I was the squires' trainer until I gave the job over to Sir Larimer. I trained your father, young Miriam, and I trained the King. The King asked me to do the same for you." He paused significantly. "But I won't."

I gaped at him, and I wasn't the only one. Was he defying Papa's orders?

"I'm going to train you all differently," he continued. "The way I *should* have trained young Geniver in the first damn place."

His voice got a little rough, as if he was holding back emotion. "I made the mistake of training him like a knight. Honor and rules and chivalry. Pretty jousting and swordplay meant for tournaments, not the battlefield. We hadn't had a war in decades, and I never thought—well, leave it at that. I didn't *think*. Jousting manners are all very well for people like His Majesty and me, but it won't do for you. It will not do. I'm training you like *fighters*. Every trick and no rules. Miriam, you asked for companions, and I've asked these five if they would volunteer, and they've agreed; I believe they are all smart and quick to pick up on training. You'll all be trained in the filthiest of dirty fighting because Aurora's enemies will be; they'll give you no quarter, and you should learn to fight like cornered badgers. I made a mistake in how I trained Geniver. I am never making that mistake again."

His voice caught for a moment and he blinked rapidly. Then he straightened and went back to being the authority he'd been when he walked out of the Knights' Tower. "The King has charged me with making the six of you into not just good fighters but a unit, people who know how to fight *together*. And together you'll be called Aurora's Companions. Now let's go to the armory. The first thing to do is get you all fitted up in your practice armor."

So off we went in a straight line, following Sir Delacar like chicks following a big fat hen. When we got to the armory, Delacar took us to the part where all the practice gear was and opened three chests. From these, he took heavily padded canvas tunics and loose trews, held them up to us, and shoved them in our arms when he was satisfied that they were going to fit. Then he went rummaging in a box on a shelf and handed us girls each a long canvas band that looked like a bandage.

"What's this for?" I asked.

But Elle was already wrapping it tightly around her chest while the boys were pulling on their padded leggings. I copied her, and so did Anna. When we were all dressed, Delacar found battered helmets that fit us, gave us each a quarterstaff, and paraded us out to a part of the yard where none of the squires were practicing or polishing their masters' mail or otherwise doing chores for their knights.

"Have any of you learned quarterstaff yet?" Sir Delacar asked, with the air of someone who expected us all to say no.

But Giles and Elle both held up their hands. Sir Delacar blinked in surprise, then quickly recovered. "All right, Giles, please pair up with Miriam. Raquelle with Robert, and Susanna with Nathaniel. Raquelle, you and I will demonstrate the first exercise, then everyone will do it with their partner—slowly."

The exercise was pretty simple. One person would use the upper third of the quarterstaff to strike at the partner's head from the right, and the partner would intercept the blow. Then the striker would do it again from the left. Then he or she would try to strike for the knee from the right, then from the left. Then it would be the partner's turn to try the four strikes. Then it would go back. We all watched closely, then followed Delacar's orders. "I didn't know you knew quarterstaff," I said as Giles and I took turns going through the moves.

He smirked. "There's a lot you don't know about me." He was teasing me, but I didn't rise to the bait. Which is just as well, because a moment later, Sir Delacar began pounding his quarterstaff on the ground, setting a beat we were supposed to follow. And he kept speeding up. I was using all sorts of muscles

I wasn't used to using, and the faster we went, the harder I had to concentrate to keep from being whacked. This was like dancing lessons—except the dancing master had never whacked me as hard with his little pointy stick as Giles would if either of us slipped up.

When we were starting to fumble and dripping with sweat and Elle had caught poor Robert a sharp rap on the forearm by accident, Sir Delacar called a halt. "Go get a drink and come back and practice on the poles." He pointed to a row of poles with targets marked on them in chipped red paint. We each had a turn at the bucket and ladle, then followed his orders. Once again, Delacar waited until he thought we had the pattern down, then began setting a pace for us.

By the time he let us go, my clothing and armor were sodden, my hair wringing wet, and my arms so sore that I could barely lift them. We left our padding in a soggy pile to be taken away, rinsed out, and dried; and we went our different ways. I would have thought that all the work in the kitchen would have given me better muscles!

I stopped at the kitchen and asked for food, and someone thrust something to eat into my hands and shooed me out. It was a couple of legs of cold roast chicken, some warm bread with jam stuffed into the middle, and a handful of radishes, and by the time I reached my room, I had eaten the lot. It was a good thing that I'd stopped down there because Belinda was *still* in a mood and my sweaty state did not do anything to change it.

She made me strip to the skin and rubbed me down with a rough wet cloth—which I *could* have done myself, but she was clearly not going to miss the chance to scrub me thoroughly, as if by doing so she could erase all my ideas about being Aurora's Champion. When she was done, she waved her hand at the gown and underthings she'd laid out. While I was putting it all on, she was carrying out my morning clothing to be dealt with by the laundresses and wearing an expression of extreme distaste on her face.

But instead of going to eat the noon meal with Mama and Papa and the rest of the Court, I flopped down on my bed with my arms outstretched to ease them. Right now, an hour or two of rest sounded better than food.

Belinda came back in and looked at me, still wearing the scowl. It was clear that her feelings about what was right and proper for a young lady were running roughshod over any concern for how vulnerable Aurora was. I don't know what she *expected* me to do. Maybe wear a Fae gown and wave a wand prettily? "You asked for this," she said accusingly.

"Yes, I did," I replied. "It's worth it. It will get better." I didn't say it would get easier because it was pretty clear that Sir Delacar was not going to make this easy on us. But squires had been doing this for a very, very long time, and I figured that I could do what they were doing. I'd never heard of a squire who died of too much exercise.

Belinda sniffed and stalked out. But just as I started to doze off a little, a servant arrived with a big wooden tray with a bowl of soup, more bread, and a pitcher of watered wine. The wine was extremely welcome even if Belinda's idea of what someone should be eating after a heavy bout of quarterstaff training left something to be desired because I could probably have eaten an entire baron of beef by myself. At least it was a nice thick soup, not a broth. I ate very slowly, both because my arms hurt and because I knew that if I lay back down, I *would* fall asleep.

When I had finished eating, I knew it was time for me to meet whichever Fae had either volunteered or been ordered to teach me. I managed to stagger down to the kitchen stair, and by the time I was at the bottom of it, my muscles were a little less sore and no longer stiff. The directions I had been given yesterday had been very explicit. I was to go to my favorite ancient oak in the overgrown part of the garden. I couldn't imagine why I would be going there instead of someplace outside the palace, but I assumed that the Fae would transport me from there to somewhere else. How? No idea. They were Fae.

I was very much hoping that the Fae teaching me would be one of the ones I recognized.

Through the vegetable and herb garden, then into the pleasure garden, and then into the overgrown section I went. Not moving briskly, may I say, but not crawling, either. And when I pulled aside a vine curtain and revealed my oak, who should I see waiting there for me but Brianna Firehawk, and I sighed with relief. Here was someone who had proved that she had a deep connection to the Royal Family in Tirendell. That was a definite point in her favor, but I had some other notions about her based on all the discussions that had gone on in Mama's solar after the christening. I trusted her, and I felt that I could count on her to be thorough and practical.

"Oh, my," she said as I used a great root as a step to get to where she was standing and winced a little. "I see your weaponry teacher has had no mercy on you."

"None whatsoever, Lady Firehawk," I said, and tried not to groan. "It's Sir Delacar."

She tapped her lips with her finger. "Hmm. I believe I can see why he is being…rigorous. Well, this will be your first lesson in magic," she continued, switching subjects abruptly. "There is an ancient door in this oak, a Fae door that I have used a great deal in the past. The first thing I want you to do is *find* it."

I was momentarily distracted by the astonishing news that my favorite tree had a *Fae door* in it. And one that Brianna had used a lot.

Now what on earth did *that* mean? Had I been drawn to this tree *because* there was magic here and I had inborn magic? Was it just a coincidence?

But Brianna was waiting, and I shook off the distracting questions. I thought about feeling the enormous trunk for telltale cracks, but something told me I wouldn't find anything that way. So I stared and stared until I was cross-eyed, but I couldn't see a door, either. I stopped trying to spot it and closed my eyes so I could think. Then it was as if something whispered to me, *Don't think. Feel.* So I let my mind drift off into a blank and stepped forward until I was right at the trunk, holding out my hand until it rested just above the bark. I moved it slowly back and forth, and suddenly I *felt* it! A tingle and a sensation of warmth. I traced it with my hand downward in a gentle curve across the base of the trunk and back up again in another gentle curve until I reached my starting place.

I looked over at Brianna and saw her smiling with approval. She tapped the oak with her finger, and the outline I had just traced lit up for a moment.

"Now I am going to teach you how to open it," she said. "For the near future, you'll be required to come here, open the door, and step through to have your lesson."

"But—can't other Fae use this door too?" I asked in alarm, thinking of the Dark Fae.

"Of course. But *only* Light Fae, and it won't take them to my home. That destination is locked to you and me. The way into the palace via this door is also locked to you and me." Her smile widened as she saw me take that in.

"But...that means the door can go to more than one place!" I cried, bewildered. "How is that possible?"

"Among many other things, that is what you are going to learn," she chided gently. "First, you must find the place inside you where your power is. That is the same place you reached when you deflected the curse and the dark magic."

I closed my eyes again and thought back to the moment when I realized my baby sister was about to be struck with a magic curse that would send her to a horrible fate. I pictured it very vividly in my mind—and as I actually started to feel some of the fear I had felt then, I sensed it. It was like a snake uncoiling and rising to strike.

And at the same moment that I felt this stirring within me, Brianna said, "Now send that power into your hand, hold it in the middle of the door, and will it to open. It might help to picture the power as a hand pushing it."

That was what I did, and for a while, nothing happened. But

then I felt some of the power leaving me as a bright line formed around the edges of the door, and then the door *did* slowly swing inward!

It opened on another garden, but it was nothing like the one behind me. As I looked past it, I saw it led to another garden that was quite clearly a garden only a Fae could create. This one was full of plants I didn't recognize, flowers in shapes that made no sense—one was shaped like three pyramids stacked on top of one another—and with perfumes I had never smelled before. There were trees that had been somehow contorted into seats, like the roots of my oak, and bushes that had been coaxed into amazing symmetrical shapes. I had trouble taking it all in, but Brianna took my hand and led me inside through the tree. I heard the door in the tree close behind us, but I was too busy looking at the garden to worry about that. The fantastic landscape was not limited to plants. There were butterflies everywhere and a veritable chorus of birds. Listening closely, I heard frogs and crickets too.

In the middle of all this was a sort of miniature castle. That is, it was built to look like a castle, and a very fanciful one at that, but it was about the size of the manor house Mama and Father and I had shared.

Then again, I supposed that a Fae could make her dwelling as big or as small as she cared to.

"We're going to work out here in the garden for the first little while," Brianna said, leading the way to one of the trees that had been formed into what looked like a rather comfortable bench seat for two. "Until you gain control, I would rather not risk anyone else's property, and to be honest, it's safer for *mine* that we practice out here in my garden. Once I am certain you won't be knocking down walls, we will practice inside my home. When your control is even better and I need not be concerned about any accidents, we will move to a spot in the forest near your own home."

I nodded, acknowledging the justice of that. "But why are we starting here instead of there?" I asked. "If you're worried about accidents, wouldn't the forest back in Tirendell be better?"

"Magic is easier to move here in the Fae Realm."

"Oh." I thought about that a moment. "Well, how do I start?"

"You felt the magic within you when you concentrated on the peril your sister had been in, and you managed to control it," she observed as we both took our seats on the velvety greenish-black bark of the trunk of one of the seating trees. I couldn't help running my hand over it. I'd never felt bark like that—

Then I realized that it wasn't bark; it was moss, the thickest, softest moss I had ever seen.

"Um, yes," I said, belatedly realizing that she was still waiting for an answer. Brianna raised an eyebrow at me.

"You mustn't allow yourself to be distracted when you are dealing with magic," she warned. "Human magic, such as your wizard practices, is dangerous enough. Fae magic is generally much more powerful and capricious. And you may have both; I am not certain yet."

I knew that there was human magic and there was Fae magic, and that they weren't the same thing. But I'd had no idea that it was possible to have both.

"Yes, my lady," I responded, flushing with embarrassment.

"Now I want you to find the center of your magic when you are *not* agitated," the Fae instructed. "Take your time. Tell me when you have it."

I closed my eyes to shut out all the extremely distracting sights of the garden and concentrated on how that magic had *felt* inside me.

It had felt like a coiled snake.

But I want something gentler—kinder. I don't know where the thought came from, but it was loud and strong in my head and somehow *right*. Righter than a snake. I wasn't going to attack something, after all, or even defend against something. So when I finally found that deep well of warmth and force, I thought of a flower instead of a snake.

I imagined a flower inside me opening up, spreading its petals, filling me with its perfume.

I felt something tickling my cheek that was *not* that power, and I almost lost it. But I managed to get control of it at the last second before it slipped away from me, and I opened my eyes.

I was covered in butterflies. They clung to me everywhere, my dress, my hair, and the tickling on my cheek had been one of them trying to land there.

Brianna smiled broadly, much to my relief. "Excellent," she said. "Not exactly what I wanted you to do but near enough. Now send the butterflies away without frightening them."

What would the butterflies in a Fae garden be attracted to? *Well, they came to me when I called up magic. Maybe they eat magic?*

Carefully, without disturbing them, I turned my right hand over so it was palm up. I had forced power out of my hand when

I opened the door, but I wanted something gentler now. So I coaxed the power instead, moving it by degrees until it started to flow of its own accord, and I pooled it in the palm of my hand. It formed into a softly glowing golden puddle there.

The butterflies immediately responded, fluttering off my dress and hair and moving down onto my arm. So far, so good. Now they were all competing for a spot on my hand and arm.

I lifted my hand, imagining that the warm little pool of power was a ball, a ball as light as a bit of thistledown, then I imagined a breeze coming and blowing it out into the garden.

And it did! It lofted off my palm and bobbed out into the garden, the butterflies following in a joyous, fluttering multicolored cloud.

I coaxed the ball into setting down on a bush of what looked like roses and turned to see what Brianna thought of my solution.

She watched the butterflies drinking up the magic with her head tilted to one side. "Interesting. That is not a solution I would have come to."

"Is it wrong?" I asked, concerned.

"No, not at all. Just not the way a Fae would have done it." I felt uneasy and a little anxious.

"How would a Fae have done it?" I asked, hoping that I was hitting the right note of humility and eagerness to learn. Because, after all, this was not just one of the Fae, this was the Fae who had taken the Royal Family literally under her wings, and the last thing I wanted to do was displease her.

She smiled, much to my relief. "Well, it would depend on the Fae. A Dark Fae would just have blasted them into dust.

Someone like Domna would make them feel her irritation, and they'd leave on their own. But a Fae would not have separated a piece of her magic for them to feast on because we conserve our magic whenever possible."

"Oh." I considered that.

"Magic is food for us, as it is for those butterflies," she replied. "Or rather, the energy that is transformed into magic is food for us."

"And you don't waste food," I said solemnly.

She smiled again. "So show me a way you could have sent them on their way without frightening them and wasting magic."

I thought about this as a few of the butterflies that had missed their chance at the feast drifted back over to me hopefully. Poor little things. My heart wanted to feed them, but I had my instructions.

Then it occurred to me; I must be putting off some sort of magical scent, luring them the way flowers lured butterflies in my own garden. So I concentrated again and closed the power up like a flower furling its petals for the night. When I opened my eyes again, the butterflies were drifting off elsewhere in slightly baffled confusion. And Brianna nodded with approval.

We didn't do anything more exciting than that for the rest of the afternoon. Where today's lesson with Sir Delacar had been the very rudiments of quarterstaff work, today's lesson with Brianna was the very rudiments of magic. How to call it up and close it down, and a very little bit of how to direct it. Nothing complicated—but a great deal of repetitive practice. When she dismissed me for the day, I felt sore inside in the same way that all my muscles had felt sore after this morning. My mind was very tired, and that place in my chest where the power came from ached vaguely.

I opened the door in Brianna's kingdom—that was how I thought of it—all on my own and found myself in the palace garden again. From the position of the sun, it was probably very near suppertime, and I was starving.

At least I wouldn't have to change or bathe.

I made my way to the Great Hall, where the servants were just starting to lay the table for dinner. For working people, lunch was the big meal of the day, and supper—the word literally came from the word "soup"—was generally soup and bread and butter and perhaps some fruit or vegetables in spring, summer, and fall, or fruit and cheese in winter. When Father was alive, we had kept the common custom since we seldom had much to do with the Court. Perhaps once or twice in a week, Father and Mama would take dinner with the Court, and I'd eat in the kitchen with our few servants. But since Mama and I had come to live in the palace, I'd had to get used to eating this big long meal at the end of the day.

And it was a *long* meal. Seven or eight courses on an ordinary night, ten to twelve on special occasions, and as many as twenty for a great state affair. And for a great state affair, each one of those courses might have multiple dishes. All that food generally made me feel overstuffed even when I was careful not to eat too much, and serving it took a long, long time. The dinner after Aurora's christening was supposed to have been one of those, but virtually everyone had fled in the wake of the Dark Fae's attack, so we would probably be eating the various foodstuffs in some form or another for the next three days at least. Even though a lot of it had already gone to the poor.

It was a good thing that old Gerrold, the palace wizard, had renewed the preservation spell on the pantry just before we started making the food for the feast. If he hadn't, Papa being Papa, he probably would have declared a feast for the whole town below the palace to keep it all from going to waste.

Sure enough, when the rest of the Court and the palace staff had gathered, the very first course was the clear broth that had been intended to start off Aurora's christening feast.

Halfway through dinner, I was starting to nod off, but I shook myself awake long enough to finish. I even managed to make polite conversation with the other people near me at the high table, but being young meant that I was mostly supposed to listen to what they had to say and nod in the right places. I was pretty good at that; Belinda's lessons on Court manners had stuck even if nothing else much did. As soon as the plates were cleared and the benches and tables pushed back for the evening's entertainment, I excused myself and headed for my room using that private stair behind the dais.

Belinda started to follow me, but I waved her back. "I undressed myself for years; I'm perfectly capable of doing it now," I said, making sure to soften my tone so she wouldn't take it as being snappish or pert. "You enjoy the minstrels." I knew she loved music and dancing, and I didn't want to deprive her of either. I don't hate Belinda; I'm actually rather fond of her. When she's not trying to stuff me into some sort of mold or trying to curtail my reading on the grounds it will "make me look bookish," she's a decent governess. She knows Court manners better than most and the proper way to address anyone of any station; she can sew as well as a seamstress; and she is as good a housekeeper as Mama. She's even conversant in managing the land of a manor house.

She swayed back and forth indecisively. "If you're sure…"

"I'm sure," I replied, and winced. "Right now, all I want is bed." And before she could lodge any further objections, I started up the stairs.

I think maybe if I had been older, she might have come anyway. Suspicious that I was having a rendezvous with someone I shouldn't and all that. Belinda had the most suspicious mind I'd ever seen when it came to people having meetings with people they shouldn't. Then again, that is part of her job—to keep the young lady in her charge from getting herself into trouble thanks to a too-romantic mind. But so far, I hadn't had any suitors at all, suitable or unsuitable, and Belinda didn't know about Giles's being my friend because she never came down to the kitchen. So she didn't have any suspicions on that subject, and I was allowed to go up to my room in peace, undress in peace, and fall straight into bed in peace.

Thank heavens.

"How did you know what the breast bandage was for?" I asked Elle a couple of days later.

She grinned and pulled her mass of curls up into a loose knot on the top of her head. "Archery. It's ever so much easier to shoot with everything flattened down a bit. Back home, I practiced every day."

"I should have taken up archery," Anna grumbled. "My mother might actually have allowed it." She glanced over at me.

"You know what that's like; you have that bear of a governess. The only reason I was allowed to join the Companions was because the King ordered it."

I looked around at the five of them, all of us resting after the first round of our workout. "How *did* you all get picked, anyway?"

Elle and Anna looked at each other, and Anna nodded to Elle. "The Queen suggested us, and I don't know about Anna, but I couldn't agree fast enough."

Anna bobbed her head. "I've been envying all the interesting things you've been getting to do, Miri, and this? I've wanted to be a lady knight since I was little."

I glanced at the boys. "I went straight to Delacar and told him I wanted in," said Giles. "I couldn't let my best friend go into this without someone to have her back!"

"Nat and I are best friends too," said Robert. "Sir Delacar came to a bunch of us who were beginning squires and asked for volunteers. We both thought that this would be a whole lot better 'cause we get archery and some interesting stuff from Sir Delacar in the afternoons instead of squire chores."

Oh, that made a lot of sense now. While I was getting lessons in magic, they were getting lessons in things knights absolutely would not be caught dead doing—archery was for women and peasants to their way of thinking. It's a bit of snobbery. Anyone could afford a bow and arrows—you could make them yourself if you had to—but swords and armor cost real money. And it's a bit of masculine preening.

But before I could ask anything else, Sir Delacar got us up and moving again.

I was right. The weaponry lessons *did* get "easier" in the sense of feeling *good* at the end of them and not so tired and sore that I wanted to give up. I got better at it too, enough better that Sir Delacar had me measured for my own set of riveted chain mail. Giles had gotten measured for his right away, and not long after I got my armor, so did the other four, although beyond making sure it fit, we weren't using it yet. Soon we were practicing with bows and swords as well as quarterstaffs, though when I asked about jousting, Sir Delacar snorted with contempt.

"Jousting is for knights playing games of honor," he said, making sure his voice carried to all six of us. "You can't afford to play games—and you can't afford honor, either. If an enemy comes for Princess Aurora, he won't come riding in on a high-bred warhorse to issue a challenge. He'll come sneaking up a back stair with a knife. Or he'll ambush her in the garden when she's playing. Or—well, I have the other possibilities covered with the plans I am discussing with the captain of the Royal Guard." He coughed. "I'm counting on the six of you to be her bodyguards against more direct threats."

Now I saw why Delacar had Papa's respect. There was so much more to him that I was beginning to think that the "fat, lazy knight" persona was all a ruse to cover up his clever, even devious, mind.

We all nodded and went back to practicing in the yard we shared with the other squires. I couldn't help but notice how different the style the other squires were being taught was from ours. Theirs was full of rules. Disarmed meant defeated. No low blows. No dirty tricks, like maneuvering your opponent so the sun was in his eyes, or kicking dust into his face, or even getting him to face into the wind so his eyes dried out.

These rules were exactly what had brought my father down. I wasn't supposed to know the whole story, but I'd overheard people talking about it when the King brought us to Court.

The whole story is this: In war, knights are supposed to be a solid line of force meant to shock the enemy. The heavy armor protecting them, the war-trained horses, all these are supposed to strike the front line of an enemy's forces and break it apart. And in the event that the enemy also has knights, your knights are supposed to break *them* apart so they can't do the same thing to your foot troops. Not every kingdom has knights; not every kingdom can *afford* them. Knights are expensive to train and equip. Warhorses need special training and are heavier than ordinary horses. Full armor is extremely expensive to make and has to be fitted to each knight individually along with the weapons they have proficiencies with. They and their horses also have to be trained, housed, and fed even when they aren't fighting. Then you have to add to all that the squires with their own training, feeding, and housing.

And the knights are often nobles, which means you have noble families to answer to, so they're valuable to another kingdom. If they are unhorsed and surrender, you're supposed to ransom them back.

One of Tirendell's knights got cut off from the rest. He tried to surrender, but the enemy foot troops swarmed him and clearly intended to kill him instead. Father saw this happening, went to his rescue, and also got swarmed and cut down along with his fellow knight.

Delacar knew that we could absolutely count on the enemy being ruthless, so he was training us for that. Tripping. Rushing and headbutting. Grappling. Shield bashing, aiming for the hands or wrists, finding all the weak points in your opponent's armor. It was a good thing that we were practicing with wooden swords, the edges padded with wool, or we'd probably have killed one another a dozen times each day. And you might have thought that when the grappling and headbutting and all that came into play, he'd have had the girls practicing against the girls and the boys against the boys. Not a bit of it. It was boys against girls, and Delacar showed us girls tricks we could use to make the boys' weight and reach work against them. Which was fair, since he taught the boys not to hold back against us girls.

I'd gone into this driven purely by the determination to protect my baby sister. But I was discovering that I *liked* all this for itself. I liked feeling strong enough to take care of both of us. I liked having skills that could keep both of us safe. I loved the pride in Papa's eyes when he came down to review my progress with Delacar and the relief in Mama's when she understood everything that Delacar was teaching me. So what if some members of the Court looked at me with pursed lips and disapproving expressions? There were others who approved, tacitly and openly; and there were at least as many girls my age who looked on Anna, Elle, and me with envy as there were ones who watched us with contempt or puzzlement. Sure, there were female knights—but there weren't any at Papa's Court, and some people just didn't understand why *any* girl would aspire to the white belt of a knight. And there were not that many girls here in the first place.

As for the six of us, tales of knights always spoke of the brotherhood and camaraderie of being brothers-in-arms, and to tell the truth, since I didn't have a romantic bone in my body, I'd always thought that this was a lot of nonsense.

Now, though, I realized that it wasn't. I had friends, real friends, for the first time in my life! Not just Giles, either, but also Elle, Anna, Nat, and Rob. We spent a lot of time together in the mornings encouraging one another when we were not actually training, resting, or recovering. And during the training, it was as much about helping one another as it was gaining skill. I *know* the others were enjoying this as much as I was; we were never late; we were often early; and for me, at least, there was a pang of disappointment when we broke up for the day, and I really wished they could join my magic lessons.

And we weren't *just* friends. We were a lot more than just friends by now. We knew we could count on one another no matter what; we each had five people we could trust with our deepest secrets. We were what Sir Delacar had called us when we met that first day in the yard.

We were Aurora's Companions. And we would guard her and one another against all odds.

CHAPTER
FOUR

I MIGHT HAVE BEEN FITTED FOR MY ARMOR, BUT IT TOOK TIME to make. And this would be only the first set; master craftsmen would be working on a better, lighter, stronger version. By the time I got my first riveted chain mail (and, holy angels, it was *heavy*!), Brianna had moved our practices from her little kingdom into the real world. I understood now why she had started things in her home in the first place—it was the location where she was strongest, where her protections were layered and centuries old, and if I made a big powerful mistake, it would be relatively easy to contain the damage to a small part of her garden. When I had gotten enough skill, we moved to a practice room inside her castle. But now I had enough control that she felt it was safe to bring me and my power out into the "real world."

So she created a protected place in the forest close to the palace for both of us to use for further lessons. Outwardly, it looked like a peasant's cottage, old and nestled in the trees, cleverly made to look as if it had been there for centuries. There was an actual path to the cottage that branched off from one of the main roads the Court used when going hunting, and she had made sure that I knew the way, but I usually used the tree-trunk door to get there. In fact, that was the last lesson she taught me in her kingdom: how to use the tree trunk as a gate to any place she had set this particular door to go to. Doors, I had learned, were available for any Fae to use—but *where* they went was locked to each individual, and to allow another to go to the same destination, the information had to be shared.

The door in the tree trunk didn't drop me right *at* the cottage; that would have been very risky for Brianna. An enemy could magically watch the forest and find her cottage as soon as she crossed the destination threshold. She explained to me that while she could fortify her own kingdom against interlopers, especially against Dark Fae, she could not do that with the forest.

So the door opened onto a path in the middle of the deep woods, and you had to know where you were going in order to find Brianna's cottage.

On the outside, you'd never know it wasn't the dwelling of some particularly prosperous peasant. It stood two stories tall, with a thatched roof of straw that had turned silvery gray with age. Two huge oak trees cradled the walls between them, as if they had been saplings when the cottage was first built. Whitewashed cob walls held red-painted window frames with red shutters. There was glass in the windows rather than horn or oiled parchment, which indicated a certain amount of wealth. A flower and herb garden with a whitewashed fence stood between the cottage and the end of the path. All perfectly normal. A decrepit-looking cottage might tempt someone to try to get inside to see if there was anything left in there to steal.

On the inside, it was one single room with warded walls to prevent anything we did inside from leaking out—and quite often the room was larger on the inside than the cottage was on the outside. It gave me quite the start when I first realized that the size changed. Maybe one day I'd learn how she managed such a feat.

But even though I might learn how, at least in theory, I doubted very much I'd ever be able to do it. The Fae were not only the masters and mistresses of magic, they'd also had centuries to learn every nuance of the craft. As half-Fae at best, more likely only a quarter, I might live longer than a human but not long enough to learn all I'd have to know to do what a Fae like Brianna can.

Anyway, the point of this place was to have a practice area out in the real world, where Fae magic could be a bit more unpredictable and where human magic could come into play as well. Brianna intended to teach me defensive magic first—something a lot more refined than my brute-force shield against that Dark Fae had been.

That was why I now stood in the middle of the odd empty room feeling horribly vulnerable. I wished I had my suit of chain mail despite its being really heavy. My own breathing seemed ridiculously loud in the silence of that room as Brianna studied me carefully.

"Bring up your power," she said when I guess she thought I was ready. "Now concentrate on the forearm of the arm you use to hold your shield."

I already knew where she was going when she said that, so I called the power into my arm and created a round shield of it, and I looked at Brianna over the edge of it. It weighed nothing but looked as if it were made of solid gold. She smiled with approval.

"Make it more dome shaped," Brianna suggested, and I subtly altered the shape. "Now I'm going to launch levin bolts at you, and you are going to deflect them. For right now, I will center my attack on your shield."

That was so I could get used to how the attacks felt, I guessed. I'd been in such a panic with the Dark Fae that I'd been working on pure instinct and fear, and all I remembered was the pressure on my impromptu shield trying to push me back. Now I understood her approach. Brianna intended to teach me how to handle an attack exactly the way Sir Delacar was training me—deal with any attack by paying attention, analyzing, and planning counters.

She thrust out her hand, and what looked like a ball of white fire hurtled from her toward me. I held steady; it hit my shield and splattered off, as if it had been a ball of liquid.

I felt the impact as a definite jolt in my arm. And the shield got hot for a moment before cooling again. Brianna nodded at me, I nodded back, and she repeated the attack.

Each time she sent a levin bolt hurtling at me, I understood a little more. Not the "thinking" sort of understanding, though. This was more feeling than thinking, and the feelings had to have time to work their way up into my head so I could take them apart. *It's power that acts like fire*, I realized. *Except it has weight and it hits me like a stone about the same size, and it also acts like water. Like molten metal, I guess.* She continued to send these levin bolts at me, and I held steady, braced against the impacts.

My shield became warm, then uncomfortably warm, but I didn't dare dismiss it, not while those fiery levin bolts hurtled toward me. I had to do something about that heat. A few more of those things hitting me and I was going to get burns! *Can I make the shield more reflective? Like a mirror?*

The second I thought that, the shield obeyed. The next levin bolt that hit splashed off with a lot more show, and the shield cooled a little. Brianna smiled ever so slightly and let her arm drop down to her side.

I let out a huge sigh and absorbed the shield back into myself. Sweat dripped down my back and clumped my hair, and my muscles ached exactly as if I had been working out under Sir Delacar. "Now tell me what you've learned so far," Brianna ordered as I sat right down on the floor.

"What you used on me wasn't like what the Dark Fae was using," I replied. "It had weight and heat—like molten metal."

"That's a good analogy," she replied. "And the levin bolts would have gone right through that instinctive shield you used with the Dark Fae. I suggest you try not to use that crude tactic again, at least not in that form. You did it in front of nearly every Dark Fae in the kingdom, and even the few who didn't attend the christening will know what you did by now."

I sighed. Of course they would.

"So tell me more," she continued.

"The physical shield you had me make started to get hot, so I made it reflect more. But why am I so tired?"

"Because you aren't in my realm anymore, where using Fae magic is more effortless. You're in the human realm, where it is harder for you to control Fae magic. The only reason you can in the first place is your Fae blood—here your human blood works against you. That was why you were completely exhausted after you defended your sister."

"Please tell me that this gets easier with practice," I begged.

Brianna laughed. "It does. It's just like your weaponry practice. You'll strengthen your ability to wield Fae magic, and your control will become more precise." She gestured at me to stand. "Now let's get back to practicing. This time I want you to make that shield so reflective that none of the heat penetrates to your arm."

We worked all afternoon until I was ready to drop, soaking wet with sweat, and Brianna finally called an end to our practice. She did do one thing for me that Sir Delacar couldn't, though.

"Hold very still for a moment," she said, and I obeyed. She made a few little gestures with her hands, and I nearly jumped out of my skin as my sweat dried and my hair unbraided itself, floated around me in a cloud, then braided itself back up as neatly as you please! And suddenly there was a scent of lavender about me instead of the stink of sweat. I looked down at myself. I was as neat and clean as if I'd been spending the afternoon in the solar reading.

"There," Brianna said, nodding. "That should keep you out of trouble with your fearsome guardian."

I had to laugh at that. "She *is* a bit of a dragon," I agreed. "Do I walk all the way home?"

"This late? Of course not. You'd arrive late for dinner, and your dear father and mother would probably be certain that something dire had happened to you. Go back to where you entered the forest and 'look' for the door in the tree you came here by. You'll find yourself in the palace garden again." She made a shooing motion with both hands, and I didn't hesitate.

Sure enough, when I went out and retraced my steps, I made out a very faint glow of magic from one of the trees just off the path. I opened the trunk door, and it let out into our garden from the oak. I stepped through.

Since I didn't need to change, I went straight to the nursery. Melalee had Aurora lying on her stomach on a lambskin on the floor. Her little arms and legs waved happily; it was clear that she liked the new position. I plopped down on the floor next to her, and for once, Melalee didn't *humph* in disapproval. Aurora looked straight at me, held out her arms, and said "Mi mi."

Melalee and I both stared at her in astonishment. "Was that her first word?" I gasped. Melalee nodded, dumbstruck for once.

I picked Aurora up and turned her to look at Melalee. Aurora crowed, and said, "Meh meh." Quite different from "Mi mi," and it was clear that she had said both our names and that it wasn't just random baby babbling.

"What a *good* girl!" I told her, and jounced her until she laughed, then put her down on the lambskin, where she wiggled all her limbs happily. "If you don't tell Mama, I won't, either," I said to Melalee conspiratorially. "'Mama' should be her official first word."

The nurse nodded, and I headed down to dinner.

I wasn't as exhausted as I had been after my first couple of weeks of weapons practice, but I was definitely too tired for dancing and entertainment once dinner was done. I excused myself and started for the privy stair, but to my surprise, I found Giles waiting for me there. With the door closed and the only light coming from the candles lighting the landing, it was surprisingly private and a lot quieter than the Great Hall.

"Are you all right?" he asked with concern.

"I just feel as if Sir Delacar singled me out for extra bouts today," I replied, and sat down on the bottommost stair. He took the hint, edged past me, and sat down a few steps above me. "Hey, I'm curious. Have you been taken off kitchen duties?"

"Don't worry about it," he said, waving the question off. "I'm officially a squire now. I rank right there with Nat and Rob." He eyed me. "So...you avoided the question. Are you all right? You've left dinner early every night since we started fighting lessons."

"I'm..." I hesitated for a moment, then decided that it wouldn't hurt to let Giles know what my afternoons were filled with. Outside of the Privy Council, Belinda and Melalee, and the King and Queen, no one knew what I was studying in the afternoons. "One of the godmothers took me as a kind of apprentice. So in the afternoons I'm learning how to use magic to protect Aurora."

His eyes got huge. "Really? You're learning *magic*? I didn't know you had wizard powers!"

I hesitated again. Should I tell him? I hadn't been told that I was allowed to....

But I hadn't been told that I *wasn't* allowed to. And this was Giles. If I couldn't trust him, whom could I trust?

"I don't know about the wizard powers, though I may have that," I said slowly. "But according to the godmother, I'm at least a quarter Fae-blooded. Maybe half."

I'd thought his eyes had gotten big before. Now they practically covered half his face.

"How is that even…" Then his mouth snapped shut.

"Father," I said softly. "So now I know why his mother took him straight to Sir Delacar." I'd shared that story with him as soon as I had learned it.

Giles stared at me for a very long time. "Do you think she enchanted Delacar into accepting him as a squire?" he finally asked.

"I don't know," I confessed. It was something that had been bothering me. What if Father's mother was a *Dark* Fae? Because none of the *Light* Fae seemed to know who his mother could be.

But nothing I had ever heard about him or seen for myself could make me think that he was bad. And he had died trying to save another knight. Surely a Dark Fae would not have done that.

We both sat there and looked at each other as the music from the minstrel's gallery filtered down to us in the stairwell. "Does that make a difference?" I said. "Between us, I mean."

"No." The way he said it lifted a load of worry off my shoulders. It wasn't too quickly, as if he wasn't sure. And it wasn't too slowly, as if he'd had to think about the answer for too long. It was just good old solid Giles. "No. We're the Companions, right?" Then he shook his head. "Actually, that makes it better, 'cause if we have to defend Princess Aurora against more Dark Fae, I'd *really* rather we didn't have to wait for your wizard to totter down out of his tower to come to our rescue. So what are you learning?"

"It's kind of strange stuff," I confessed, and gave him the shortened version of everything I'd done. His face lit up when I described what I'd been doing with the magic shield earlier that day.

"I wonder if we could do that with *our* shields," he mused. "Make them shiny, I mean. Would they reflect magic too?"

"I can ask tomorrow. But I bet we can get enchantments put on them that would do the same thing. Maybe I can learn how."

"That would be a really good idea—" He stopped when I yawned. "You should go to bed."

"Yes, I should. If I'm going to be fit for anything except getting shouted at by Sir Delacar in the morning."

"Then I'll let you do that." Giles got up and started to sprint down the stairs, then turned back for a moment, his face full of unsuppressed excitement. "Do you *realize* how incredibly *terrific* this is?" he gushed. "My best friend! Is half *Fae*!"

Then he ran off, leaving me to take my time getting to my room and my lovely, lovely bed.

"Is it true?" asked Anna breathlessly. Her dark eyes flashed with an excitement that I had no explanation for. What sort of gossip had she overheard yesterday when I was busy working myself to a lather with Brianna?

"That you're half Fae!" she exclaimed, her dusky cheeks flushed. "Is it true? Giles says it's true!"

I gaped at her. Then I turned to stare at Giles incredulously. I mean, I hadn't sworn him to secrecy or anything, but I hadn't expected him to blurt it out the moment he saw the others this morning! This could be a problem. There was a reason why Gerrold didn't socialize much. A lot of people don't like magicians and magic—they don't like power they can't see and don't understand. And Fae magic was worse than human magic in that regard.

Anna continued to stare at me as her curly black hair slowly escaped from the topknot she'd tried to tie it up into, her expression equal parts glee and excitement.

"Uh—yes, I guess." Which was *all* that I managed because Anna and Elle squealed and began hopping up and down like a pair of overexcited crickets, and the boys pounded one another's backs for no good reason, grinning like fools. And in another few moments, the rest of the squires were going to come into the yard, and they'd want to know what the fuss was all about and then—

Well, I didn't know what would happen then except that the rest of the squires would know, and by lunchtime, the whole palace would know. I got hot all over and would very much have liked to sink into the ground at that moment. "Look," I said to all of them. "Don't spread this around. Not everyone in the Court trusts the Fae, even the Light ones—"

It was fortunate that Sir Delacar emerged from the Knights' Tower at that moment and bellowed, "*What's all this, then?*"

Everybody froze except me since I hadn't been doing anything. But Giles blurted out, "It's Miri, sir! She's half *Fae!*"

"And what of it?" he growled back, amputating their excitement. "Fae blood doesn't make her stronger or quicker. It doesn't make her smarter. And she'll have a *hell* of a lot more to learn before Fae tricks do her any good in fighting." He cast a sour glance at me, but I just shrugged, trying to convey without words that *I* wasn't the one responsible for all the nonsense. He grunted, looked at me with narrowed eyes, then nodded brusquely. "You all seem to have plenty of energy this morning, so ten rounds of the courtyard at a trot in your mail. On the double!"

I groaned inwardly. It wasn't fair! I wasn't the one who'd been bouncing up and down on my toes! I wasn't pretending to be anything special!

But squires don't argue with their knight, so I darted into the armory, shrugged on my padded surcoat and heavy chain-mail coat, and began trotting around the courtyard with everyone else. Meanwhile, the rest of the squires finally came to the courtyard to start their practices and gave us a look of sympathy as we circled the courtyard. After ten rounds, I was mortally glad to shrug out of the surcoat and armor, and sit panting on the bench in the armory while my sweat dried.

Delacar was fair; he let us get our wind back and get a couple of dippers of water before we returned to work. Which was, since we had just finished sweating in them, dunking our padded surcoats in diluted limewater to clean them, then rinsing them in clean water. A pole went through the arms, and the surcoats were hung on the wall of the courtyard to dry in the sun.

It occurred to me at that moment that an *awful* lot of a squire's job was cleaning. Even when we weren't cleaning our knight's armor, we were cleaning our own. Then again, we had to know how because what if we were all on our own with no servants to help? Like if the palace was under siege and the servants were all doing more important things and helping those manning the walls? Cleaning your armor, as Delacar told us often, was the same as cleaning your horse. If you don't clean your horse after he's had a workout, he gets sick. If you don't clean your armor after you have exerted yourself, it will rust, and rust means weak spots, and weak spots get you killed.

"Since you've gone all flibbertigibbet this morning, I expect every lesson I've taught you has been driven straight out of your heads," Delacar growled as the last of the surcoats got heaved up on the pegs set into the wall. "So it'll be the pells for the rest of the morning for the lot of you while I decide what's left of my careful training."

The pells, of course, was the proper name for the marked poles we used to practice sword strokes and quarterstaff against. I found working on the pells soothing, though I knew a couple of the others hated it. Sir Delacar came to each one of us in turn while the others practiced attack and defense patterns, and he called out sword moves at a lightning pace, moves that we were supposed to execute as soon as the words were out of his mouth, while he stood there frowning fiercely. He rattled all of us, but at least we were able to give him a credible show, and no one fumbled or, most heinous of sins, dropped his or her weapon. By the time he gave us the curt signal to stop, the other squires had left—no doubt wondering what we'd done *this* time that had gotten the old man so riled up.

Delacar put a hand on my shoulder to hold me back while the others put their padded weapons away and made their escape. I looked up at him, but his stony expression gave me no hint of what he was thinking.

"I didn't tell them, Sir Delacar," I finally said. "I mean, I told Giles, but I didn't think he'd tell the others."

Delacar sighed. "Well, that horse has escaped now, and it's no use closing the stable door. We'll just have to see what comes of it."

"What should I do?" I whispered.

"I don't know," he replied frankly. "Hellfire and damnation, *I* didn't even know your poor father was Fae-blooded until the King told me after the christening! I just—I just thought the lady who came to see me had been extraordinarily persuasive." He pulled a kerchief out of his sleeve and mopped his brow with it. "Truth is, I don't remember much about that, only that it seemed important that I take your father as my squire after she left."

I understood immediately just how unsettling this might be to the rest of the Court. They'd had my father among them for decades. He'd been the King's Champion. And all that time he'd been Fae and nobody had known. People would wonder if *he* had known and why he'd seen fit to keep it secret. And what did that mean about me?

"People are going to wonder about that," Delacar continued. "So I'm going to be in for it too. After all, I'm the way he came into the Court. And they're going to wonder why one of the Fae placed her child among us in the first place."

I gulped, because I didn't have any answers. Brianna didn't know—in fact, she didn't even know who Father's parents could have been. A web of unknowns stretched in front of me, and I knew instinctively that some of the answers to all these questions might be very bad.

"We'll just have to make the best of it, I suppose," he said, which wasn't any kind of answer at all. "Just be yourself. You're a good child. You want to protect your sister. Just keep telling yourself that and try to ignore people who look at you sideways. Maybe this will all blow over."

But he said that as if he didn't actually believe it. And neither did I.

In fact, the first signs that word was spreading like flames in dry grass came as I went to get luncheon in the Great Hall. When I came in, some conversations stopped dead, and others broke out in whispers. It felt as if *everyone* was watching me as I quickly ate and just as quickly left.

People watched me as I went to the garden. No one followed me, but I sensed eyes on me. But now they would be talking among themselves about how no one ever saw me *in* the garden, because I went in right after luncheon and didn't come out again until almost dinner. So where did I go? And what was I doing? Did I grow wings and fly away somewhere? Surely the guards would see that. Did I make myself invisible? Did I creep around the palace *spying* on them?

I knew *I* could make up a dozen alarming theories about what I was doing, and they had dozens of busy little minds to make up a whole lot more. By the time I came back, the entire palace would be buzzing.

But what could I do? All I could do was what I did every afternoon: open the door in the trunk of the oak tree and go to Brianna. Staying here wouldn't solve anything; people would just gather in corners away from me and whisper where I couldn't see them.

So, with a heavy heart, I opened the door and stepped into the deep forest.

"Well, this is a bit of a problem, isn't it?" Brianna said when I finished the recitation of my troubles. "Let's go outside into the garden. You look as if you could use a little fresh air."

We left the big empty room, and Brianna and I sat down

on a couple of seats made from peeled logs gone as silver with age as the thatch on the cottage roof. I didn't so much sit as plunk myself down. I felt like dropping my face into my hands but didn't. Instead, I took deep breaths of herb-scented air and tried to calm myself down.

Birds sang all around us, twittering in the thatch of the cottage and caroling from the trees overhead. Bees blundered around the herb flowers, lending a drone to the birdsong that might have been soothing if I hadn't been so worried. I fixed my gaze on a lush basil plant and watched a bee harvesting pollen from its tiny flowers.

"I haven't been successful in discovering the name of the woman who delivered your father to Sir Delacar," Brianna said at last, her voice pitched low. "She clearly used magic to persuade him to take the boy. There are more questions there than I care to think about. Was she Fae or was she a human? If she was human, she must have been a sorceress, but in that case, why did she have a Fae child with her? Of course, your father could have been her child and half Fae, but from the strength of your abilities, most of us feel your father must have been fully Fae. And if he was fully Fae, where did he come from in the first place? Why bring him to Sir Delacar—why not place him with a human family or a childless couple? I just don't know." She shook her head.

"Could she—could she have been a Dark Fae?" I ventured, which was the worst possible fear I had. "Did she intend for Father to become her agent against the King?"

To my relief, Brianna laughed, and it sounded genuine. "If she did, she picked one of the *worst* possible ways to go about it!" I looked up. Brianna shook her head at me. "Think about it.

Would you send a little boy who is easily swayed to one of the kindest men in this kingdom if you intended him to turn into a serpent at its heart?"

"It...doesn't seem...logical," I said slowly.

"I don't think there *was* any intention." Brianna reached out and idly picked a sprig of rosemary and crushed the evergreen-like leaves between her fingers. The sharp scent—one of my favorites—wafted over us. "Except to put that child into a safe place."

"How would putting him with Sir Delacar be safe?" I asked.

"It is the very last place that any enemy would look for a Fae child." Brianna dusted the crushed leaves from her hands. "On the rare occasions when a Fae child is placed with humans by Fae, it's always been with a kindly but childless couple who live in the forest, where it is easy to watch over the child without being detected by the human family. And it's not done by walking up to the couple and persuading them with magic to take him in. The couple always finds the child in the woods or in their garden, tries to find his parents, then takes him in themselves. I'm sorry to tell you that a good many human children are abandoned that way by parents who don't want them or cannot afford to feed them, so *Fae* is not the sort of thing a couple assumes when they find such a waif. That way there is no suspicion among other Fae, or humans, either, that the child is Fae."

"Why would a Fae child be in danger?" I asked.

"That is something we should not discuss. Let's concentrate on your dilemma. What we need to do is encourage people to be less suspicious of you." Brianna tapped her finger against her lips as she thought. "The best thing to do is make use of your friends, the other Companions. And Sir Delacar. He'll be the most important of all."

"Then can I bring them all here to train with me?" I asked. "With magic?"

"That was going to be our next step," Brianna said with a smile. "You anticipated me by about a day. Bring them tomorrow—but not in your usual training gear. You'll need to learn how to handle yourselves without armor as well as with it, and you'll start that now."

Melalee was knitting in the dark by the cold hearth when I went up after supper and checked on the nursery. I have no idea how she can do that. It seems a skill as mysterious as magic to me. She looked at me when I poked my head in, and whispered, "She said 'Mama.' The Queen was over the moon."

I grinned. That explained why my mother had looked so happy even though she was stuck talking at dinner with Lord Chrilen, who is as deaf as a post and never talks about anything but his dogs.

I tiptoed over to the crib and looked down. Aurora was sound asleep, all silvered by the moonlight streaming in the nursery window. I wanted to touch her soft little cheek, but I also didn't want to wake her up. I settled for air-kissing her and went to my room.

I'd tried to slip out without Belinda noticing, but she was waiting to undress me. "A body would think you were that baby's mother," she said, and shook her head as she unlaced my dress. "You're besotted."

I just laughed as she dropped my nightgown over my head. "Yes, I am."

The next afternoon I led my five friends (dressed in their ordinary clothing, not squire's gear) through the tangled, wild part of the garden, with Sir Delacar bringing up the rear. I had expected the old knight to huff and puff his way in, but he was surprisingly nimble and negotiated the path as well as any of us.

When we came to the old oak and stopped, Giles looked around dubiously. "There's nothing here," he said. Then I placed my hand on the trunk, the outline of the door glowed, and the door opened, and he yelped and jumped back, bumping into Sir Delacar.

The old knight glared at the opening in the trunk suspiciously. "Has that always been there?" he demanded.

"If by 'always,' you mean since Brianna rescued the baby Prince—probably." I shrugged. "It's Brianna's. She made it. But she lets me use it."

"Ah, all right then." Delacar calmed down a little, although my friends were still staring round-eyed at the forest on the other side of that door. "Well, lead on."

I could tell from the way Giles acted that he recognized the part of the forest we came out in almost as soon as we got on the trail. That meant this must be somewhere reasonably near the palace, though farther than *I* had ever been before. Sir Delacar recognized it too; he nodded once, thoughtfully, as he looked around. No one else seemed to know where we were, though. And when we got to the cottage, both Sir Delacar and Giles looked startled to see it, which cemented my conviction that it hadn't been there until recently.

I had my hand on the door latch when I realized that the rest were still standing uncertainly at the garden gate. I turned back to them. "You know, this is not the time to stop trusting Brianna Firehawk," I said quite calmly. "That horse left the barn and died of old age three centuries ago."

To my relief, Sir Delacar snorted and smiled a little. "Quite right," he said. "Form up, squires." And he marched up to the door, which I opened for all of them.

There were oohs and aahs as they took in the fact that the room on the inside of the cottage was much larger than the outside of the cottage. Brianna stood over to one side, letting the squires get over their surprise, but Sir Delacar marched right over to her and gave her a full court bow, complete with a sweeping hand. "My lady," he said as he straightened up.

Brianna was wearing something entirely new to me, probably the Fae version of a knight's fighting gear—it wasn't unlike what the rest of the squires and I wore to work with Sir Delacar, but it was ever so much more splendid. She had a coat of gleaming golden mail over a surcoat of scarlet, scarlet breeches, and boots with golden embroidery. The mail and surcoat even had openings for her wings. She nodded and smiled. "Sir Delacar, now that we know you trained and sheltered an apparently orphaned Fae or half-Fae child, I think you should be aware that you have achieved considerable respect from the Light Fae as a whole. I have been asked to tender our thanks."

Sir Delacar blushed a brilliant crimson. "I'd like to think it was something any good and decent knight would have done."

"But you were the one the unknown chose," Brianna pointed out. "And *I* think it was because she saw something very noble and kind in you."

He continued to blush but snorted a little. "I suspect if you'd asked Geniver about it, the lad would have told you I was anything but kind."

Brianna laughed. "Well, your young squires are likely to say the same about me soon." She raised her voice a little. "Come here, if you please, Companions, and form a line in front of me."

The rest stopped gawking and scrambled to obey her. I took my place at the end of the line. With Sir Delacar at her side, Brianna made a show of inspecting us as if she were our commander.

"You'll do," she said approvingly. "Do any of you have any questions before we begin?"

Giles raised his hand. "My lady, Miri told us about how you were training her with a shield she made out of magic. If we got especially shiny shields, would those work as well as her magic one?"

"That is a fine question, Giles," Brianna replied. "And the answer is both yes and no. Your shield would have to be so shiny that it could serve as a mirror, and the least little scratch or scuff on it would allow the levin bolt to penetrate through to you."

"And just imagine how much work it would be to keep the shields that shiny," Delacar pointed out shrewdly. "In a pinch, you could use a mirror to reflect that kind of magic weapon. But I suspect the ploy would not last very long."

Brianna nodded. "No, it would not. It's one that is quite well known to both Light and Dark Fae. Miriam was very lucky that her foe was so enraged by the unexpected resistance that she didn't think and reacted instinctively by blasting back with pure power. I can tell you that this doesn't happen often."

"Fae fight dirty," muttered Nathaniel. He probably hadn't expected Brianna to hear him, but she did. She looked right at him, and he flushed with embarrassment.

"You are quite correct, Nathaniel," she said solemnly. "The Dark Fae fight dirty. Exceedingly so. If it weren't for the Rules and the Compact constraining them, they'd fight even dirtier. As it is, they are always trying to find a way around the Rules."

"What if they *break* the Rules?" Nathaniel asked, made bolder by the fact that Brianna had answered him. Then he flushed again and added a belated "my lady?"

"They lose their power," Brianna said. "Just as we do if we break the Rules and attack them without being attacked first."

Nathaniel's brow puckered with puzzlement. "But—how? And why, my lady?"

But Brianna only shook her head at him, so I knew then that this was a Fae secret that wouldn't be told to humans.

I wondered if one day it would be told to me.

But that was all the talking we got for the afternoon.

Brianna made magic shields for everyone but me. I had to make my own, of course, and I had the distinct impression that Brianna intended for me eventually to be the one making shields for everyone. And then she began lobbing levin bolts at us—even Sir Delacar. Everyone flinched and winced at first (except me), but as they got used to the idea of fireballs hurtling at them and began to actively deflect them instead of passively letting them hit the shields, Brianna changed her aim so we all had to react and move the shields to protect ourselves.

The Fae was utterly merciless, and from the look on Sir Delacar's face, he approved. I really don't know what would have happened if any of those things had hit us, but thanks to our training under Delacar, we were all quick enough (or Brianna was deliberately being slow enough) that it didn't happen.

She did give us frequent breaks, but by halfway through the afternoon, we were really feeling it. And by the time she let us finally end the session, we were as dripping with sweat as I had been the first time. Giles didn't seem to care, but the other four looked dismayed at what they probably thought was the ruin of good clothing.

"Hold still, Nathaniel," Brianna ordered, and worked her magic on him. And truth to tell, I think his outfit was cleaner when she finished with it than it had been when he walked in. She did all the boys first. Then Brianna turned to us girls.

Brianna laughed as we (I'll admit it) preened a little after she was done with us. "All right, young ladies. Off with you. I expect to see you back here the day after tomorrow."

And she turned to me. "Because tomorrow will be something new for you."

As I followed my friends out the door, I realized that I was actually looking forward to that.

CHAPTER
FIVE

AFTER THAT WORKOUT SESSION, BRIANNA'S PLAN, WITH SIR Delacar's agreement, was for us to spend every other day with her in her cottage learning how to defend ourselves from magical attacks. On even-numbered days, I studied alone with her. When I trained with the Companions, we used either conventional shields that had magic applied to them by Brianna or magic shields she created. We certainly worked as hard under Brianna as we did under Delacar—but we certainly left smelling sweeter and cleaner. Delacar would watch from behind defenses created by Brianna and sometimes suggest things to her that always resulted in us working even harder.

Even Giles began looking a little worn, and he told me in confidence that he'd never been worked so hard in his life, not even when he was the wood hauler for the kitchen. I went to bed exhausted every night, and sometimes I didn't even make it as far as the subtleties at dinner before excusing myself and going to bed. The only thing I spared time for were my morning and afternoon visits with Aurora, who just kept getting more adorable with every new thing she learned. Even Belinda left me alone and stopped giving me the disapproving stare all the time. I guess she figured that what I was doing was punishment enough. Or maybe, since two other girls of rank were doing it, she had grudgingly decided that it was all right for me to train as a warrior.

After two solid weeks of extremely hard work, Delacar suddenly declared that the next day we could rest, that we'd earned it fair and square. And that included me. I was going to be excused for the day from both my sets of lessons.

Anna and Elle said that they were going to spend the entire day lounging about in the garden with some of the ladies who weren't Mama's ladies-in-waiting and do nothing but eat fruit, embroider, and listen to the minstrels.

All three of the boys decided on a boating expedition—I have no idea why unless they planned to drift on the lake all day, sleeping, with food at hand. Both the girls and the boys asked me if I wanted to join them, but I had another idea.

You would think that with a day of leisure ahead of me, I would sleep late, but no. I was so used to waking at just after dawn that I woke then anyway. I think Belinda was expecting me to sleep in because she wasn't awake, so I was able to get into a pair of my practice breeches and one of those sturdy smocks, and sneak out through the kitchen before she even knew I was gone. I told one of the cook's helpers what I wanted, and while I was eating a breakfast of plums and bread and butter, he got me some food for luncheon and did it all up in a napkin. I knew exactly where I was going too: straight to the stable. I got my old pony—thank goodness the grooms had been keeping him exercised for me, or he would have been very grumpy—saddled him, hung my luncheon and a bag of oats for his meal on my saddle, and rode out, heading for the forest track that would eventually lead me to Brianna's cottage—I figured it might be interesting if I could see how far the cottage actually was from the palace. I could have walked, but I hadn't ridden in weeks, and I liked Brownie's easy pace. As we got to the edge of the forest, his ears perked forward. He seemed quite pleased with where we were going. He should be; we used to do this all the time before Mama married the King. But we hadn't gone nearly as far into the forest as I planned to do today because we usually took the road that skirted around the edge.

We weren't alone, by any means. There's always someone collecting something along the forest edge. There are not a lot of forestry laws in Tirendell, and the ones that exist are just common sense. And anyone can search the forest for edible plants, nuts, fruits, mushrooms, and herbs. So there are always people foraging at the edge of the forest.

I rode past them, and no one recognized me. I looked nothing like a noble, of course, and with my long hair braided and tucked inside my shirt, I probably looked like a boy on his farm pony coming back from the city on an errand. At any rate, some people ignored me, and some people waved to me, but everyone was too busy to talk to me.

The deeper we got into the forest, the fewer people we saw, and as we continued going farther in, we soon didn't see anyone. It was just Brownie and me, the great trees arching over the road, and the track leading on ahead of us. I felt absurdly happy. This was the first time I'd been properly alone in . . . much,

much too long. I enjoyed being with the Companions, but I was more used to my own company. I hadn't realized just how much I missed *not* hearing other people's voices constantly chattering at and around me. I intended to ride as far as I could until about noon, stop at the first brook I found, have my luncheon, and ride back again. Peace! No Belinda scolding me, no gossiping around me, and no one giving me a side-eye because I have Fae blood. A day of peace was worth any price.

The road went from hard-packed dirt to having grass growing on the ridge between the wheel ruts to having short grass growing all over it, which signaled the fact that the only folk who traveled this road were the ones brave enough to traverse the forest instead of going around it. The trees were thicker and taller, and there was a wild hedge of mixed brambles and wild roses and thorny blackberries between the road and the trees that discouraged trying to go off the road into the forest itself. Oh, the scent! Oak and the grass Brownie crushed under his hooves, hints of pine and spruce, and just a little bit of wildflower. Better than any perfume I could buy.

And peace. Distant birds, the drone of insects, the breeze in the leaves, and *nobody talking.*

"Hello, Miriam," said a very deep, rather gravelly voice behind me.

I nearly jumped out of the saddle. Poor Brownie was just as startled; he whipped around to bring us face-to-face with—an enormous wolf. I mean, an epically big wolf. Tiny pony size. He gave me this long penetrating look while I was trying to figure out if Brownie could outrun him, then he did the kind of fancy bow you can train a horse to do. "Hail to the conqueror of Lady

Thornheart," the wolf said. "Hail to Miriam, who trampled the killer of pups, to the young woman who ended the crusher of hopes, to the brave soul who destroyed the destroyer of dreams." He took a deep breath and might have gone on further, but despite my fear, I was blushing so hot my cheeks burned. It was pretty obvious what he was talking about even if I hadn't known the name of the Dark Fae who had tried to curse my sister.

"Actually, that was mostly an accident," I admitted, interrupting him. "I was just hoping that the curse would hit me, not my baby sister, and I wasn't really thinking."

The wolf rose from his bow. "Usually 'not thinking' is a very bad idea. But in your case, combined with your brave heart, I would say it worked out well." He lolled out his tongue in what I figured was a wolf grin since dogs do that too. When he grinned, he showed all his teeth, so this didn't help to put me at ease nearly as much as he must have thought it would. "If she was Thornheart, then you are Briarheart, the young warrior whose mettle is as strong as the briar that can pull down castle walls."

"How do you know who I am?" I finally managed to ask. A talking wolf is not something you see every day, and even though every time he opened his mouth I thought of the story of Little Red Hood, he hadn't shown any disposition to murder and eat me or swallow me whole—so far, anyway.

"All of Brianna Firehawk's friends in this forest know who you are," he replied. The wolf continued to stare right at me, something an ordinary wild animal won't do because that's considered a challenge. It was very hard not to get mesmerized by those huge yellow eyes.

"Is that the killer of the Dark Fae?" came another voice from behind the hedge at the side of the road, this one sounding a little less thundery. A huge red deer stepped out of the forest to my right. I had no idea how he'd done that. I wouldn't have thought that even a rabbit could squeeze through the intertwined branches.

Then again, the huge deer was another talking animal. Oozing through a bramble hedge was nothing for them. Everyone knows about the rare magical talking animals in the forests of our kingdom, but nobody, least of all me, ever expects to see one!

Brownie must have smelled him because this time he didn't start. The deer turned his head so he could look out of his right eye at me. Predators like wolves can look at you head-on, but prey like deer and horses have to look at you out of one eye or the other to see you clearly. The deer nodded gracefully. "Oh, it is. Lovely. I'm so glad she came to the forest today! Would you like to tell her or shall I?" The red deer bowed his head toward me, then raised it. He must have had twenty spikes on each antler, which made him *old*. "Forgive me for speaking around you as if you were not here, my lady," he added.

"I was getting ready to, but she might feel more comfortable alone in the forest with something that is *not* a meat-eater," the wolf said. "If you want to—"

"I'm sure anyone who faced down Thornheart the Wicked isn't in the least afraid of you, but let's let her decide, shall we?" the red deer replied.

Two things made my decision easy for me. These two natural enemies were speaking to each other like old friends, and the wolf had claimed that Brianna was a friend of *his*. And both of them seemed to think that telling me what they wanted me to know was very important and possibly an honor. When something like that happens in the Court, whoever gets there first has the right to impart the information and get whatever reward might come with it. "Sir Stag, I very much appreciate your offer, but Sir Wolf has a prior claim," I said, with my best Court manners and a little bow in the saddle.

"There, see? Perfectly at ease with you," the stag said, and bowed to me as the wolf had. "And thank you; my antlers are inclined to get tangled where Lobo is taking you. It's a bloody nuisance having to stop to say 'Wait a minute' every two or three steps. I'll be on my way, then. It was a pleasure to meet you, Slayer of the Dark Fae." And before I could get anything out, the stag reared up, pivoted on his hind feet, and leapt over the hedge into the forest and out of sight past the brambles.

A very impressive exit, but I didn't hear hooves on the forest floor, so I suspected that he was lurking out of sight, waiting to hear what the wolf had to say.

The wolf and I regarded each other for a moment. I was pretty sure he was looking at me with amusement. Which was perfectly all right because that was a lot better than being regarded with hunger.

"Well, Clarion seems to have let the proverbial cat out of the bag, so...I'm here to take you somewhere very secret if you'll trust me," Lobo said at last. "I *have* eaten, though even if I were starving, you would be safe with me." He paused the barest instant. "But if Brianna happens to be about when we return, I would not hesitate to call on her with you. She makes the best butter cake." He sighed. "Ooey, gooey butter cake..."

"He'll get too fat to fit in his den entrance!" came the stag's voice from somewhere on the other side of the hedge. As I had thought, he was lurking.

"I heard that!"

"You were meant to!"

I suppressed a smile. The wolf looked at me again. This time his expression was definitely pained. "I'm quite sure you would never get fat," I said firmly.

"Thank you for that. And please call me Lobo."

"I'm just Miri, without all that other stuff," I replied, waving my hand dismissively. "But you're being awfully mysterious about where you're taking me."

"That is because we are constrained to not tell you, only show you." Lobo coughed. "We—or rather, Clarion's family and mine—were appointed as guardians of it, and we have very specific instructions that have been passed down through the generations. And as far as I am aware, this is for only you or your mother, and I doubt that she has the qualifications for...something I can't tell you." He looked at me hopefully. "Will you trust me anyway?" I couldn't help but notice that his tail was wagging.

Well, this wouldn't be the strangest thing I'd ever heard of. Or seen, for that matter. My life had certainly gotten interesting. I nodded and turned Brownie around. "Lead and I will follow," I replied, figuring I could eat in the saddle if this was a longer distance from home than I'd planned to go. "I just hope that it's not so far that I'm so late coming home that Papa sends out the Royal Guard to look for me. That would be very bad for both of us, but mostly for me. I'm bound to get into some kind of trouble or be restricted on what I can do if I do something that makes him think I'm not responsible enough."

"I'll make sure that you won't get home late," Lobo promised.

Lobo loped along ahead of me, forcing Brownie into a canter to keep up. I did ask him to stop as we crossed a nice clear brook so all of us could get some water and Brownie could catch his breath. "How far now?" I asked, keeping an eye on the sun as I took a moment to eat. Lobo didn't answer immediately; his mouth was full of my bread and cheese.

"Not far," he said, and looked at my parcel. "That's uncommonly good cheese," he added suggestively. I was almost positive that he deliberately widened his eyes to make them look more puppylike.

"I'll happily give you bread and cheese to keep *girl* off your menu," I teased, because I felt very sure of him now. With him, I was as safe as, or safer than, I was with Sir Delacar. I decided that I had had more than enough and gave him the rest. I would be going home to another huge Court dinner soon enough.

"*Mrmph!*" he said indignantly around another mouthful. "I wouldn't *touch* human. You humans may think you rate high on the deliciousness scale, but the reality is that only creatures who are too slow to catch anything else bother with you. You're not horrible, but rabbit is much nicer."

"I can't say that disappoints me," I retorted dryly.

"Besides, I don't eat things that can talk," Lobo said. "Clarion is right off the menu."

"I'm sure Clarion will be happy to know that," I said with a grin.

I found myself hoping that once Lobo showed me whatever it was he was so eager to have me see, he'd continue to find ways to meet with me. Perhaps on the walk to Brianna's cottage I made every day?

When he had literally wolfed down the last of my lunch, including a custard tart I discarded in favor of a nice juicy plum, we got back on our way. And he hadn't lied; after he turned off the main track, the path we took quickly became a game trail, then a rabbit trail, then a barely perceptible trace through under-brush that was unaccountably thick considering that it was all under a dense forest canopy.

When you read about "dark impenetrable forests" in books, you get the impression that an old forest is all vegetation from the ground up to the treetops.

That's not usually true. The older and thicker that old trees are, the more they shade the ground, and that means that a lot less can grow there. In an ancient forest, very little light reaches beneath the canopy, and it's usually as easy to walk there as it is on a groomed garden path.

Not here. As I ducked over Brownie's neck to avoid getting my hair snagged in branches, I could see why Clarion the stag had not wanted to come along. Either he'd have had to walk along with his nose to the ground like a hunting hound or we'd have spent most of our time untangling his antlers from the branches. Neither would have been very dignified. This really *was* a dark impenetrable forest.

It was practically twilight in here. Not an uncomfortable

dark but a deep-green herb-scented dark with hints of evergreen in the air. The undergrowth was like nothing I had ever seen before—mostly huge ferns and dense bushes a little like holly but without the thorns. We pushed our way in among the dense vegetation, which came up to Brownie's ears. Ferns don't need a lot of light, so that explained how they could grow here, but where had they come from? I'd never seen ferns like this anywhere in the forest.

Brownie began shaking his head with irritation, and the moss-covered ground looked awfully comfortable to walk on, so I finally dismounted and led him, following the swish of Lobo's tail ahead of me.

Because I was paying attention, I saw the glow up ahead when it was just barely visible and watched as it increased as we drew nearer. Finally, Lobo paused and looked over his shoulder. "Come up beside me."

I did and saw that we were at the open arched doorway of a little building made of stone. It looked a bit like a tomb except there was no sarcophagus. Despite the fact that it was as dark as pitch in there, I had no trouble seeing the inside of the mostly empty building because of the softly glowing sword hanging on the back wall.

"I—uh—assume that's what you wanted me to see?" I said to Lobo.

"Actually, we want you to do more than look at it. We want you to take it. It's yours. Or rather, your great-great-great..." He shook his head until his ears made a flapping noise. "Too many greats. The grandmother from Prince Lionel's time. On your mother's side."

So—this wasn't Fae. This was a human thing. My human many-times-great-grandmother had had a magic sword, which, apparently, was now mine. My knees felt a bit wobbly. "I think I need to sit down," I said, and did so right on the moss.

"It's an easy explanation." Lobo licked my ear. I think he intended it to be comforting, so I didn't yelp from surprise when he did it. "Your many-times-great-grandmother was a stable-master's daughter at the palace who was the same age as Lionel. When Lionel's father died, virtually everyone in the palace was aware that Lionel's uncle was going to usurp the throne, but they hoped that his knights would put a stop to it. But they didn't, and the wicked uncle tried to throw Lionel off the tower. Brianna intervened, and everyone who could flee fled, knowing that he was going to purge loyalists, which was everyone at that point. Brianna led them all to Caer Fidelia in the mountains."

"I know that part," I said.

"Well, what you don't know is that instead of being raised as a stablehand, your four-times-great-grandmother showed quite the aptitude for combat, and despite her low birth, she was made a lady knight and eventually the King-in-Exile's Champion. The wizard of the time, Ian Steward, was extraordinarily powerful, and fearing that Lionel's uncle was in league with the Dark Fae, he made *that* for her against the time when she would lead the King-in-Exile's troops into battle to regain his throne." Lobo nodded at the sword.

"It's magic?" I asked. Then I felt stupid because of course it was. Swords don't just glow randomly.

"Actually, it's antimagic," said Lobo, which was a reply that I wasn't expecting. "It's proof against Fae offensive magic, Light *or* Dark. Obviously, a Fae could not have made it. And if you strike against true evil, it will never fail you. Wizard Steward made the sword and Brianna made the scabbard, which heals all wounds that are not immediately fatal. And when Lionel was again on the throne, your great-great-great-great-grandmother came here, left the sword until it was needed again, told only Brianna where it was, and retired to raise horses and lots and lots of children. About the time you destroyed Lady Thornheart, it started glowing. I was the one who first saw that, and I told Brianna since she was the one who bound my line and Clarion's to it, and we both assumed that this meant it was for you. Or there may be another girl out there of your great-great-great-great-grandmother's bloodline who could take it if you don't." He blinked for a few moments. "Or a boy, I suppose; Brianna didn't say anything about the sword being exclusive to females. And your great-great-great-great-grandmother had quite a litter. Eight, I think. By now there must be great-great-great-great-grandchildren scattered all over this kingdom."

"All right then, so this isn't a chosen-one thing?" I asked, somewhat relieved.

"More like an appropriate-one thing."

I giggled a little, and he lay down in the doorway beside me. "But why bring it here? My four-times-great-grandmother, I mean. Why take it all the way out here and hide it if it was meant to be found and used? Why not leave it in the palace armory or something?"

"It's proof against *all* Fae magic," Lobo reminded me. "Just because it's 'meant' for you to take, it doesn't follow that no one else can use it. It's not intelligent, after all; it's just an enchanted tool. Imagine if someone got it who was in the pay of the Dark

Fae. A human, that is. He could go on a wholesale slaughter of the Light Fae without ever breaking the Fae Rules." He scratched his ear with his hind foot. "If something like this had even been thought of at the time the Compact was made, there likely would have been Rules binding humans too."

"I...hadn't thought of that." Now leaving it in a stone building in the middle of the forest seemed a lot more sensible than it had a few moments ago. "So what do I do to claim it? Is there a spell? Do I have to perform a quest or some ceremony?"

Lobo shook his head. "You come from a long line of great-hearted, brave, loyal, and fundamentally common people."

"Oh." I got up. "I'll just go take it down off the wall, then," I said, walking into the building.

"Please. Then we can get you back before your father starts to worry."

The sword stopped glowing as soon as I touched it, and I lifted it down off the two stone pegs it was resting on, as if it were quite like any other sword in our armory. But it had obviously been made for the smaller hand of a woman to use single-handedly with a shield. For being many centuries old, the leather of the scabbard looked practically new. A little scuffed and worn with use but not brittle. It didn't look any different from the swords I'd seen my father using: perfectly plain and completely undecorated, which I suppose was the point. You don't want to have something that practically shouts *I'm a powerful magic sword!* It didn't even have a common agate as a pommel jewel, just a practical steel nut. I threaded the holders onto my belt and put it on. And just like that, we were on our way again.

We did stop at Brianna's cottage, but she wasn't there, much to Lobo's disappointment.

He left me at the part of the forest track that started to see more use. "I'll try and visit when you are taking your lessons," Lobo said. "And if you are alone, I shall sniff that out and escort you to Brianna's. It was a great pleasure meeting you, Miri."

"It was wonderful meeting *you*," I replied, and I impulsively threw my arms around his neck to hug him. He didn't pull away, so I guess he liked it. "I hope we'll be friends."

"Oh," he said, lolling his tongue out in a wolf grin. "We already are. Good night, Miri. Tell your King and your wizard about this, but no one else. Remember what I said about someone getting hold of it and going on a slaughter of Light Fae. This is not a weapon we want many people to know about. I'll let Brianna know that you have it if she doesn't already. She's like that."

CHAPTER
SIX

I GOT BACK TO THE PALACE WELL IN TIME TO CHANGE. AND I toyed with the notion of hiding the sword under my mattress, but once I thought further, that seemed like a really bad idea. I knew Belinda checked under there all the time—not because she suspected me of hiding anything, but because she suspected the serving maids of not doing their job of turning the feather bed and chasing all the dust out of the bed frame every day. If this sword was important enough to have been left where no one would find it all these years, I probably shouldn't do anything like stick it under the mattress. So, before Belinda came in to "help" me dress, I got into my gown and strapped my new sword on over the gown but under the surcoat and went to see if Papa and Mama were still dressing.

They were, although their body servants were just now putting the finishing touches on their outfits. Papa was facing the door as I came in, and both his eyebrows shot up into his hair at the sight of my new "accessory." The sideless surcoat didn't hide it nearly as well as I had hoped it would.

"I think we can manage ourselves now, thank you," he said to the body servants who were hovering over both of them, tweaking seams and twitching sleeves into place. All four of the servants bowed and retreated to join the other servants filing into the Great Hall for dinner. "I trust you have an explanation for this?" Papa asked as soon as they were out of earshot. Mama turned, and one hand flew to her lips as she started with surprise.

"I do," I said, and I did. Explain, that is. When I was done, there was absolute silence in the room.

"I didn't know anything about this," Mama admitted. "So far as I know, my family is just of a line of gentlefolk and esquires with the occasional knight."

"Well, this does answer the question of how they got to be gentlefolk and esquires in the first place," Papa said thoughtfully. "It also tells me why Lionel's Champion was always called the Nameless Knight—it wouldn't have done for the Champion to have been revealed as a woman back then. You know the rest of the story, don't you, Miri? The Usurper got backed into a corner by Lionel's army and demanded single combat. The Usurper chose a Dark Fae as *his* Champion. He obviously intended to cheat by using magic rather than pure combat. But he got put down in three moves and was forced to yield." Papa gestured at the sword at my side. "Well, now we know why. It wasn't the Infinite Light being on the side of right and good, it was Wizard Steward's magic sword." He put one hand at the back of his neck and rubbed it as he thought. "Obviously, you can't just leave it lying around in the open. And I want Gerrold to have a look at it."

"That's what Lobo the wolf said. But I can't hide it in my room, and we can't hide it here, and if I wear it, I'm going to get more wagging tongues." Squires, and I was technically a squire, were not allowed to wear weapons to meals. Only select knights known for their sober behavior and moderation when it came to drink were allowed to do that. Quarrels broke out now and again when people were in their cups, and they were bad enough when people had only eating knives available. There would, of course, always be those select knights inside the Great Hall, and the Royal Guard inside and outside of it, to take care of a surprise attack by an enemy.

"Ah!" Papa's face lit up. "I know. I'll wear it to dinner; given the events at the christening, no one will think twice about it. You and Gerrold can take it up to his tower when dinner is over. You keep it overnight. By that time, I'll have a word with the armorer and Delacar, and we'll have a secure place for it in the morning. I'll tell them as much as they need to know."

So that was what we did. And during dinner, Papa got up and had a word or two with several people; one of them was old Gerrold. Gerrold winked at me when no one else was looking. When Mama and Papa got up, I did too, and I talked idly with Nathaniel and Elle for a little bit. When Papa and Mama went to the privy stair, I followed. This was a little later than I had been retiring lately, but by this time, everyone knew the Companions had gotten a day to rest and weren't surprised to see me up so late. At the stairs, Papa passed me the sword, belt and all; and Gerrold and I went up the back stair while Mama and Papa went back out to the Great Hall and then went into the garden, where there was going to be music.

Once we got up into the Royal Suite, Gerrold and I made our

way through the maze of rooms above it until we got to the little staircase that went up into his tower.

Wizards always have a tower. That's because wizards are known to keep odd hours, and there are often noises and lights and sometimes bad smells coming from their quarters. A tower keeps that sort of disturbance away from the rest of us. Gerrold's was very nice. There was a long spiral staircase that came up through the floor to what looked like a pretty stone cottage in the round with two floors and a really excellent set of fireplaces. You would have thought that it would be drafty and cold, but it was always cozy unless it was a warm, sunny day and he had the windows open. The windows had exceptionally thick glass in frames that you could open to let the bad smells out and stout shutters to keep out winter winds. I guessed that Gerrold slept on the second floor; I never went past the first, so I never saw that part of the tower.

Every inch of wall on the bottom floor was covered in shelves. Some had books, some had bottles and jars and boxes of ingredients, some just had interesting things on them. Even Papa isn't old enough to remember the wizard before Gerrold; I was told he had a much more disturbing notion of what should be on display—he went in for preserved animals and animal parts. Everywhere. On the shelves, on the floor, and hanging from the ceiling.

Gerrold prefers his animals whole and alive. He has a pet crow, a pet ferret, a pet tortoise, three cats, a hedgehog, an owl, and an ancient raven that rarely moves except to look at you out of one rather bored eye and dismiss you before it goes back to sleep.

As usual, I looked around for a chair that didn't have anything in it, and I ended up picking a stack of books out of one at random and sat down. I laid the sword across my knees. It was promptly sat on by the tortoiseshell cat, which jumped up into my lap.

"Trust a cat to find the center of attention and occupy it," the wizard chuckled as he moved another cat off his chair and sat down across from me with the cold hearth between us. "Now, before I have a look at it, give me the whole story, will you?"

It didn't take long, and while he thought about what I had to say, I relaxed and looked around because there's always something interesting in his tower.

He had all the windows open, and glass-and-horn wind guards over all the candles, but there was only just enough of a breeze tonight to keep the room aired out and comfortable. No one had ever told me how old he was, but wizards do tend to live longer than most people, so he was definitely at least seventy. His hair was a silvery gray, cut in a slightly untidy bowl cut. Gerrold liked to wear comfortable tunics and loose trews in colors that didn't show stains and burns, and if you didn't know who and what he was, chances were you'd take him for some faithful family retainer or a slightly eccentric old uncle of someone in the Court. He dressed up in fancy velvet robes with lots of gold and silver symbols that no one else knew the meaning of when he wanted to impress, but I think he preferred being nondescript most of the time. And Gerrold rarely wore his pointed hat. He hated the hat even though it's the one thing that people know about wizards, that they always wear a pointy hat.

It was impossible to tell what color his eyes were. In some

lights, they looked gray; in others, a smoky brown; in others, there was a hint of green. He's a wizard. Mystery is what he's made of.

"I wonder," Gerrold said, looking keenly at the sword on my lap, "if being immune to Fae magic means that you won't be able to use Fae magic when you're wearing it?"

"Well, that would be inconvenient. Shall I try?" I asked. I liked that about Gerrold; he got straight to the practical side of things. I've often heard wizards described as "vague" or "fuzzy minded." Neither of those applied to Gerrold.

"Something harmless, please," he said, his eyes getting crinkles at their corners as he smiled. "We don't want to alarm the cats. Or the birds. Or both."

I did the most harmless thing I could think of: making a little light at the end of my finger. He had me try it again with the sword unsheathed. I still had no problem—although I got the distinct feeling that if I had tried to pull Fae magic into the hand that rested on the sword, I wouldn't have been able to.

"Excellent. I think we can assume that you'll be able to use human magic as well," Gerrold said. "Yes, Miri, it appears to me that you have the ability to do human magic as well as Fae. And, yes, I know you don't know how; once you have a reasonable mastery of the Fae side of magic, I'll take you on as a pupil." He paused and looked at me speculatively. "Although…there are a few simple things I should teach you that will be immediately useful, so perhaps we can add the occasional lesson after dinner."

I didn't groan, but it took an effort. I was already exhausted by the end of the day, and now Gerrold wanted to add more lessons. Really?

"Meanwhile, may I examine this sword?" Gerrold asked,

and he did not hold his hand out for it until I picked it up and offered it to him hilt first. Which showed a nicety of feeling, I thought.

"Wizard Steward never mentioned this blade in any of the writings he left behind," Gerrold said, perching a pair of wire-wrapped glass lenses on his nose and peering earnestly at the hilt. "Of course, if he'd done so, the weapon wouldn't still be a secret, would it?"

This was clearly a rhetorical question, so I kept my mouth shut and petted the purring cat. I noticed that there was a faint scent of balsam in the room now, and it had a hint of warmth to it that told me it was coming from the candles. Gerrold had been experimenting with scented wax again, and I hoped that he'd share his new recipe with the household chandler.

"However, I cannot believe he did not leave the formula for creating it *somewhere*. After all, what if it was lost or destroyed in some way? Someone would need to make another, wouldn't you think?"

Another rhetorical question. Now he bent over the steel blade. "So, if he didn't leave the secret behind in his writings, then where did he..."

He stopped talking, as if he had spotted something. And he sketched a few symbols—at least I think they were symbols—in the air with his index finger. He paused, then sketched a few more. He paused again, then sketched one final glyph.

And the entire length of the blade lit up in lines of tiny glowing words. Gerrold didn't say anything. He just smiled in satisfaction.

He passed his hand over the sword as if he was wiping something from the blade, and the writing vanished just like that.

"That was how to make another sword," I said. "He wrote the instructions on the blade of this one! So the next wizard to see it could memorize it just in case!"

"Exactly so. I'll have another look at it when I'm prepared to commit it to memory, but for now, I think I shall give you this fine blade back and let you get your rest."

I tried not to, but I yawned anyway.

Gerrold chuckled. "You are obviously in need of it, and my day is just beginning." He stood up and escorted me to the stairs leading downward, like the kind gentleman he was. "This has been a very exciting and profitable day for all of us."

"It has. Good night, Wizard Gerrold," I said, starting down the stairs and holding the hem of my gown up with both hands. It would be pretty stupid of me to get this far and break my neck on the stairs because I didn't hold my gown up!

"Good night, Squire Miri," he said from the square of light above me.

"Squire Miri." That had a very nice sound to it.

The look on Belinda's face the next morning when I pulled the sword out of my bed was beyond price, because the very last thing she would have suspected of me was that I would be sleeping with a sword. And even better was the look on her face when I said, "Papa's orders," before she could think of a single word to say.

Her mouth opened once, then shut firmly, and she nodded. I had been prepared to argue some more, but it looked as if I wasn't going to need to. Whether it was my dogged persistence in the face of my own exhaustion and her disapproval or her respect for the King, she was going to accept this without an argument.

When I got down to the courtyard, Sir Delacar and the armorer were both waiting for me. Delacar put the rest of the squires through a trot around the courtyard to warm up; the armorer crooked his finger at me and I followed.

The armorer is probably the most important man in the palace who's not a noble. He is the man every fighting person in the entire palace depends on to keep them as safe as they ever can be in a battle. He knows when to call them in to make alterations, and he chooses the right weapon for them.

He's always in light armor except when he's in the smithy working on some specialized piece that needs tricky adjustments. He doesn't do most of the actual work of making the armor we all wear; that's for his three smiths. But they are there to get his detailed knowledge pounded into their skulls with the relentless steady beat of hammer on anvil. And one day, the best of them will take over his job and select a new journeyman to take *his* place. Not too soon, though, I think. The armorer's body is the body of a man half his age, corded with the muscle of someone who has spent his entire life making things to save ours. He can wield the heaviest of hammers with scarcely a sweat and carry entire armloads of chain mail as easily as I can carry a stack of clean gowns.

As I had half expected, he led me into the armory, but we went deeper into that building than I had ever been before to a room filled floor to ceiling with racks holding shallow man-size chests. He pulled one off one of the top shelves. And considering that the chest itself was heavy and probably contained a full set of battle armor, that was quite the feat.

The lanterns on the wall between each rack gave us plenty of light to see by, and the room smelled of oil and leather, with a faint hint of damp. The armorer bent down, opened the chest, and unfolded the oiled leather that lay over the top of the armor in it.

"This is yours," he said. He had a pleasant baritone voice. "This is your combat armor. Try not to grow too fast."

As I'd expected, it was chain mail, which was the lightest of the metal armors, the one that offered the best protection from everything but crushing weapons and that was the easiest to move in. It was a much better set than the one I'd already been given; the links were strong, riveted like the other set, but much smaller than the links in my practice suit. At his nod, I bent to pick up one sleeve.

It moved like very heavy fabric. It actually felt liquid, sensuous in my hand. For one moment, I contemplated what an entire gown of the stuff would be like....

Don't be ridiculous, I told myself as the armorer bent down and picked up the contents inside the oiled leather. "Feel along the inside top of the chest for the catch," he told me. I did, and I pulled up the entire bottom of the chest. Which, obviously, was a false bottom. I could already see where this was going, so I laid the sword and belt inside it and lowered the false bottom again. It didn't quite fit right, so I pulled it back up, took the sheath off the belt, took the blade out of the sheath, and laid them side by side. I tried the bottom again and felt the catch click shut properly. The armorer arranged my chain mail back in the chest, closed it up, and put it up on its shelf.

"This will do for now," he said. "But I'm having a proper lady's chest with a false bottom brought up to your room as soon as I can finish it. I was told there's not room to spare in your chamber for an armor chest, so you can stow your gowns in it too. I'll transfer the sword myself before it goes up. There's no use in your having such a thing if you can't keep it where you can get to it in a hurry."

That was more words at once than anyone I know had ever gotten out of him. I puffed out my breath with relief, since having the sword where I could get to it was exactly what had been on my mind.

"Your knight is waiting," he said meaningfully, and I headed out at a trot.

Four days later, there was a chest in my room when I came up to change for dinner. Because we Companions were essentially doing combat training all day long, I was almost never *out* of my trews and tunic until I came in for dinner. The six of us ate luncheon together, rested together, and did pretty much everything except eat dinner together, which was when the ranks became all too apparent. Giles was all the way down at the far end of the room at the servants' tables. The rest were scattered all over the room. I had some ideas about this that I was brooding over, but the sight of the new chest knocked them right out of my head.

Unlike the very utilitarian chests that held the armor down

in the armory, this one was beautiful and I couldn't imagine how the armorer had had it made in a mere four days. Unless—of course. He'd found a craftsman with a chest of the proper size and had the false bottom built into it rather than starting with the false bottom and building around it.

At any rate, the chest was a beautiful piece of work. The color of honey, the top was carved with tiny wild briar roses and vines, and it was polished and waxed so smoothly that the wood felt like silk under my fingers. Belinda caught me sitting beside it and nodded with approval. "First time you've been given anything that befits a *young lady*," she said, which told me that she still had not forgiven me for turning into a warrior and that she probably never would.

"Shall I move some of your things in there for you?" she asked, looking as pleased as a cat with a choice of cream or fish.

"Yes, but be careful," I told her. "The armorer gave it to me, and my new chain mail is in there all wrapped in oiled leather. Make sure you put some canvas in the chest so the gowns won't get spoiled by the oil."

The look on her face was worth the hair pulling I was going to get when she did my hair tonight. It was a blessed shame that my hair was so long that I couldn't easily do it myself. And the thought of that hair pulling I was about to get gave me an idea to distract her from the chest.

"Maybe I should cut my hair," I said aloud, knowing what she would think of *that*. She was always going on about how "a woman's hair is her crown of beauty" and how "at least your hair is appropriate." Belinda turned crimson.

"Proper ladies do not cut their hair," she said primly. She

left out the part about how only women shameless enough to conduct themselves as if they thought they were equal to men cut their hair because I always added, "And women in holy orders, and those who are very sick, and those who are trying to show they aren't vain about their looks." Belinda had stopped using that nonargument weeks ago.

"But I'm not a proper lady, am I?" I replied. "I'm Aurora's guardian and one of the Companions. I'm a proper warrior, or I'm going to be, and woman warriors cut their hair all the time."

The more I thought about the idea of cutting my hair, the better I liked it. I was always waking up with my head at odd angles if I wasn't careful to drape my braids over the top of my bed or off to the side. And although my hair made good padding, it was also a damned hot nuisance inside a helmet. If I'd had scissors handy, I'd have done the deed right then.

Belinda, however, was now furious with me, her face a mask of barely suppressed rage. "Very well, then," she said, and marched off. I thought I was going to get some peace and quiet, but no, she came marching back with scissors. And before I knew it, she was shearing me right off at the chin.

For a minute, I was shocked. Then I started laughing as she whacked the second braid off.

From the look on her face, this was not what she'd expected me to do. She stared at me, stunned, the scissors still in her hand.

I could hardly believe how much *freer* such a simple thing made me feel. All my life I'd had this weight of hair holding my head down, tugging at me, getting in the way. It had been far more of a burden than a sign of beauty. My head felt *light*. In a good way.

Belinda had expected me to be shocked that I'd gotten what I asked for and start crying because now all my "beauty" was gone. She did not know how to react when I didn't do that. I ran both hands through my hair, then ruffled it up like you would a dog's fur. To my slight disappointment, it didn't curl. I'd rather hoped for curls. Curls always look good no matter how wet or windy the weather.

I stood up, the two braids of hair falling down to my feet like a pair of coiled snakes, and ran my fingers through my shorn crop again. "This is marvelous, Belinda! Thank you!" I said merrily, and snatched the chaplet she'd left on my little table and put it on my head. "I can't wait to show Mama and Papa!"

"Wait!" Belinda bleated, suddenly aware that if anyone got into trouble for this, it was going to be her—but it was too late. What could she do? It wasn't as if she could glue the braids back on again.

Mama and Papa were already gone to dinner, so I ran down the stairs and made my "entrance" from the private stair. I really didn't know what to expect, but the immediate reaction from those who could see me was side-eyed, as if *they* didn't know how to react; Mama caught that and turned and looked at me, and her hand flew to her lips. "*Miri!*" she gasped. "*Your hair!*"

But Papa just nodded. "Very practical especially considering you are one of Aurora's Companions now. It looks both competent and becoming. I strongly approve." And he said it loudly enough that his voice carried at least to the middle of the Great Hall, which stopped some of the side-eyes.

"Thank you, Papa. I like it ever so much better than long hair." I took my place at Mama's left, then when it appeared that he was not going back to another conversation, I said, "And about Aurora's Companions...would it be presumptuous of me to ask that we all be seated together at meals from now on? I think we need to..." I searched for the right words. "I think we need to really become like the knights are. Brothers and sisters. Right now, we don't have much to do with one another outside of training." Not that we weren't spending most hours of the day training, but still.

Papa considered that for a moment. "Not *all* meals," he responded. "Not state occasions or great occasions when you really must be with us because of your rank and position. But ordinary meals, yes. In fact, you should all be seated with the squires. It will give them a chance to get to know you, and you them. They will be knights one day, and you will all be as well."

"Thank you, Papa!" I replied gleefully. Because that meant no more dressing up for dinner; I could and *would* arrange for some practical tunics and trews to wear at dinner among the squires, so we and the squires would be dressed equally rather than according to rank. The arms on my tunic would be the Royal Arms, of course, rather than Sir Delacar's, but that would be the only difference among us. I'd make sure that all the rest had the same sort of outfits too—if Papa didn't give the orders himself, which he just might. He was very good at taking care of the details that made a difference.

Belinda had started this, but I was going to finish it to my satisfaction.

"I think your mother wants to have a word with you after dinner about the genesis of your new hair arrangement," Papa added, after a long look exchanged with Mama. I nodded. For once I was entirely blameless, so I was actually looking forward to this.

When Papa signaled the end of dinner, he went to mingle with the Court. Mama and I, however, went back silently up the stairs. When we got to her rooms, which by now had been lit by lamps, I expected that she would finally say something. Before she could, however, we realized that Belinda was sitting on a stool in the common room of the Royal Suite with my braids on her lap and a face full of woe.

My governess sprang to her feet, clutching the hair in front of her, then went to her knees and sobbed. "Oh, Majesty! Forgive me! It was all my fault; she vexed me so, and before I knew what I'd done, the scissors were in my hand and the hair was on the floor!"

Now that was a bit of a fib, because we both knew she'd had to go out of the room for the scissors, and she'd had plenty of time to think about what she was going to do while she was looking for them. But I kept my mouth shut since she'd owned up to its being her doing and her idea.

"Miri, is that true?" Mama asked. Rhetorically, of course, since Belinda was now sobbing theatrically about how sorry she was, with her face buried in the braids. I just nodded.

"I do truly like it much, much better than long hair, though," I said. Now Belinda was groveling and weeping into Mama's hem. "I'd like to keep it this way. Though a bit tidier. I think it's lopsided."

In the candlelight, poor Mama looked as if she couldn't make up her mind what to feel. Annoyed with Belinda? Pained that I wasn't turning out to be like her and taking pleasure in being feminine? Amused at my lopsided haircut? Since becoming Queen, she had learned how to control her expression so well that I often couldn't figure out what she was thinking. Which was good for the Queen but a little hard on me. Finally, she just nodded and turned to Belinda, who was still noisily weeping.

"That will be enough, Belinda," Mama said, using that flat, matter-of-fact tone she trotted out only when she needed to. It certainly made Belinda shut up and drop the hem of Mama's gown. "It's very clear now that you are entirely the wrong sort of governess for Miri. I believe you'll have to have another position elsewhere."

Belinda looked up, her face frozen in horror, and for the first time, I actually felt sorry for her. Very sorry, in fact, since Mama had just told her that she was being turned away. She was rather old to have to go out and find a new position—not to mention the fact that virtually every lady in the Court who needed and could afford a governess already had one. Now it was my turn to feel guilty. As angry as I'd been with Belinda in the past, she didn't deserve to be turned out! "Mama—" I began hesitantly.

But Belinda spoke over me. "Majesty—you're turning me out?" Her face crumpled, and two huge *real* tears welled up out of her eyes.

"I'm—good heavens, you silly thing, of course not!" Mama laughed. "No, I'll need you for Aurora, who will certainly need the kind of early training you can give her once she's too old for Melalee. But for Miri, you're all wrong. So until Aurora is old enough, you'll be the mistress of my chamber and in charge of my maids. See to it that they keep the Royal Suite, the nursery, and Miri's room clean, and instruct them in the sorts of needlework needed for mending our apparel and linens. Take them off any other duties but those. It's time I made some changes to the immediate household anyway. I can make quite a difference in the costs of the Royal Household with some new economies." Mama made a little face. "Just because I am the Queen is no reason to act foolishly improvident. I wore my gowns turned four times, then cut them down for Miri before I was the Queen, and the King and I can certainly cope with having everything but velvet turned at least once."

Now Belinda was back to sobbing into Mama's hem, this time in burbling gratitude. Mama and I exchanged a look of exasperation. But I was elated. This was exactly the sort of thing that Belinda was good at, and it would be a step up for the maids, who would learn how to refurbish an expensive wardrobe. That was literally a priceless skill—and what was more, it was one they could teach when they were too old to work as maids anymore.

Right now, they were just chambermaids, part of a crew that cleaned every room in this part of the palace every day. Now they'd only have to clean the Royal Suite, the nursery, and my room. The heavy work they'd been assigned to had been cut in half in favor of needlework. I knew from Belinda's relentless tutoring in running a household back when we were in our own little household that, while we'd have to hire two more maids, the money the household would save would be made up three or four times over by being economical with our wardrobes.

"But if Belinda isn't to be my governess anymore, who is?" I asked. I couldn't think of anyone *I* would want. Most of the other governesses I knew about were cut from Belinda's cloth.

"You won't have one," Mama replied, which shocked me. "You don't need one any more than a boy your age would still need a tutor if he was training to be a knight. These past weeks, I've been watching you run from one lesson to another and never shirk. I don't think a governess would make you work any harder, and you already know everything Belinda can teach you that is going to be useful to you." She sighed and smiled. "I should have known all along that you were destined to become a lady knight even if Aurora *didn't* need you as her Champion. Swords instead of needles it is."

I wanted to hug her in gratitude, but Belinda was still in the way. Mama looked down, a brief flash of annoyance on her face. "Thank you, Belinda, that will do. You're a good and faithful servant, and I know I can count on you. You might as well keep to your current bedchamber; it's as convenient to the Royal Suite as any other would be. You may go."

That was the royal dismissal, and Belinda knew it. She clambered to her feet and left, walking backward until she came to the doorway, where she curtsied, turned, and left.

"The struggle between her and Melalee is going to be entertaining," Mama mused with a slight smile. "I suspect age will defeat Melalee before Belinda does."

"And even then, she'll sit in the nursery and wait for you and Papa to produce a little brother for me," I said, and Mama flushed prettily.

"Well, my dear, even though you are not a princess, you are still my daughter, and as such, the King and I have decided that you should have a pair of ladies-in-waiting of your own." And I was about to protest that I didn't need any ladies-in-waiting because what would they do all day except sit with Mama's ladies and be redundant? But she went on before I could even open my mouth. "Lady Raquelle and Lady Susanna might as well take those positions. Lady Felicity and Lady Iris are both leaving me to return with their husbands to their family estates, I don't intend to replace them, and I can reshuffle the others so Raquelle and Susanna can have that small bedchamber nearest yours."

"Oh, *Mama*!" I cried, beside myself with happiness because nothing could be more perfect. The two girls were each crowded into a bedchamber with their sisters in the chambers occupied by their parents. Actually, crowded into a *bed*. Anna shared one with her two younger sisters, and Elle with *three* other sisters. This was the norm for most of the younger members of the Court whether they were here or on their family estates. In fact, all of Mama's unmarried ladies slept two to a bed, and more often than not, four to a room. Space in the palace was at a premium, and there were many people here at Court. My friends would be so happy to get some space of their own even if they had to share the room!

"I'll give the orders to their parents in the morning," Mama said, because, of course, she was the Queen, and it really didn't matter what their parents thought. Not that they were likely to object. This was a tremendous honor for both of my friends, not to mention taking one source of sisterly quarrels out of a crowded "suite" that probably consisted of only two or three bedrooms.

"I won't have you three staying up half the night gossiping, mind you," Mama added, shaking an admonishing finger at me. "If that happens—"

"It won't!" I promised. It was a safe promise because chances were that we'd be yawning at the end of every day. The only reason I wasn't now was because of all of the excitement…which was wearing off. And just as I thought that, I yawned.

Mama laughed. "Do you still remember how to put yourself to bed?"

"Yes, Majesty," I replied, and dropped a saucy curtsy. "Oh… if I'm going to be eating with the squires—"

"I already left orders for tunics and trews to be brought up in the morning," Mama said, turning to leave.

I got back to my room without stumbling—and without having yards of hair to deal with, I got ready for bed in a fraction of the time I usually did. I already knew Belinda's act of intended punishment was one of the best things she had ever done for me.

I heard from Papa over breakfast that since my female Companions had been elevated to ladies-in-waiting, he felt that it was time to do some rearranging of housing all around. So the boys would move from their parents' suites—or in Giles's case, the servants' dormitory—into the Knights' Tower.

Obviously, I didn't help in the Knights' Tower when the boys moved into the empty squires' room in Delacar's suite, but I had quite enough entertainment with helping the girls.

Elle and Anna giggled at my hair, giddy with their elevation in status and thrilled to bits with the prospect of no longer sharing a bed with *anyone*. Servants brought up their chests of clothing; two of the strongest chambermaids stayed to help shuffle the furnishings around. The girls were utterly delighted with having separate beds. Their beds weren't the sort of immovable canopied monsters that had to be disassembled and reassembled in place. They were a couple of little box beds you could fit a wool mattress into, and they had separate canopies for the bed curtains that could be put up once they decided where to put the beds. "I've had quite enough of elbows in the eye and cold feet where no foot should be!" declared Elle.

Anna nodded vigorously. "There," she said, laying a sheepskin down between the two beds. "Now neither of us will step on cold stone in the morning. I think this is as much room as we're going to be able to manage and still have two beds. We can put up the frames and canopies now." The chambermaids nodded and began assembling the frames.

"Well, there was barely enough room to move around in my old chamber and no sheepskin on the floor, either. I'm happy!" Elle said, throwing herself backward onto her bed. Then she sat up abruptly. "Do you think Sir Delacar will want *us* to cut our hair?"

"I think Sir Delacar won't care," I said. "I think he'll even approve if you can figure out some way to use your hair as a weapon."

I meant that facetiously, but Elle took me seriously. "Hmm," she mused, pulling her long braid over her shoulder and examining it. "Not long enough to use as a whip, but I bet I could strangle someone with it."

Anna stared at her. "And I'm sleeping in the same room with you?" she said in mock horror.

"Don't worry, you're safe. As long as you don't snore!" Elle uttered an evil laugh.

And right about then, a maid delivered sets of the same kinds of tunics and trews the squires wore, and they were in approximately the appropriate sizes. I say "approximately" because the squires got their clothing out of a common pool so nothing was actually fitted. Still, that could be fixed as long as we didn't actually cut any of the material. Since these tunics and trews would eventually have to be handed on to other squires, we had to return them in the same condition we got them except for normal wear and tear. Elle and Anna each seized a tunic and held it up to themselves, trying to gauge where alterations needed to be made. There weren't any badges on them yet; the badges would have to be made before we could apply them to the tunics. Well, there it was, Belinda's sewing lessons were going to come in handy after all.

"Clothing later, lunch now," I admonished. "Or we'll be late for Brianna."

I didn't need to remind them twice. Whether they fit or not, all three of us got into our tunics and trews and boots, and with me enjoying the freedom of movement and freedom from my hair, we competed to see who could get to the Great Hall the fastest without actually breaking into a run.

CHAPTER SEVEN

It was obvious from the moment we sat down with the squires that we were going to get tested. Luncheon fare with the squires was pottage and bread and butter served on common platters and in big common bowls. The other squires filled up their bowls until there was no room left, leaving us with only scrapings. This was far more food than anyone could reasonably eat, especially if they were going to train right after luncheon, which, of course, they were. They were just trying us to see if we raised a fuss over being left with nothing to eat.

But the servants, unperturbed, just brought another bowl of pottage and plate of bread, which we helped ourselves from—with much more reasonable portions for someone who was about to get a heavy workout. The oldest boy, who sat in the middle of us all, smirked at the looks of dismay from the others when they realized their attempt at making us upset had backfired on them. "That's what you get for pranking the new squires. And you're going to eat all that, you greedy little pigs. Every bit. And if you vomit it all back up when we go back to training, *you'll* be the ones cleaning it up."

So, the Chief Squire is on our side, I thought.

That was proved a little later. "How do you like slumming down here, Your Maj—" one began, but he ended with *"Ow!"* when the Chief Squire smacked him on the top of the head with a particularly long-handled spoon that appeared to have been made for just that purpose.

"Manners," the Chief Squire said mildly. He was a good-looking young man, probably just about to be made a knight, with tidy brownish-black hair and chiseled features.

"I'm not royal," I said, politely ignoring the smack and the admonition. "I'm certainly not a 'Majesty.' My name is Miriam. And I like the food down here very much. It's what I was used to before, when my father was alive."

That was a reminder that I used to be a simple knight's daughter and liked it that way.

The next test came when Elle got up and one of the other squires leered at her. "I see you still have all your hair," he said. "I can use it against—"

Before the Chief Squire could stand up to rap him on the head with the spoon, Elle stepped swiftly behind the other squire, whipped her braid around his neck, and pulled.

"*Urk*—" he said. The Chief Squire sat back down and watched in amusement.

"The thing about using my hair to garrote you," Elle said conversationally as he tried and failed to loosen the noose, "is that, unlike using my hands to choke you, you can't escape my hold by prying up a finger and trying to break it."

He clawed at her wrists to no avail.

"And I can tighten it at will, which I can't do with my hands." His face got a little redder.

"You've made your point, Squire, and a good point it is," the Chief Squire said, and Elle released the boy and whipped her braid back too fast for him to grab it. "Gentlemen, please remember your fellow squires are being trained by Sir Delacar. Sir Delacar has trained the last three King's Champions. Don't ever mistake his girth for a sign of incompetence as a trainer. Now, if you're quite finished, I'm going to be interested to see if any of you can keep that triple portion of pottage you hogged down where it belongs this afternoon."

He gestured with one finger, and the other squires got up a bit shamefacedly and filed out the door. He stopped at my seat and held out his hand. "Wulf," he said as I took it. "Don't mind them. The puppies think they have to prove themselves." Then he grinned wryly. "Or rather, they thought they had to make you prove yourselves. You'll be pleased to know that during their move to the Knights' Tower, the three male Companions took no prisoners, either." I glanced over my shoulder and saw the three boys grinning sheepishly. Well, that explained the bruise on Giles's cheekbone.

"We expected it," I replied, although I hadn't. "Call me Miri. This is Elle." Then I introduced the others. "I don't envy you this afternoon. If nothing else, they are going to learn the folly of training on an overfull stomach."

He made a face. "I'd advise you to avoid the training yard until tomorrow."

*　　*　　*

It was a good thing for us that we were training with Brianna in the afternoon. When we got back, changed, and went down to our first dinner with the squires, a good half of the seats at the table were empty, and Chief Squire Wulf wore a smug little smile on his face. It appeared that his prediction had come true. The rest of the squires were quite subdued.

And very polite. There was no attempt to hog all the better offerings, and dinner was quite nice even down at this end of the table. Everyone shared. Wulf more or less monopolized the conversation, directing most of it at us, asking us how far along we were in our training with Sir Delacar, and giving us some very useful tips.

Although, to be honest, he was paying attention mostly to Elle. Anna looked a little put out but soon reconciled herself when a new knight got up from farther up the table and came back to us when the last course was being served. She didn't even have to exert herself, as he made it quite clear that while he was ostensibly there to rib his old comrade Wulf about not being made a knight yet, his interest was really in Anna.

They both looked disappointed when I cleared my throat gently and stood up, and they stood up with me. Now, it was true that Anna and Elle didn't strictly *have* to go up when I did. As long as I made it clear they could stay, they could. But we all were pretty young, and for that reason, they'd certainly hear about it from their parents if they didn't accompany me. In a few months, they could probably get away with staying in the Great Hall after I went up, but not now, and all three of us knew it.

Besides, there would be lots of opportunities for flirting. We'd had a long morning of moving things and a longer afternoon of training, and if they weren't feeling tired now, they would be as soon as those boys' eyes were off them.

And—all right, I was a little jealous. I was in a very awkward position socially. Although technically I was probably the same rank as the young squires and knights, having the Queen as my mother made things...odd.

This is where Belinda's lessons had been spot-on, and I was reluctantly grateful for them. My behavior with young men had to be beyond reproach because what I did could have political repercussions. Missteps on my part meant potential things that could be used against my mother. While I was not a princess, I was still valuable material for a political marriage, so I couldn't engage in anything that even appeared like light flirtation with young men.

I knew this in theory, but this was the first time I'd come up against this in practice. So I said good night politely, the other two said good night reluctantly, and Giles got a friendly nod and a wave of my hand. Then, with a summoning gesture from Wulf, Giles and the other two boys moved farther down the table and took our vacated seats so they could all talk. Which was a very good thing; it meant that the Chief Squire had decided that they measured up to his standards. Having the Chief Squire as your ally meant that even if you were lowborn like Giles, no one would dare try to snub you.

Since we were nowhere near the head table, we went out the usual entrance and up the main stair. As soon as we got out of earshot of the boys, Elle giggled. "Please don't tell me you two are going to stay up all night talking about Wulf and Sir Karel." I sighed. "You'll regret it in the morning if you do."

"Well, what do *you* think about them, Miri?" Elle demanded.

I could see that I wasn't going to be allowed to keep my opinions to myself. "I like them both. Wulf is smarter than Karel, but Karel is probably a better fighter. Did you see how he caught the tankard that was about to fall off the table? Those are quick reflexes." I shrugged. "They both seem nice and not as full of themselves as that one idiot was." I didn't have to specify which idiot.

"So you *were* watching them!" Anna exclaimed.

"Of course I was." I smirked. "And listening too. We're more or less attached to the squires now, so it makes sense to pay attention to the Chief Squire. And it doesn't hurt that he's handsome."

"Oh, is he?" Elle sighed. I laughed.

By this point, we were up on the fifth floor passing through the maze of rooms to get to ours, and she was obliged to keep her feelings to herself. Both Elle and Anna must have learned what I was taught at an early age: Don't say anything you wouldn't want spread about where there are ears to hear it, staff *or* Court. People will gossip regardless of rank. I have no doubt at all that Belinda shared plenty about me with her fellows.

It was still light outside although dusk wasn't far off, so it was easy to weave our way through the palace, and the only people we encountered were servants. Everyone else would be outside in the garden enjoying the balmy night air and the minstrels. It was only when we got to the room Elle and Anna were sharing that they could both talk freely again.

In their absence, the frames for the bed curtains had been set up around the little beds, and the heavy curtains and canopies had been installed. Theirs were a heavy wool rather than the velvet of mine, but they were a nice shade of green. They weren't needed now, but when winter came, those curtains were really good to have to keep out the cold drafts. Elle looked as if she was about to fling herself down on her bed, then she suddenly remembered that she had duties and started to follow me into my room.

"Oh, don't bother," I said, waving them both back. That was one of the many things that drove me insane about Belinda. "I'm perfectly capable of undressing myself, so you two—"

"When you're ready for bed, would you rather come in here for a good long gossip, or would you rather we come to you?" Anna asked, looking to me expectantly. And I was startled, because I'd never actually *had* friends before, and it had never occurred to me that they'd want to include me. They were my ladies-in-waiting, after all. On the other hand, we were also Aurora's Companions. I thought quickly and said, "Come to me. I've got one of those beds big enough for a family; there'll be room enough for all three of us in comfort."

I had just finished a good brushing of my hair when they peeked in, with dressing gowns wrapped around their night-dresses. We all clambered into my bed, and I used a tiny bit of Fae magic to light the candle in the headboard. By now, it was fully dark. I'd left my window open, and the hooting of Gerrold's owl drifted in the window on a breeze cool enough that we all wrapped part of the blankets and velvet coverlet about ourselves.

But I really didn't want to hear them coo and sigh over boys until we all got too sleepy to stay awake any longer. "So, are you properly settled in?" I asked. "Everything put away? Happy with the furnishings?" They nodded happily. "Oh, and I have good news and bad news for you about being my ladies. The good news is that one of your privileges is that you get the pick of my old gowns. The bad news is that Mama told me that the Royal Household is going to be a model of economy and that our gowns are going to be turned at least once before they are handed down."

They both laughed at that, genuine laughter that I was happy to hear. "The way you like to run about in tunics and trews, your gowns are never going to see enough wear to be turned once before all the muscles we're getting make you outgrow them, Miri." Elle chuckled, pulling her knees up to her chin so her dressing gown and nightdress covered her toes. "I must admit, I like the squires' clothing better myself except for the way we look in it."

Anna made a face. "Shapeless."

"We can fix that," I reminded them. "That is, if you're willing to give up a few free hours to alter your tunics. I'd leave the trews alone if I were you."

They exchanged a look. "Mama's dressmaker will alter them for us…but we'll need something to give her for her trouble," Anna said after a moment. I nodded; Anna's family was much better off than Elle's, and it was lovely of her to think of helping Elle out.

"Well, I get money from the estate the King gave me, and I haven't touched a copper yet," I told them. "That's my 'household money' and you're my household, so there you go, that's something I'm responsible for. The only complication is that when we get our tunics back from the palace laundresses, we'll have to be careful that we get the right ones."

"We can mark our initials inside the collars in ink," Elle suggested.

"So, were you both maids of honor to any of the Queen's ladies-in-waiting?" I asked, before the topic of boys could come up.

"I was actually between ladies, I guess you could say." Elle laughed. "My mother had decided for some reason I never learned that I shouldn't attend to Lady Diona anymore, and the Queen hadn't requested I attend to anyone else."

Anna sighed. "I was attending old Lady Katrion. She may be a bear on the Privy Council, but she was actually very sweet to me. I like being a Companion better, but I quite miss her."

"So tell me about being a maid of honor," I urged.

Elle and Anna happily chattered away, the topic quickly turning to how they wanted to alter their gowns since now they were my ladies-in-waiting and would have to make a better show of things. I offered to let them dive into the chest of trimmings that Mama shared with her ladies-in-waiting—when a gown is spoiled by staining, tearing, or burning, and there's not enough good fabric to remake it for someone smaller, the trim and embroidery are cut off and salvaged, and the remaining fabric made into something for a child.

While I certainly like the comfort of wearing squires' clothing, I do adore a pretty gown, so that was a much better topic for gossip than the boys as far as I was concerned. Truth to tell, my feelings about young men are very complicated. I can't just flirt willy-nilly like other girls can. I'm not really free to do what I want unless Papa says I am. And while he did promise that I could be whatever I want, I am very aware, thanks to Belinda, that this promise does not extend to random flirting that could lead to jealousy or worse among his allies.

Mind you, now that I was the chief of Aurora's protectors

and everyone knew I had Fae blood, things might be very different. But until I knew for certain that they were, well, when it came to boys, I needed to keep my feet on the ground and my wits about me. And as soon as Elle and Anna started to yawn, I chased them back to their beds.

I blew out the candle feeling absurdly happy. Tonight had shown me that I had *friends*.

Bring your wolf present to the tower tonight after supper, said the note left on my bed a few days later. It wasn't signed, but it didn't need to be. Gerrold must want to look the sword over again.

But now there was a complication. Elle and Anna.

I'd been told by Lobo not to tell anyone but Mama and Papa and Gerrold about the sword—but then Papa had told Sir Delacar, and Sir Delacar had told the armorer. And if I was going to tell the girls, I should tell all the Companions. It wasn't fair to the boys not to have them in on it. They were going to have to find out sometime.

That night, when we were all eating together at the squires' table, I gave the lads little signals that we needed to talk. Giles caught on first, then Nat, then finally Rob. So instead of going up to bed followed by Anna and Elle as I usually did, I had them follow me to the main door. They were probably pretty puzzled when, instead of going to the garden like everyone else, I went to the training yard, where we were least likely to be overheard.

"What's going on, Miri?" asked Giles as we gathered in the dim light coming from the windows of the palace above us.

"I have a bit of a story to tell you," I said, and I told them as much as I could about Lobo and the sword. "And this is absolutely to go no further than us. This sword is *dangerous* because it protects anyone who has it against Fae magic."

"Which means if someone bad got hold of it...," Nat said, catching on first.

I nodded. "Exactly."

Nat was more interested in the wolf than the sword. "Has Lobo really been escorting you to Fae Firehawk's cottage?" he asked, his eyes wide with what looked like delight.

"Yes, from the tree door to the cottage and back when you and Delacar aren't with me. I think he's probably lurking in the underbrush after luncheon to see if I come through Brianna's door alone and going off when I'm with you."

Nat's face fell. "I don't suppose—" But I already knew what he was thinking.

"Tomorrow I'll go through first and see if he doesn't mind meeting all of you," I promised, and his face lit up. "But that's not why I wanted to get us all together. Wizard Gerrold wants to look at the sword tonight, so it's a good time for all of you to see it."

"But that means going up to the Wizard's Tower," Nat replied, sounding dubious. "I've heard things...."

"You'll like it," I said. "Go up to the foot of the staircase, and I'll get the sword and meet you there." That seemed like a better idea than all of us traipsing through the ladies-in-waiting's rooms. Especially the boys, who wouldn't be especially welcome there.

When I got to the doorway at the base of the tower, they

were all there. I beamed at them and led the way up to the rooms at the top.

The wizard looked surprised to see us all as we crowded into his relatively small workroom, but Brianna Firehawk, who was also there, looked as if she had expected us. Before Wizard Gerrold could recover from the intrusion of having seven people in his usually private space, she smiled and said, "I can see I am going to have to do something about this. Gerrold, can you give Miri one of your insulating cloths to wrap around her sword?"

I would have thought that in all the clutter, Gerrold would never find what the Fae had asked for, but he squeezed between Nat and Rob, and pulled a slightly smudged thick-twilled patch-work cloth from a basket on the floor. I took it from him, real-ized with a bit of a start that it was made of silk, and wrapped every inch of the sword in it. It was clear that Gerrold got first chance at pieces of silk not large enough to use for clothing and had special cloths patched together out of the scrap.

Brianna closed her eyes and put her hands together palm to palm at chin level, as if she were praying. I watched her in the way I had learned to watch for magic, and I immediately saw a glow about her that increased with every intake of breath. Then, slowly and gracefully, she moved her hands so the palms faced outward, and the glow became a shell surrounding her at the level of her palms. She pushed gently, and the shell of light expanded until it touched the walls of Gerrold's room.

And the walls *expanded*!

My eyes practically popped out of my head, and I wasn't the only one.

She dropped her hands when the walls were as far apart as

the ones inside her cottage, uttered a sigh, and opened her eyes. "We won't need more than a couple of hours, I would think," she said, a little breathlessly. "But since you are all here, there are some experiments I would like to conduct with Gerrold's help."

There was the circle of clutter where the walls had originally been, then an expanse of clean stone floor from there to the walls. The owl had already gone off into the night. The cats had leapt up to their padded perches, tails bushed with alarm. The ferret had swarmed up Gerrold's leg and was now huddled in his arms and shaking. The crow was so frozen that you'd have thought him stuffed. Only the raven and the hedgehog seemed unalarmed. The hedgehog was still asleep in half a cup on the hearth even though the hearth was several feet away from where it had been. And the raven eyed all of us before yawning and closing his eyes again. I could only suppose he had seen all this before, or at least something enough like it that he didn't care.

That this had all taken place in complete silence only made it more unnerving.

"You can unwrap the sword now, Miri, and unsheathe it," Brianna said. I did so, then something occurred to me.

"If the sword can't be touched by Fae magic, why does the sheath work?"

"Ah, excellent question. It *doesn't* unless the sword is well away from you or sheathed. Once the sword is sheathed, because the lining is silk, you don't have its protection anymore," Brianna said, then Gerrold took the sword from me and laid it down on a workbench. "Remember this for the future, all of you. Silk insulates against all magic. If you need to pick up or carry something you suspect to be bespelled, wrap it in silk first."

Gerrold made several gestures over the sword, muttering things under his breath, and the words on the blade lit up with a soft yellow glow. He and Brianna bent over it, heads together, while Brianna took the words down on vellum. Then they turned the sword over and did the same on the other side.

"I'll keep these safe," Brianna said, folding the pieces of vellum as soon as the ink was dry, and—well, I didn't exactly see what she did with them. One moment they were there, the next they were not.

"And I have it all up here," Gerrold replied, tapping his head. He made a wiping motion above the blade, and the words on it vanished. I took this chance to look around at my fellow Companions. They weren't as startled or as alarmed as they had been the first time they saw magic, but they were certainly enraptured.

"Come take it, Miri," Gerrold said to me, gesturing to the sword. "I'd really rather you handled it just to be on the safe side."

I came and got it, but Brianna shook her head when I went to sheathe it. "I want to make some experiments first," she said. "I never got the chance when your ancestor had it, and the more we know, the better use we can make of its powers. Go stand there, if you please." She gestured to a spot about halfway into the clear stretch of floor. "Now hold it in front of you, straight up and down."

She looked over her shoulder at Gerrold. "Get some chalk, would you? You'll see why in a moment."

As he went to a box on the far wall for a piece of chalk, I took my place and stood as she had directed. "This is completely harmless," she told me. "But the important thing is that the magic is visible." And with that, she held out one hand, her palm toward me.

Her hand lit up like the setting sun, and the entire room lit up with an orange radiance.

Everywhere *except* behind the sword. I glanced behind me and saw a cone of shadow. It was quite out of proportion to the thin blade of the sword, so I could only assume that the effect of the blade was wider than its actual breadth.

Gerrold saw what she wanted immediately and moved behind me, scribing the limits of the cone on the floor with the chalk. Brianna closed her hand and the light stopped, and the two of them examined the lines on the floor.

"We'll do this again, but this time hold the blade horizontally at chest height," Brianna said at last, and I obeyed. Again, there was a cone of shadow behind me, this time much broader. Gerrold scribed the boundaries of this as well. Then Brianna had me point the sword at her. To my surprise, although the cone of shadow was narrower than it had been the first time, it was not as narrow as I had thought it would be.

"Why...?" said Brianna as she stared at the lines.

"Aha!" Gerrold's face lit up. "Of course. I know what is going on here. When Miri holds the sword, the size of the cone of protection behind her is relative to her body size, not to the sword or how it is pointed."

"But—"

"But when she holds it horizontally so the sword forms a bar across the front of her chest, *that* expands the shadow."

Brianna actually laughed. "I would never have been able to intuit that. And this is why human wizards are better at these deductions of logic than Fae, who rely on intuition." She gestured at my friends. "All right, younglings, fit yourselves into this shadow and memorize where you may be in safety. That way, if some Fae sorceress decides to blast you, you may emerge unharmed."

My friends all crowded carefully inside the chalk marks, and we quickly figured out a formation that kept everyone's arms and legs inside the safe zone. Gerrold and Brianna seemed very happy with the night's work, and if they were pleased, then I was certainly content. I was thrilled that they had figured out a way that the sword's protection could extend to cover all of us. I wasn't eager to lead my friends into combat that I alone was immune from.

Well, relatively immune. There were still perfectly ordinary weapons and some Fae used them.

We all filed down the stairs, which were lit relatively well with oil lamps in sconces, but Giles lagged back a little. I guessed that he might want to talk, so I stayed next to him while the other four clattered and chattered on ahead. "How is life with the squires?" I asked. "Are you all right?" I was concerned for him; he was probably the only boy who wasn't of noble blood in the lot. And we hadn't really had much of a chance to chat, just the two of us, for weeks.

He shrugged. "Today was hard, but Wulf didn't let them keep at it for long. After that, I proved I was as good or better at fighting than any of them, so they've let me be. In fact, a couple of the fellows are all right. It helped that there were three of us, and Nat and Rob stood up for me." He glanced at me out of the corner of his eye as we reached the bottom of the stairs and saw that the other four were nowhere in sight. "I must say, the squires' quarters are worlds better than my old bed, though to hear the complaints from the rest, you'd think they were sleeping on hard stone in front of a cold hearth. Have Anna and Elle kept you up half the night with nattering?"

I laughed. "They would have if I'd let them. They have their own room, so I'm not sure what they do after I tell them in my best Sir Delacar voice that it's time to go to sleep."

"I kind of miss when it was just the two of us in the kitchen making bread," he said after a moment of silence. "Things were a lot simpler then."

"No matter what, they wouldn't have stayed that way for long," I reminded him as we lingered near a torch so anyone passing by could see we weren't up to shenanigans in the shadows. "Not with my having Fae blood. And not with my being the Queen's daughter. Something was bound to happen sooner or later."

He scratched the back of his head. "I guess, when you put it that way. I *like* being in the Companions, Miri...but I liked it better when things weren't so complicated."

What could I say? I'd liked it better too. "We never seem to have much time to just be ourselves," he added.

"Neither do the squires," I said, and Giles uttered a small chuckle.

"Responsibilities," he said.

"The only person I've ever noticed who doesn't have them is the jester." I was trying to make him laugh again, and it worked. I didn't point out that the jester has the responsibility, sometimes very heavy, of finding humor when things seem darkest.

"I suppose we must be adults now," he said. "Well, it looks as if we are going to have adventures as well as responsibilities, and there's not much adventure in dough."

"Not unless someone casts an evil spell on it, and it rises from the bowl as a monster." *Now* I made him laugh, a real laugh.

"You'd better go catch up with Anna and Elle, and make sure they get some proper sleep tonight. Sir Delacar won't like it if they turn up yawning."

"Off to my responsibilities." And I bid him good night.

But I couldn't help but agree with him. It *had* been so much easier back when I was just the Queen's other daughter. I had to keep even Giles at arm's length now, because if there was one thing that traveled faster than arrows, it was gossip. It hadn't mattered in the kitchen because we were under the eyes of many people all the time. But now? With our being together a lot and often on our own, it mattered. It mattered a lot.

CHAPTER EIGHT

NOW SIR DELACAR HAD AN ENTIRELY *NEW* SET OF SKILLS FOR US to learn. No sooner had Brianna acquainted him with the "safe" zone that the sword and I cast than his cunning mind began to think of ways to use it—more than just the obvious of "everybody hide behind Miri"—and we began working on Delacar's group maneuvers.

I was also working on control and consistency with the Fae magic. When I practiced in our world, sometimes the power drew up instantly and did exactly what I wanted it to. Sometimes it was sluggish and weak, and it was all I could do to light a single candle. Brianna thought that this was probably because the human magic in me fought with the Fae magic for control, and Gerrold reckoned she was right. It's not just wizards who have magic, at least according to Gerrold. All humans have at least a little bit. The difference between wizards and regular humans is that wizards have a lot more of it and are willing to invest every waking moment in learning how to build and control their magic, how to use spell components to help them, and how to create verbal components of spells. And I was going to have to deal with whatever magic I had inside me. So I needed to train myself so I could call on either to get what I needed instead of having them fight with each other.

At the moment, Brianna was teaching me illusions—those came easily with Fae magic but were a piece of complicated spell casting when it came to the human version. But the Fae version didn't last if the magician lost sight of it, and the human version lasted as long as the spell components did.

When I was a child, there had been a wizard who had come to the palace in the guise of a jewel merchant and offered fabulous stones for prices just low enough to seem like a reasonable bargain. But Papa was not as naive as the wizard had supposed, and he had Gerrold with him whenever a merchant came to present goods. "It's much easier to dispel an illusion than it is to cast one," Gerrold told the King, which was a failure in human-cast illusions that Fae illusions didn't suffer from. Moments after Gerrold touched the stones, they were revealed for the flawed, inferior things they actually were, and the merchant wizard found himself languishing in a jail cell until the King determined whether or not he'd defrauded anyone in Tirendell. I never learned what happened to him after that, but he wasn't in the cell by the time we came to the palace. But that was something to keep in mind when Brianna and I worked out together, and dispelling illusion was very high on my list of things to learn.

I'd just gotten used to the new pace of my life when it was all shattered. Shattered by the wail of a baby that woke me up out of deep sleep. There was only one baby in the palace, and I was already halfway to Aurora's nursery before I realized that I was even out of bed.

I wasn't the only one to come running, but only Mama and Melalee beat me there. Melalee had my poor, precious sister in her arms, vainly trying to soothe her. Even in the dim candle-light, I could tell that there was something wrong. Her beautiful rosebud face was screwed up in an expression of pain, and she was white with fever.

This wasn't something I knew how to fight, so I backed into a corner while the doctor and Gerrold were both sent for and Melalee and Mama did their frantic best to soothe her—to no avail. I don't think that anyone noticed I was there, to tell the truth. The more Aurora cried, the more people crowded into the room, all of them stiff with fear, none of them useful.

The doctor came and pondered and prescribed and went off to his stillroom to make medicines. Gerrold came and stayed. I stood in the corner, anxiety and fear consuming me, as Gerrold sprinkled Aurora with powders and dusts while motes of magic surrounded his fingers and he sketched signs in the air. He must have been doing that for a good half an hour when something tapped on the window and every one of us in the room jumped and squeaked or yelped, Gerrold included. The spell Gerrold had been working on misfired in a flash of orange light.

I was the first to recover and the closest to the window, so I flung it open, and as I had hoped, Brianna was hovering outside, her scarlet wings a blur. She caught the edges of the window with both hands and deftly swung herself inside with folded wings, then dropped lightly to the floor. The maneuver was impossibly graceful, but I suppose when you have centuries to practice, you can make anything look easy and graceful. My heart rose. Surely Brianna would be able to put everything right again!

She didn't say a word as she huddled over Aurora with Gerrold, the two of them putting their heads together, murmuring in tense voices, and occasionally casting some magic. My heart began to sink again as I took in the expression of tense worry on both their faces—and as nothing they did made Aurora any better.

The doctor came, dosed Aurora with something that also made no difference even past the time it should have taken effect, and he left muttering to himself. The sky lightened to predawn gray. Aurora continued to cry, but now it was the thin wail of a baby losing strength. My heart was in knots, and so was my stomach.

Now Papa and Mama joined the tense conversation over the cradle. I strained my ears to hear. "Unicorn's horn," Gerrold said, when I could finally make something out.

Mama looked puzzled. "Why?" she asked.

"Whatever this is, it's not a poison; and it's not a spell that either of us recognizes. Magic is involved and, we think, a disease. And I am certain that *someone* caused it, but we are running out of time and options. Unicorn's horn can cure anything that isn't a wound," Gerrold explained.

"There hasn't been a report of a unicorn in this kingdom in a century," Papa said. "That was why King Stefan banned their hunting, but by then, I am afraid, it was too late. And I've never seen even a sliver of horn."

"Send out a proclamation!" Brianna exclaimed. "Surely *someone*—"

By this time, I had stolen out, dressed in a heartbeat, belted on my dagger; and I was running for the garden and the door in the tree. There might still be unicorns about; just because no one had seen them didn't mean there weren't any. They were notoriously stealthy, and after being hunted relentlessly, they weren't going to take the chance that someone would ignore the law.

And if anyone would know if there were any unicorns left, it would be Lobo and Clarion.

I burst out onto the road to Brianna's cottage well into the forest. Under cover of the dense trees, it was still dark. The forest was a very different thing at night than it was by daylight, and with a chill down my backbone, I regretted that I hadn't brought my sword or at least *a* sword and a lantern. Things scuttled about in the undergrowth, and I felt many eyes on me, not all of them friendly. Would illusions help me against wild beasts? But I hadn't really learned how to create them yet.

Stupid! I scolded myself, still so knotted up with fear for Aurora that I had trouble thinking. *Make a light.*

My Fae magic came to hand at once, and I made a little globe of light and set it to float over my head. I trotted in the direction of Brianna's cottage. I suspected Lobo had his den somewhere nearby. It would make sense; they were friends and allies, and it would be smart to be close enough to come to each other's aid. "Lobo!" I called as I ran. "Lobo!"

I was just about to Brianna's cottage when there was the sound of something crashing through the bushes on the right side of the road. My heart jumped into my mouth; I staggered back a few steps, my hand on my mostly useless dagger; and I came very close to shrieking as Clarion leapt out of the undergrowth into the middle of the road.

"*Wretched* child, what do you mean by running down the road shouting like that?" he asked, panting and clearly out of breath, all four hooves planted firmly in the dust of the road as if he expected to receive the charge of…something…at any moment. "Something terrible might have heard you!"

"Something terrible has already happened," I said, and I told him quickly about Aurora. Well, as quickly as I could in and around the occasional sob of fear. All I could think about was how my baby sister had looked just before I left.

His attitude changed immediately.

"This is dreadful!" he proclaimed, just as Lobo, also out of breath, pushed his way through the same set of bushes. "Lobo! Something appalling has happened to the little Princess!" Clarion repeated what I had told him, without the crying, as I stood there wiping my eyes on my sleeve and trying to get my emotions under control.

"Gerrold said the only thing he could think of was unicorn's horn, and Brianna agreed with him," I said. "But there isn't any in the palace—"

"And you were hoping I would know if there was a unicorn in the forest," Lobo said, and looked at me steadily. "Were you intending to kill it with that little knife of yours and take the horn? Because I can't permit that. Not even to save the Princess."

Clarion took a step back and looked at me as if he suddenly doubted my trustworthiness.

"Wait, what? *No!* That's *horrid* and *wrong* and—I was

just hoping maybe it would let me shave a little off the horn, or something!"

Clarion and Lobo looked at each other for a long time, their eyes reflecting the light of my little Fae-magic globe. I stood there shivering with fear and grief and cold as a chill mist seeped out of the forest and wreathed around us. I got the sense that they were talking to each other in a way that I couldn't hear.

Clarion turned to look at me sternly. "And what would you give to be brought to a unicorn?"

I bit my lip and trembled. Oh, the danger of questions like this was in half the Fae tales I had ever heard! I could quite literally find myself giving up something important, even vital, if I answered that I would give anything. It could be my magic—it could be my sword—it could be my life. The talking animals didn't play by quite the same rules as humans or the Light Fae did—their rules were more primal, and if I'm to be honest, often bloodier, just as life in the forest can be.

But I didn't have to think long. Warnings be damned. "Whatever is required," I said steadily.

Clarion and Lobo looked at each other again. Clarion turned back to me. "Will you do what is asked of you without question at some time in the future no matter what the cost?"

Ah. Yes, I had heard of this sort of thing in tales before. And if I agreed—no matter what else was urgent—I'd have to do what I was asked.

But this was Aurora....

"Yes."

They stared at each other. "It's worth asking," Clarion said aloud, and he turned to me. "You're light and small enough that you can ride on my back. We need to hurry if we are going to catch him."

He knelt down and I climbed onto his back, sitting farther forward on him than I would have on a horse since I was planning to wrap my arms around his neck to keep from falling off. "Who?" I asked as I got on. "What—?"

But I didn't have time to get an answer. As soon as I was secure, Clarion was off like a shot.

Riding a deer is nothing like riding a horse. They don't run. They leap. And there are no pauses between the leaps the way there is when a horse jumps. It was just one leap after another as I was being thrown forward and back, clutching the deer's neck desperately to keep from being thrown off. It must have been even harder on Clarion than it was on me, but he didn't falter and he didn't slacken his pace at all. Lobo ran beside us, tongue lolling out of his mouth. Dawn finally crept into the forest, which made it somewhat easier to see, but I wasn't looking at much of anything. I was too busy holding on to Clarion's neck for dear life and trying not to choke him at the same time.

I was doing as much work just staying on Clarion's back as if I'd been running, and before too very long, I got a stitch in my side and I was panting like a dog. And just when I was sure I couldn't hang on for a single jump more, Clarion came to a dead stop, and I fell off. I slid right off his back and tumbled onto ground that was covered in thick, soft moss. I looked up quickly and saw that we were in a tiny clearing with an equally tiny spring bubbling up out of the center of it, the water running away in a little brook that cut its way through the moss and vanished into the forest.

And standing next to the spring, eyes wide with surprise, was a unicorn.

He wasn't very big, perhaps the size of a half-grown yearling fawn, and he was not as bulky as my pony, and he didn't look anything like a horse with a horn in the middle of its forehead. The closest description I could come up with was that he looked like an incandescently white goat with an elegant long neck and legs and a delicate head like a deer's. That long neck sported a horse's mane, but it was silkier by far, and he had a long tail with a silken tuft on the end, but otherwise his coat was smooth and looked like that of a fine palfrey. His legs ended in silvery cloven hooves, and, of course, there was the horn, a tiny delicate spiral bud of pearl in the middle of his forehead, no longer than my little finger.

He stared at me as if he was about to flee, his enormous pale blue eyes filling with terror.

"*Viridity!*" Lobo said urgently, making the unicorn start and look at him instead of me. "It's all right! There's a terrible emergency! She's not here to hunt you, she needs your help."

Speaking rapidly and finishing each other's sentences, Lobo and Clarion explained what had happened, which was just as well because I was staring breathlessly at this incredibly beautiful creature of myth. I managed to gather my wits when Lobo said, "And Miriam was hoping that perhaps she could shave a little bit from your horn."

But all three of us looked doubtfully at the tiny nubbin. And the unicorn's next words confirmed that. "It's still growing,"

Viridity said in a sad, sweet, breathy voice. "If you damage it, it will die, and so will I."

Clarion and Lobo looked at me, but I was already shaking my head no. "It's not worth it. I won't take the chance that I might kill another creature—not even to save Aurora." I choked on the last words and sobbed once, but I meant it. *Maybe somewhere, someone in the city has an heirloom, a piece of unicorn horn....*

But at those words, Viridity drew himself up, raised his head high, and flagged his tail. "And I will not let the baby Princess die!" he declared. "There is another way! Take me to her!"

And so we began another wild run through the forest to the road, then raced along the road at a breakneck pace. And just before we reached Brianna's cottage, when Clarion's flanks were already foaming with sweat and his sides heaving under my legs, we caught sight of Brianna flying straight for us. The four of us literally skidded to a halt in a cloud of dust as Brianna back-winged and hovered in midair. It would have been hilarious if things were not so serious.

But her eyes were only for Viridity. "There's no time to lose!" she said urgently. "The cottage! Quickly!"

We managed to race the remaining distance to her cottage. Brianna flung the door open, and on the other side was the palace garden.

I slid from Clarion's back, sending him and Lobo back to the forest while I ran for the door. I didn't have to urge Viridity since he stuck right by my side as we ran into the garden. And at that point, I realized that there was no way we could go through the normal entrances. The people of the Court would mob us. We'd lose precious time getting free of them, time that Aurora clearly did not have.

"Kitchen!" I gasped, and headed for the kitchen garden and the entrance there. "We'll take the servants' stair!"

We rushed into the kitchen—and everything stopped. Complete and utter silence fell, something that never happened between the hours of dawn and dusk because of all the work going on there.

Odo recovered his wits first. "Lee! Run ahead and clear the stairs! Take three breaths, Miri, you'll need them!" He came to me and held me back by my shoulders while I took those three precious lungfuls of air. "Now run!"

Run we did, with Lee ahead of us to make sure we had clear passage all the way up. We burst out of the upstairs entrance and raced for the nursery. "*Move!*" I screamed as we hit the door and everyone in sight jumped back a pace, giving us a clear sight of the cradle.

My heart broke. Aurora had gone from white to a strange pasty color. Only little flutters of the lace around her cradle showed that she was still breathing. I didn't know what to do.

But Viridity did.

With three goatlike bounds, he reached the cradle, nuzzled her, and breathed on her cheek. A little color came into them, and she gave a little mew and reached up with both of her hands and seized the end of his horn.

He stood as still as a rock, head lowered into her cradle, while she held on steadily to his horn. Color flooded back into her, her breathing eased, and slowly but surely, she returned to the healthy little baby she had been just yesterday.

But as color flooded into her, vitality visibly drained from Viridity. He lost his glow, his brilliantly white coat became dull and lifeless, and a film of white fogged his eyes. When Aurora finally let go of his horn with a sigh, he staggered a few steps to the side and almost fell.

Almost. But my dear papa was there to catch him, and then he helped Viridity lie down on a bed that Mama and Melalee had hastily built with cushions and a blanket thrown over them.

Viridity looked awful.

"Water, quickly," Papa said to Lee, who ran for a basin. But my Fae magic had something else in mind. I felt it impelling me, and I knew exactly what I needed to do to help Viridity.

I went to his side, sat down next to him, and took his head in my lap. It was my turn to cup my hands around his horn, but this time, power was not flowing *from* him. It was flowing *into* him from me. As soon as this began, I understood instinctively what had happened; he had used his own inherent magic power that had been transmuted through his horn into something that could heal Aurora. Now I would restore his magic by giving him mine.

I don't know if anyone else could see it happening—Brianna, certainly; Gerrold, perhaps—but I saw it clearly. A steady golden glow around my hands drained into Viridity's horn as if the power were a liquid and he were drinking it in. I *felt* it too, and I willed it to flow faster. And the more of my power that flowed into him, the better he looked. His coat slowly regained its proper color and luster. His mane went from straw-like to silken again, and the skin under his coat took on that glow it had had before. And finally, the horn, which had faded to a gray like weathered wood, took on its proper pearly sheen. He heaved a huge sigh and finally opened his eyes. They were no longer filmed with white but looked as beautiful as a cloudless sky.

Just then Lee brought a basin of fresh water, and I recognized it as the bowl from my mother's dressing room. With a nod of thanks, Viridity lowered his head and drank daintily. When he raised his head, there were little droplets on his tiny beard that sparkled like crystal beads.

"I don't suppose," he said in that sweet, breathy voice, "that I could have some of those strawberry tarts I smelled baking in the kitchen?"

It was Papa who answered since Mama was too busy with her arms full of Aurora as she made sure that she was all right and babbled tearful nonsense over her. Papa went to one knee— and, of course, so did everyone else in the room, since when the King kneels, *everyone* kneels. "Sir Unicorn," he said in his proclamation voice. "You have saved my daughter. Anything in the kingdom you want, save only my family, is yours."

Viridity laughed a little. "Strawberry tarts will be very nice. And also more water."

Lee practically fell over himself getting to the stairs before Papa could order him to go to the kitchen. And it was Anna who took the basin and brought it back full, placing it in front of the unicorn with her eyes so big and round that they practically took up half of her head. I hadn't even noticed her, or Elle, but there they were. And Giles and Rob and Nat, all of Aurora's Companions were there to do what they could. Elle brought more water; Anna draped Viridity in her best shawl; Giles and Rob and Nat kept people from crowding the beautiful creature so he wouldn't feel surrounded and perhaps threatened. I was so proud of them at that moment! And so was Brianna, for seeing that we Companions had it under control, she took her leave of us.

Since Viridity had no hands to lift the tarts to his mouth, everyone in the room vied for the chance to feed him one. I was torn between being enchanted and feeling amused, with a healthy dose of exhaustion thrown in. But I wasn't going to leave him, not before he was ready to go back to the forest. Short of going through the palace and the city, which was not a wise thing for him to do, his only way back would be by my opening the door in the oak. And to be absolutely honest, when I had first finished emptying myself into the unicorn, that was exactly how I'd felt—empty. If I'd had to open that door then... well, I couldn't have done it.

But the longer we sat there surrounded by relief and joy, the faster my power returned. And I remembered what all the histories and the tales had taught me, that Light Fae magic came from the joy and pleasure felt by humans.

Light Fae magic... surely this meant that my father had been Light Fae! I felt almost dizzy with relief at that thought.

When Viridity had licked up the last crumb of tart from the last trembling hand and drunk the last drop of water from the basin, he got up from his nest of cushions, and so did I. Only he did it a lot more gracefully than I did. It was a good thing that all eyes were on him because I more or less staggered to my feet. "It is time for me to return home," he said with great dignity. "Miriam will escort me."

"Is there nothing more we can do to thank you?" This time it was Mama who spoke, having finally relinquished Aurora to Melalee, her hands now clasped before her as if she was prepared to pray to him.

Viridity shook his head. "Not at all. It was my pleasure. That was a terrible thing someone did to your child. It was a disease carried on the wings of a spell." He turned his gaze toward the exhausted wizard. "You should search this room for the way it got here—and when you find it, discover who brought it. There will be a physical object, and it may be quite small."

Gerrold bowed. "I will. I will not rest until I have found it."

Viridity bowed in return. "Then I will leave you to it. Come, Miriam."

We walked down the servants' stair in silence but it wasn't an uncomfortable silence. I think we were both too tired for anything but intense relief and gratitude on my part and intense satisfaction at having saved the day on the part of Viridity. He deserved that satisfaction because he had certainly risked his life, betting on the fact that I was not tricking him into a trap. And then he had exhausted his magic without knowing how long it would take for him to get it back, which would have left him helpless until he did.

"I like you, Miriam," he said abruptly as we were about to enter the kitchen. "You are steadfast, loyal, and true. We are friends."

I opened the door for him, and when he entered the kitchen, complete silence fell once again. A silence that was immediately broken by tumultuous applause.

Viridity accepted it with casual aplomb, then stepped forward and led me through the kitchen to the door to the garden as everyone in the kitchen clapped hard enough to bruise their hands. But when he reached the door, Viridity stopped and turned back for a moment to face all the kitchen workers. Silence fell again.

"I would like to thank you all very much for the strawberry tarts. They were excellent."

Then he turned back and led the way out the door. Behind me, I heard Odo shouting, beside himself with joy. "Did you hear that? Did you *hear* it? The unicorn liked my tarts!"

Somewhat to my surprise, Giles was waiting for us in the kitchen garden. After figuring out how I would probably get Viridity back to the forest, he must have run down here without my noticing that he'd left. I was awfully glad to see him, because by that point, I was getting to the end of my strength and I was very happy to lean on him a bit. He didn't say anything, but he didn't have to. But I did introduce him to Viridity, of course.

"I hope I will see you again someday very soon, Giles," Viridity said when we reached the oak. "I am inclined to think Miriam has excellent taste in friends."

"I'm inclined to think you're right, Sir Unicorn," Giles replied with a wink, and Viridity chuckled. It sounded like water gurgling over rocks.

Viridity nodded at the tree, and I opened the door—although it took such an effort that my eyes swam for a moment. Then he stepped through it, and I closed the door and swayed, and Giles caught me.

"Are you going to be all right?" he asked anxiously.

"I just need a little rest is all," I said, and lowered myself carefully to the ground with his help. "I think I'll just sit here for a bit."

It was more than a "bit" since the next thing I knew, Elle was shaking me awake; Anna was offering me a basket with a meat pie, a turnip pie, and a pair of strawberry tarts in it; and there was a blanket sliding off my shoulders.

*   *   *

I'd missed practice, of course, but I was pretty much absolved of that. Sir Delacar gave me a piece of his mind for running off without at least *one* of the other Companions, and I knew he was absolutely right. Things had worked out because Clarion had heard me calling for Lobo, but what if he and Lobo hadn't? I'd been stupid and stupidly lucky. I'd acted impulsively again; and again, it had worked out well, but how long would such luck last? I took my tongue-lashing with proper humility.

"You need to remember that Elle and Anna are there not because they are your ladies," Sir Delacar said. "They are there because they are two of the six. So what should you have done?"

I'd already been over this in my mind. "Gotten both of them right away. When unicorn's horn came up, and I realized that Lobo might know where there was a living unicorn, I should have told one of them where I was going and taken the other one with me. Brianna obviously used the door in the oak to get to the forest, so she could have brought the other four to help if I'd been in trouble."

Delacar nodded curtly, but I could tell that he was somewhat mollified. "There are six of you for a reason. Never do this again."

"No, Sir Delacar," I promised. And having gotten my just deserts, I went to find Wizard Gerrold. I figured that he must have found something while I'd been sleeping since the maids were setting the nursery back to rights when I checked.

As I expected, he was in his tower workroom. But I had not expected to find him dead asleep at his workbench with his head on his arms. I debated waking him, but the raven let out a loud warning *quork* from his perch and Gerrold started awake.

"Wha? Wha?" he managed to say, and I spoke up very loudly and clearly.

"It's just me, Wizard Gerrold. Miriam. Your raven thought you should wake up."

He shook his head, dislodging the soft cap he had on it, which was probably his nightcap. "Bloody bird," he muttered, and shook his fist at it. Then he turned to blink at me. "Oh, you're all right again. Good. Don't need another sick little girl for a good long while, thankyouverymuch."

"I just needed some rest. Did you find what made Aurora sick?"

"Aye. Told the King already. Waiting for Brianna to help me trace it." He motioned toward a drift of white silk lying on a stool pushed up against the wall. "*Don't touch it!*" he snapped as I made an abortive move in that direction. "Don't even get near it. It's not the cradle curtains themselves, it's *in* them. A little white thorn. When I found it, the residual magic must have affected the maids because they couldn't keep their hands to themselves, and I very nearly had to slap them to keep them away. We're just lucky neither of them came to harm, though likely the curse was meant only for Aurora." He looked very annoyed, but I couldn't tell if he was annoyed at the maids or himself. Maybe both. "It's *probably* spent, but I don't want anyone finding out the hard way."

But that set my now-rested mind going. "Could it be that the reason they tried to touch it was because one of them put it there?" I asked slowly.

He frowned. "Now why didn't I think of that?"

"Because you were drunk with lack of sleep?"

He started to get up, then sank back down on his stool. "No use in going after them. If one or both of them are guilty, they've already fled the palace. And if they aren't, it won't matter."

"I'll tell Belinda; she's in charge of them now. She'll be better at questioning them than you will. She won't let them get away with bursting into tears and wringing their hands. If they know anything, she'll have it out of them."

But it really troubled me, as it obviously troubled Gerrold, to think that the Dark Fae might have agents among our own staff.

"Bloody hellfire," he muttered. "There's no hope for it; I'm going to have to bring in help. Whatever is going on that makes the Princess so important, it's obvious the Dark Fae have taken to using other races to do their work for them to get around the Rules. Aurora should have been safe for years as soon as the christening was over."

"What do you mean, 'bring in help'?" I asked, not liking the sound of that.

"Call on some of my former apprentices to come back here to help me. I'm going to have to—"

"But can you trust *them*?" I shook my head. "How can you know that the Dark Fae haven't subverted one or more of them?"

He groaned. "I can't, of course, you're right. Bloody hellfire." He took a deep breath. "Right. Don't panic. Don't go haring off in all directions. Get some sleep. See what Brianna says."

Since it was clear that he was talking to himself, I kept my thoughts to myself. He finally realized that I was still standing there and smiled at me. "That's all the information I have for now, Miri. I'll make sure you know whatever else I find out."

"Thank you, Wizard Gerrold. And...until Brianna gets here, maybe you'd better get some sleep on something other than your workbench."

"Good idea." He sighed and went to his favorite hearthside chair, putting his feet up on a pile of books. Within moments, he was asleep again. I put one of his discarded robes over him as a makeshift shawl and left. I had just enough time to dress for dinner, which I desperately needed to do, because I was still in the tunic and trews I'd thrown on when Aurora started wailing. I'd slept in them, and they looked like it. But I intercepted Belinda first and told her what Gerrold had said about the maids and what I suspected. For the first time ever, she didn't tell me that I was a silly girl and that I was imagining things. Instead, her mouth went into a thin line that didn't bode well for the maids. "I'll look into it, my lady," she said, giving me the very first "my lady" I'd ever gotten from her. "If they're naught but silly girls, no harm. But if they've been up to mischief in this matter, the King shall know about it."

Thank heavens this was one of those nights when I ate with the squires. People were babbling about the unicorn and how he had miraculously cured Aurora. The same people didn't seem to realize that I was the one who had found and brought him; they all assumed it was Brianna because she had left and returned about the same time I had. I decided that I would keep my mouth shut about that. But over the course of the meal, I managed to signal to the rest of the group that we needed to meet up in the practice yard again.

I left first, claiming that I was tired, and since I actually was, it wasn't a lie. Elle and Anna came with me, and we hurried to the practice yard before anyone could intercept us. It wasn't too many more minutes before Rob turned up, then Nat and Giles together. It was almost midsummer now, and it was still light out here, making the meeting seem less clandestine. As shadows filled the bowl of the practice yard and the upper walls of the palace turned softly red gold in the light of the setting sun, I told them about the thorn that had sickened Aurora.

"We need to tell Delacar," Giles said immediately. "One of us needs to be watching Aurora all the time now, which means skipping lessons now and again."

I nodded, because he was right. "We are still young enough that we could easily be overlooked, especially if we get our hands on pages' tabards. And I think I have an idea." Because my Fae magic was stirring again, I knew what I needed to do. "I hope this isn't a nuisance for you all, but I need to give you the ability to see magic and magic creatures that are generally invisible. Like ghosts and will-o'-the-wisps."

"You can do that?" Elle said incredulously.

"Why?" asked Giles.

"I think I can. I need to do this because there are more magical things out there than just the Dark and Light Fae, and the Rules don't bind *them*. They can be coerced, or bribed, or... well, some of them are just evil and only need turning loose to wreak havoc." I shrugged. "It won't do us much good to watch if we can't see what we're watching for."

"Then do me first," Giles said, clenching his jaw as if he didn't like the idea much but was going to do it anyway. Which, if he really didn't like the idea, was awfully good of him. So I did, and it was much, much easier than I had thought it would be. It was as if my Fae power and my human power both agreed with what needed to be done and how to go about doing it. I just had to put my hands on either side of his head and will him to be able to see what was otherwise invisible. And the test, of course, was that when I had finished and moved on to Elle, Giles exclaimed that he could see the magic lighting up my hands while the rest saw nothing.

When I was done with them, I was just a little more tired than I had been when I started. "You're probably not going to like this until you get used to it," I warned them. "Because anything that has even a little magic about it is probably going to look like it's got a light inside of it."

"Well, that sounds easy enough," Giles said, and stretched and looked up at Gerrold's tower, which was just catching the last red rays of the sun. "Well, we've done what we can for now. Let's all get back to where we're supposed to be before anyone misses us."

"The best thing we can do right now is not be noticed," Nat said. "Why is it that this is never part of adventure tales?"

"Because it's not exactly adventurous?" Elle said. "Don't worry, when they make up tales about us later, I'm sure they'll add a heroic speech for you."

"Just what I want to be known for," Nat grumbled. "Making speeches."

But I noticed that he didn't object.

CHAPTER NINE

SIR DELACAR HEARD US OUT THE NEXT MORNING, AND I GOT the impression he was listening to us seriously. I explained about the thorn, the speculation that it could have been a human *or* some magical creature who was an ally of the Dark Fae rather than one of the Dark Fae themselves. Giles pointed out that if the Dark Fae were bending and going around the Rules like this, we needed someone keeping watch on Aurora all the time and that this someone needed to be a person who could actually see magic creatures and objects. "And Miri made sure we all could last night," he said, causing Sir Delacar to raise an eyebrow. I shrugged.

"Have you heard anything more from Wizard Gerrold?" he asked me.

I shook my head. "No, but I didn't expect to. He was asleep when I went to see him before dinner, and I left him sleeping again and waiting for Brianna so he could show her the thorn. If he and she worked all night, like I think they did—"

"He's not going to wake until dinner, obviously," Delacar

said, and rubbed his head. "Damn the man. Why is he so stubborn about taking another apprentice?"

"Because he's afraid he'll die and leave the apprentice half-trained?" said Nat quietly. From the way he said it, I got the feeling that he wasn't just guessing. I decided to ask him about that later.

"He wanted to try to call back some of his former apprentices, but I pointed out we have no way of knowing if the Dark Fae have gotten to any of them," I said.

He sighed. "All right then, I will compromise with you six. Miri, I want you to work your magic on some of the regular guards so they can see magic too. I'll have them stationed in the nursery at night. In the dark, we can find places where they can watch the cradle without being seen. I'll also have a guard there during the day, but you six will take turns spending half the daylight hours there as pages." He looked up at the palace. The nursery window wasn't visible from here. "And we need a way for you to sound an alarm if you see something." He rubbed the back of his neck as if it pained him. "And what the hell all of this will do against something that can move through walls, I have no idea."

I didn't quite know what to say, but it was Giles who spoke up. "Maybe we should wait until Gerrold is fit to talk, then you and he and the captain of the Guard can figure out what to do?" He stated it as a question, but it was really good advice—especially since people, including me, weren't thinking all that clearly after yesterday.

Sir Delacar nodded. "That's good sense. Miri, do you think you can repeat that magic of yours on all the guards?"

"Maybe," I said, feeling a bit doubtful about the "all the guards" part. "I don't know if it will work on ones who don't like magic. I mean, trying to put a spell on someone who doesn't want it is coercion, isn't it? I don't actually think I can do that." And I had no doubt that there were plenty of the guards who didn't like, or distrusted, magic. And who could blame them? Magic was something they had no means to counter or control, and why should they trust some girl who was said to be Fae-blooded to be able to do what she claimed to be able to do without harming them?

I wouldn't trust me, either, if I felt that way.

Delacar passed his hand over his eyes. "Let's all just stop and think a moment. We're haring off in all directions." By "we" he meant mostly himself, since the Companions hadn't actually done anything so far, but point taken. "We have both too much information and not enough. I'm going to arrange a meeting with the King, the wizard, and Brianna if she'll come. I'll make it for this afternoon."

"I can take care of that last part. She'll be waiting for me after luncheon at the cottage for lessons." Was this the day for lessons alone or with the group? I couldn't remember and it didn't really matter. "I'll bring her back with me."

"Good. I want you six there, but Miri will speak for you." He looked around at all of us, but no one appeared to have any objections. "We need to pool our information before we can have a plan. And for now...business as usual. Warm up, then pair off; for the first part of our exercises, you're going to do drills back-to-back."

Returning to drills almost felt normal.

Almost.

But then again, not much was normal around here anymore.

We were all seated at a table in the Royal Suite that Papa used when he needed to speak privately with his councilors. Gerrold was awake and in his full wizardly regalia. Brianna had been quite willing to come back with me. Because of her wings, someone found her a stool to sit on instead of a chair. Papa had dropped everything to attend this meeting and sat at the head of the table. Sir Delacar and the captain of the Royal Guard sat in the fifth and sixth seats, and my five friends had decided to make themselves useful as pages.

I just listened as Gerrold and Brianna spoke first about the thorn and how it got into the curtains around Aurora's cradle. The thorn carried a curse. The curse, as Viridity had said, was a disease. Brianna suspected that Aurora had been pricked with it before it was placed in the curtains, although she could not say that beyond a shadow of a doubt. She *was* certain that one of the maids had been under a spell and done the dirty work. Gerrold was just as certain that one of the maids had *not* and that it had been some other creature, even a perfectly normal bird or animal under the Dark Fae's control. They argued back and forth for some time before Papa stopped them with a look.

"Gerrold, on the chance that Lady Brianna is right, you will need to armor every servant who comes into contact with Aurora against such enchantments." He turned to the captain of the Guard. "It will be your job to place men who have been fortified in this manner at the door to the nursery day and night so no one goes in or out who is not on the approved list."

Gerrold looked strained. "But, Sire—"

Papa ignored him for the moment. "Lady Brianna, on the chance that Gerrold is correct, how can we prevent magical creatures from invading the castle?"

"Well..." She pondered the question. "The easiest would be to get a very large circle of witches to bless the walls themselves."

Now it was Papa's turn to look strained. "My lady, there is no such thing in this kingdom."

Brianna's brow creased with annoyance, and her wings fanned impatiently. "Of course there is. They were originally called the Order of Everon Isle, but these days they call themselves the Sisters of Saint Everon. There are at least two hundred of them all told. That should be enough. Talk to your Archbishop, I believe he is nominally in authority over them."

Papa's jaw fell open. Actually, everyone's jaw dropped, including mine, because the last thing I would have called a Sister of Saint Everon was a *witch*!

"But—but—but—" sputtered Sir Delacar.

"Witches use chants, invocations, and their will to create spells, do they not?" Brianna asked tartly.

"Yes, but—"

"And the Sisters use chants, invocations, and their will to create blessings, do they not? Which are, when it comes down to it, nothing more than benevolent and beneficent spells."

Delacar had been rendered speechless. In fact, it took a very long time before anyone recovered from that shocking, even blasphemous, statement. And yet there was no way to refute it.

It was Papa who finally regathered his wits and turned to Nat. "Find Archbishop Thomas, please, and ask him to attend this council." Nat nodded and ran off. Papa turned to Brianna. "My lady, your suggestion will certainly be acted upon. But do me the favor of *not* referring to the Sisters as 'witches.' At least not in the hearing of the Archbishop."

She gave him an odd look, and I was suddenly struck with how *alien* she was in that moment. That it had never occurred to her that her statement would be outrageous was a mark of how little she actually had in common with humans. "I don't understand," she said finally. "But I will do as you ask."

It took a bit of time before Nat returned with the Archbishop, but it was just as well he'd taken that time since it took that long for everyone except Brianna to recover their wits and their aplomb. Brianna, of course, was still in possession of hers. She clearly still had no idea that what she had said was offensive.

Once *I* got over my shock, however, what Brianna had said made perfect sense. And I quickly thought that I knew why the Sisters—if they had, indeed, originally been a coven of witches—had decided to transmute themselves into a holy order.

Witches had a mixed reputation, as did wizards, which made sense, since they were only human, and were good, bad, or indifferent as all people were. But here was where wizards and witches were different—witches practiced magic not up in towers at the behest of the high-and-mighty but down among the people. So if you were suspicious of magic, you were suspicious of the witch who lived on the edge of the village (as most of them did). You couldn't do anything about Lord Something's pet wizard if you suspected magic was at the root of some misfortune. But you *could* do something about that pesky witch.

Unless, of course, you knew that she was powerful enough to defend herself if you came calling with unpleasantness in mind.

Which only made you *more* suspicious of her.

Sorceresses were like wizards, basically the female equivalent—they were very powerful individually, and they spent their entire lives studying magic rather than living among ordinary people and doing things like growing and selling herbs or weaving. And they were generally in the employ of the same sort of people who hired wizards—the rich, the mighty.

So I could see how a powerful order of witches would decide to turn themselves into a convent of holy Sisters for their own protection. It wouldn't even be a lie if they took the proper vows and devoted themselves to good works and prayer. And why wouldn't they? Unless you were actually *evil*, we all worshipped the Infinite Light, mortals and Light Fae alike. Becoming a holy order was the ultimate form of protection. In fact, it made perfect sense because it wasn't as if witchcraft was evil in and of itself. It just *was*. It was how you used it that made it good or bad.

I didn't say any of this out loud, of course. The others had already had a big enough shock, and when this meeting was over, they'd probably convince themselves that Brianna could not possibly be right about the origins of the Sisters of Saint Everon—that the name was a coincidence and that Brianna, being Fae, had not completely understood what we mayfly humans were doing. Or she'd confused the Sisters with some long-ago master coven that had died out because the Sisters had taken over the same place and the name by coincidence.

Archbishop Thomas, when he finally appeared, was only too willing to talk to the Abbess immediately. "I'm chagrined that I did not think of this myself," he confessed. "I thank you, Lady Brianna, for recalling that the Sisters of Saint Everon have the power to reinforce objects against the forces of evil with their holy prayers."

Brianna looked as if she wanted badly to correct him with the word "spells," but she just nodded gracefully.

"A message sent on swift young feet can travel faster than I." And before the Archbishop could say anything more, I brought him parchment and writing equipment. He wrote a note, sanded it to dry the ink, and sealed it with his signet ring. Rob practically snatched it from his hand and ran off with it so fast that you would have thought his feet were on fire.

The rest of the people in the room were discussing how else Aurora could be protected—or they were attempting to think of ways she could—when Rob came back a lot faster than I had thought he would; he must have run like the wind. "The Abbess agreed immediately; I almost didn't have to say anything. She is on the way with all the Sisters," he said breathlessly. "They want to do this right *now*!"

Well, that certainly got everyone's attention. As everyone got to their feet and went down to wait for the Sisters, I signaled to the Companions that they should stay behind.

"Rob, Anna, you stay up here and guard Aurora," I said, and they nodded. "If you see anything—find a way to make a lot of noise to summon help even if you have to pitch something out a window."

"Then we try to keep ourselves between it and her until you and Brianna come." Rob made it a statement, and I nodded.

"Be on your guard. I don't think they'll try anything this soon, but who knows how Dark Fae think?" I said, and headed out the door with the rest of the Companions.

"I'm not sure I understand how *Light* Fae think," I heard Rob muttering as we left.

The Archbishop was old, and the steps were steep and narrow. He took them slowly and carefully, and since we were behind him, we were stuck at his pace. If I'd thought about it, I'd have led the others down a different set of stairs, but it was too late now. By the time we emerged, blinking into the light of day, somehow the Abbess and her entire abbey of Sisters, novices, and postulants were already arraying themselves in a rough circle outside the palace walls.

Evidently, they didn't consider it necessary for anyone to leave or stop what they were doing, because they were silently and cheerfully getting themselves evenly spaced around the palace, with the novices and postulants sandwiched in between full Sisters.

Except for the color and simplicity of their gowns and the fact that they all wore full wimples and veils—which almost no one but the most old-fashioned women did anymore—they didn't look all that different from ladies of modest means who were a few decades behind the fashion. The postulants were all in a faded blue gray—that particular color achieved, I was told once, by heavily diluting the woad-based dye used on the wool. The novices were in the natural gray you got by spinning the wool of black and white sheep together into the same thread, and the full Sisters were in white. They made a lovely pattern against the green grass at the foot of the cream-colored stone wall. At some unspoken signal, they all raised their hands and their eyes, and began murmuring something under their breath in a kind of plainchant. It was strange and pleasing even if I didn't understand a word of it.

While I watched, Brianna moved silently to stand beside me. "See?" she whispered to me. "Spells."

Well, I had to nod because it certainly sounded to me like a spell—a human spell, that is, because so far everything I had learned about using Fae magic involved internally persuading it to do what you wanted.

And what they were doing looked like a spell because their hands glowed faintly with golden light, and after a while, so did the palace walls. This was clearly magic, at least as I understood it. Human magic, though, not Fae magic; I felt that part of me awakening and rising to meet and join what was going on in front of me even if I didn't understand it consciously. Brianna gave me a sideways look. "Relax and concentrate on protecting Aurora," she said, so that was what I did, and I sensed some of my human power flowing out to join that of the nearest Sister.

Nat, Giles, and Elle watched with their eyes wide; they obviously saw what was going on too, as little motes of power, like fireflies or bursts of dust or pollen, drifted from the hands of the Sisters to the walls of the palace.

Now that I was experiencing very powerful human magic in person at a time when I was not concentrating on defending myself or Aurora, it was easy to distinguish Fae magic from human. Fae Magic felt cool, like a welcome spring breeze; it smelled of fresh green grass after a rain and tasted—yes, to me, magic had a taste!—like sweet spring water. Human magic felt like warm sun; it smelled just like fresh bread; and it tasted like toasted grain. And the Dark Fae magic? I vaguely remembered that it was bitter to both smell and taste.

I think they must have been chanting for an hour or more when they finally stopped all at once with no signal that I could see. It hadn't seemed that long, though; I felt as if I had been lazing about in a half drowse on a perfect summer day the entire time.

The Sisters didn't seem in the least tired, although they could have been hiding it, for all I know. The Abbess, whose robes, wimple, and veil were all of white linen instead of white wool, approached Papa, who bowed to her as she nodded her head in acknowledgment. They spoke together in low voices; Papa sounded relieved; the Abbess, kind. But I couldn't make out what they were saying. Once or twice the Abbess looked at Brianna and me, and the third time I *definitely* saw her give Brianna a merry wink. I don't think Papa saw it, but Brianna did, and she had an expression of satisfaction on her face.

The Abbess put her hand on Papa's arm once or twice, as if to reassure him, and he certainly looked as if he felt better when she left him. I wasn't completely surprised to see her come up to me as the rest of her order assembled on the road in four columns, like an army about to march.

"Greetings, Sister," the Abbess said to Brianna.

"Fair greetings to you, Sister," Brianna replied. "The Light Fae know their allies of old."

"I know you do. And thank you for thinking of us. We had no notion that the situation had turned so dire in so brief a time." The Abbess *tsk*ed. "So the Dark Fae are finding ways around the Rules, are they? The Princess must be more important than we knew."

"It certainly seems that way, and the Light Fae are looking into it. There's nothing in the past to tell us, so the answer must lie elsewhere." Brianna's wings waved, which by now I knew was a sign that she was uneasy. "We're going to have to be just as clever."

"Fortunately, we have this child." The Abbess put her hand on my shoulder, and a gentle warmth radiated from it. Once again, I smelled fresh bread and tasted toasted grain. I welcomed it. After all, this was the Abbess! As with the Archbishop, I had been taught to trust and look up to her all my life.

I felt emboldened enough to ask a question. "What was that chant you were all doing? I never heard it before, not in holy services, anyway."

The Abbess laughed. "That, my dear," she replied, with humor in her voice and her piercing blue eyes, "is because the Church is above such simple and humble magic in its services."

Brianna's eyes flashed with satisfaction to hear her own words confirmed.

"It's the Cradle Song, my love," the Abbess continued. "But in a language older than Tirendell itself. It's the most potent spell we know for warding against evil, all the more potent for its simplicity."

I knew it, of course, when she named it. Every child in Tirendell knows it; we're taught to say it when we're frightened or wake up from a nightmare or find ourselves alone in the darkness.

> *In darkest night, when shadows fall,*
> *Infinite Light, on thee I call.*
> *My sword and shield, my arrow drawn,*
> *I shall not yield, Shadows begone!*

"It channels strong human magic even in the hands of the uninitiated, Miriam," the Abbess said. "Never forget that, and don't hesitate to use it. While Gerrold is a fine man and a good wizard, and he may be able to teach you many things that have specific applications and purposes, I very much doubt that he will ever teach you anything more powerful."

She took her hand from my shoulder, and I almost begged her to put it back. It felt as if she had been filling me with energy and strength, which, after the last few days, I sorely needed. "Live in the Infinite Light, my dear," she said, both a blessing and a farewell.

"Live in the Infinite Light, Holy Abbess," I replied as she turned and walked to the head of her army of Sisters. I no longer doubted that it *was* an army; my only question was why she wasn't leaving some of them here to guard Aurora.

But as they broke into song and began gliding back to the abbey in the town below us, Brianna answered that question as if she had been reading my mind.

"The Sisters' duty is to more than just Aurora or the Royal Family. Their duty is to the entire kingdom. She and the Sisters will now be bending their will to seek out any incursions of the

Dark Fae and doing their best to stop them since every incursion gives the Dark Fae more power to attack the kingdom as a whole." Brianna patted my shoulder. "And truth to tell, the Sisters are not...well equipped for the kind of offensive work that you are. Think of them as a wall. You and your fellow Companions are the guards on the wall."

A few weeks ago, my worst problem was to make sure my manchet bread rose properly. Now I was a guard on the wall.

Too bad I couldn't throw bread at the shadows to make them go away.

"Why are you so jumpy?" Anna asked when I requested that she and Rob watch Aurora while the rest of us had dinner. "The Sisters made the palace impregnable."

"Against the stuff we know about, but not against things that use doors and gates like regular people." I rubbed the back of my neck; it ached. "Just because Gerrold says the thorn wasn't put in place by the maids, that doesn't mean the Dark Fae haven't thought of using human agents. I'm having dinner sent up to you from the head table; you won't starve."

"Well then," Anna said, mollified. "I can stand to have Melalee glare at me every time she thinks I'm about to make a noise for a share of High Table goodness."

"Just stay sharp. The Dark Fae may be counting on the fact that now the Sisters have done their work, everyone will be off guard." I was going to be at the head table tonight, so I couldn't do this myself, though I wanted to. Papa had invited the Abbess and Archbishop tonight, which meant inviting every other high-ranking ecclesiastic in the city as well so no one would feel affronted, which meant the whole family had to be on show. I suspect that Papa was doing this to reinforce the fact that, although we were depending on Fae and a wizard to keep Aurora safe, we were not forgetting that we were human and were also relying on the power of the Infinite Light. Or something. It was times like this that I was very glad I wasn't a princess. Balancing all the fragile egos and politics would drive me mad.

So, within the hour, there I was in my second-best gown with a silver chaplet around my short hair and making polite talk with a Bishop on one side of me and a Sister of some order other than Everon who was supposed to be a noted scholar on the other. Of what, I couldn't tell you. She mostly used me as a way to ask questions about some tricky theological point of the Bishop, who was slightly deaf.

And all the while I was thinking, *We've missed something. I just know it. We've overlooked something.* At first, I just felt uneasy. Then I felt a growing urgency that made it hard to sit in my chair and pretend that there was nothing going wrong.

I finally got a little signal from Papa that it was all right to excuse myself, and I did, but I didn't take the back stair directly up to the nursery. My instincts led me into the rooms that lay just above the dungeons.

And that was when I saw it.

If it hadn't been wincing away from the walls and looking as if it was trying to find a way out, I might not have spotted it, a shadow within the shadows, something like a knight in full armor but only from the waist up. From the waist down there was...nothing.

A Wraith. Not that I had ever seen one before, but I knew what it was from descriptions in ghost stories. This couldn't be a Wraith that was tied to the palace, could it? Surely those had been banished long ago, and to make sure that no new ones awakened, the Archbishop performed a banishing ceremony every nine years. This had to be a Wraith that had been sent here from the outside. Last night, maybe, and then it found itself trapped by the Sisters' blessing.

Normally, it would have been able to go right through walls to get to the nursery. But thanks to the spell the Sisters had put on *all* the palace walls, the Wraith was having to find its way through open physical doors and rooms and stairways like any mortal would have to.

But it wouldn't take long for the Wraith to get to the nursery, where it could kill Aurora with a touch. I had to run.

I hauled up my skirts above my knees and ran, grateful that Papa had allowed me to wear my sword even though I was in a dress.

I knew where all the shortcuts were, and I kicked off my soft-soled slippers so I could run in my bare feet. Otherwise I'd have broken my neck on the polished floors. I pelted up the servants' stair two at a time and skidded into the nursery, startling Mela-lee, Anna, and Rob.

"*Wraith!*" I gasped, dropping my skirts and pulling out the sword as I turned to face the only door into the room.

"I'll get the others," Melalee said instantly, and she ran off *much* faster than I had given her credit for being able to do.

"What are we going to do?" Anna asked, unsheathing her own blade.

"I have no idea, but we need to figure out something because it's on the way and no one will be able to see it but us, Gerrold, and probably the Abbess of Everon." I took a moment to pull my Fae power into my left hand and give both Anna and Rob magic shields because all they had with them were ordinary swords, which were not much good against a Wraith. Then again, without knowing whether I could use Fae magic, was my sword any better? Would what little human magic I had even work against a Wraith? While I was doing that, Melalee returned, panting like an exhausted horse and being towed between Giles and Nat, with Elle bringing up the rear.

Melalee staggered to the cradle and imposed herself between it and the rest of the room.

Just as the Wraith appeared in the doorway, I pointed my sword at it. The others gasped.

"Begone," I said, hoping that I sounded confident. It just stared at me, and I felt my human magic stirring along with my Fae magic. But how should I use it? What should I do with it? Where should I put it, assuming that I could figure out how to channel it?

I should feed it into the sword, I decided. That would at least make the sword look more formidable, and maybe it would reinforce the enchantments against evil. Fae magic probably wouldn't touch this thing; the Wraith used to be human, so maybe human magic *was* the only way to attack it. If only I knew so much as a single spell!

Wait—I *did*!

"In darkest night, when shadows fall..." My voice wavered a little. *"Infinite Light, on thee I call."*

By the time I got to the word "Light," Giles had already figured out what I was doing. He placed his hand over my hand that was holding the sword hilt, grabbed Anna's hand, smacked it on top of his, and picked up the chant.

"My sword and shield, my arrow drawn." Then Rob and Elle added their hands to the stack and their voices to the chant. There wasn't any room for Nat, but he put his hands on my shoulders and added his voice to the rest. *"I shall not yield, Shadows begone!"*

We started the chant again, and as my magic flowed into the sword, I felt something coming from them that followed my power into the sword as it flared into light and grew brighter and brighter with every moment. Just as Gerrold had said—every human had a little magic in them—and now mine was drawing theirs in with it.

The Wraith screamed in what sounded like defiance rather than fear. But it didn't seem as if it could get past us to Aurora, and I was perfectly prepared to stand here all night chanting and holding it at bay—or at least until one of the holy people downstairs figured out that there was trouble and that they were needed to exorcise this thing.

However, it seemed that my human magic had another idea in mind.

As we started on the third iteration of the chant, my sword got so bright that I couldn't look directly at it, and I felt the magic winding tighter and tighter, like a bowstring being pulled, until the finale *"Begone!"*

Then something like a bolt of lightning shot from the tip of the sword and struck the Wraith directly. I winced and looked away as the light flared up and covered the doorway. The others did the same or tried to cover their eyes.

The Wraith screamed again, but this time it was clear that it was a scream of pain.

When I looked again, the Wraith was still there, but it was not in good shape. In fact, there was a hole blasted right through the middle of it. The edges of it were on fire as if the whole creature were made of parchment and I'd just stuck a red-hot poker through it. It screamed again and stared down at itself in horror. All the Wraith seemed to be able to do was freeze and stare as the fire devoured it. And with one last scream, the Wraith was gone.

Then a mob of guards and ecclesiastics and Papa and Mama poured into the room.

Mama went straight to Aurora, who evidently thought the entire thing had been a great deal of fun. The six of us were surrounded by various robed dignitaries, including the Abbess, who patted my cheek and winked before telling the others how clever and brave they had been.

The ecclesiastics who couldn't get near us and Gerrold went over every thumb-length of the doorway to make sure that there wasn't a trace of the Wraith left. I felt as limp as an overcooked carrot.

Those of us who had our swords out sheathed them before someone pressed up against the edges or the points and got hurt. I heard Sir Delacar's voice booming above the babble of the crowd. "You heard it! That was the Cradle Song! Pure human magic calling on the Infinite Light! Blasted that Wraith right into the next world, they did!"

And I realized exactly why Sir Delacar was making all that fuss about it being "pure human magic."

People were still giving me side-eyes about my Fae blood even though the revelation had been weeks ago.

With any luck, this would put those fears to rest. I had called on the Infinite Light and had been answered.

Nothing could be more human than that.

I slowly worked my way out of the mob of people to the side of the room where Mama and Aurora stood, defended from encroachment by Melalee. With five others to fuss over, people didn't seem to notice that I had moved away from the crowd.

"She's fine," Mama said, without my asking. "I think she liked the bright lights."

"The screaming frightened her, but she's a brave little girl," said Melalee proudly. "Not a whimper out of her."

In fact, despite all the hubbub in her room, my baby sister was smacking her lips and blinking drowsily as if she was ready to go back to sleep again. I just hoped being frightened by the screaming Wraith wasn't going to give her nightmares.

The Abbess and Gerrold worked their way over to us as well, and I asked the questions I had wanted to ask since I'd seen the Wraith. "Where did that thing come from? How could it get in the palace?"

"It might always have been here," the Abbess said. "The history of this building has not always been a good or happy one. Don't tell poor Thomas, but that 'banishing' spell he does merely puts whatever dark thing is here to sleep. The Dark Fae may have awakened it before we set the protective spell in place."

So another of the things that we had been assured of as

children was wrong! As if the world weren't a dangerous enough place, the palace could still be haunted. Lovely.

"Then I think we should ask your fellow clergy to help me make a sweep of the palace from top to bottom to make sure there are no other surprises lurking in the shadows," Gerrold said grimly.

"I quite agree, Sir Wizard," the Abbess replied, linking her arm with his. "Let's go collect the useful ones before they begin going homeward or get involved in a jolly old theological debate that lasts the night."

I, however, was not going to be part of that. Because the next thing I knew, Sir Delacar had swept me up with the others, herded everyone out of the nursery, and led us down to the Great Hall, where we could, singly and together, tell the tale to everyone who wanted to hear it again…and again…and again until we were given too much wine and sent to bed because we were stumbling over our words.

CHAPTER TEN

I WOKE UP WITH A BIT OF A HEADACHE; BUT IT WAS ENOUGH TO remind me that I probably should not have accepted that last cup of wine last night. From the looks of things, Elle and Anna were feeling the same. Still, it was only eight days to midsummer and setup for the Midsummer Faire had surely already started down in the town. After our sterling performance as a team last night, I had high hopes that Sir Delacar would let us have half a day off to visit it.

The only thing I was really worried about was how frightened people living in the palace would be now that we'd had a Wraith ghosting through our rooms. But when the three of us went down to breakfast, it seemed I needn't have worried at all.

Our fellow squires practically fell all over one another to make sure we had our share—more than our share, really—of everything on our end of the table. And they all wanted to hear about last night. So we took turns—I told about spotting the Wraith and running for the nursery, then Anna and Rob told about me bursting in, then Giles and Nat told about Melalee coming to get them just as everyone else was leaving the Great Hall. And Elle finished up by describing what happened when we all chanted.

Well, they all wanted to hear about the Wraith being destroyed several times more, so Anna, Rob, Giles, and Nat all took turns describing it.

I ate slowly so as not to disturb the slightly precarious state of my stomach. But I could not help but notice that the same faces that had watched me suspiciously yesterday were all wide-eyed and friendly this morning. Sir Delacar had been right! The mere fact that I had used something every person in Tirendell had learned as a child to destroy a Wraith meant that I had gone from being considered dubious to utterly trustworthy. Suddenly, I had gone from a thing to be wary of to our beloved Princess's loyal defender. My Fae blood had eclipsed my human blood a mere day ago. Now the reverse was true.

This was, well, wonderful!

And sharing this attention was, I thought, extremely good for my five friends. There was no helping the fact that I was the leader of the Companions, but the more I could be the leader among equals, the more comfortable I was going to feel. I honestly could not imagine being Papa and ordering people about all the time, with everyone looking up to you and expecting you to provide answers.

"All right, lads, enough," Wulf said, pitching his voice so it carried over everything. "Time to get to work for all of us." The tone of his voice warned that he wasn't going to tolerate any nonsense.

"Whew!" Giles said as we headed for the training yard and

Sir Delacar. "Wulf doesn't put down his foot often, but he boxes ears if he gives an order and you don't jump to it. There was no talking after we all went to bed, and nothing to slow us down this morning." But his eyes showed me how excited he was. "I can't believe we all did magic!" he exclaimed. "I just can't believe it!"

"Well, you should, because we all certainly did," I said as we entered the training yard. "If I was the arrow, you all were the bow."

Sir Delacar huffed with approval. "That's a nice way to put it, young Miri. And it's a fine thing to know that you can work this way. Once Gerrold starts teaching you more-proper spells, you'll likely be glad of the bow behind you."

I kept quiet about the Cradle Song not being a "proper" spell, since both the Abbess and Lady Brianna certainly seemed to think it was.

"And speaking of Gerrold, you two are going to work together to put that spell on the guards that will let them see magic and the creatures of magic." Then Sir Delacar turned to the others, who looked a little disappointed. "You're not being left out. After last night, it is quite clear that somehow Miri can use you to help her. So you'll be taking turns to do just that." He chuckled as their faces lit up, and he sounded extremely satisfied. I soon found out why.

Before yesterday, the members of the Royal Guard had been recalcitrant about allowing me to do anything with them involving magic.

Today, they were falling all over one another to have the spell cast on them.

So Gerrold and I had a line waiting for us down in the training yard. I went ahead and started, with one of the Companions liter-ally lending me a hand with one hand on my shoulder. And just like last night, even though I was using Fae magic, I was somehow able to get power from my friends; maybe because they were prac-tically glowing with enthusiasm and happiness, and that is where Fae magic gets some of its power. When one started to feel tired, another came to take his or her place. As a result, we got through every single member of the Royal Guard and some of the knights as well, with me doing about three-fourths of the work so Gerrold didn't exhaust himself. And we did it all in the space of the morning.

Brilliant.

I was feeling awfully proud of us when we went in to eat—though, mind you, we ate like a pack of starving animals when we got there.

And to be honest, what I wanted to do when I finished eating was lie down and take a nap. But I went out to the tree and Lady Brianna's cottage because I'd gotten used to doing things when I was tired, sometimes so tired that I didn't think I'd be able to do them at all.

Lobo was waiting for me, and to my surprise and pleasure, so was Viridity. "I understand you had an exciting evening," Lobo said conversationally as I emerged from the door in the tree that let me out on the road.

I stared at him in shock. Wolves don't smirk, but I thought I heard something like a smirk in his voice. "A little bird told me," he said. "Or rather, a big bird. That raven of Wizard Gerrold's is a dreadful gossip."

I rolled my eyes but laughed a little anyway. "It all came out right in the end, but we were pretty scared."

"Why would you be scared?" Viridity asked. "A mere Wraith is nothing compared to one of the Dark Fae."

"Because I didn't *think* when the Dark Fae attacked," I told the unicorn. "I just jumped in. I had plenty of time running up the stairs to the nursery to think."

Lobo barked a laugh. "And now you *know* enough to be scared."

"I wish I knew what it was that was so special about Aurora to attract all this terrible attention," I said as we trotted along under the deep cool of the trees. "It doesn't make sense. She's not Fae-blooded, I am. We're not a great kingdom. We're too small to start wars with other people. We're not really all that important."

"We don't know, either," Viridity confessed. "We've decided to take an interest mostly because the Dark Fae have, and anything bad for them is good for us."

The little unicorn looked quite recovered from his ordeal—and I had no doubt that healing Aurora had been an ordeal for him. "By 'we' do you mean the Light Fae in particular or all the magical creatures that aren't already allied with the Dark Fae?"

"Hmm," Lobo said, before Viridity could answer me. "There are always going to be creatures that insist on staying neutral."

"At least until something attacks *them*," added Viridity.

"That's no different than humans," I admitted. "Some people think that staying neutral will keep them safe. Some think that good and evil are relative and that they can't possibly judge."

"Some people—and creatures—are idiots," Lobo replied crossly.

Just then Clarion leapt over the bushes at the side of the road and landed beside Lobo. "I heard you mention idiots. Are you making fun of me behind my back?" Clarion asked, although I could tell from his tone of voice that he was joking.

"No, if I want to insult you, I'll do it to your face, it's more entertaining." Lobo snapped playfully at him. "What brings you here when you could be eating leaves?"

"Brianna asked me. I have no idea why."

"And Brianna has butter cake," Lobo said, drooling a little.

"Butter cake?" Viridity asked curiously. "Is this something I should know about?"

Both Lobo and Clarion began to describe the wonders of Brianna's butter cake—which I had not yet tasted—and ran over the top of each other with superlatives. Viridity was highly amused. Truth to tell, so was I. That a plant-eating creature like Clarion would be mad for baked sweets didn't surprise me—my Brownie loved bread with a little honey on it and naturally sweet things like apples and pears. But that a meat-eater like Lobo would be so in love with a cake was both unexpected and hilarious.

Brianna was waiting for us in her little garden outside the front door. She was wearing an illusion that got rid of her wings and had her gowned like any ordinary middle-aged peasant woman. If I hadn't seen the glow of magic about her, I probably would not have recognized her. What little of her hair that showed under her cream-colored kerchief was brown; her modest dress was a dull dun, with a smock over it that was imperfectly bleached.

But the only one who would be sitting out in front of that cottage was Brianna or someone she had specially asked to do so. And her face was still Brianna's when you looked closely enough—just Brianna coarsened and aged in a way I had never seen on a Fae's face. We approached, and the first one of us she greeted was Clarion.

"Clarion, I found something in my storeroom that I thought might be useful for you and Miri," she said as the other three went in single file through her little gate and I closed it behind us.

"Oh?" Clarion's guarded tone told me that he suspected Brianna was about to ask a favor of him on my behalf. "Well, say on."

Brianna stepped aside to show us what her skirts had been concealing.

A saddle. But it was a distinctly odd-looking saddle, smaller than the one I used on Brownie, with an odd pommel, and very light.

Clarion bent his head down to nose it. "Huh. Interesting. So you're proposing that I should serve as her horse now?"

"Not exactly. Only in an emergency, when she needs to get somewhere swiftly." Brianna was using her most persuasive tones. "This isn't just any saddle. It's one specifically fitted to a deer's back. Look."

She pointed out all the ways it was different from a horse's saddle—it was meant to sit farther forward over the shoulders; it had a wider chest band and rump band to keep it from sliding back and forth as a deer leapt; and it had a very tall pommel to hang on to. "The stag that wore this centuries ago was no more minded to wear a halter and reins than you would be, so we gave the rider something to hold on to for added safety. I remember when I had it made for him."

Clarion raised his head, an expression of acute interest in his eyes. "And who would that be?"

"Valiant," she said. The name meant nothing to me, but it clearly did to Clarion, who took a step or two back.

"Oh," he said thoughtfully. "Well." While Brianna waited patiently, he contemplated the saddle and brought his head down to sniff it. We were all quite silent as Clarion thought; the only sounds were the bees droning in the garden and the birds chirping overhead. "Well," he said again, after a very long pause. "There's no harm in trying it on."

Brianna lifted it as if it weighed nothing, and as I looked at it more closely, I realized that it did weigh next to nothing compared with saddles I was used to. Which made sense, since there was no way that a stag could carry the sort of weight that a horse could. Except for a very light frame, the saddle was thin and mostly padding. Saddle leather was usually extremely weighty, made from the heaviest part of the hide. I don't know what sort of leather this was, but it was perhaps only glove weight. But it must be tough to have lasted for centuries. I wondered what sort of creature the leather had come from and if the leather had had the same sort of magic done to it that kept the sheath of my sword in good condition.

Brianna adjusted the saddle on Clarion's shoulders, then tightened up the chest and rump bands. Clarion pranced in place a little, shook himself all over, then gave an experimental jump or two. "Hmm. Comfortable. Surprisingly comfortable. I suppose there's no harm in having Miri try it out as well."

Brianna boosted me into the saddle, which had leather loops instead of stirrups; and the loops were up high so my knees were much higher than they were when I was riding a horse. That forced me to shift my weight slightly forward and hold on to Clarion's trunk with my entire leg, not just my thighs.

Clarion snorted a little. "Well. This is much better than I expected. Let's go for a little run, shall we?"

And before I could say yes or no, he reared up, spun around, and leapt over the garden gate.

I clung tightly to the pommel, which was actually a loop of something hard covered in leather so it was easy to grip. And the difference between riding with this saddle and without it was night and day. I wasn't sliding all over Clarion's back, I didn't have his sharp spine poking me in regions best left unpoked, and I actually felt secure. In fact, I started to enjoy the ride once I got used to shifting my weight over his shoulders to assist him as he bounded through the trees. He was much, much faster than Brownie or any other horse I had ever ridden.

I felt a pang of regret when I realized that he had turned around and was bounding back toward the cottage. With a last leap, Clarion landed on the garden path, and I dismounted properly rather than sliding off and landing in a heap on the ground. I realized that I was grinning because that had actually been fun!

"All right," Clarion said, holding his head up and looking straight at Brianna. "You've convinced me. I'll serve as Miri's mount in the spirit of my ancestor Valiant. But *only* in an emergency."

"I wouldn't ask anything else of you, Clarion," Brianna said soothingly. "I'll keep the saddle in the storage seat of this bench; if there is a great emergency, I can call you for Miri rather than having her run through the forest shouting your name and attracting who knows what kind of trouble."

Oh, so she knew about that. I flushed with embarrassment.

"Come over so I can take it off you, then there is butter cake for everyone while Miri tells us what happened at the palace last night."

I almost groaned, thinking that I was going to have to repeat that tale yet again. But then…there *was* butter cake, which I was now quite eager to taste. Maybe it wouldn't hurt to tell it once more.

"But first, Miri, as a test of what I have taught you, I want you to dispel my illusion."

So that was why she hadn't dropped it when we arrived.

Well, I was rested, and feeling quite good, but I had never done this before and I didn't want to be humiliated in front of my friends.

I gathered my Fae magic together and stared hard at Brianna while Lobo, Clarion, and Viridity watched me with great interest as I *willed* Brianna to look the way I knew she looked.

I had the magic settle over her like a cloud. I held it there as long as I could, then when I couldn't hold it any longer, I let it dissipate. And as it faded, it took the illusion with it.

Brianna smiled. Viridity nodded as if this was entirely what he had expected. Clarion chuckled with satisfaction, and Lobo wagged his tail.

We all went inside and settled in the cottage's single room, which now had enormous cushions for Viridity, Lobo, and Clarion to recline on, and a cloud-soft not-exactly-a-chair thing for me. Brianna sat on a soft pouf. We each had a little table with refreshments at a convenient height, and other than that, there wasn't a splinter of other furniture in the room. I told my tale (and the butter cake was every bit as good as Clarion and Lobo claimed), then I asked a question that had been preying on my mind for some time.

"Lady Brianna, I've read all the official records of the last time you acted on behalf of Tirendell—and you didn't do half so much as you're doing now."

"Well, I *did* supply a stronghold to hide in and guides to get everyone there. But you're right. I've been much more...present in the current situation. And I expect you would like to know why."

I nodded eagerly.

"We Light Fae are not precisely *ruled* by the Council of the Elder Fae, which is what it sounds like, a council of nine of the oldest Fae among us, but they are very important to us. We've always had such a council; it is in charge of dealings with the Dark Fae, humans, and all the magical creatures who are not Fae."

"Like us," Lobo said helpfully.

"They assigned me to you, Aurora, and Tirendell as soon as we realized that the appearance of the uninvited Dark Fae at the christening had to have been carefully planned," she said, with a frankness that astonished me. "And the more that has happened since, the more certain we have become that this time we *must* intervene in these affairs. The Dark Fae are bending and evading the Rules, and we think Tirendell is a test to see if they can get away with it. If the ploy works here, they can try it in larger, more aggressive kingdoms. This does not bode well, and if we are to survive, we must do the same as they and find ways to get around the Rules as well."

"I never heard of a council that governs the Light Fae!" I said in surprise.

"Not *governs*, precisely. They act more as advisors. If I had chosen to act against their recommendations—which I most certainly would have once I knew you were Fae-blooded, my dear—nothing would have been done to stop me. But nothing would have been done to help me, either."

That took me rather aback as well. To cover it, I went on to describe what we'd done this morning with the guards—and how suddenly eager they all had been to have a spell cast on them after I used the Cradle Song to defeat the Wraith last night.

"That is excellent news," Brianna said, and there was real relief in her voice. "It's not going to be easy for you, being Fae-blooded, but having the backing of the Royal Guard is going to help you a great deal."

"I don't care what the Court thinks as long as the Royal Guard trusts me," I said stoutly.

Brianna raised an eyebrow but made no comment. I suppose she thought that I would probably change my mind, but as long as I had the Companions, I really *didn't* care what the Court thought about me because I could never be sure who was sucking up to me for Mama's favor. But maybe Brianna didn't understand that part of my life.

Or maybe she didn't understand human rulers and Court politics at all. It's sometimes easy to forget that the Fae aren't like us; they look so much like us, and yet, I don't think even Gerrold knows much about how they live day-to-day. What do they do when they aren't swooping in to rescue humans from their Dark kin? I have no idea. We see them only when they choose, and we see only *what* they choose.

I guess I should just be glad they're on our side.

"I was going to wait until I was certain you had mastered Fae magic before allowing Wizard Gerrold to teach you human magic, but I am having second thoughts about that plan," Brianna said, though she sounded very dubious. "I think the sooner you start learning human magic, the better."

But I shook my head. "Except for the christening, the Court hasn't 'seen' me do any magic until last night. It's all been rumor and gossip until now. I don't think they could even tell the difference between human and Fae magic."

Brianna laughed at that. "I'll take your word for it, my dear. Very well then, we'll just go on as we have been."

That sounded very good to me. I was only now getting used to how I was being trained!

After we'd settled that, and Lobo, Viridity, and Clarion were stuffed full of treats, Brianna sent them off and it was back to work for me. By the time she let me go for the day, I had worked so hard, I was starving again.

One day passed, and nothing horrible happened. Two days. Then a week. It was almost midsummer and time for the great Midsummer Faire in the town. I hadn't been but a handful of times; first, I was too young, then Father went off to war; and after that, we were in mourning and it wouldn't have been appropriate. Then Papa proposed, and things were too complicated for me to go.

But I had hoped (before the christening, when everything got complicated again) that I might be able to go this year. The christening certainly put an end to that hope. So now I just listened to the squires rattle on about when their knights were going to give them a morning or afternoon off, and what they planned to do, and how much (or little) pocket money they had to spend, and I tried not to feel too envious. Even my friends were pretty sure Sir Delacar was going to give them leave to go at some point during the seven days of the faire.

I kept reminding myself how privileged I was. I mean, I had not just one kind of magic but two! And I was Fae-blooded! And I spent significant amounts of time with the Fae! Surely I should feel as if I were living in a wonder tale, right? And we were already taking turns to guard Aurora, so I could scarcely expect to be let off from that duty.

So on the morning before the first day of the faire, when Sir Delacar lined us up (except for Giles, since it was his turn at morning guard duty) and said, "I expect you all want to be let off for the faire," I had already made up my mind that he was going to tell us that we were doomed to disappointment.

"I'm going to let you off two at a time every other day in the morning. And if you are not back at the table for luncheon, even if you've stuffed yourselves too full of faire food to eat it, none of you will ever get an opportunity for an excursion for as long as I'm your trainer."

He glared at all of us, which kept us from jumping up and down. "Elle and Anna, you will go tomorrow. Nat and Rob, you will go the third day of the faire. Miri, you and Giles will go the fifth day. I'll adjust the schedules so Aurora does not remain unguarded. Now get your minds on your training."

I have to say that keeping my mind on my training that day was one of the hardest things I have ever done.

Everyone else's mornings at the faire went off without an incident, although Elle and Anna confessed to me later that they had only *just* squeaked into their places at the table mere breaths before Sir Delacar came in to see if they were there. Now it was just Giles and I, and we got up while it was still practically dark and snatched bread and butter in the kitchen in order to maximize our time. "After all," he'd said, when we conferred about what we wanted to do, "we're going to stuff ourselves when we get down there, so why ruin it by eating much breakfast?"

So by the time the performers and stallkeepers were just getting in place, we were walking around the faire well ahead of most of the crowd. We'd followed our noses to a stand that was clearly patronized mostly by the people working the faire and had gotten fried dough twists sprinkled with salt. Then we made a quick circuit to find out where the performers everyone had raved about had their tents.

The first ones who were thoroughly awake and ready to perform were a troupe of players who performed a comedy that involved a lot of running about and people being in the beds of other people where they had no right to be and people imagining that their spouses were doing that and getting their comeuppance for their suspicions. I thought it was absolutely hilarious, though poor Giles was as red as a strawberry before it was all over.

He was hungry again, and we went looking for food before

finding the rope dancers. And that was when I noticed something and stopped him before he spent a penny on another snack.

"Giles—almost everything you want to buy is just *bread*. There's fried bread sprinkled with salt, fried bread sprinkled with sugar, fried bread sprinkled with sugar and spices, baked bread with onions and garlic and herbs and seeds in it, baked bread with spices and sugar in it, and dough wrapped around a tiny bit of cheese or meat or jam. This is all stuff you could make or get for free in the palace kitchen if you put your mind to it. Are you *sure* you want to spend money on bread that isn't even manchet bread?"

That made him pause a moment. "You're right. That doesn't make sense."

"There's a fruit seller," I said, pointing out a little old lady with a tiny stall. "If you are going to spend money, try there."

And she had a golden-yellow apple she called Honey-Sweet that neither of us had ever seen before. So we each got one of those, which were a bit more expensive than plain old red apples but were absolutely worth it, then we went to watch the jugglers.

Our court jester juggled but nothing like this family. They not only juggled, they were acrobats too, which our jester was not (to be fair, Tamarline was an older gentleman, and I think his joints were a bit stiff for acrobatics). By the time the family had finished their show, bodies, balls, staves, flags, and torches had flown through the air and my eyes were as big as the apples we'd just eaten.

And just as we left the tent, there was this huge *boom* that made me jump out of my skin. I thought something horrible had happened and was wishing I had worn my sword—but none of the vendors or performers even stopped for a second, and only people like us looked startled.

Then Giles suddenly laughed. "I know what that is! Come on!" And he grabbed my hand and hauled me through the crowd. He dragged me all the way to the edge of the faire, where there were some really small stalls and people were gathered around one of them. People were lining up and coming away with cones made of woven grass full of little white puffs. There was an odd, pleasant, nutty smell in the air, and we waited our turn until we could get close to the source of the smell.

At that point, there weren't any more of the white puffs to be sold, just a few on the ground. A man was standing close to a very hot coal fire near a round-bottomed barrel made of thick cast iron with a crank on the rounded end and a cast-iron lid with clamps that looked as if it sat inside the barrel. He was wearing clothing like I had never seen before—not a costume, as the acrobats wore. More like something from a land quite far from here—robes of light linen or something like it and a long scarf that wrapped around his head and neck, all a sort of orangey-ocher color. We watched, I in puzzlement and Giles in anticipation, as he poured a little oil into the cast-iron thing and followed it with a double handful of wheat kernels. Then he clamped the iron lid into place and tightened the clamps down— it was a *really* tight fit—and lowered the barrel over the coals and turned it with the crank while working bellows with the other hand to make the fire really hot. Then, without any warning at all, he flipped the barrel off the fire, popped a big cloth bag over one end, and hammered a protrusion on the clamps that were holding the lid to make them let go.

Boom!

I jumped and shrieked, and I wasn't the only one.

The bag suddenly inflated, and when he pulled it away from the mouth of the barrel, I saw that the bag and the barrel were full of those little white puffs. He sprinkled salt and herbs over them, shook the bag vigorously, and began scooping the contents into those grass cones he had waiting.

"Give me two pennies," Giles demanded, as he pulled two more out of his own belt pouch. Two pennies was pretty exorbitant for faire food—but I had never seen anything like this, so I figured it was worth it. Besides, watching the man work had been a one-penny show all by itself.

Giles got us both cones of puffs before the man ran out and started the whole thing all over again. Some enterprising souls had brought their own containers, and he measured out the same amount into them that went into a cone. I waited to try the puffs until we were outside the crowd.

They were tasty, although I couldn't have said what they tasted of besides salt and herbs. I liked them, though, and the novelty and show were more than worth the cost. "Where does he get the grass cones?" I asked Giles, figuring that since he'd known about the treat in the first place, he'd know about the cones.

"Nat says that he has two wives and six children in a tent outside the faire and that they spend their time weaving the cones from grass they collect at the roadside, then clean and dry," Giles explained as we headed for the rope dancer's tent, slowly munching our—well, I am not sure what to call them. Wheat puffs, I suppose. I finished my cone and found myself wanting more.

The rope dancers were just as good as Anna had said they

were—and when we left the tent, we didn't have a lot of time left before we had to be back up at the palace. I was about to suggest that we start strolling up there so we didn't have to run when I felt someone pulling at my elbow.

It was a young girl. Like the man with the puffed grain, she wore a costume I didn't recognize: a blue knee-length tunic with embroidered cuffs, a little standing collar with embroidery around it, and an asymmetric opening in the front. This was worn over leather trews and knee-high boots. Her black hair was done in two braids.

I wasn't sure what to expect. She looked at me with large, slightly scared eyes and said, "The lady will come with me? Puri Daj says I am to bring you to her."

Giles eyed her suspiciously but said nothing.

"Puri Daj sends me, most urgently!" the girl insisted.

"I think I should go with her," I told Giles.

"All right," he growled. "But I'm coming too."

CHAPTER
ELEVEN

With Giles trailing a little behind me and watching everything and everyone as if he expected an attack at any moment, we left the faire proper and entered the section of common land where the performers and stallkeepers camped at night. And I didn't argue with his attitude at all because this was exactly the sort of scenario I could imagine being used as a trap.

Of course, if it was a trap, that meant that there was someone up at the palace who had known Giles and I were coming down to the faire this morning and had informed whatever miscreant wanted me. After everything the captain of the Royal Guard had done in verifying the loyalty of our servants, that seemed unlikely, though not impossible. And if we had been *really* clever, both of us would have feigned indifference. Giles, unfortunately, was not that good an actor, so I was left to pretend that all I was interested in was finding out who this Puri Daj was and what she wanted with me while Giles glared murderously at anyone who even looked at us.

The young girl took us to a part of the camp where her

people had set up their traveling wagons, which stood out like proud pheasants among their drabber brethren. Each round-topped wagon was carved and painted on every available surface. Exceedingly colorful but not gaudy, to my eye at least. This area, like the rest of the encampment, was relatively empty. The women were mostly dressed like the girl, although some had a longer gown-like version of her tunic. The few men I saw were dressed as she was and wore an odd sort of round cap with a pointed top. A few old women looked after the smallest of the children like hens with big broods of chicks. The little mites were hardly what you'd call "clothed" at all, but it was a warm summer day, and I personally didn't see the harm in letting them run about mostly naked in the sunshine.

Seeing nothing but peaceful people going about their business, Giles stopped scowling as much, which was just as well, as I really didn't want him frightening the children.

The girl led us to a caravan right in the middle of the encampment. The back door was wide open, and beside it, sitting on a chair that looked suspiciously as if it had been carved to resemble a small throne, was a tremendously old lady.

She was bundled up in so many shawls that it was hard to tell how big or small she was, but I got the impression of fragility, which was immediately contradicted by her sparkling, shrewd dark eyes under a pair of snow-white eyebrows.

I curtsied to her as I would to a lady of rank. This amused her no end. "The forest is full of tales of you, Companion," she said in a reedy though not unpleasant voice with a trace of accent I couldn't identify. She gestured for me to sit on the ground next to her, so I folded my legs under me and did just that. Giles, she ignored.

"I certainly hope not, Puri Daj," I replied. "I am much too young to have tales whispered about me."

She slapped my upper arm with the tail of one of her shawls, but she smiled as she did so, so I was pretty sure she was pleased with my reply. "Give me your hand," she ordered as she grabbed it. She studied my palm with great care.

"You will lead but never rule," she said, and I got the sense she was testing me.

I shrugged. "I never want to," I replied honestly.

"You are not a chosen one. Instead, *you* made the choice to act out of love and that propelled you into the course you are now on."

Now she bent over my hand in earnest. "You will face many trials," she said, after studying for so long that I began to feel uncomfortable. "But there is one thing that unites them all." She looked up at me. "Love, compassion, and kindness are the strongest weapons you have. Stronger than magic, stronger than steel. Never doubt that and never lose hope. And when you have a choice—choose kindness and compassion."

I felt an odd sort of chill when she said that—not the scary sort of foreboding chill but the chill that felt as if she had said something very, very important.

And that was when she coughed dryly, and the girl who had brought us there moved toward her with a look of fear and concern on her face.

The old woman waved her away. "Enough, little one. Even hearts wear out, and there is nothing you can do about it."

But once again, my human magic rose up inside me, rebelling against that statement. *It* wanted me to do something!

But I'm no healer! I thought. *I don't know how to focus the power to actually do anything like healing!*

But I had to try. The Abbess had said that spells were a way to mentally channel and focus human magic. *Puri Daj said it was her heart…maybe I can…make something up!*

I don't know where the words came from, but I found myself whispering them under my breath, and the magic responded to them in the same way it had to the Cradle Song. "Not yet is your story ended! Weary hearts can still be mended. Kindness shown when unexpected, now your kindness is reflected!"

The human magic seemed to approve. I sensed it flowing into Puri Daj and concentrating on her chest as Giles watched in puzzlement.

I continued to hold the old woman's hands and let the magic flow into her until it stopped abruptly. Taking that as a sign that I had done everything I could, I let go of her hands and straightened up.

I might not have been a healer, but even I could tell that whatever I'd done had been an improvement. Underneath the weathering of many, many years of being in the sun, her face had been pale with grayish undertones. Now she was flushed with new vigor. She was breathing easier too, and she stared at me with surprise and delight.

"I'm not a healer," I said apologetically. "And I'm not even sure what I did, but I hope it helped."

She said something in her own tongue that I didn't understand, but the girl burst into tears and ran off.

"What did I do?" I asked in alarm, starting to get up to run after her.

But the old woman motioned for me to sit back down. "She is just happy," Puri Daj said. "I told her that, thanks to you, my *drubarick* would be serving the clan for many more years and that she should run to tell her father, who is my son, our leader."

Before I could say or do anything, the girl was back, dragging a middle-aged but still handsome man by the hand. Actually, he was awfully handsome. He had expressive dark eyes that were slightly slanted, hair as black as a shadow on a moonless night, a chiseled face that should have graced the statue of a hero, and a very long, handsome moustache. Anna would have fallen in love at the sight of him despite the fact that he was at least as old as Papa. The girl babbled at him in their tongue, and he cut her off with a kindly gesture to ask something of his mother. She replied, and to my acute embarrassment, he went to one knee in front of me, bowing deeply.

"Our clan can never repay you for your gift, dear lady," he said as Giles stared from me to him and back again with his mouth hanging open. "But if you ever need help from any of our people, tell them Batbayar of Clan Uru'ut requires it of them."

I flushed so hard that it felt as if my face were on fire, but I tried to act like Papa or Mama and thanked him sincerely even though I had no idea what he was actually offering. I still didn't know where these people had come from or who they were. But I certainly would be able to recognize them if ever I saw them again! And then I realized how late it had gotten.

"I don't mean to be rude, but we have duties and we are going to have to *run* to get back to them!" I blurted out.

But Batbayar smiled and rose to his feet. "No need to run. I can give you a tiny payment for your great gift now."

He said something to the girl, who ran off and came back within mere moments with two of the most beautiful black horses I had ever seen. They had heavily feathered feet, white stars on their foreheads, one white foot, and manes that reached down to their knees, and they were saddled with light saddle pads with leather-loop stirrups and bridled with hackamores. "Take these as our gift," Batbayar said, and before I could protest, he had boosted me into the saddle. Giles was already in place, as his mare stood like a rock. "They can run for days and will serve you long. But never put a bit in their soft mouths. They are daughters of the wind herself!" And then he gave them each a light smack on their rumps, and they launched themselves into a canter, taking us out of the camp and on the road to the palace without a chance for me to say anything more.

"Oh! My! *Infinite Light!*" Anna squealed. "They gave you a *horse*?" She seemed much more impressed with the horse than with the fact that I had healed the lovely old woman without actually being a healer. She skipped around the horse and clapped her hands, which did not seem to disturb the horse in the least.

"They gave me a horse too," Giles pointed out, pasty in one hand, horse's reins in the other. For those of us at the bottom of the table, lunch had been pasties—crescents of pie crust stuffed with chopped leftovers. Which had made it convenient for Giles and me to leave our horses in the hands of the grooms, dash in, grab a couple of pasties, collect the rest of the Companions, and lead everyone back to the stable yard.

"Miri's is prettier," said Anna.

"They're practically identical," I said. "Except that the white foot on mine is the left foreleg and the white foot on his is the right hind leg. That's the only difference. They're even both mares."

This was when Sir Delacar came lumbering into the stable yard. "Let's see these gift horses, and tell me what happened," he huffed, taking the reins from Giles and putting his hand on the horse's nose to get it to lower its head. "Hmm," he said, looking into her mouth. "Young." He looked over all four of her feet, felt her hocks, and ran his hand over her coat while I explained how we came to have the horses. "Sound legs and feet. No sign she's been dosed. I did not expect this." Only then did he turn to look at me. "You've made yourself some interesting friends, young Miri. For your information, those folk call themselves the People of the East Wind, and they travel about during the summer months selling horses, horse tack, and a kind of wool, and in the fall, they vanish. No one really knows where."

"What are you going to call her?" Anna demanded.

I said the first thing that came into my head. "Star."

Giles smirked. "Not exactly original."

"I could have picked Blackie to match Brownie."

Sir Delacar laughed. "I do see the reason behind their gift, though," he said as Nat and Rob gazed on our horses with unconcealed envy. "There are two of you but six Companions, and I have no doubt that your new friends know this. If they'd only given *you* a horse, Miri, well, that would be one thing. But they gave Giles one too. They knew the others would be wanting horses to match, and that's money in their pockets."

Anna and Elle looked stricken, and I knew why; there was

no way their families would buy them horses to match mine and Giles's—and now that I thought about it, there was no reason why they *should*. My father's armor and horses had always been supplied by the King because he was the King's Champion, but everyone else, the knights included, had to supply their own. So by all that was proper—

"Sir Delacar, may I go run a quick errand?" I asked.

He raised an eyebrow at me and gave a slight jerk of his head at my horse. I nodded. "Be quick about it," he said.

He kept the others there talking while I ran off. The last thing I heard him say were the lines from a poem about horse buying that I'd heard before. "One white foot, buy him; two white feet, try him; three white feet, send him far away; four white feet, keep him not a day."

I remembered my father telling me that as I looked at his massive chestnut warhorse with four white feathered feet. And he'd laughed. "Silly poem," he'd said. "White feet often mean pale hooves, and foolish folk think that pale hooves are weak hooves. Not true. Remember that, my love, and don't let four white feet keep you from taking a fine horse."

I returned as quickly as my feet could carry me, having determined from the seneschal that, yes, my household income would extend to buying four horses and housing six. "No more extravagant expenses, however," he cautioned. "No more gowns or other costly items until the harvest. You can afford this only because the costs of your estate are reasonable and you had a good profit last autumn." And he had given me the exact amount of coin that he considered appropriate for spending on horses for my Companions. Sir Delacar was still pointing out all the things that made Star and Giles's mare superior animals for the sort of work we'd need them for. "They don't need to be war-horses; you aren't going to war. But you likely *will* need them for travel when the King and Queen take Aurora on the Royal Progress and when Aurora gets older and goes out hunting, so they need strong hocks." He heard me coming in the stable door and turned, smiling when he saw the pouch in my hand. "And now, I presume, this afternoon's lesson will be one in horse buying?"

I nodded. He fetched the stablemaster for a second opinion, and to the dazed glee of the other four, we all went back down to the faire. And we soon had four more black-and-white horses, three geldings and a mare, all bought from my new friends after much palaver and bargaining. Three of them had two white feet; one of them had only one. They all had some white on their faces, from a little dot to a long, fat stripe, and we'd all learned more about buying horses in that one afternoon than any of us had in our entire lives.

"Now we'll add new lessons," Delacar proclaimed as Nat, Rob, Elle, and Anna led their new mounts up the hill—Delacar had deemed them too green as riders to ride unknown animals through town. "I suspect you are going to find yourselves sorer after the first day of riding than you were after your first day of fighting practice."

Giles looked a bit smug at that. I already knew I would be all right; if I could survive a bareback ride on Clarion's back, I could take anything. Giles had seemed to me to be a perfectly competent rider, but I wondered about the others. It didn't necessarily follow that if you were a noble, you automatically knew how to ride the sort of horses we'd just bought. Especially if you were a girl. Most boys learned to ride so they could hunt, but I knew that many girls never rode anything more exciting than a gentle palfrey, and that at an amble.

But Anna and Elle just smirked. Well, time would tell.

We all assembled at the stables the next morning and saddled and "bridled" our new horses under the supervision of the head groom. Sir Delacar insisted that we know how to do this quickly and competently, just as he had when he made us groom and put our charges up in their new stalls last night. I say "bridled" because we'd been ordered never to put bits in their mouths. Giles and I had the saddles our mares had come with; the rest had the lightest saddles the head groom could find.

Then we spent the morning riding in the big field behind the palace where jousts were held and the knights trained every day. I loved every minute of it. Brownie was a good little pony, but Star was just...*elegant.* Sir Delacar made sure that we could all competently ride every pace from a walk to a full gallop, first singly then as a group. "I confess I am pleasantly surprised," Sir Delacar said, before he dismissed us for lunch. We dismounted as he crossed his arms over his chest and wore a satisfied expression, then we led our horses to the stable. He gave us permission to leave them in the hands of the grooms so we would have time to wash up before luncheon.

We'd all passed his trials with flying colors and that included our horses too. Anna and Elle smirked again, and all the boys looked exceedingly pleased with themselves. But Delacar's next words changed those expressions to surprise tinged with alarm. "We'll be jumping tomorrow. And if that goes well, we'll start accustoming the horses to fighting. You'll be practicing against the pells while mounted."

I could tell that Star had been well trained in the basics—but I very much doubted that she'd ever had someone whacking a stick around her ears. This could be a problem—for us, not the horses. They would certainly react, at least initially, with alarm. And an alarmed horse usually bucks and sometimes bolts.

On the other hand, Sir Delacar was *the best* trainer. I was sure that he knew this already. I decided to put it out of my mind and get fed before I ran off to my magic lessons. I had a *lot* to tell Brianna.

I was afraid that the other squires were going to be jealous of us, but to my relief, they weren't—and it turned out, as I listened to everyone talking over lunch, it was because having a horse just meant having extra work as far as they were concerned. "It's not as if you're ever going to get a chance to ride for fun," one of them said with a knowing smile. "And you *are* going to have to take care of that tack all on your own. You're just lucky you don't have to feed and muck out too."

And I could see their point. We weren't at war. None of their knights went on tourneys to earn prizes and money. All the squires ever did—all they had *time* to do—was train and take care of their knight's property. Even if they had a horse of their own, when would they have time to ride it and enjoy it, much less have the money to feed it? They were perfectly happy to make do with the stolid retired warhorses that belonged to their knights that they were allowed to use in training. To them, a horse was just another thing, like a sword or armor, that needed taking care of, not something to enjoy.

But we weren't like that. In a way, we were almost knights even though we didn't have the rank. We would have time to ride as well as train with our horses. Well, the others would, anyway. And because we were Aurora's Companions and I had my household income, the feed and upkeep were taken care of for my five friends.

It was a relief to know that the squires weren't going to resent us for our new acquisitions. This wasn't going to upset the fairly decent rapport we'd finally forged with them.

I ate in a hurry, hardly tasting anything, and debated as I ran to the oak tree whether I should tell Lobo about how I had cured the old woman. I decided I had better wait to see what Brianna said first, so I just told him how we'd all bought horses at the faire. He wanted to know if any of them talked, and when I said that they didn't, he snorted. "So, not interested in getting into debates with your mount, then?" he said, referring, of course, to Clarion.

"You have to admit that conversation could be a problem. For one thing, I doubt that Star would be willing to carry me into an actual battle if she was able to talk to me and decide things for herself."

"Probably not." Lobo laughed.

Brianna was *far* more interested in the fact that I had essentially "made up" a human spell on the spot that had worked. A healing spell at that!

"Human magicians are not necessarily able to heal," she told me. "Nor are Fae, actually. Did you sense any of your Fae magic working while you were doing this?"

"Nothing," I said with confidence. "This was all human. And the verse I made up—I think it was very specific to Puri Daj and what she had done for me. I don't think I could use it a second time even on someone with a similar ailment."

"Fascinating," Brianna murmured. "Well, I hope that Gerrold can keep up with you. It sounds to me as if you are going to be a challenge to his abilities as a teacher."

That took me aback. It certainly didn't sound auspicious!

"I would like you to talk to him tonight and tell him exactly what you told me. And in the meantime, it is time for your lessons. You have the basics now, and I'm quite pleased. Now we are going to start lessons about concentrating on very fine control."

Brianna wasn't joking. The only thing I can compare this to was when I was trying to learn how to embroider over one or two threads at a time with a thread no bigger around than a hair. Today I practiced on levitating a single grain of wheat in the air in front of me while simultaneously peeling off its outer husk. Neatly. Without shattering, crushing, or otherwise mangling what was inside. And when I said that it was impossible, after destroying twenty grains in a row, Brianna showed me that it was *not* impossible by deftly doing the same—to a moonflower seed, which was a quarter of the size of a grain of wheat.

By the time she dismissed me, I was more than ready to be finished for the day.

And I was not looking forward to climbing all those steps to Gerrold's tower. But I was fortunate that I didn't have to. As I left the table and the Great Hall, he intercepted me on the stairs before I got very far. I wondered if he'd ended his own dinner early to make sure he caught me.

"I heard something of your adventure with the People of the East Wind from Sir Delacar, and I was wondering if you could spare me part of your evening, my lady?" he asked me politely enough. "And what would you say if we repaired to the garden for a discussion?"

"I'd say it's better than climbing all the way up to your tower, Sir Wizard," I replied politely. He laughed.

It was still light outside; I loved these long summer evenings. I always have. But it was a pity that it looked as if I wasn't going to get much chance to enjoy them this year.

I wasn't surprised when Gerrold chose that wild part of the garden I liked so much. I *was* surprised when he led me to a little overgrown bower behind "my" oak, where two small seats sat facing each other. They were made of smooth river rocks cemented together in the shape of a tilted cup. I hadn't even known that they were here!

We sat down in them in the fading light of sunset, and they were a lot more comfortable than you'd think for being made of stone.

When I had finished my tale, he sighed. "Well, I am going to tell you what I think Brianna has already guessed. I cannot teach you."

"Wait, what?" I said, bewildered. This was not what I had expected to hear. I'd expected that he'd insist that I immediately double up on my lessons with him.

"That is, I cannot teach you *much*. Let me explain. There are two kinds of human magicians, wizards and sorcerers."

I nodded because I knew that already.

"Witches and wizards must study, learn great control, and memorize specific ways of implementing that control. Spells, in other words. Witches are less powerful than wizards—much like the difference between a hearth fire and a forge fire. This is why witches work in groups when they need to do something that requires a great deal of power. But for sorcerers—and sorceresses, of course—control is instinctive. They make up spells to focus their power on the spot if they need to." Gerrold shrugged a little. "Wizard magic is predictable. A sorcerer's magic is not quite as predictable. Sometimes it works, sometimes it"—he made a little *pfft* motion with his fingers—"just vanishes in a shower of sparks. Wizards are reliable. Sorcerers, not so much. And sorcerers are incredibly rare. They're like musical prodigies; there is perhaps one born for every five hundred wizards. In fact, now that I think about it, sorcerers are *exactly* like musical prodigies. Magic is something that comes naturally to them."

I blinked. I wasn't sure I liked the idea that my magic was unreliable. But on the other hand, if I kept my sword sheathed, I would have Fae magic to use if the human magic didn't work.

"I'm just supposed to make spells up on the spot?" I asked.

"But they aren't reliable. You might think you have the perfect spell, and something will go wrong with it. It's almost worse than having no magic at all."

"Except I do have the Fae power, and that's reliable."

But the look on Gerrold's face made me bite my lip.

He tried to manage a smile. "But the positive side is that in very small things, you'll be able to do anything you like with it, and you can make up a spell on the spot that will work as well as anything I could teach you."

"Like what, for instance?"

He looked around and picked up a dead twig. "Try lighting that," he said, handing it to me.

I took it and peered at the end of it through the gathering darkness. *Hmm. Darkness. Dark...* "Hasten, hark!" I said to the magic. "Light the dark!"

And just like that, with a tiny drain of power, the end of the twig blossomed into flame.

We tried several more little tricks after I made one of those glowing balls of Fae light to give us something to see by. Not only could I create fire, I could also distill pure water out of the air; I could make a plant go from bud to bloom within a few moments; and I could make small objects float and fly just as I could with Fae magic. But I couldn't get it to work to cheat at dice (and with Fae magic, I could).

Gerrold pulled at his chin a little, then looked as if he had decided something. "Let me repeat what Brianna has probably already told you about human magic. Most people don't have magic that is strong enough to be useful, and of the ones that do, about half don't have the will, the patience, or the ability to stick to mastering it to make it useful. It's like being musical. Everyone can sing. Not everyone is willing to undergo the discipline and training to be a minstrel. Fewer people than that can compose music. Even fewer can compose and perform to a standard that makes them into legendary performers."

"So...it's more than just having it, it's having it strong enough and being willing to work at it?"

"Exactly so," Gerrold said. "Not everyone magical has the drive. Because they don't have any control, they can't even wish a drop of water into existence at first. But if someone is determined enough, it's possible for almost anyone with sufficient magic to become a competent magician—a witch. Not brilliant but certainly competent enough to make a living. People who have more power and devote time and effort into mastering control become wizards. But unless you are a sorcerer, and they are very rare, it takes a lot of work to master control, as you are learning. Without that work, magic dries up in most people for lack of use." He chuckled. "Wizards don't like people to know that."

"Because then there'd be no jobs for wizards?" I asked, only half seriously.

"No," he said, sobering. "Because then wizards and witches and other folk like them would spend all their time cleaning up the messes that people who don't think before they act would create. Remember the fable of the Wishing Fish?"

"The one that gave a man and his wife three wishes?" I asked.

"And you remember what happened. The first thing he wished for, because he didn't think, was a sausage for dinner. Then his wife got so angry that he'd wasted a wish that she wished the sausage onto the end of his nose. But he wished it off again—and there they were with nothing to show for the great gift but a single sausage."

I chewed my lower lip. "But *I* didn't think at the christening, either. I just jumped in between Aurora and that Dark Fae."

Gerrold smiled. "That's a very different sort of 'not thinking.' You could be trying to use Fae and human magic for all sorts of things to make your own life easier—and you're not. What you *are* doing is learning control and discipline."

"That's probably because every time I use magic, it drains

me. So the lesson is, don't use it unless you have to?" I shook my head. "No, that's not right. I have to have a different sort of discipline than it takes to memorize hundreds of spells. I have to learn how to focus *everything* fiercely when I need to use human magic. I can't let myself be distracted no matter what is going on around me. My concentration has to be perfect or nothing will happen."

Gerrold looked up at me, his eyes solemn in the light from the Fae globe. "I honestly would not care to have that sort of magic."

"Only because you like to have complete control and predictability." I don't know why I said that, but once the words were out of my mouth, we both knew I was right.

He looked chagrined. "I'm inclined to think of magic as my tool. I must admit that I don't much care for the tool possibly twisting in my hand and failing to accomplish my goal because my concentration slipped an infinitesimal amount for a mere moment."

"Maybe that's another reason why I have this sort of magic. I don't mind that." Then something occurred to me. "But that means that I didn't get chosen by it?"

"It's just an accident. And you could have decided to reject something you couldn't completely control. I'll be honest. If that had been the only way I could be a wizard, I might well have decided to follow in my father's footsteps and be a blacksmith. I hope you're not too disappointed that I won't be able to teach you anything."

"Well, to tell you the truth, I'm relieved." I stood up.

"Why is that?" Gerrold asked, doing likewise with a little groan for his old knees.

"It means that I'm *not* getting another set of lessons." I rubbed my head, wondering if the vague hollow feeling in it was the prelude to a headache. "I'd need a day and a half of time each day to fit everything in."

He grimaced and dropped a comforting hand on my shoulder. "I'm very sorry, Miri. We seem to be loading you up with more responsibilities every day, and you didn't ask for any of them."

"But I did. I asked to be able to protect Aurora. At least now I *can* instead of sitting back and wringing my hands." I was very good about not adding "like Melalee." And as I parted company with Gerrold at the door to the garden, I said, "I'll take being able to act over being a spectator, no question about it."

But I had another reason for being relieved that my human magic was going to require only the ability to make up rhymes on the spot and focus hard. Even though the Companions and I had very little free time at night, there was something I wanted to do, but I was going to need help.

A lot of help.

When I had given the others the silent signal that I wanted to meet up after dinner, we all went to the training yard as usual, which was the one place that was guaranteed to be deserted at this hour.

"Are we going up to Gerrold's tower again?" Nat asked excitedly as soon as the last of us (me) arrived.

"Well, no, actually." And before his face could fall, I said, "I've been thinking about something I need your help with. And this is the best time of day to do it."

"All right, what is it then?" Giles asked.

I took a deep breath. "You all know my father was Fae, or half Fae. But none of the Fae seem to know who his mother could have been. That's what I want to see if I can find out."

Rob's brow wrinkled, then his face cleared. "Oh! I see where this is going! We need to go through all the records of the Fae in and around Tirendell and see if we can find a match!"

I gulped a little because what I was about to say was, well, scary. But it was a possibility, and we—I—needed to consider it. "That includes the Dark Fae."

Anna looked shocked. "Why?"

"Because the Dark Fae are constantly bickering with one another, one of them might have had an enemy, and how better to protect her son than place him with humans?" I was pretty sure that this was the thing Brianna had been dancing around and not saying. "So we also need to look at the Dark Fae to see if there are any females who might be a match and who disappeared shortly after my father was handed to Sir Delacar. Because the best way of explaining why a Dark Fae wouldn't come back for her son would be if she was dead."

They all wore varying expressions of consternation, ranging from Giles, who looked mostly as if he was thinking hard about this, to Nat, who looked seriously alarmed.

It was Nat who finally spoke up. "But why pick Sir Delacar? Why not just steal a human child and leave hers as a changeling? Everyone knows the Dark Fae do that."

"Because he's kind, and she wouldn't want her son harmed in any way. And because her enemies would certainly look for a changeling. They might look in all the traditional places where a

Fae or half-Fae child is left—like remote cottages. The last place anyone would look for him was here." I then repeated some of what Brianna had told me. "If she expected to confront an enemy and win, she probably assumed that she'd be back for him within months at most and that all this would become an amusing tale about how she had duped the humans into caring for her child, then left them bereft when he vanished again."

"That would explain why none of the Light Fae know anything about it—or at least claim not to," Elle finally said. "But—"

"I know. I've thought of everything you can think of. What if he was planted here to do mischief in the Court? Except he didn't. What if he was evil? Except he wasn't. What if he was intended to betray the King and the kingdom? Except that didn't happen—"

"And what if the real difference between the Light and Dark Fae is just as simple as what they do and how they get their power?" asked Giles sensibly. "What if you took a Light Fae child and gave it to a Dark Fae parent to raise and vice versa? What if the Fae aren't two separate races but two different attitudes?"

And that was exactly what I had been wondering about after I realized that the Companions' courage and determination had empowered me against the Wraith.

There was silence for a very long time, until Nat finally spoke up slowly. "Well, there *are* Fae allies who are completely good or evil as far as I can tell. And there are some who are supposed to be neutral. Take Goblins, for instance—"

"I'd rather not," I said, but it seemed that I had won over my Companions.

"So we'll be spending our lovely summer evenings cooped up in the Records Hall ruining our eyes." Anna sighed.

Nat spoke up suddenly. "No one locks up the records. There's no reason why we can't get the pertinent record books and read through them somewhere nicer than the musty Records Hall, at least until the sun goes down. Tomorrow night after dinner, I guess."

And just as easily as that, it was decided.

CHAPTER
TWELVE

WE FOUND THE TIME TO GO TO THE RECORDS HALL AND
retrieve the books we needed to start our search, and we had
about two hours to peruse them before it got too dark to read
anymore. Then we had to replace the books since I didn't want
anyone to ask questions about why we had them.

It was actually pleasant doing this even if the reason was
potentially disturbing.

We found a corner of the herb garden with great light until
sunset, and no one ever went *there*, since that garden and the
kitchen garden were right by the kitchen door. Which turned out
to be very nice because Odo would come out with cool wine and
leftover pastries for us once he had finished banking the ovens
for the night.

Nat was the best of us at deciphering the crabbed hand-
writing of the clerks who had made the entries. Elle was best
at determining if a name was an alternative spelling of one we
had already noted down. However, it became clear from the first
evening that this could take a long time. Assuming that my father

had actually been his apparent age of six or seven when the lady brought him to Sir Delacar, we had started with the books that recorded the Fae of the kingdom about nine years before that event, and I wanted to look through all of them right up to three years after his arrival. That was twelve years of records to check.

It would have been even harder if the Fae frequently changed their appearance. But once they found a look they liked, they tended to stay with it and only varied their costumes. That meant that once a Fae was identified by name, we could be relatively sure that as long as the appearance matched, it was the same Fae every time.

In the process of carefully making lists of the Fae we thought were likely candidates for what would be my grandmother, we discovered something else. The lists also made note of who had identified the Fae in question, where they had done this, and how the person had determined who the Fae was. The "how" was usually "because this Fae matches the description of an existing Fae," but there were other far more interesting answers. Like "bargained for the information at the Goblin Market" and "was told of the Fae by Grothar, the King Bear."

On the third night of our list making, I mentioned this aloud, and the others all looked up. "That sounds as if asking Clarion, Lobo, and Viridity about Fae might be a good idea," said Nat. "And any other talking animal they know. I wonder if that Grothar is still around."

"Well, when we get done with our list, we could see what Lobo says," I replied. "We could ask him on our way to Brianna's."

"He should know the safe ones to talk to," agreed Giles, because as we knew from tales, not all the King animals were exactly "safe." Just because Lobo wouldn't eat anything he could talk to, it didn't follow that other King animals were that picky.

By the fourth night, we were finished. We had lists of both Light and Dark Fae females who were probably of an age to have children and the years they were in Tirendell. I planned to ask Lobo for his help.

The next day, Brianna met us at the tree in the garden. "The Council of the Elder Fae is calling a full meeting of all Light Fae," she said, before I could ask her why she was here. "I'm leaving now, and I will be gone at least a week." She smiled, and I could tell that it was intended to reassure us. "I'll send a message when I am back. In the meantime, you'll have a week to entertain and rest yourselves in the afternoons. Enjoy it, my dears!"

"Wait—"

But she had already stepped back through the door and was gone.

We looked at one another. "Should we tell Sir Delacar?" Rob asked.

"No," I said firmly. "This is our chance to have a nice long talk with Lobo, and I'll bet Brianna forgot to tell him that she was leaving. I'll ask him to bring Clarion tomorrow and any other King animals he can persuade to talk to us. Let's go."

As I had hoped, Lobo was waiting for us on the other side of the door. "Brianna was called to a Fae council," I told him, "I don't know when she'll be back."

His ears flattened. "That's disappointing, I shall miss you."

"No, you won't," Nat said, before I could say anything. "We're not telling Sir Delacar. You'll get all of us on our usual days, and Miri alone on hers. We have a project—"

Nat turned to look at me as if he was afraid he had spoken out of turn.

"Go right ahead, you're doing fine," I told him.

"That's...very interesting," Lobo said thoughtfully, when Nat had finished. "What do you want of me?"

"Well, if we find female Fae who disappeared in the three years after my father came to the palace, we're hoping you can tell us about them. And if we *don't* find any who disappeared, maybe you can help us narrow down the list in some other way," I said.

"Or if not you, then any other King animals you know that are willing to speak with us," Nat added.

Lobo opened his mouth but didn't get a chance to say anything because Viridity crashed through the bushes at just that moment. The unicorn panted franticly, and his eyes rolled wildly as he skidded to a stop beside us.

"You—you—you—you—have to—help me! My friend Serulan—is in—terrible—trouble!"

"Who's Serulan?" Rob asked, before I could.

But it was Lobo who answered.

"Serulan," he said, "is a dragon."

Dragons were rare and powerful, and there were three that lived in Tirendell that I knew of, and all three were treasured by the provinces they lived in. Serulan was one of Tirendell's resident dragons. They were hermits for the most part, and they were renowned for their wisdom, which makes sense seeing as they lived as long as Fae. They spent most of their time adding to or brooding over their hoards—and most of those "hoards" weren't treasuries of gold and silver. Dragons could collect almost anything, from books to seashells; the one commonality was their obsession over their hoards. They hunted for objects of desire, they traded for them (in either goods or knowledge), and they spent entire days admiring their collections when they weren't being consulted by those brave enough to approach them for advice.

So all I could think was: *How could something that big, that powerful, and that old be in trouble?*

And how in the name of the Infinite Light could *we* possibly help?

But it was Viridity asking, and I owed him more than I could ever possibly pay back. And—I *had* promised him that I would do whatever he or Lobo or Clarion wanted from me when he saved Aurora.

"How far is it?" I asked. "And how can we help?"

"I don't know!" Viridity cried in anguish. "But without Brianna here, I don't know what to do!"

We didn't even have to exchange a look; I already knew what we would say. "We'll try," I said, and I caught the others nodding in agreement out of the corner of my eye.

I won't list all the machinations we endured to get our horses into the garden and out the door without anyone noticing. I was thankful that I could persuade the door to enlarge enough to fit the horses through. It took longer than I would have liked, given how frantic Viridity was, but finally we were following the unicorn at a gallop on a road through the forest that branched off before we got to Brianna's cottage, a road I had never traveled before. And all I had going through my head were questions—and fear that when we got there, there would be nothing we could do to help.

And in the back of my mind, as we urged our horses to keep up with the surprisingly fast unicorn, was the nagging question: *Would we be able to get back before we were missed?*

The dragon did not look right.

It was broad daylight, and he should have been sunning on some rocks. According to the books I had read, the reason dragons didn't need to eat as much as you would think they would for their size was because they "ate" sunlight. They absorbed it somehow. I suspected that it had something to do with magic; like Fae, dragons are inherently magical creatures, so they don't work exactly the way normal creatures do. Like I did with so many other things, I had intended to ask Brianna about dragons, but it hadn't seemed to be all that urgent compared with learning whatever was relevant—whatever could protect Aurora—so now all I could go on was my memory.

But this dragon certainly didn't look right.

The valley he was in didn't get a lot of sun, so the trees were higher up on the sides, and the bottom was mostly covered with bushes and shade-tolerant plants. From where we were, we had a pretty good view of him. He was blue, but his scales looked more gray than blue. Instead of sunning himself on the highest part of the hill, he had wedged himself into the back of this dead-end valley where the sun wouldn't touch all day long, as if he was trying to avoid it. In fact, it looked as if he'd dug himself a partial cave in the end of the valley to hide in.

The six of us, plus Lobo and Viridity, lay prone on the top of the hill and looked down at him. We had left our horses tethered in the next valley, and with Lobo's help and instruction, we had managed to crawl up here without the dragon noticing us. Now I motioned to the others that we should crawl back down again so we could talk.

"That's Serulan, all right," Lobo said thoughtfully. "Although his color doesn't look right. It might be me, though; we wolves don't see color the way you humans do."

"Well, his color looks bleached and grayed out," Giles replied. "I thought all dragons were supposed to be very brightly colored."

"They are." Elle spoke as if she was an authority. "Every single mention of a dragon in any book I've ever read, or any story I've ever heard, says how brilliantly colored they are. And I think I've read every book in the palace except the ones Wizard Gerrold keeps up in his tower."

"So if it's Serulan, then he's seriously ill or the Dark Fae did something to him that also affected his color. Or else it's a stranger." I didn't like any option, but I liked the notion that one of *our* dragons had been subverted even less.

"It's Serulan," Viridity moaned. "I'd know him no matter what happened to him. But he doesn't know *me* anymore!"

"Beyond not knowing you, he's not acting like a normal dragon at all, so I think we can probably assume that he's been bespelled." I gritted my teeth. "I think I have an idea. It all depends on my sword."

"Miri!" everyone said, absolutely aghast.

"*Shh!*" I hissed, before they got the dragon's attention. "I'm not going to fight him. That would be stupid. But my sword cancels out Dark Fae spells, so what if I could touch him with it? Wouldn't that break the spells on him?"

Viridity pawed a hoof in the ground in distress. "I think you're right," he said. "And I think he's fighting it. I think that's why he burrowed himself down in the bottom of that valley, so he couldn't fly or do anything terrible."

"You know him better than I do," I told the unicorn. "But if he's fighting a spell, doesn't that mean that I'm the only one here who can break it?"

"I...guess," said Giles. "But how are you going to get close enough to touch him before he turns you into a cinder?"

"Got any good ideas?" I asked.

So that was how I ended up creeping down the steep side of the hill just above the dragon's excavation with a rope tied around my middle and all five of the others braced on the hill and paying out the rope a little at a time. And that was why Lobo and Viridity appeared at the mouth of the valley and approached the dragon.

"Serulan?" Viridity called. "Is that you? It's us. Your friends. Lobo and Viridity."

The dragon's head rose, but it said nothing. It also didn't do anything, which suggested that he might be fighting something.

Lobo and the unicorn drew nearer. "Serulan?" Viridity said again, which completely focused the dragon's attention on him. "If there is something wrong, we can help you."

The dragon began to tremble. Small rocks tumbled down the hill on either side of him as he shook. Was our guess right? Was he fighting a spell?

Only one way to find out. I silently unsheathed the sword, gathered myself, aimed, and jumped.

I landed astride the dragon's neck, the flat of the blade hitting his spine at the same time as I landed. We'd all come to the reluctant conclusion that with something as big and armored as a dragon, the only way for the sword to break any Dark Fae spells that were on him was for it to be in direct contact with his body. It wasn't as if I could wave the sword at him and expect the magic to work.

And I stayed there on his back for about as long as it took to draw three breaths. The dragon froze, with not even a twitch to show it was alive.

Then in the middle of my fourth breath, the dragon convulsed, and I found myself in the air. There wasn't any warning. I had only a glimpse of heaving back, then I was falling.

And then I was swinging. *Swinging*, not flying. He'd bucked me off, but that was why I had five Companions hanging on to the other end of the rope around my waist. Instead of arcing across the valley and cracking my skull open on a rock or breaking my neck, I got thrown up and off, then with a jerk of the rope around my waist that made me grunt with pain, the fall turned into a swing, and while I did end up crashing into the side of the valley, it was more controlled and nowhere near as hard.

And I managed to keep the sword in my hand too.

Beneath me, the dragon had fallen on his side, spasming and twitching. I shook my head to clear it, and half climbed, half staggered, down the side of the valley. Whatever the sword had done in that brief contact looked as if it had accomplished something close to what we wanted, but it wasn't enough. And the only way I knew to do "enough" was to hold the sword against him some more and hope that he didn't roll over on me. That was a lot of dragon. I'd end up squashed like a bug.

Unless, of course, the Companions managed to pull me out of the way while he was still rolling and I was trying to scramble backward. I had to count on them.

No time to think; I scrambled back down the slope to where he was thrashing; there seemed to be the least amount of movement halfway down his back, so that was where I aimed for, and I slapped the sword against his scaly hide as soon as I got there. His convulsions turned into spasms and twitches, and though it looked as if I was in no danger of being squashed, it was hard to keep the sword in place.

Everything came into sharp focus: the sword, which was faintly glowing again; the dragon's back, which was covered in scales the size of my hand that kept changing from a dull blue gray to an iridescent blue green and back again in ripples across his hide.

But we seemed to be at a standstill. I tried helping the sword with human magic, but that didn't change anything, although I could sense the draining feeling in my chest that meant that the magic was going somewhere. Plus, I couldn't for the life of me think of a rhyme to trigger anything, and I couldn't use Fae magic because the sword would negate it.

"This isn't quite working!" I shouted. "Anybody have any ideas?" Inside, I was a wreck. I hoped that I sounded better than I felt, which was absolutely frantic. We *had* to save this dragon from the enchantment he was under because he would eventually become so exhausted that the spell would take over—and then something horrible would happen or he could turn on *us*. Maybe we could get away from him. But the odds weren't good.

I hadn't really expected an answer to my question, but suddenly I heard hooves scrabbling up beside me. "I have an idea!" called Viridity, who was behind a pile of churned-up dirt; and a moment later, he jumped over it, landed next to me, and butted his tiny horn right into the dragon's side.

I sensed the tremendous flow of magic out of him into the dragon, and the pulses of color changed again. The grayed-out color didn't last as long. The iridescence stayed longer. And I felt my human magic building up to be used—finally!

I leaned all my weight onto my left hand, which was holding the sword against the twitching dragon, freed my right—which I put on Viridity's back—and let the human magic flow into him. And then a chant finally came to me.

Help Viridity to fight! Help us all to make this right!

I concentrated on that, putting my entire will and mind into it. Dimly, I sensed some of the others scrambling down the hill to stand next to me and put their hands on my shoulders. Just two—one on each side. Giles and Anna, I realized after a moment. I hoped that they had ropes around their waists too. Otherwise, if this didn't work...

It has to work!

Help Viridity to fight! Help us all to make this right!

I heard shouting. First Lobo, then the others, encouraging Serulan to fight back against the magic that was trying to control him. "You can do it, Serulan! Fight it! Don't let the Dark Fae control you!" And anything else they could think of to cheer him on. I was drenched, with sweat running down my face and my back and beneath my hand. Viridity's silky coat was soaked with sweat too. We were both near the limits of our endurance, and I felt a sick uncertainty. I had been so confident that this would work, but the dark magic was so strong! If this spell didn't break soon—

The world went white, and I lost track of everything.

The next moment, I was lying flat on my back in the churned-up soil, half on top of Giles. To my right, Viridity sprawled in a decidedly undignified position, covered in dirt.

And a gigantic blue dragon head loomed over me, the great beast becoming cross-eyed as he attempted to focus both eyes on me. I was too stunned to think, too stunned for the moment to even feel fear.

All I could do was stare into those golden-yellow eyes like a rabbit caught in the gaze of a serpent.

For a very long time, nobody moved and nobody spoke.

Then the great jaws opened.

And a sweet, gentle voice, quavering with concern, emerged from them.

"Are you all right? Oh, please tell me you are all right!"

I blinked at the dragon stupidly as little rocks and bits of dirt fell in my hair from the three scrambling down the hillside behind me. Elle got there first and shook Anna, who seemed more stupefied than I was. Nat got his hands under my armpits and hauled me to my feet; Rob did the same with Giles, then helped poor Viridity to roll over and get up. Lobo came trotting down the hill a moment later with the sword's hilt in his mouth, holding the whole thing high up off the ground like a dog with a tree branch too big to carry easily.

Meanwhile, the dragon continued to gaze down at us with an absolutely unreadable face. If I hadn't heard it speak a few moments before, I would have thought it was about to eat us, flame us, or both.

"Serulan, are *you* all right?" asked Lobo, after depositing the sword at my feet. Cautiously—because my head was swimming—I leaned down, picked it up, and sheathed it properly. "We thought we would never break you free of that spell."

The dragon coughed, and hot breath scented with something not very pleasant that I couldn't identify washed over us. "As all right as I can be, after being ensorcelled like that, thank you for asking, King Wolf." Serulan ducked his head in what looked like an apology. "I beg your pardon, but other than Viridity, I don't know any of you."

Viridity shook himself violently, and all the sweat and dirt shook right off him, leaving his coat pristine again. "Serulan, this would be Lobo. And the humans are Miriam, Giles, Susanna, Raquelle, Robert, and Nathaniel. They are Princess Aurora's Companions. They are here because I found you here and you didn't seem to recognize me, and I knew something was wrong."

"Oh...," Serulan said, then I suddenly felt heat coming off him in waves. "*Oh!*" he exclaimed in dismay. "Oh no, what have I done? What *have* I done?"

Gingerly, I reached up and patted the end of his nose, which was very hard and metallic. It was also extremely hot, so I wasn't tempted to leave my hand there long. "Nothing yet. You were fighting it as hard as you could. You had even wedged yourself down here so you wouldn't be able to do anything if the spell did take over."

"Oh!" Serulan replied, now sounding stricken with guilt. "*Oh no!* Oh, I am so horribly, horribly sorry! I will never forgive myself!" He collapsed limply down into the little valley and sobbed brokenheartedly. "Oh, this is horrid, horrid, horrid! I am a disgrace to dragonkind! I should be tarred and feathered and driven from the kingdom! And I'll *deserve* it! And all because I saw that beautiful statue there and... and I shouldn't have touched it, because it *obviously* belonged to someone else, but I thought that I'd just take it back to my hoard and find out who it belongs to and pay them... and how could I have been so *stupid*? And *greedy*? It was such an obvious trap! Oh, what a fool I am!"

And sure enough, lying a little way away from him was a truly amazing marble statue of a mermaid surrounded by swirling water and her own swirling hair. It was breathtakingly lovely. If he collected statues, well, it was the perfect bait. I unsheathed my sword and slapped it against the statue—but nothing happened. The spell was gone, and with it, any way to tell it had ever been there.

Well, what could we do but try to comfort him? We surrounded him, patting and reassuring him, Viridity, Lobo, and I at his head, the rest at his neck, as he sobbed, huge steaming tears splashing down into the dirt from his eyes.

Finally, Lobo had had enough. "*Serulan!*" he barked. "Calm yourself. You were foolish to fall into such a trap, but now you know better. Enough."

Serulan stopped and looked up for a moment, but burst into tears again. "I could have done *horrid, horrible* things!" he wailed. "Horrible things! And I'm sure you're here to punish me now! I'm sorry! I'm just so sorry!"

Then he dropped his face into his claws and went back to hysterical weeping. Now, in the time that Mama has been Queen, I have seen quite a lot of hysterical weeping. But most of all, I have seen a lot of *faked* hysterical weeping. This sounded and looked absolutely genuine.

But Lobo was right. I drew myself up and put on my best imitation of Mama chastising her ladies. "Serulan, that is *quite enough*!"

This time the dragon gulped audibly and took his claws away from his face to look at me.

"Everything's all right," I said. "There is no point in crying about what you could have done because you didn't do it. Serulan, you actually did all the right things—you hid yourself, you fought off the spell with your will, and you managed to last long enough for one of your friends to find you and bring you help. Right?"

Serulan gulped and nodded slightly.

"No one was hurt. The only damage was to your self-esteem and the bottom of this valley." I glanced up at the sky. "And if we ride like the wind, we can get back home before anyone notices we're gone."

Now Serulan glanced at me shyly. "But I hurt *you*," he protested. "I can see the bruises."

That actually made me laugh. "And Sir Delacar has given me much worse." Then it occurred to me. Serulan had been in this kingdom for more than a hundred years. Maybe *he* knew who my father's mother was! Or could guess! "There is something you might be able to help me with, though."

Serulan raised his head and gasped. "Anything! Anything in my power!"

"Is there any chance that you know or have heard anything about a Fae child left at the palace in Tirendell about thirty years ago?" I asked, and held my breath.

For a moment, the expression of intense concentration on his face gave me hope.

But then those hopes were dashed.

"No," he said sadly. "There have been no Fae children born, Light or Dark, in the last fifty years to my knowledge. And if there was a Fae child born in secret, there would have to have been a good reason to keep the birth unknown, the child hidden, and an equally good reason for the child to have been left among humans. Not even a Dark Fae mother would abandon her child."

"But if the mother died?"

Serulan sighed. "I don't know of any Fae deaths, Light or Dark, in the last half century."

I didn't betray my disappointment, but Rob wasn't so controlled. "Three nights! Three perfectly good nights we wasted going over all those musty old records!"

Serulan looked crestfallen. "I'm so sorry—"

"This is *definitely* not your fault," I said firmly, because the dragon looked as if he was going to start berating himself all over again. "And we didn't waste that time. There might be another explanation. My father might have been only half Fae."

"But how would that explain that the lady who brought your father to Sir Delacar obviously bespelled him?" demanded Rob.

"Oh, that's simple. She was a human sorceress." I sighed. "Which means another set of lists to go through."

*　　*　　*

The horses were pretty tired by the time we got back, and it took some creative scrambling to stable them and change in time for dinner—seeing as some of us had a lot of cleaning up to do before we entered the palace. But currycombs worked to get all the dirt out of my hair, and a quick wash under the pump took care of all the ground-in soil on my skin. As for our tunics and trews, well, they were the same color as the dirt we'd been rolling in, so nothing showed.

I was the one in the worst shape, so I hid under the chatter of everyone else at the table. I actually felt very sorry for the rest of my friends because they were only just now realizing that they had rescued a *dragon*. I could tell when the realization hit each of them; their eyes suddenly lit up, and they had to bite their lips or suck in their cheeks to keep from bursting out with it. But they knew that they couldn't tell, not this time. We'd talked about it. This little excursion had not been authorized, and if we were found out—well, I was not sure what Papa would do. *Someday*, I'd promised. *Someday we can tell. When we're knights and it will be too late to punish us for it.*

Dinner revived me enough that I gave them all the little signal that said we were to meet in the training yard again.

"Well," Nat said, his face reflecting the fact that the elation from saving Serulan was fading and the realization that we had probably wasted three evenings of research was setting in.

"It's not wasted," I said firmly. "Just because Serulan doesn't know of any female Fae who disappeared, it doesn't follow that the Fae didn't have some other reason for not reclaiming her son. We should still think about asking other King animals and trying to think of other ways we can get information about the Fae. And we do need to add sorceresses to our search."

Nat perked up. Rob groaned. "I don't mind the talking-to-animals part," he said, rubbing his head. "It's the going over the records that's murdering me."

CHAPTER THIRTEEN

THE NEXT DAY WAS ONE OF MY DAYS WHEN I WAS SCHEDULED to visit Brianna's cottage alone. Lobo was waiting for me when I came through the door in the oak, and with him was a badger.

It was a much larger badger than I had ever seen before, so I knew immediately that this would be another of the talking King animals, and I gave the fine-looking fellow a little bow of respect.

"This is Haldur," Lobo said. "Of all the animals I know, he's the one who knows the most about the Fae."

"Which is not much, damsel," Haldur admitted. "But I do collect stories. I know all the ones told by all the badgers in my line and all the ones that anyone I have met has been willing to tell me. Now, I do have a story. But I only tell stories when I am told a story in exchange. Have you a story?"

"Do you know about my baby sister Aurora's christening?"

"Only that there was a great deal of excitement that went on about it. I would love to hear this story."

So I sat right down next to the oak and told him everything in as much detail as I could. And when I was done, he sneezed three times and said, "*That* was a story worth hearing! Now here is mine.

"My family has always had their burrow in a part of the forest that most creatures won't venture into."

Lobo shook his head vigorously. "That's an understatement! You're practically on the doorstep of the Serpent Sisters!"

Thanks to our reading, I knew who the Serpent Sisters were. They're among the rare Dark Fae who live together in a family group; at this point, it was more like a clan of about a dozen Dark Fae females (no males, none that humans have ever seen at least). The entire clan seems to have adopted a serpent theme; they wear sinuous snakeskin gowns, they have wings like dragons', their ornaments are all serpent themed, and the clan leader has a snake-headed staff. There are probably all sorts of internal squabbles going on in that group, but none of that is allowed to show on the surface. When they appear in public, one or more of the subservient sisters play attendant to Sessoranu, the one humans call the Queen Snake.

"It's nice and quiet, the way we like it," Haldur said complacently. "They leave me alone; I don't trouble them. Oh, I should mention this because it's important. They actually live in a very large cave complex with multiple entrances. One of them—never used but once in my memory—is near my den."

"I really wish you'd move," fretted Lobo. "What if one day one of them takes a fancy to a badger-fur collar?"

Haldur chuckled. "It would clash with their theme. They are as set in their ways as I am. But to continue, it was a day in deep winter when I would ordinarily have been hibernating that I was awakened by rumbles in the ground. It was not unlike an earthquake, and I cautiously poked my nose out only to discover the forest and the air above it swarming with minions of the Dark Fae—in this case, of the Serpent Sisters, who seemed to be hunting for something. I retreated deeply into one of my three dens, and for a time, all was quiet. But then I heard something crawling down my entrance tunnel."

Haldur was a very good storyteller. By this point, I was holding my breath.

"I gave a warning growl, but what I heard was not the frantic scrambling of something trying to get out of my tunnel before I charged but a soft female voice. 'King Badger, King Badger,' she called. 'Will you let me hide here?' I sniffed the air and smelled Fae. But more than that, I smelled something so rare that at first I did not recognize it. I smelled a Fae with child."

I really had to bite my tongue and sit on my hands so as not to interrupt him at that point. I was afraid that if I did, he'd take offense and storm off without telling me the rest.

"Now I know you are bursting to ask me if she was a Dark Fae or Light." Haldur tilted his head at me. "Well, they smell the same. So I just said, 'Do you swear by the Compact and your power that you mean me no harm?' and she said, 'I swear,' and I gave her leave to go to the right-hand den, and I went back up my tunnel to sit at the entrance and mask her scent. A few of the Serpent Sisters' minions came snooping about, but a growl convinced them to look elsewhere. By nightfall, they had given up searching around my den. I went back down the tunnel, told the Fae that I thought it was safe to depart. 'King Badger,' she said. 'Do you know of any place safe where I might go? The Serpent Sisters will kill me if they find me.' I told her that I did not, but

I suggested that she seek out the Goblin Market and told her where to find it. 'They'll sell you anything for a price, including safety.' She thanked me and crawled out into the forest, and that is the end of the story."

I thought about that for a moment. "So if anyone knows the next part of the story, it will be the Goblins?"

"Perhaps," Haldur replied. "I never found out if she decided to look for safety on her own or went to the Goblin Market. Trying the market is a desperate move, but she sounded desperate to me." He nodded gravely to me, with ponderous dignity. "And that is the end of my story."

"Thank you, Haldur. So far you have been the most help I have been able to find in trying to determine just who my father was."

The badger nodded again, nodded to Lobo, then turned and ambled back into the forest. He didn't bother with the road. Then again, he was a badger. There wasn't much that he couldn't shove his way through.

Lobo sighed and lay down on the moss next to me "Well, that wasn't *much* help."

"It was more help than you'd think. I'm reasonably certain that this female Fae is my father's mother. So far, there hasn't been anyone else who corresponds to the person we are looking for. And what do *you* know about the Serpent Sisters, Lobo?"

"They're very minor on the scale of things within the Dark Fae," Lobo replied thoughtfully. "In fact, it's speculated that the reason why they all stick together is that singly they're quite weak, magically speaking, and that they'd end up someone else's minions if they didn't pool their powers and their resources. And no one knows how many there are."

So the mysterious Fae could have been…a dissenter. Or a Light Fae they had somehow captured who then escaped. Or someone who thought she was being recruited as an equal but who found that she was intended to become a minion.

Or one of the Serpent Sisters who dared to become pregnant.

But somehow that didn't feel quite right. I would have thought that the Serpent Sisters would welcome a new birth into their clan; after all, they would have the opportunity to instill loyalty to the clan from birth. And the child might prove to be a more powerful magician than any of the current lot, making it extremely useful to them.

I nodded. "And that might be why we don't have knowledge of any Dark Fae disappearing—you can't know of one disappearing if you didn't know about her in the first place."

Lobo licked his lips. "It does sound," he said tentatively, "as if your father's mother was a Dark Fae."

"Unless she was a Light Fae captive who was taken prisoner secretly by the Serpent Sisters so long ago that even her own people stopped looking for her. And in either case, if she knew the Serpent Sisters were about to find her again, it explains why she left Father with Sir Delacar and never came back for him. She might even have allowed herself to be recaptured in order to throw them off his trail."

Lobo nodded. "It does seem as if the Serpent Sisters are where you should start your researches. When Brianna gets back, you should ask her. In the meantime, I will keep asking the others if they know anything. You never know. Perhaps we can find a creature that saw her or encountered her now that we know where and what we are looking for."

But I already had an idea of where and how I was going to look. "I have to get back. I need to talk to the others."

"What about?" Lobo asked, his brows suddenly furrowing with what looked like worry.

But I was in too much of a hurry to tell him.

I waited impatiently—lurked was more like it—just out of sight near the archery butts where the other Companions were training. It was easy enough; there was a huge wall around them to prevent misses from hitting anything, and bushes to make the wall less...obvious, I suppose. So I hid in the bushes. It was fortunate that Sir Delacar left early so I was able to slip inside the archery range once he was gone. I whistled softly to get the Companions' attention and had them gather around me.

"I need you all to leave dinner early with me," I said, feeling a bit breathless and very nervous because this was a spur-of-the-moment plan, but I didn't think we'd get another chance at it. "We'll need to get our horses and take them into the garden before anyone else gets there." I took a deep breath. "We're going to the Goblin Market."

They all just stared at me as if they couldn't believe my audacity. Since no one immediately objected, I continued talking.

"You know you can buy almost anything for the right price at the Goblin Market. Including information. Maybe we can find out where Lady Thornheart came from and what creature she was working for." And I quickly related Haldur's tale.

"I see where you're going with this, Miri," Giles said slowly. "But 'the right price' more often than not is something *bad*. The Goblin Market is supposed to be neutral, but everyone knows that it's not. And you don't know for sure that this Fae who escaped from the Serpent Sisters was your father's mother, and you don't know that she went to the Goblin Market."

I didn't feel like arguing with him. "Are you going to help me or not? Because no matter what, I'm going there tonight. The evenings are still really long, and we can get back before anyone will notice that we were gone. I'll never get a better chance."

Rob and Elle looked excited, Nat and Anna were interested but apprehensive, and Giles was disapproving. I honestly wanted to shake him, I was so annoyed with him. This was my best chance at finally finding out something about my own heritage, and he didn't want me to do it! Couldn't he see how important it was to me? And, of course, it was also our only chance at finding out anything at all about the late, unlamented Lady Thornheart!

"Of course we'll go, Miri!" Rob burst out. "It's a brilliant plan!" I smiled at him, relieved, because I knew once one of them agreed, they'd all follow. And, of course, they did.

Even Giles, although he still looked reluctant as we all split up to get ready for dinner.

And thank goodness it was a stew night. There was only one bowl to pass and the platters of bread were within the reach of everyone. We were able to hurry through the meal without seeming to hurry and got out while the other squires were still lingering over their second bowls. They were used to our doing that and didn't even look up when we left. Even Wulf didn't give us a second glance.

And it was still daylight, so taking our horses out for a late ride was not unreasonable. The only tricky part was getting them through the garden to the oak before people inside came out to enjoy the early-evening breezes, the flowers, and the minstrels.

Once through the door, we turned in the opposite direction of Brianna's, and about a mile down that road, we took the first track heading north. This path wasn't a secret; everyone in this part of the kingdom knows where the Goblin Market is—mostly so they can avoid it. And the farther along we went, the narrower the track became. The trees were closer together, their bark and leaves got darker and darker, and the branches and trunks became more crooked and twisted. Fewer and fewer were "friendly" trees like oak and ash, and there were more yews, willows, and thorns. Spiderwebs glinted among the branches, and black-and-white molds patched the trunks. The undergrowth looked rank and somehow unhealthy. The others kept glancing uneasily at the forest on either side of us. "Look confident, like we belong here," I whispered. If there was one thing I knew about Goblins, it was to never show your fear in front of them.

In theory, the Goblin Market is a neutral place; although they are not strictly Fae, the Goblins are a kind of Fae creature, and they have to hold by the Rules. But beyond that, even Goblins need to trade for things they can't produce for themselves, and a few of the things they want are produced only by humans. If you're brave or audacious enough, and smart enough to not get outmaneuvered by them, you can make quite a good living selling the things—and the information—you can get from them to humans who don't dare venture to the market themselves. But the neutrality of the Goblin Market is hedged with a great many "maybes." While they can't attack a human directly, nothing in the Rules prevents them from tricking anyone they trade with, and while the Rules say they can't lie while inside the market, nothing prevents them from withholding truth.

There's no point in acting coy around them, either. Everything I've ever heard or read says to state what you want straight out and let them compete with one another to sell it to you. It also doesn't pay to act too eager, and if they aren't being reasonable, you should walk away because there's always the chance that you can hire someone who is a better trader than you are to get it for you. Sometimes the point of coming out here to the market is to find out *if* the thing you want exists at all. Of course, *that* was not what I wanted. I wanted information, and since the last thing I knew about the unknown woman was that she had been advised to go to the Goblin Market, I was pretty sure that this was where she had gone.

There was light ahead of us now—a bright light that, as we continued to ride forward, resolved itself into several light sources that were warm yellow, red, and blue and that stood in stark contrast to the shadow-dark, spiderwebby forest around us. Then I heard music, faintly at first, but it became louder the closer we got. From here, the Goblin Market sounded and looked no different from the Midsummer Faire. I pulled up Star, and the rest came to a halt beside me.

"You all know not to eat anything here, right?" I asked urgently.

They all nodded, but Giles spoke. "I know not to. I mean, that's what the tales all say, but *why*?"

It was Nat who answered, his voice a little harsh. "Because

if you do, you'll never be satisfied by human food again. You'll keep coming back here again and again and again, giving everything you have to the Goblins in exchange for their food. And eventually, all you'll have is yourself, and that's what you'll end up giving them."

Giles licked his lips. "And then what?"

"No one knows," said Nat. "No one knows if you become a slave to them, or if *they* eat you, or even if you become a Goblin yourself. All anyone knows is that if the addiction isn't broken, you'll finally go to them and never come back again."

"It's not easy to break, either," I added, relying on my knowledge of the wealth of Fae tales I'd read. "It takes a Light Fae, a powerful sorcerer, or a wizard. And you'll still never be the same again afterward. So don't eat anything. If juice is squirted on your face, keep your mouth tightly shut and don't lick your lips. And don't draw weapons inside the market; that's an offense, and it will mean they can attack us."

I nudged Star into a walk and the rest followed me toward the enticing beacon of the Goblin Market.

We stopped just outside the bounds of the market and dismounted. Giles volunteered to hold the horses. We didn't want to take any chances on breaking any rules by bringing them inside—and we also didn't want to discover that the Goblins would only trade the information I wanted for the horses!

We walked through an arch made of the intertwining branches of two trees, one on either side of a weedy track. The arch was covered in thousands of tiny moving lights, which looked to be some sort of firefly. But this sort of firefly had a glowing head rather than a glowing tail, and the tail was home to a wicked-looking stinger. And the market looked remarkably like the faire, complete with stalls—except the stalls were woven of still-living, intertwined, black-leaved vines, and the canopies were hanging swaths of moss full of those fireflies. There were also glowing globes of light everywhere, the source of the red, blue, and yellow light we'd seen from the distance. And in every stall was at least one Goblin.

They were taller than humans, with gray skin and long pointed ears and hair like dandelion puffs. They wore tight-fitting, elegant clothing in extravagant patterns and colors. Most of them had many rings hanging from their ears; some of the rings were plain gold or silver, some had chains hanging from them with tiny gems suspended at the ends, and some were thick bands of carved metal or gemstones. And I spotted one or two Goblins who had encased the tips of their pointed ears in filigreed metal. They didn't wear any other jewelry except those ear ornaments.

Most of the Goblins stood behind the counters of their stalls feigning indifference, although their black eyes darted everywhere beneath half-closed eyelids. A few Goblins sauntered down the aisles between the booths and idly looked over what was on offer. Most of it was food. And it was really, really tempting-looking food. There were heaps and heaps of fruits, some I recognized, most I didn't. There were trays of sparkling candies that looked like enormous jewels. There were pastries that looked like glazed carvings of some pale, pale wood, and some of them were dotted with succulent currants or glazed nuts, and others looked like fat little loaves bursting with nuts and preserved fruits. *Interesting. It's all sweet stuff. The sort of thing that would be the hardest to resist.*

The rest was very much a mixed bag. Here was a stall full of dried roots, each one carefully labeled with a little tag; and there was a stall selling bunches of fresh herbs and packets of dried ones. Across from it was a stall selling...well, it looked as if it was selling parts of animals; there was a tray of feet, another of ears, a bunch of tails hung up in one corner, and the preserved heads of what looked like foxes, wolves, and badgers. One stall sold nothing but bones, most of them loose; but some were cunningly wired together. Another stall sold tightly rolled scrolls, which I assumed were probably magic spells ready to be cast by just reading them aloud. Although for all I know, they could have been maps.

We were not the only humans strolling the aisles between the stalls, but all of the others were—well, they didn't look very much like us. They all looked like hardened adventurers; they were well armed, dressed in leather, often with chain-mail tunics on top; and they had expressionless faces and shuttered eyes. I knew that human magicians and both Light and Dark Fae were known to frequent the Goblin Market, but I didn't see any here tonight, at least not that I recognized, although I suppose any of the adventurers who were perusing the wares could have been magicians. They don't *all* wear robes and pointed hats.

The others kept close to me, although I thought they were being pretty good at not betraying how much this place unnerved them. It certainly unnerved me. A couple of the other humans gave us passing glances followed by little smiles. Not reassuring smiles. More like *these children have no idea what they've gotten themselves into* smiles. But no one spoke to us; I suppose they (rightly) figured that if we discovered that we needed help, we'd come to one of them, proverbial cap in hand.

Then there were the stalls displaying nothing. Some of these were Goblin mages willing to sell their services. But some sold information. The ones who sold information, according to what I had read, were designated by the sign of an eye above the stall.

So I looked for the sign of an eye, expecting either a painted sign or (just as likely) an actual *eye* preserved in some way. But what I spotted was a lot more unnerving.

It looked like a mirror, but in the mirror was a great big pea-green eye, complete with lids, that continuously scanned the crowd. And when it spotted us, it fixated on us and blinked rapidly. And the moment it began looking at us, the Goblin tending the booth turned to stare at us as well.

I gulped. *So much for being subtle.* There was no point in subterfuge. I led the others straight to the booth.

Ever since I was a little thing, I've collected odd objects. Very few of them are actually worth anything, but they are definitely very odd. While digging around in the forest behind our old home, I uncovered a series of lumps of black amber. I did some experimental carving on them, polishing them until they looked like strange, contorted flowers. No humans use black amber for jewelry because it's not very pretty, and the results of my carving attempts looked so weird that I certainly would not have considered wearing them myself.

But magicians valued it highly. And I thought I would open the bargaining with them. So I put some steel in my backbone, stood tall, and looked up at the Goblin, doing my best to ignore the giant eye above us looking down at me. The Goblin's eyes were the same shade of pea green as the eye on his stall. I fumbled in my belt pouch and brought out one of the black amber sculptures and put it on the counter in front of him.

I was watching his eyes rather than my own hands as I did this, and I thought I caught a flash of greed before he schooled his features into a mask of indifference. He raised an eyebrow at me, and I nodded and took my fingers off the sculpture so he could pick it up. He picked it up carefully between his elongated thumb and forefinger, both of which sported nails long and sharp enough to be called talons.

"Hmm," he said. "Interesting. What is it you wish to know?"

I should start with the least important thing. "Where Lady Thornheart came from," I said casually. "She wasn't from Tirendell, or at least she hadn't been here long."

He smirked at me and pocketed the gem. "That's easy. Nobody knows. But since that's an unsatisfactory answer and not worth the price of your gem, I'll add something else. The first anyone knows of her is that she appeared out of nowhere and took over the Shardstone Tower about a month before the christening where she got herself immolated. And I only got that much from the Hobs living near the tower. If you want to know more, you'll have to go exploring there yourself." And he leered at me, because *obviously* we were all far too young to go that deeply into Dark Fae lands and poke around the dwellings of dangerous Dark Fae.

Now he looked at me with expectant greed, because he surely knew—even if he didn't recognize me—that this was just my first question. So I took a deep breath, reached into my pouch, and brought out two more carvings, placing them on the counter. "Now I want to know about something that might have happened approximately thirty years ago that involved the Serpent Sisters."

"If you want to know about anything involving the sisters, you'll need two more of those."

"One more," I said, and put my hand in my pouch while my other hand hovered over the carvings as if to take them back. He licked his lips, then nodded.

"One more then," he agreed, and a third carving joined the other two.

"About thirty years ago, someone escaped from the sisters in the middle of the night," I said, trying to choose my words carefully and watching his expression for the tiniest of signs that he recognized the situation I was describing. "She was advised to come here, to *this* market, to bargain for safe haven. Did she come here?"

"No," he said quickly—too quickly, because a direct denial that she had come here meant that he *knew* what I was talking about and didn't intend to give any additional information, or at least not without being paid a lot more for it. He scooped up the three carvings before I could touch them—he *had* answered the question—and deposited them somewhere under the counter.

I quickly fished out the last of my carvings, all five of them, and put them on the counter so I could ask who the escapee was. But to my astonishment, he shoved them back at me. "No more questions. At least not on that subject," he said flatly, and before I could react, he raised his voice and called out, "Brothers! These young humans look hungry! I think we should feed them, don't you?"

I got a cold feeling in the bottom of my gut, and the hair on the back of my neck rose. And out of the corner of my eye, I could see every other human in the market backing away from us and making their way as quickly as possible to the entrance. Some of them were even running, not caring what the Goblins thought.

I scooped up my carvings and stuffed them in the pouch as the others crowded closely around me. "We appreciate your concern," I replied, my voice cracking a little with strain. "But, really, that's not necessary—"

"Oh," he replied as the Goblin fruit sellers picked up some of their wares and began weighing them in their hands. "I do think it is. I really do."

I motioned to the others that we needed to get out of there, although I am pretty sure they'd already figured that out. "I think we'll just be on our way now," I said with forced cheer. "It's been a pleasure doing business with you."

We clustered back-to-back and started to move toward the entrance. I was walking backward so I could cover our rear, and I couldn't help but notice that we were the only humans left in the market now; everyone else had vanished. Goblins with fruit in their hands came from behind their stalls, huge grins on their faces. Since their teeth were all needle-pointed, this was anything but reassuring. "Keep moving," I said under my breath. "Don't stop. And keep your mouths shut. Don't let *anything* get past your lips!"

The Goblin I'd been talking to emerged from behind his stall and accepted a beautiful purple thing that looked like a plum the size of an apple from another of his kind as he continued to advance on us. "I think they'll change their minds after they get a taste of our wares, don't you, my brothers?" he crooned.

And before I could blink, we were surrounded by Goblins, all of them with fruit in their hands. The first one held his giant plum up in front of my eyes and squeezed it slightly so it oozed juices from the punctures his nails made in the skin. The scent was like nothing I had ever smelled before, like honey and almonds and cherry blossoms, and it made my mouth water, it was that good. I didn't say anything, though, because I was pretty sure that if my lips parted even a little, he'd shove that fruit into my mouth. I seized Elle's hand with one hand and Nat's with the other so the Goblins couldn't separate us, and I fought down the rising panic that made me want to break and run.

We continued to head for the entrance as the Goblins crowded closer and closer, juices oozing from the fruit they held and intoxicating scents wafting over us until my eyes watered from the urge to taste them.

Then, with a lunge, the first Goblin rubbed the plum he held over my mouth. My teeth cut into my lower lip, and my lips hurt with how hard I was holding them together, and the scent was maddening. But terror kept me from giving in to it.

Now the Goblins were all over us, rubbing their prizes into whatever parts of us they could reach, shrieking "Eat! Eat!" at the tops of their lungs. I had pulp in my hair and juice in my eyes, and suddenly I was being dragged along backward by my hands as whoever was at the front of our group broke and began running for the entrance. I let go of the others' hands and whirled and ran with them as the Goblins began pelting us with fruit.

But what would happen when we reached the entrance? We

wouldn't be safe! In fact, once we crossed out of the market, we'd be out of the neutral area! And then what? My mind gibbered with terror at the prospect.

At least we can draw our swords then!

But they outnumbered us three to one at least!

It was hard to run with fruit flying at us from every direction. "Eat! Eat!" the Goblins shrieked as they threw. "Come back, guests! Come and eat! Come join us and eat!"

I couldn't see for the juice in my eyes, I was running blindly toward where I remembered the entrance to be, and I knew the others must be trying desperately not to get so much as a particle of fruit or a drop of juice into their mouths and not thinking much past that. The bright lights of the market were nothing more than haloed blobs as I tried to dash the juices out of my eyes and succeeded only in making my vision more blurry.

Then out of nowhere, a huge gust of hot wind buffeted us and nearly knocked me to the ground.

And we stumbled into something blue that was as big as a house and very warm.

"Fancy meeting you here, Miri!" said Serulan, his voice coming from far above me.

I crowded with the others into the shelter of his chest and finally managed to rub the juices out of my eyes with my sleeve just in time to see that we had crossed the threshold of the market. Serulan brought his head down to our level, his long neck curved in a graceful blue arc, and his face was almost nose to nose with the Goblin who had been bargaining with me.

"Hello, friend," Serulan said in a cloyingly sweet tone of voice. "Is there anything I can do for you?"

The Goblin lost his grin. The fruits he'd been holding dropped from his hands to the ground as if he no longer had the strength to hold them. "No," he said breathlessly. "No, there's nothing you can do for me. Thank you."

And then suddenly we were in darkness.

The Goblin Market had vanished.

CHAPTER FOURTEEN

A SOFT WHITE LIGHT APPEARED FROM BEHIND SERULAN'S right foreleg, and a moment later, the source of the light trotted quickly into the midst of us. It was Viridity, of course, who brought his own light with him in the form of his glowing horn. "All of you!" he exclaimed. "Crowd around me! Touch my horn! Miriam, help me with your magic as you did before!"

I didn't think; I just did as he said as his beautiful little spiraled horn vanished under all our hands. Since my sword was sheathed, I fed him with every bit of Fae power I could muster, and the light from his horn leaked out from between our fingers, then became so powerful that it flashed for a moment right *through* our hands, blinding us all.

Then the light went out, exhaustion hit me like a hammer, my knees gave out, and I dropped to all fours on the bare earth, panting. And then I noticed something.

The tantalizing scents were gone, replaced by something harsh and bitter with a hint of rot.

"It's safe to open your mouths now," Viridity said, sounding very tired.

I looked up. His horn was glowing dimly, and he looked as tired as if he had run flat out for a mile.

"*Argh!*" Rob exclaimed, and retched. "Don't lick your lips! It's horrible!"

"Viridity purified the evil," Serulan said, sounding very annoyed with us. "That's what's left."

I scrubbed my mouth and face with the hem of my tunic and my sleeve as hard as I could, but when I opened my mouth...I could still taste it. Take all the worst things you've ever accidentally bitten into—the sourest, the bitterest, the most rancid. Mix them all up. It was like that but probably worse. Vomit would have been better. I spent a long time gagging and trying to control my stomach.

Finally, I looked up and saw that Giles was looking at me with an expression that said, *You deserve this.* He still held the horses, which were reacting to the stench we were soaked in with distaste and head tosses.

Serulan curved his head down to stare at all of us—but me in particular. "You are very, very lucky that Lobo realized what you were about to do," he said sternly. "He came to Viridity and me and told us. He followed you to the market, and we followed him at a distance. If we hadn't come when we did..."

He didn't have to say anything more.

"Thank you, Serulan," I replied, feeling worse than I had ever felt in my life. "Thank you, Viridity. I know that thanks are not enough, but that's all I have."

"Well," Serulan said, sounding mollified. "You *did* save me, after all. Get on your horses if you can get them to stand still. You should be getting back before you're missed. You should be all right without us now."

I managed to create a light over our heads that the horses could see by, and we put them to a fast trot. I had no idea how long it had been since we left the palace, but Serulan was right—we had to get back before we were missed.

But when I stepped through the door in the oak with Star, I realized by the quiet in the gardens and the position of the stars that it had been longer than I had thought. And we were still a mess. The foul taste and smell had faded to almost nothing, but we had sticky stuff all over our faces and clothing, and fruit pulp in our hair. We were going to get looks and questions from *anyone* of rank we might run into.

Well, maybe we can clean up at the pump at the stables enough to get to our rooms without anyone noticing something's wrong.

I headed for the stable before Giles was more than partway through the door. And when I got there...

I knew we were in trouble when I was intercepted by one of the King's guards, who was waiting for us at the stable. I knew we were in a lot of trouble when he told me sternly to wait until everyone had reached the stable, then had the stable boys take all our horses.

I knew that we were in much more serious trouble than I could have imagined when we were escorted up to the Privy

Council Chamber, and I saw that Papa was wearing his crown and sitting in his throne, and that none of his councilors were with him.

Because this was the King, not Papa, I gave him a full bow rather than a curtsy since curtsies look stupid when you are wearing trews. The rest followed my lead. We stood there silently and waited for him to address us.

"Lady Miriam," he said, after looking at us soberly for a very long time. "Explain yourself."

So I did, taking my time about it and laying out my reasoning—but I didn't say anything about asking about the Fae who was probably my grandmother because that seemed like a very bad idea, but I had to explain why a dragon had rescued us, which meant also confessing to that unauthorized expedition to help Serulan. And I could tell from the darkening of his expression that the King did not approve of that, either.

The King—not Papa when he was in this mood—pondered all this. "Lady Miriam," he said very, very sternly. "I am gravely disappointed in you."

I froze. I knew better than to try to speak. I just listened with my head bowed as he read me a long and entirely accurate lecture on exactly how careless and willful I had been, how I had let my impulsive nature lead my friends *and* me into a situation that could have had extremely serious consequences for all of us. He described exactly what it would have taken to rid us all of the addiction to Goblin fruit and how costly it would have been to Gerrold and the Crown. Many of the components were rare and expensive. One of them was available only from the same kingdom that had tried to invade us when I was a child. There was no telling what sort of concessions he would have had to make to get it out of them. "And whatever made you think that I had *not* sent agents of my own to the Goblin Market to discover what I could about Lady Thornheart?" he demanded, his tone so cold, it made me shiver. "Did you really think I was *that* foolish? Did you actually think I was *not* moving heaven and earth to discover why Aurora was the sudden target of the Dark Fae?"

I hung my head because he was right. I had been so caught up in my own concerns and so sure that I was the only one looking for answers that I had not bothered to think past what *I* wanted. Those words struck me dumb, but what followed was worse.

"And as if that was not bad enough, you tell me you cajoled your Companions into an unauthorized, unsupervised mission to help Serulan the dragon! Without bothering to tell anyone! And to top it all off, you kept it all a secret, and I do not doubt that you did so because you already knew that I wouldn't be treating you as a hero but as a foolish, willful little child." I could feel his glare. "Didn't you?"

I kept my head bowed.

"I am confiscating your horses and leaving word that you and your Companions are not to be permitted to ride, even in training, for at least a year, so you will not be able to indulge in any more escapades. If we go on the Royal Progress, and you will, of course, need to go with us, you will ride ponies. The horses will be boarded at the royal stud farm until that time. And for a year, you and your Companions are not to leave the palace grounds except to go to and from Lady Brianna's establishment, and then only in the company of Sir Delacar. When you go alone, Lady Miriam, it will be on foot, and you will be escorted by one of the guards. Your Companions are relieved from their shifts guarding Aurora; we have enough of the Royal Guard who have been given the ability to see magic that we will not need their services, and I do not think that they are worthy of being trusted with that duty anymore. You are to be together when training, and only when training. Perhaps that will curb some of these wild schemes that you have been concocting together."

Behind me, my friends gasped. My heart dropped, and I felt dizzy. This was *wrong*! This was a *terrible* decision! Couldn't he see that?

But I didn't dare argue with him. It was clear that he was speaking in his capacity as the King, and to disobey him was treason.

He looked over my head at my friends. "Your parents will be informed of what happened tonight. You may continue to train at your parents' discretion, but if they choose to withdraw you from the Companions, I will honor that decision. There will be no more 'adventures.' No unauthorized expeditions. Lady Miriam, I was wrong in encouraging you to be like your father, because it seems that you are prey to the same impulsive behavior that got him killed."

That hit me like a physical blow, and I looked up at him incredulously.

He frowned. "Yes. Impulsive, unthinking behavior drove him to attempt to rescue a single knight at the expense of leaving the men he was supposed to be commanding. And it got him *and* that knight killed. His life was not his to throw away like that; it belonged to me, and to the kingdom. And your life is not yours to squander, either. It belongs to me, your mother, and Aurora, whom you vowed to protect. You violated that oath just as you violated our trust. And now you will be treated in accordance with your immature behavior. You will be watched and weighed to see if you are worthy of being trusted again. And that will probably take years, given what you have done in mere weeks to destroy my trust."

I bowed and my eyes burned with tears. "Yes, Majesty," I choked out.

We backed out of the room, turning only when we reached the door. The door closed behind us and I sagged against it, the tears that had threatened to fall now burning down my face in earnest.

"He can't do that!" Rob exclaimed.

"Oh, yes, he can," Giles said unhappily. "He's the King. To disobey him is treason. We don't have a choice."

I looked up at their miserable faces. "I'm sorry I got you to agree to come with me," I said through my tears. "If you hadn't, only I would be in trouble now."

"And you would probably be hurt or worse," argued Nat. "No, Miri, it's not your fault, and he might be the King, but he's *wrong* and you were right."

"And that doesn't matter when he's made up his mind." My throat closed up and I couldn't even talk. I just shook my head as the rest stood there helplessly. Finally, one of the guards we had been ignoring coughed pointedly and jerked his head toward the way out. Dragging our feet, we took the hint and went our separate ways, with only Anna and Elle staying with me.

And to cap it all off, Belinda was waiting for me with a bath full of cold water—not in the privacy of my room, either, but at the beginning of the Royal Suite, right at the stairs. I took off my ruined clothing and cast it aside; I doubted that it could be salvaged. I laid my sword down.

And she didn't let me bathe myself. She made me stand in the tub and scrubbed me from my hair to my soles so hard that I started to cry more without saying a single solitary word. When she was satisfied I was clean, Belinda pulled me out of the tub, toweled me off roughly, handed me my sword and a nightshift, and finally spoke.

"Go to your room."

I went.

Once there, I had the horrible feeling that Papa might send someone to take my sword once I left the room. So I opened the chest where I normally kept it, formed the chain mail to make it look as if it were still there, closed the chest, and hid the sword behind a tapestry until I could find a better place to put it. I thought for a moment that the sword pulsed with light in protest as I let the tapestry fall flat, but that might just have been because I was crying. I curled up on my bed and wept. I didn't know what Anna and Elle were doing; what I *did* know was that I was the most miserable of all of us. They weren't the ones to blame for it. I was, and everyone in the Court would know it by morning.

Mixed with my misery was utter despair. How could I protect Aurora when no one trusted me now?

By the time Anna and Elle arrived, presumably after a confrontation with their parents, I had wept myself into a state of complete exhaustion. My throat was raw, my eyes were swollen, my cheeks felt scorched, my stomach was in knots, and my head throbbed.

I looked up. They both had that slightly raw look about them that told me that someone—probably their mothers—had ordered them scrubbed until the first layer of skin came off along with the Goblin fruit juice, just as Belinda had done to me.

"We can stay Companions and be your ladies," Anna said for both of them. "But—well, it's only because our mothers think that no one would have us as maids of honor now, least of all the Queen."

"I did this to you—" I choked on the words.

"We all did it, Miri," Elle said, then she sighed and handed me a pot of salve. "You should use this on your skin. You look like you've been peeled."

They went off to bed, and I used the salve, which did help a little but eventually only made things worse because now I could concentrate on my own misdeeds. I started crying again and cried myself into an uneasy, nightmare-filled sleep.

In the morning, I woke at dawn, now in the state of grief where I was indifferent to everything. I couldn't eat, didn't want food, so I didn't go down to breakfast. And I didn't care what Mama and Papa thought about that or what the Court would think or say. I knew Elle and Anna had gone down only because at some point after breakfast they peeked timidly into my room, Elle with a cup and a pitcher, Anna with a platter.

"Miri, you need to eat," Anna said.

"Can't," I croaked, somehow managing to erupt in a fresh spate of tears.

"Have something to drink at least," Elle urged as they both came into the room. Anna put the platter down on the foot of the bed, and Elle poured a cup of wine and held it out to me with a hopeful look and a little gesture of invitation.

I didn't want that, either, but my mouth was as dry as stones in the desert, and my throat hurt from crying. So I accepted it even though my eyes were so swollen that I could scarcely see the cup, and I managed to get the contents down in sips.

Encouraged, they moved the platter over and sat down on the foot of my bed. "Aurora will be fine," said Elle. "All the guards can see magic, and the King seems to have doubled up the watch on her. I'm sure the Dark Fae won't try anything again. And we'll get back the King's trust sooner than you think."

I wanted to believe that. I really did. But the sheer dread that avalanched over me when I thought of Aurora convinced me that Elle was wrong. I just shook my head, refusing to be comforted by anything so unlikely. In fact, it was far more likely that the *Dark Fae* would assume that *we* would assume exactly that—and think that Aurora would be safe for years and drop our guard—and they would strike again.

Or worst of all, and even more likely, they had a spy or spies in the Court. They would know that Papa had hobbled the Companions and forbidden us to do anything that wasn't authorized by himself or Sir Delacar or Lady Brianna. They would know that there was one less barrier between themselves and Aurora. And one less barrier might be all they needed.

At the thought of that, I broke into hoarse sobs and threw myself down on the bed to hide my head in my arms and weep inconsolably.

At some point, my friends figured out that there was nothing they could say or do to make me feel any better. Anna moved the platter to my little desk, and Elle put the pitcher and cup down beside it. And I cried until I couldn't move, and at some point, I fell asleep again from sheer emotional and physical exhaustion. By the sun, it was about noon when I woke up, but I had no more appetite for luncheon than I'd had for breakfast.

I got dressed and splashed some water on my raw face. Just in case, I took the sword from its hiding place, strapped it on over my chemise but under my overdress, and left the room. I didn't take the public ways, either; I slipped silently down the servants' stair to the garden and my oak.

As promised, there was a guard waiting for me at the oak. I didn't say a word to him as he followed me through the door. Then I ran all the way to Brianna's cottage, leaving him to follow as best he could, burdened as he was with armor and weapons.

Brianna was waiting out in front, looking anxiously up the road for me. She was back early. I flung myself into her arms, and I couldn't help it, I broke out into hysterics again.

She just held me and stroked my hair, and when *some* of the crying eased up, she led me into the cottage, which now looked no bigger on the inside than it did on the outside and held pretty much what you would expect a neat little cottage to hold. But I wasn't paying any attention to all that, only to the settle she led me to, where we both sat down and I buried my face in my hands and sobbed.

I didn't weep for as long this time, but when I finally got myself under control, I felt utterly drained and hopeless. Brianna gave me a cloth that was cold and damp and somehow managed to ease my sore nose and eyes. But it didn't help my depressed spirits and hopelessness.

"Lobo and Viridity told me about the Goblin Market," she said. "And, obviously, you are in great trouble with your father now. Tell me the rest."

So I did, pausing now and again when my voice broke in a sob.

"The King persists in not understanding how constrained we are against the Dark Fae," she said somberly. "I cannot protect Aurora as he demands I do."

That only sank my spirits further.

"Did he take your sword?" she finally asked.

"No," I said, and pulled up my overdress to show her. "I was afraid he was going to so I hid it last night and took it with me this morning."

She nodded with approval. "I think that he probably will not ask you for it. After all, possessing it gives you no special powers that would enable you to disobey him. But to make certain, avoid him as much as you can."

I sighed, because that didn't make me feel one bit better. Her face went very still and closed for a long while; I hoped that she was thinking, because I couldn't. My mind was still turning in endless dizzy circles as I thought about how Aurora was in danger more than ever before and that there was nothing I could do about it.

Finally, there was only one thing I could think of. "Is there any way you can teach me a spell or something that can get me to Aurora *immediately* if she's in danger? I mean, I know *you* can, right? Can I?"

Brianna's face went very still for a moment. "It is true that I can, indeed, come to a set place where I have a link in the blink of an eye. It is also true that I can make an amulet for you that will do just that. It is how I appeared at the top of the tower when your young ancestor was in danger. But I am a Fae in the fullness of my power, and I was going into a situation where I knew that all I needed to do was snatch him and fly away. If you use such an amulet, you will have no notion of what you are about to step into."

"It's my duty and my responsibility," I said, remembering Papa's words of last night. "If Aurora is in danger, I have to go to her."

"Very well. Can you get your hands on a lock of Aurora's hair?" Brianna asked.

"I already have one," I replied, a bit surprised, and pulled out the silver locket where I kept a lock of Mama's hair, a lock of Aurora's, and a lock of my father's. Each one was tied tightly with a length of silk thread. I pulled out my baby sister's and handed it to Brianna.

"Clarion should probably hear the whole story as well," Brianna said, taking it from me. "Go outside and call for him. I have some things to do with this, and it is better if I work alone on it—and then we'll use your human magic to finish the job. Don't forget, Miri, the King can take your armor, your sword, and your title, but he cannot take your magic. And that is what we will concentrate on."

From anyone else, those words would have been treasonous. But although Brianna and the other Fae lived in Tirendell, they were not Papa's subjects, and he had no right to rule them nor any way to control them.

My spirits rose—not a lot but at least I wasn't so sunk in despair that I couldn't even move. I went out the cottage door and called for the stag, ignoring the stolid presence of the guard at the door. Clarion came bounding toward me out of the forest after what seemed like an age. And, of course, he took one look at me and demanded to know what the matter was, and I had to explain it all to him. At least I managed not to cry so much this time.

Clarion looked at me gravely. "It is not the end of the world, Miri," he said as the guard tried to pretend that he wasn't in the presence of one of the King beasts of the forest and stared straight ahead. "I know that it feels as if it is, but it is not."

But before I could reply, there was a buffeting of wind from overhead, which now was quite familiar, and down through the trees came Serulan. The guard's eyes nearly popped out of his head, and when Brianna emerged from her cottage in all her Fae glory, I thought he might faint.

Serulan walked up to the front gate and dropped his head down to our level. "I heard what happened, Lady Miriam," he said, sounding as if he felt this too were his fault. "I am so very sorry to have gotten you into trouble. You probably wouldn't have gotten into nearly so much trouble if you hadn't come to help me when Viridity asked you to."

Well, this only made things worse as far as I was concerned. I really had to work not to cry, because I knew if I began to cry, Serulan would cry, and we'd both reinforce each other and probably not recover for hours. "It's all right," I lied. Then I added something that was true. "If it hadn't been helping you and then going to the Goblin Market, it would have been something else.

And you *did* rescue us at the market. The debacle at the Goblin Market was all my fault. I didn't think it through. Papa would never have found out about how we helped you if I hadn't made up my mind to go there last night."

"Yes, but…" Serulan swallowed audibly. Very audibly, given how large he was. "Please give Lady Miriam what I brought this morning, Lady Brianna."

Brianna picked up something at her feet and handed it to me.

It was a small but beautifully carved statue of a woman in full armor in an antique style that was about as tall as my fore-arm was long. I couldn't identify the stone; it was a little like moonstone but not as transparent, and there was a subtle shift-ing of light under the surface as I moved it.

Before I could ask, Serulan said, "It is your great-great-great-great-grandmother, the one who first carried your sword. I had it commissioned when I was a younger dragon. I thought you should have it."

Startled, I searched what I could see of the face beneath the helmet visor though I was not sure what I was looking for. Some resemblance to me, maybe? I didn't see any, but I was looking at the face of a woman at least twice my age and with a hundred times my experience. It was a strong face, with the expression of someone inclined to take neither nonsense nor prisoners. It was not the kind of gift I wanted at the moment, since it just reminded me of how much I had managed to mess up not only my life but the lives of my friends.

But I'd spent the last two years learning how to counterfeit emotions I didn't feel—you learn that sort of thing very quickly at Court if you want to maintain harmony. So I thanked Serulan by mustering up every bit of gratitude that I had, praising him for being so thoughtful. Which, as it turned out, was more than enough to make him flush under his scales and mutter about how it was nothing compared with what I had done for him. Eventually, he trotted off down the road to the place where the tree canopy had a break in it that he could fly up through, and I looked at Brianna with the statue in my hands, unsure what to do next.

"It's a good likeness," she said, looking down at the statue. "But leave it at the door. We have work to do."

Her words sparked another bit of hope in me, and I followed her into the cottage, leaving the statue at the door so I wouldn't forget it. Somehow, although he was as white as a bleached shift, the guard had managed not to faint at all the strangeness and Faeness. Apparently, no one had told him what he might encounter when he was given this assignment.

The interior of the cottage hadn't changed appreciably. The only difference was that now there was something like Wizard Gerrold's workbench in the middle of it, albeit on a smaller scale. And in the middle of that workbench was a bit of gold jewelry in the shape of a wild briar rose that looked as if it had been woven and braided out of thin gold wires hardly bigger than a baby's hair. When I looked more closely at it, I saw that the gold wires were braided with actual hair. Aurora's hair?

"I've done what I can with this," Brianna said. "The mechanics of the spell are all in place. It will be your task to empower them and bring them to life. But I must warn you that it could be—probably *will* be—very dangerous for you if you actually have to trigger the spell. It will bring you to Aurora's side wherever she is even if that means right into the middle of a gathering of Dark Fae or worse."

I thought about my great-great-great-great-grandmother, what she had faced, what she would say about this, and the expression on the carved face of that statue. "Tell me what to do," I said—not steadily but with absolute certainty. "I don't think I would be able to live with myself if something happened to Aurora and I didn't at least *try* to save her." Because I could think of one thing that would be worse than death, and that would be to live knowing that I could have gone to my baby sister's rescue and hadn't.

It was the right thing to do, at least as far as the human magic inside me was concerned, because it all but poured out of me, filling that rose, until I found my sight dimming and I started to sway. Brianna snatched it out of my hands, breaking the connection, and I quickly caught myself on the workbench.

"Give me your locket," she demanded, and I gave it to her. The rose just fit inside, flattening the other two locks of hair behind it. She closed the locket and gave it back to me.

"Anytime you are alone with the baby, open the locket and take the rose out and place it on her under your hand to charge it more," Brianna ordered. "But please take care not to drain yourself doing so, or you'll draw attention to the fact that you are doing something the King would probably not approve of. I am not altogether certain that he intended anything like this when he reminded you of your responsibility to Aurora."

I put the locket around my neck and staggered over to the settle. Brianna plied me with a drink that tasted like honey and sage—which was better than it sounds. "I want you here every afternoon," Brianna said sternly. "The King can take away freedom, but at least he is still allowing you to train, and we will take advantage of that. And I will have a word with him about doing away with that useless guard. I value my safety and my privacy, and he contributes to neither."

I nodded, my spirits falling again at being reminded of how much I was watched, measured, and judged.

After that, we practiced until I was as tired as if Sir Delacar had been working me, and she sent me home just in time for dinner. This time the guard had no trouble keeping up with me. I wondered what he was thinking. Nothing in his expression gave me any clue.

But I was not going to eat with the Court. Not unless I was ordered to. The very last thing I wanted right now was to eat with a hundred or more pairs of very disapproving eyes on me. I went straight to the kitchen, grabbed a slice of trencher bread and one of the wooden mugs, and slipped around the kitchen helping myself, then I went back out into the garden to that secluded little stone bench Wizard Gerrold had shown me. I ate very little, but I hadn't taken much in the first place. I crumbled up the remaining trencher bread and scattered it for the birds in the morning and sat in the gloom.

I had left my statue at the foot of the oak tree when I went to the kitchen, and after a while, I got up and brought her back to my seat. I stood her on the seat beside me, and she seemed to have a faint glow in the dusky darkness.

"And what would you do?" I asked the statue. "Sir Delacar

is going to continue to train me, but is he going to put his heart and soul into it? There's no reason why he can't keep us doing the same things over and over, and never teach us anything new. And why should any of the others continue in the Companions when we've been so restricted?"

"Because we're your friends?" I nearly jumped out of my skin as Anna and Elle came around the oak. "We were looking for you all afternoon," said Anna as she moved the statue off the bench so she and Elle could sit beside me. "Were you with Lady Brianna?"

"Yes," I said, aware that they wouldn't be able to see me nod in the gloom.

"Good, now she knows what the King did to us." Anna was next to me, and she seemed to be staring at her hands, which were pleating and repleating the fabric of the skirt of her gown. "And what did *she* say?"

"That she's going to continue to train me in Fae magic regardless of what the King says," I replied, and I felt my desperation ease a little as I said that. "She advised me to continue wearing my sword, but she doesn't think the King is going to take it."

Anna looked up, her hands dropping the fabric as she clasped them together. "Oh, thank heavens! I was afraid he'd already taken it!"

Elle nodded. "If he had, I was planning on figuring out a way to break into wherever he put it and get it back. I'm pretty sure I could sneak into the armory and get it without anyone noticing."

"You'd have done that?" I was astonished.

"Miri, we love you, and we love Aurora. The King can say

whatever he wants, but nothing he says will break up the Companions," Elle said firmly. "Anna and I talked to the boys, and they feel the same."

The boys! I hadn't even given a thought to them. "Where—"

"Delacar made them all his squires absolutely and officially, remember?" Anna said. "So they're all still living with the other squires *and* they're all still training with Sir Delacar."

"I don't know why he didn't make *us* squires too," Elle said darkly. "It seems extremely unfair to me."

"Maybe because our parents wouldn't approve of it. I know mine wouldn't; they were only going along with my training because of the prestige of being a Companion. Or maybe Sir Delacar didn't to throw the King off the scent. Or maybe because there is no way that he could make Miri his squire without getting the King's permission first, and there is no way that is going to happen," Anna said sensibly. "This is the only way Delacar can keep the Companions together."

"But we are together!" I exclaimed, and a wash of warmth came over me as I realized that the others weren't going to abandon me. "There's no reason why we can't train in Lady Brianna's cottage, either! I'm still allowed to train with her, and—"

"And we just won't tell anyone that we are going too as long as Sir Delacar approves," said Anna, with a nod.

But Elle laughed at that. "Oh, I promise you, he'll approve. He was probably pretty angry when he found out about Serulan and the Goblin Market, but by now, he's over it. And I know Sir Delacar doesn't like all the restrictions the King has put on us—or the way he tried to get our parents to take us out of the Companions."

I hugged them. "You're brilliant, both of you!"

They hugged me back, Anna sniffing a little. "We aren't going to let the King stop us from doing what's right," Elle said fiercely. "And what's right is helping you protect Aurora."

"If he finds out, the King might demand that your fathers take you away from the Court altogether."

"Then we have to make certain that he doesn't find out," Elle said. "You keep moping around the way you have been today. Avoid meals. Avoid your parents. He'll be sure that you're not up to anything because you're sulking. That should put him right off the scent."

"Sulking" and "moping" were very unflattering descriptions of how I'd been acting, but Elle did have a point, and I was sure that this was how Papa and Mama were thinking of my behavior. They were adults, and when adults are annoyed with you, every demonstration that you're feeling bad is sulking and moping.

Well, I could keep right on sulking, but I'd have to be very careful about it. Too much and they'd get impatient with me and get me another governess to "occupy my time properly."

Just then, Elle changed the subject.

"Why on earth are you carrying around a statue?" she asked. "And who is it? Do you know?"

"Serulan gave it to me. He said that he had it made ages ago and that I ought to have it because it's my great-great-great-great-grandmother."

"Really?" Elle picked it up and peered at it. "It's not as heavy as it looks. Your great-great-something was a knight?"

So I had to tell the story about my many-times-great-grandmother and being the Nameless Knight and the first holder of my sword.

They weren't as curious about it as I thought they might be; they were more interested in the fact that the dragon had chosen to give the statue to me. Anna took it from Elle and brought it out of the shadows into a shaft of moonlight to look at it more closely—and all three of us gasped as the statue seemed to light up softly from within once the moonlight struck it.

"What is this thing made of?" Anna looked as if she was afraid to put it down.

"I have no idea. Serulan didn't tell me. It's not magic; it must be a trick of the stone."

Anna took the statue out of the moonlight, but it glowed for a little while longer before the light inside it faded. She handed it to me again. "I've never seen anything like that."

"I don't think anyone has. Or we'd have heard about it by now." I thought about it some more. "Wait, there might have been something…something about transforming quartz with dragonfire?" I shook my head. "It wasn't important then, and it's not important now."

"You're probably right. You take care of Lady Brianna tomorrow and leave the rest to me," Anna said. "When you come back tomorrow night, we'll all have dinner in our room and we can catch up with one another."

"Snatch luncheon and breakfast from the kitchen. I'll get a tray for you from the kitchen for suppers," Elle said. "There's a lot of sympathy for you among them. Giles told me that, and he still has those friends."

Of course he did, and he wouldn't have deserted them just because he'd been made a Companion and then a squire. I knew from my own experience that everyone in the kitchen knows what's going on all over the palace.

I'd have tried to talk to him alone, but that would have been a very bad idea at this point. The King was livid with me not only because I hadn't checked with someone before running off to do things on my own but also because I'd kept the fact that I was doing so a secret. But if I was spotted with Giles alone, without a chaperone and acting in a clandestine manner, my reputation could be utterly ruined, the King would *certainly* be sure that I was back to keeping things secret from him, and I would probably be exiled to my little property under the strictest of guards to make sure I wasn't caught alone with a young man ever again.

I hugged Anna and Elle once more. "If you weren't sticking with me, I—I don't think I could bear this."

"But we did, and we'll keep right on sticking with you," said Anna fiercely. "No matter what. For Aurora, yes, but most of all for you. Because we're friends. And that's what friends do."

CHAPTER
FIFTEEN

By the time three days had passed, we were back to a modified version of our old routine. I say "modified" because we were no longer learning horsed combat and Sir Delacar had us doing an *awful* lot of remedial exercises, but in the second half of our training sessions, he'd take a moment to make sure we weren't being watched by anyone, then we'd switch to more advanced work. He didn't say anything, but within two days, I was pretty sure that although he was still very irritated with me, he was also determined to continue training us exactly the way he'd started. And I was certain that he was just as irritated with the King as we were for pulling us off guarding Aurora.

We were back to the same schedule of weapons training in the morning and combat involving magic every other afternoon. And, of course, I had my solo sessions with Brianna. I had been skeptical that she would be able to do anything about my bird-dogging guard for those sessions, but after two days, he suddenly didn't show up. I still don't know how she convinced the King to pull him off.

But then again, I'm not sure even the King was willing to deal with Brianna when she was angry.

Brianna and I talked a little bit about the Serpent Sisters' captive, who I was sure was my father's mother—but she didn't have anything to add, and at this point, I had realized that...it didn't matter.

That's right. It didn't matter. I had let my own selfishness rule over what was important. I already knew that my father had been a good man, the best of men, and *that* was what mattered. Not whether his mother was Dark Fae, Light Fae, or a sorceress. He had been a good, kind, wonderful father, and it was up to me to live up to that—and not obsess over details that made no difference to the person I was.

I'd stop at the kitchen for breakfast and luncheon, and Elle and Anna and I would have dinner in my room to avoid having any meals in the Great Hall.

I really didn't like this arrangement. It had me out of the palace most of the day, which left Aurora vulnerable. But at least all the guards watching her nursery had been given spells to enable them to see magic and magic creatures, so they weren't totally "blind."

As often as I could, I put more magical energy into my amulet, and as often as I could manage it during my visits to her without getting caught, I attuned it to Aurora. She seemed to enjoy it when I did; she giggled and cooed as if she were being tickled and played with.

And I avoided my parents. Which is easier to do than you might think when your parents are the King and Queen. They were busy all day long and often well into the evening, and what little time they could spare from their duties they spent with Aurora. Since they didn't confide their thoughts about what I was doing to anyone I spoke to, I didn't know how they felt about the way I was behaving. When Father was alive, I was pretty solitary, so maybe Mama thought I was reverting to my old habits: keeping to myself and reading in quiet places when I wasn't training. Without Belinda around to disapprove, that would have been logical. And it wasn't as if I had any actual duties to attend to, nor was there any pressure on me to make a brilliant marriage. I could, in fact, do whatever I wanted to. And since my duties were to train right now, and that was what I had been doing, I suppose they figured they'd wait out my sulks.

After all, they had plenty to worry about, and until I'd gone off rescuing dragons and visiting the Goblin Market, I had always been obedient, never questioning anything they asked of me or told me to do. So they probably assumed I had gone back to being that strictly obedient daughter.

If they wondered where the oddly luminous statue of the armed and armored woman in my room had come from, they didn't ask. Or maybe they never looked in my room to preserve something of my privacy. Not that you were ever really private in the palace, with servants running into and out of rooms all day long.

I never saw any signs that Papa had had my room searched for my sword. My armor remained in the chest where I had left it, and the sword never left my side. Then again, it was possible that he assumed it was in the armory, which was the logical place for it to be. If he'd asked Sir Delacar about it, I'm fairly certain Delacar would have said something like "As far as I know, it's where it belongs," which certainly wasn't a lie, but it would allow Papa to draw his own conclusion (wrongly) about where it was. Just the same, I was glad I had it with me at all times because there was always a chance that he'd go looking for it. Not a *likely* chance, because Papa was anything but a fool, but it was a chance I hadn't been willing to take.

By the end of the week, we had a routine, and my parents and I were carefully avoiding each other, each of us for reasons of our own.

And things might have stayed that way indefinitely.

Melalee's screech woke half the castle.

I was one of the first to reach the nursery, where the two night guards lay insensible on the floor and Melalee was on her knees beside the empty cradle, screaming her lungs out in panic and grief.

Empty...cradle.

Part of me wanted to drop to the floor and howl with Melalee; part of me wanted to kick the comatose guards until they were one bruise from head to toe. And a little bit of me grimly whispered, *I told them so. And they wouldn't listen.*

Melalee's incoherence wasn't helping. How long ago had she last checked on Aurora? Had she seen anything at all? Smelled anything? Seen the curtains moving at the window? All these things could tell us which way her kidnappers had taken her or even if they were still in the palace!

But I didn't get the chance; within moments, I had been shoved out of the room by more guards and Mama and Papa and Gerrold, and I could only hover impotently at the door while

Gerrold worked a spell that might tell him who or what had taken her and possibly where.

I strained my ears to listen while I did the little I could think of by performing both Fae and human magic on the unconscious guard not far from my feet. I didn't wake him, and I couldn't figure out how he'd been rendered into this state except that it *wasn't* by magic.

At least he was breathing regularly, and it didn't look to my untutored eyes as if he was going to die anytime soon. Though when he woke, the watch commander was probably going to make him *wish* he were dead.

Or so that cynical little bit of me was thinking. The rest of me was having a complete panic. Because my darling baby sister was *gone*!

"Goblins?" said Gerrold, sounding puzzled. "Goblins?"

But the word was taken up with increasing certainty and wrath by everyone else in the room, and before I knew it, people were shoving me out of the way again as they headed—somewhere. Probably even they didn't know where. All they knew was that they had an answer, that Goblins had taken Aurora and that they were going to *get* those Goblins.

And a tiny sane voice in the back of my head said, *Goblins? But...why, exactly? And—how? How did they even get as far as the palace without being noticed, much less inside it?*

Because even though I might have ruffled their proverbial feathers by having a dragon face them down in their own market, Goblins didn't indulge in revenge. They were absolutely pragmatic about that sort of thing—because they knew that eventually I'd want information from them again and they'd make me pay for it in a much more satisfying and lucrative way. There was nothing the Dark Fae could do to them to force them to take Aurora. They certainly would never do the Dark Fae's dirty work for them for any amount of pay. Not only was there no profit in it, they already knew by now that doing anything to Aurora would bring the wrath of the entire kingdom down on them and possibly even the wrath of the Light Fae. They'd have to give up their market forever, and it would be unthinkable to lose that much profit.

Aurora would be of no use to them.

And that little piece of me remained calm and grew and grew until it took over as I stood there while the palace healer and Gerrold tried to revive the fallen guards and everyone else hared off into the darkness in search of Goblins. It tamped down the panic and sent me running for my room to change, then I leapt down the stairs and raced out of the palace into the garden. But I wasn't going to the forest. I was going to try to get the door in the oak to take me to Brianna's little "kingdom."

I hadn't gone there for an awfully long time, but I hoped Brianna hadn't locked the door against me.

I put my palm on the tree and concentrated, and for a moment, I could feel the spell resisting me. But then I let my panic flow into it, and the door sprang open, and I dashed through.

It was night in Brianna's little corner of the world too, but so much of her garden glowed in the dark that it was easy to race from the oak to her front door, where I stopped and pounded on it, sobbing a little.

What am I going to do if she's not here? Was there some way of contacting her from here that I didn't have in the ordinary world? Maybe.

But that question was quickly resolved as every window in the place lit up and the door opened so quickly that I almost fell through it.

Before Brianna could say anything, I was blabbering. "Something stole Aurora! It knocked the guards out and took her!" I clutched my hands together to keep them from shaking. "Gerrold did some sort of spell and said it was Goblins!"

"*Goblins?*" she exclaimed. "But that doesn't make any sense! They wouldn't take Aurora just for revenge on *you*, and they have *never* allied with the Dark Fae!"

"But what if they—"

But Brianna kept speaking. "They are immune to Fae powers. They have no interest in human politics. The only way they would be interested in Aurora is if she were a fully adult woman. A baby is of no use to them." Which just confirmed what I had thought.

"Take me to her room!" Brianna demanded. "And to the guards who were watching her."

We fled back to the door in the tree and went into the garden. I was running and Brianna was flying at about head height until we got to the palace, where we both ran as quickly as we could.

Taking her to the nursery was easy enough; it was totally deserted and even Melalee had been taken off somewhere. Brianna spent some time in it muttering under her breath about human magic muddling everything up and humans not being able to tell an aufhocker from a kelpie. Finding the guards was more problematic since there was no one to ask where they had been taken, but my first guess—the sick quarters attached to the palace healer's rooms—turned out to be correct.

The healer hovered over one of them as we entered, and his face was a study in conflict as he realized I'd brought Lady Brianna. I could only assume that he was one of those who didn't quite trust *any* Fae but who was far past his ability to actually do anything for the men. "Lady Brianna!" he exclaimed. She brushed past him and bent over the unconscious guard. I watched her weave spells that I didn't understand in the least, but this time she didn't say anything. Finally, she straightened up, her mouth a hard, thin line.

"It's not magic," she said, confirming what I had thought. "It's a powder, a drug that was blown into their faces. They may or may not recover since it was never intended to be used on humans. Tend them and spoon-feed them broth twice a day; they'll either wake up or they won't. There's no antidote."

The healer's face fell at this harsh news, but Brianna waved to me and we left the rooms before he could say anything.

"Trolls," she said succinctly once we were out of hearing. "That's stone-sleep dust, and only Trolls can make it or use it. And that makes no more sense than Goblins. Trolls can't be magically coerced. And there are *hundreds* of tribes of them. I have no way to tell which tribe took her." Then she gave me a stern look. "And don't even *think* of using your amulet to find her. You'd find yourself deep in some inaccessible cavern surrounded by Trolls with no way to get help. You might not even be in Tirendell; depending on how much energy you put into that talisman, you could end up halfway across the world. Do you want to deprive your mother of *both* her children in a single day?"

I wanted to scream at her that I was going to do it anyway, but she was right. What could I do for Aurora if I was dead or a prisoner myself?

Brianna made a gesture in the air and suddenly her arms were piled with books. "Here," she said, thrusting them at me, and I staggered as I took the weight of them in my own arms. "Go study these. See if you can find something. I need to talk to the King and Queen."

And with that, she was gone, leaving me standing there, my arms encumbered with books and my emotions in complete turmoil.

I did as I had been told. Since there was no way I could have gone back to sleep, I took the heavy load of books back to my room. Anna and Elle were fully dressed and waiting for me. Of course they were; no one could have slept through all that racket, and surely someone had told them that Aurora had been kidnapped.

I knew from just looking at them that they already knew most of the story. Except for the fact that the villains weren't Goblins but Trolls—Lady Brianna and I were the only ones who knew that. I made short work of that explanation and handed some of the books off to Anna and Elle. "Brianna said to search these for anything useful."

They didn't argue with me, and we lit every candle in my room, got more from the linen closet, and went to work until well after dawn. Anna used my little desk, and Elle and I worked cross-legged on my bed, using whatever book we weren't reading as a makeshift desk. Ink on the bedclothes was not a concern at this point. It felt as if I had a fever, and I was terrified and angry and grief-stricken all at the same time.

One of the maids brought us something to eat—I don't even

remember what it was—and we read while we ate with one hand and took notes on parchment with the other.

We read until we all three eventually fell asleep over the books about midmorning. We woke up with stiff necks and raging appetites. I found a maid crying quietly in the stairwell and asked her to bring food from the kitchen for us, and we all bolted it down when it came. I got dressed, then we took everything down to the library and enlisted the help of the secretaries and clerks. By this time, the word had spread as far as the clerks that we were looking for Trolls, not Goblins.

No note, no mention, was too small for us to jot down. And the chief secretary took over the notes himself, organizing them by category, and making fair copies on good parchment according to his tables of organization. Habits, known lairs, magic, weapons and warfare, interaction with humans, interaction with Fae—those are just the ones I remember. Known lairs were obviously the most important, and as soon as we were through our first passes of the books, he sent those to the King immediately.

The problem was…there weren't any known lairs in Tirendell. Or at least there were no lairs that still had Trolls in them. Trolls are huge, much bigger than humans, and have gray skin. They live underground—not exclusively, but they can't come up during daylight because the sun turns them to stone. Unlike Dwarves, who prefer to live underground but are perfectly comfortable above it. And according to the books, Troll lairs are much less sophisticated than Dwarven cities. There hadn't been any Trolls here for generations, although there were cave complexes that were said to have housed Trolls in the remote past. Papa quickly sent messengers to the rulers of the kingdoms around ours where Trolls *were* known, to ask for permission to search for Aurora, but it was going to take time for them to get there, get responses, and get back. In some cases, we'd have to negotiate for permission, and we might have to give something in return for that permission. I tried not to think too hard about any of this. There wasn't anything I could do except scour Brianna's books—and all the books in the library—for information about Trolls. The boys had joined us by this point, even Rob, who had once complained about how much he hated reading.

We went through Brianna's books again, this time much more slowly and with our old notes beside us, to see if there were any nuances that we hadn't picked up on the first time.

And all the while, time sped with no sign of Aurora, and the certainty grew that her captors were far away.

Brianna had decided to be an emissary to the Goblins just to put paid to that possibility, and she brought back messages from the Goblin Market to the effect of *What would we want with one of your mewling, useless larvae?*—messages that were rude enough to sound genuine even to Papa. Finding Trolls, *any* Trolls, was far more problematic. Because it appeared that the Trolls did not want to be found. There were no sightings, no rumors of their recent existence, and even the Light Fae of other kingdoms had not seen or heard of them for many years.

So why had they taken Aurora in the first place? What could they possibly want with her?

Mama stopped eating and took to her bed and seemed to fade more with every passing hour. Papa seemed to have forgotten my existence.

And it seemed that there was nothing I could do as my own grief and rage built to the breaking point.

Since we hadn't garnered any clues from the books, we were all taking out our frustrations on one another when we resumed our weapons training, this time in Brianna's cottage. But tempers were flaring all around, and finally I broke after missing counters three times in a row and getting painful whacks on the shin and shoulder. "That's *it*!" I shouted, throwing my wooden sword across the room and alarming Nat. "I'm not going to sit here and do *nothing*. Not anymore!"

At this point, everyone in the room was staring at me, Brianna included. But it was Anna who asked reasonably, "What can you do that everyone else isn't already doing?"

"The Trolls didn't just appear out of nowhere in the nursery, take Aurora, and vanish again," I pointed out from between gritted teeth. "They had to have gotten in somehow! And we might still be able to track them!"

"But the palace was warded!" Nat argued. "On all sides!"

"But..." We all turned to Giles. He was white. "Not from below."

Brianna rounded on him as if *he* were the one who had let the Trolls in. "What do you know?"

"Just—I was the kitchen boy who was sent most often down into the cellars for odd ingredients. And those cellars go a *long* way. I never went down as far as I could have, but there were cellars under the cellars under the cellars. The dungeon is locked and guarded—but the kitchen cellars aren't, and there's no one in the kitchen in the middle of the night." He rubbed his hand fiercely across his eyes. "What if they got in that way?"

"Or tunneled in," I said. "According to what we've read, they're not as good at it as Dwarves, but then no one is. And if they did come in that way, they had to have passed through the kitchen. That's where we can start." I turned to Brianna. "Lobo should still be able to pick up a scent if they did, shouldn't he?"

"Let's ask him," she replied, and the two of us went out to the little garden. She plucked a small silver hunting horn off her belt and blew on it. And it seemed an age before Lobo and Clarion came bounding into the garden from two different directions.

"Could you track Trolls in the palace?" Brianna asked, with absolutely no preamble. But Lobo didn't seem taken aback or even mildly surprised by her abruptness. Then again, he must know about Aurora's kidnapping by now.

"After all this time? Maybe. It depends on how many people have been trampling over things," he replied, tongue lolling out and brow furrowed. "I'll try my best!"

By this time, all of the others had come crowding out and had heard him. "I think we should all come," Giles said.

"I think we should all get our armor and real weapons." I straightened up to my full height and stared at Lady Brianna in a challenge.

But I needn't have bothered. She was nodding.

Armed and armored, we walked into the kitchen with Lobo in our midst, much to the consternation of the cooks and helpers. But they didn't stop us when Giles led the way to the stairs to the first of the cellars. In fact, they all cleared away so we could move freely when they saw where we were headed. A few of the brighter souls must have figured out *why* we were going there because I saw looks of alarm and urgent whispering. *I wonder if Papa's going to face a kitchen revolt if he doesn't put a guard in the cellar now.*

Just inside the door were lanterns and flagons of oil to replenish them. "Should we…" Rob gestured at the lanterns. But Brianna and I both shook our heads. I answered for both of us. "We can make stronger lights than those, lights that won't run out of fuel." And suiting actions to words, we created little balls of clear light that bobbed above our heads and lit up the first of the cellars. There was a faint scent of vegetables and a slightly stronger one of bacon. This cellar held barrels, sacks, and bales of stuff—flour, grains, vegetables, some fruits, things that couldn't be stored in the deeper cellars because they couldn't take the damp and would mold but were sturdy enough not to need the pantry. There was meat hung here too, and now that I knew how to look for it, there was a faint haze of magic on the walls, spells meant to retard spoilage rather than stop it altogether the way the spells did in the pantry. I could tell now that these were very old spells and probably dated all the way back to when the palace had been built.

Brianna gestured to Lobo, who began to sniff all over the cellar. And it wasn't long before he gave a *yip* to alert us that he'd found something.

"I've never smelled Troll," he said as we gathered around him. "But whatever I've found isn't human and isn't one of the things I'd expect in a human cellar."

"The trail's heading in the right direction," Giles confirmed. "That is the way into the next cellar. Lead on, Lobo."

Lobo led the way, nose to the stone floor, moving slowly and inhaling deeply so as to not miss anything. We went down a dozen stone steps into the next cellar, this one the home of preserved fruits, preserved meats, salted fish, cheeses, and vegetables that could be stored for months at a time.

I'd never been down here before. But now that I was here, it was obvious that the cellars had been cut out of the rock the palace stood on. Presumably so had the dungeons—which I also had never been to. It must have taken decades to cut these rooms out of the granite underneath the palace. I could not imagine how Trolls or anything else could burrow through this rock.

But Lobo was on the trail of *something*, and we followed him down into what should have been the last cellar, which held wine, beer, and spirits. He led us all the way to the back behind a barrel that was taller than I am—and there it was.

A tunnel.

We stared at it, then at one another.

It was definitely a tunnel, and it was new. The rock inside the tunnel was a different color from the walls of the cellar, and there was a scattering of pebbles around the entrance.

Giles spoke up. "There's no one here except the regular guards and a handful of squires. Everyone else is out there"—he waved his hand at the surface—"looking for Trolls or trying to get the Goblins at the market to give them information."

"But we can't go down that hole without telling someone," I said firmly. "We're not going to act like the children the King thinks we are. We don't go rushing into something thinking we're immortal because our cause is good. We—*I*—did that twice, and the only thing that got us in the end was a lot of trouble." Granted, it also got us Serulan as an ally, but that happened because of plain, stupid luck.

And I hated to say this because I was dying to charge down that tunnel and find Aurora and do unspeakable things to the Trolls who had taken her. She was just a baby! How were they keeping her fed? Were they keeping her warm? It was cold down here, and it would be even colder in Troll caverns.

I didn't ask myself if she was still alive. She had to be. Why would they have taken her instead of smothering her in her cradle?

The unspoken question was whom we should tell. Not the King, because he'd be enraged that we had reformed the Companions even though we'd figured out where the Trolls had come from.

I knew the answer to that. "Sir Delacar, of course. He's the only one still in the palace with any authority except the seneschal, and a fat lot of good the seneschal will do. He'll only dither about sending page boys to find the King. They've had Aurora for days." I almost choked when I said that. "The time it will take to tell—no, *show* him—won't matter that much." And before anyone could object, I ran off. Not that anyone would. Sir Delacar was our friend, after all, or at least as much of a "friend" as a teacher and mentor could be.

As if Sir Delacar had been responding to my thoughts, I ran into him right at the door of the kitchen. He grabbed me by both shoulders. "I heard—" But before he could make any queries (or worse, accusations), I freed myself from his grasp with a trick he had taught us, and while he was gaping in shock, I grabbed his wrist and pulled him into the kitchen and down the cellar stair.

He didn't resist (which was a good thing, because I would never have been able to drag him) and in minutes, there we were, staring at the tunnel entrance with the rest of the Companions and Lobo and Lady Brianna crowded behind us.

He drew a long breath. "Well," he finally said. "This explains a great deal." Then he turned to Lady Brianna. "Are you prepared to take them in your charge and guard them?"

"I am," she said. "If this is the work of the Dark Fae, then they have violated the Compact and my actions are lawful. If this was done by only the Trolls, they are not and never have been part of the Compact and I may use my powers against them. And I can make sure that we have provisions, should we need them, without burdening us with them."

"Go then," he said steadily. "I'm in no shape for a long trek through that thing. I'll give you a good head start, then tell the King."

And with that, he turned around and left. I sent my light on ahead of us into the tunnel to light the way; and with a deep breath and one hand on my sword, I followed after Lobo, who continued on, nose to the tunnel floor.

Surely there must be an end to this soon. I had been thinking this for the last several hours, and so, I am sure, had the Companions. But the tunnel stretched on before us mile after mile. Trolls are bigger than humans, and a good thing too, or we'd probably have been screaming with claustrophobia. Periodically, we came upon holes in the ceiling from which fresh air gently flowed. How had they done that? I had no idea. Wizards could do something of the sort for mine shafts, but I'd never heard of Trolls doing magic.

Then again, I'd never heard of Trolls *not* doing magic.

We had all started our journey filled with righteous wrath. I can't speak for the others, but after the first couple of miles, I discovered that I couldn't keep "wrath" going. I was running out of anger, and all that was keeping me on my feet was determination. I was tired. I was suffering slightly from the close quarters. I was hungry and thirsty and acutely aware that I should have been asleep hours ago. I hoped the others were handling the confined space and the weariness all right. I worried about Lady Brianna—her wings barely fit in the tunnel, and I couldn't imagine what this was like for a creature who could fly.

After what seemed like an eternity of trudging down an endless tunnel with nothing ahead of me but the little space illuminated by my ball of light, Giles, who was right behind me, tapped me on the shoulder. "Lady Brianna says we need to stop and take a rest and call Lobo back."

I was definitely happy to hear that, although I wished we were taking a break under an open sky. "Lobo!" I called into the darkness that was so black I could barely see the end of Lobo's tail swishing back and forth. "Lady Brianna is calling for a rest!"

The tunnel seemed to swallow up my words, but Lobo turned and padded back toward me as everyone sat down on the oddly smooth surface of the tunnel. Or in my case, I put my back against the tunnel wall and slid down it until I was sprawled on the floor.

Now that we were sitting down, I could see everyone, and it didn't seem quite so claustrophobic. And the next thing I knew, there were chunks of bread being passed up the line, and Giles handed me two, one for me and one for Lobo. Right after that came cheese, hard sausage, then bunches of radishes and carrots; and I realized that I was starving. How long had we been down here?

"Where are you getting that stuff from, Lady Brianna?" asked Rob, sounding astonished. "Are you—"

"Just apporting them from the kitchen cellars and pantry," Brianna said. "Don't worry, they aren't like the Fae food in your stories; they won't vanish and leave you hungry again."

I, for one, was glad to hear that as I crunched into a carrot. I even ate the greens from the radish and the carrot, I was so hungry. And before long, a wine flask filled with water was being passed up the line. I poured some out into my hand, and Lobo politely lapped it up until his thirst was sated. This definitely was a magic flask, since no matter how much water I poured from it, it never emptied.

As I ate, I examined the tunnel. It had a flat floor, lumpy sides, and an arching top, and it looked like the glazed inside of a brick. But this wasn't rock, so we weren't under the palace anymore. Had the Trolls somehow fused the earth into this substance so they wouldn't have to put up supports to keep it from falling in on them? More mysteries.

But as the energy I'd started this journey on ebbed, I was having qualms. I had been thinking about this for the last mile at least. *I* wasn't ready to give up—but it wasn't fair dragging my friends down this never-ending tunnel. And who knew what waited for us? My friends were all slumped over, heads hanging, as they recovered some strength. How many miles had we walked?

"When do we turn back?" I asked reluctantly.

Everyone's head came up.

"*Never!*" Giles said fiercely, before anyone else could speak. "Dammit, Miri, we're Aurora's Companions and we're not going back without her!"

Heads bobbed and everyone began babbling at once, which was unbearably loud in the close confines and caused us to fall silent. I licked my dry lips and said, "I'll take that as we're all in this till the end, then."

"Rest," said Brianna. "There doesn't seem to be anyone pursuing us; either the King doesn't know yet or he cannot spare anyone to go after us. As we have been sitting here, I've been listening to the tunnel behind us, and there has not been a single sound. So take as long as you need to recover and revive, and we will go on."

"Yes," I said, and sagged my own head to get back my energy as quickly as I could. "We'll go on until the end."

CHAPTER SIXTEEN

"There's light ahead!" Lobo called back over his shoulder. "If anyone's waiting there, I'll take them by surprise! Follow!"

His words put new energy in all of us—I was sure that by now we must have walked twenty or thirty miles. I had never walked so much in my life, and I suspect that neither had the others, except maybe Giles. But we all hurried forward now, weapons out, trotting toward that dim circle of light ahead of us that grew bigger and bigger until we stumbled out onto a platform of dirt and gravel just under the crest of an enormous hill. We stood together, baffled, under a midnight sky and a full moon without a Troll in sight.

"Well, that was...anticlimactic," said Rob, speaking for all of us, I suspect. My heart plummeted.

But Lobo's head went up, then down, then up again. "I can still smell the Trolls. Faintly, but the trail is still there."

"Where *are* we?" asked Elle.

"See that peak over there?" Brianna asked her. "That's Mount Torsee. And that one there is Mount Springrel. We're about twenty miles from the palace as the crow flies." She didn't look happy. "There are a dozen old Troll lairs in these mountains. They could have gone to any of them. If they had the forethought to confuse their trail or wade through a stream—"

Lobo snorted. "I'm not that stupid. They can try muddling their trail all they like, but I'll still find them."

I know what we were all thinking. *That will take time, and time is something we may not have.*

What were the Trolls doing with Aurora? How long could a baby live without being fed? Did they have any idea how to feed her? A sick certainty crept over me that whispered, *Time is running out.*

"I'm using the amulet," I said aloud. "And don't try to stop me."

As the others looked at me in confusion, Lady Brianna held up her hand. "Wait. I am not telling you not to—but just wait a moment. I never intended that amulet to transport you more than a hundred feet to the nursery."

"I *should* have used it the moment Melalee screamed!" I replied, thinking that if I had, I certainly could have surprised them in the tunnel.

Then what? What if there had been more than two or three?

"Just wait a moment. Let's make a plan. I can fly; Serulan's cave is not far from here, and he can carry all five of you. Lobo is limited by the fact that we are slower than he is. Wait long enough for me to get Serulan and fly back. Then use the amulet. If it's too far for your strength, nothing will happen and Lobo's tracking. If you transport yourself to Aurora and you can find a place in the lair where you can reach the outside, send up a light to show us where you are. Then Lobo can stay back. I very much doubt even Trolls will want to contend with a fully grown dragon." She bared her teeth, and I was taken aback. I had never seen her war face before. It actually made me step back a pace or two.

"All right," I said. "But hurry."

The words weren't even out of my mouth before she was in the air, leaving us on that gravel platform in a chilly breeze.

"What amulet?" Giles asked, and I had to explain what Brianna and I had made. And all the while, the moon crawled by overhead, and time seemed to be passing too quickly and not quickly enough all at once. Too quickly because it was night and Trolls could not bear the daylight. If they were still moving, they were getting farther away from me at every moment. And not quickly enough because Lady Brianna still hadn't returned with Serulan.

We'd long since taken to sitting down and huddling together in a group to keep warm when Brianna and the dragon came winging down out of the night sky. Armor and the padding under it seems horribly warm when you are fighting in it, but when you are sitting still, a cold breeze finds every single quilted seam.

I jumped to my feet as Serulan made a four-footed landing on the side of the hill next to our platform. "I'm going!" I said, before anyone could say anything; I unsheathed my sword, called my little light ball to hover over my head (though I had no idea if it could follow me or not), and grasped the locket with my left hand and triggered the spell.

I knew it had worked only because I was suddenly plunged

into inky darkness. I quickly conjured another light, a dimmer one this time.

And from somewhere near my feet, Aurora made a disgusted noise. I looked down, and there she was, nestled in furs in a knee-high stone cradle, her face screwed up in protest at the light.

I snatched her up in my left arm; she blinked at the light over my head, then her eyes focused on me and her little face lit up with a sunny smile. "Ah-glibble!" she said with delight, and grabbed for my chin.

I nearly burst into tears.

I took a quick look around. We were in a round stone chamber with an oval wooden door in it. Piles of dry moss and nappies of thin leather proved that the Trolls were aware the baby needed changing, and they were supplying the closest thing they had to cloth nappies. And then I froze as I heard voices outside the chamber.

My heart in my mouth, I quickly extinguished the light and moved to the side of the door where the hinges were.

"I don't *care*, Father! It's not right." The voice sounded high and gravelly at the same time. "You've done something horrible. When has anyone ever been able to trust the Dark Fae? And now you've gone and kidnapped a daywalker baby princess, and if the daywalkers didn't hate us before, they certainly do now!"

There came the sound of another voice, much deeper and sounding so much like rocks tumbling together that I couldn't actually make out the words.

"I'm telling you, it's not *right*," the younger voice replied stubbornly. "Someone is going to pay for this—and it's probably going to be us!"

I heard the door latch being lifted and realized at that moment that I had made a critical mistake. I'd picked up Aurora and I couldn't put her down. She'd cry. But I couldn't put the sword down, either.

So I edged closer to the door. There was only one thing that might work. But it was going to depend on my being between the Troll I'd heard coming in and the door. My heart thudded like the hooves of a galloping horse, the back of my neck was cold with sweat, and my insides were in a ball. Everything seemed very sharp and clear and focused even if I couldn't see anything.

The door opened inward, and I stood behind it. Light didn't so much pour into the room as drift in—whatever the Troll was using to light his way, it was dim. Feet shuffled into the room.

I saw a bulky shadow with a dimly glowing globe dangling from one hand. It came right up to the furs heaped in the middle of the improvised cradle. "It's me, Baby," said the young voice. "I'm here to see if you need anything. I'm so sorry—"

I kicked the door closed, made the brightest light I could conjure flare into life over my head, and pointed my sword at the creature who had cried out in pain at the appearance of the light and stumbled away from it. "Be still!" I quietly snarled, not wanting to attract any more attention than I had to. And at the moment, what little plan I had relied on having a hostage.

No one in Tirendell had seen a Troll in generations, and the descriptions in books varied wildly. In fact, the only common assertions about Trolls were that they were monstrous, hulking creatures who (possibly) feasted on human flesh, dressed in stinking skins, and (definitely) could not bear the light of the sun. But what cowered away from the light in front of me was not all that impressive.

Although he looked a little like a rough sculpture of a human being made out of smoothed rock, he wasn't much taller or bulkier than I was. He was wearing a rather nicely made sleeveless leather tunic and trews that wouldn't have been out of place on a hunter or blacksmith. He was hairless and bald, and the color of his skin was the same pale gray as the unweathered rock here in this cave. His huge eyes, which took up a good quarter of his face, were a pale blue. He shaded his eyes with his hands and still had to squint to look at me. And he hadn't let go of the lantern, whose feeble light was nothing compared with the bright orb above my head.

He didn't seem to be armed. In fact, it looked as if he had come to do what he'd said when he'd entered—check on Aurora to see if she was all right.

He was half-frozen with fear and cowering away from me, and I was almost as terrified as he was as I stood with my sword pointed at him and Aurora in my left arm. And we might have stood there forever like that, but he finally must have decided to try to placate me. He straightened and whispered, "Look—"

But that had given me another chance to act and put myself in a better position to control the situation. The moment he made a tentative step away from me, while his mind was focused on putting distance between us rather than on me, I moved. Just as Sir Delacar had taught me, I whirled on him, and when I stopped moving again, I was behind him. He was now a shield between me and anything that might come in through the door, and the edge of my sword nearest the hilt was at his throat. I'd have preferred a knife, but beggars and all that.

My heart was pounding so hard that it felt as if I had been running for a solid hour. But somehow I kept my hands from shaking.

Aurora was finding all this highly entertaining. "Gribble!" she said, and laughed.

"Don't move," I warned him. "Don't even think about moving."

"I won't!" he said in a strangled voice.

Now that I was in a more superior position, I had to come up with a plan, and the best one I could manage at the moment was to wait until someone else came through that door, make it clear that I had this fellow hostage, and make my demands. Or—wait, better still, make him lead me to the outside, where I could signal Serulan. Of course, how well that worked would depend on who this Troll was.

"Who are you?" I whispered fiercely.

He gulped. "Kol. Prince Kol. What—"

"I'll be the one asking the questions here!" I snapped in a harsh whisper, then I bumped his chin with the hilt. "Where is this?"

"I don't know!" And when I moved the sword closer to his neck, he said, "I don't know what you daywalkers call it!"

Well, that made sense even if it didn't help me. "How far is this place from where that tunnel you Trolls dug to the palace comes out?"

"I don't know that, either!" he said, choking his words off with a sob. "I'm sorry! I didn't go on that trek!"

"Well, you're not much use, are you?" I didn't mean that, of course. He was a *lot* of use. If he really was a prince, he was a terrific bargaining chip. "What are you doing with my baby sister?"

I felt a tear splash down on my hand, and if I hadn't been vibrating between fear and anger, I would have let him go right then and there. "I was taking care of her! Honest! I've been making sure she stays dry and clean and fed! Oh, I *told* Father this was going to happen! I *told* him he couldn't get away with this, that the daywalkers would come and..." Then he stopped, as if he'd just realized something. "Baby is your *sister*? You're a daywalker princess? Oh, Kreblin, now what are we going to do? You're bringing an army, aren't you? You're going to kill us all, aren't you? I mean, really murder us all! Please don't kill us! Please—"

"*Shut up!*" The babbling was getting on my nerves. He sounded like Serulan all over again—wait. "Let's try something simple. Why did you steal Aurora?"

"To keep you from killing us when we moved here! Oh, I *told* Father we shouldn't have listened to that Dark Fae. I *told* him this was a terrible idea! I—"

"Shut it," I said, cutting him off—metaphorically, that is. "Why would you think that humans would kill you when you moved here?"

"Because the histories say that you always kill Trolls." He was so sincere that I couldn't doubt that he believed it. "As soon as you daywalkers find Trolls under your land, you come down into our tunnels and fill them full of fire and drive us up to the surface and the Daystar. And then we die. That's why this cave was deserted, because you daywalkers killed everyone in it."

I'd have liked to dispute that—except the only references I had found to Trolls in Tirendell talked about how the Trolls had appeared in the night and terrorized everyone until the King sent an army to destroy them. So the part about "you daywalkers killed everyone" was right.

And what if they hadn't meant to frighten people?

"So why did you come here if you thought you were going to be murdered?"

"The Dark Fae told us what to do. He said to take the baby Princess and marry her to me, then the King would be forced to talk to us and protect us." He shook his head slightly. "I told Father that this wouldn't work! I told him that it would only make you daywalkers angrier! But the Dark Fae made him think that this was the only way...." He began crying again, and more hot tears splashed down on my hand, and it was at that point that I realized that although this Troll might *look* like he was an adult, or near to it, he couldn't be much older than the equivalent of ten.

"Stop crying, Prince Kol," I told him sternly. I was worried that someone would hear him if he cried himself into hysterics. "You are a prince of the Trolls. Remember yourself."

He gulped down a breath, sniffed loudly, and did as I asked. I lowered my sword hand a little—just enough so he could see it because I wasn't taking any chances just yet. "Do you want to keep the daywalkers from murdering your entire tribe?" I asked. "Do you want to keep living here in peace with us?"

"Y-yes?" he said, as if he didn't believe what he was hearing. And I thanked the Infinite Light that I was dealing with a child because I probably could not have come to reason this fast with an adult.

"I want you to guide me to the outside now. I am going to summon my friends. And after we have gone, you are to go to your father, tell him what happened, then I want all of you to leave this kingdom and never come back." There. That should take care of everything. Aurora would be rescued and the Trolls would be gone and no one would get a hot head and lead a mob here to slaughter them.

The young Troll's face twisted up as if he was about to cry again. "But…we can't. We can't go back! It's gone."

"What do you mean, 'gone'?" I asked sharply.

"Just that. It's all gone. We bored too many tunnels, and it all caved in. We have nowhere to go, and the Daystar will kill us." Now he really started to cry, and Aurora started to wail in sympathy, and that was when everything got out of hand.

"*Prince Kol! Prince Kol! Are you all right?*" There was shouting on the other side of the door, and before Kol could say anything, something huge kicked the door right off its hinges and loomed in the doorframe.

All I got a chance to see was something twice the height of a human that looked like a pile of rocks dressed in leather and carrying a sword as long as I am tall in one hand and a club in the other.

I made the light above me flare to daylight brightness. Aurora screeched. Kol, bless his little heart, flung himself in front of us, shouting, "*Don't hurt them!*"

The thing in the door cried out and retreated. I got poor Kol in my shadow and that of the stone crib—after only moments of direct exposure to the light, his skin had started to look… wrong.

Then the brute at the door was shoved aside by an even bigger hulk. "KOL!" the creature cried in anguish. "*You monster! He's only a child! Let him go!*"

I didn't even think; I just reached up with my will and both my Fae and my human magic and dimmed the light down to the level of moonlight, and I put one arm around Kol. The sudden dimming of the light baffled the Trolls and stopped them in their tracks even though they were still more than half-blinded.

And the sword in my hand flared up with what looked like white fire along its edges.

"We need to talk. You want to talk about children? *You kidnapped a baby!*"

The two creatures at the door stared at me as if I were a terrible beast. But a beast that had suddenly opened its mouth and emitted sanity and sense instead of a roar of rage.

"You *stole my baby sister*! How did you *ever* expect that to end well? It wouldn't matter one bit if you'd married her to your son! As soon as the King found out where you were and where *she* was, he *would* have come in here with armored knights and oil and torches and *dragons* and burned you out and chased you into the sunlight! You're just lucky that I found her rather than one of his warriors or some mercenary!"

At that point, Aurora emerged from her shocked silence and began to wail.

"And if that weren't bad enough, you're making her cry!" I said crossly and irrationally. I looked at Kol. He'd earned my trust. He'd told me everything he could. And *he* was the one I'd heard telling his father how bad an idea kidnapping Aurora had been. "Can you...?"

He nodded eagerly and held out his hands for her. I transferred her to him with one hand and turned my attention back to his father and whatever thing was with the Troll King. Kol jounced and soothed Aurora as well as Melalee could have.

"And you listened to a Dark Fae for advice. A *Dark Fae*!

What were you *thinking*?" I pulled myself up to my full height and tried to act like Mama in a full scold. She didn't give out scoldings often, but when she did, they were *epic*. And I was more than angry enough to half forget that I was yelling at two monsters whose arms alone probably weighed twice as much as I did. "Have you been living under a rock? Don't you know that they feed on pain and fear?" I realized just after I said that how ridiculous it was because, of course, they were actually living under rocks. But I kept on going. "What could you possibly have expected from them except advice that would manufacture the most pain and fear possible? What is *wrong* with you?"

It looked like I was having an effect, and a profound one at that. The guard who had first broken in looked stunned. But the one I thought was Kol's father was actually hanging his head and clasping his hands in front of him like a boy who has been caught doing something wrong that he is deeply ashamed of.

I took a deep breath, still concentrating on what Mama would have said, while watching Kol and Aurora the whole time out of the corner of my eye. I must have gone on for at least ten minutes, and all that time, the Troll King was shrinking into himself. Finally, I moved on. "And if it hadn't been for your son, *who has three times the sense of his father*, I might well have burned and cut my way through your ranks until we escaped, *then* brought the King and his knights straight here! *Fortunately* for all of us, Kol is a decent, smart, fine young Troll whom I would be proud to have as a friend, and he has persuaded me that every single bit of this has been one centuries-long horrible mistake. And that we, you Trolls and we daywalkers, finally have a chance to set things right!"

Now the Troll King looked as puzzled as a rock could possibly look. "Wait—what?"

"I said that I'm prepared to sort all this out on my father's behalf so we can live in peace with one another. But first I want you to take me to the surface so I can signal my friends. Then I want Brianna Firehawk to fly my sister back to my family before my poor mother pines herself to death, which would only bring knights and fire and all the rest of it no matter what we do. Think of it as a gesture of good faith."

"Fine!" the Troll King said hurriedly.

"No," Kol interjected. "Not yet." And suddenly there was a very unpleasant smell emitting from my sister. Kol competently changed what passed for a diaper right then and there. He took the soiled moss bundled in the used leather and thrust it at the Troll guard. "Take that to the anthill for cleaning," he ordered, and the befuddled guard took it gingerly between the tips of his thumb and index finger, and carried it out at arm's length.

"*Now* you can take her," Kol said, handing my sister back to me. "I'll show you the way out."

For creatures who had been described only in vague but terrifying terms, the Trolls were proving to be anything but terrifying. With Kol leading the way, the King following, and me stomping along as impressively as I could, glowing sword in one hand and baby in the other, the most I saw of the rest of the Trolls in this lair was the glitter of curious or frightened eyes in the shadows of side tunnels.

Then we stopped at what seemed to be a dead end. The sword flared for a moment in reaction to my surge of fear that I'd been betrayed—but then Kol did something to the wall, and the stone at the end of the dead end slid aside. We walked out onto a huge ledge that overlooked a heavily wooded valley.

I sent my light high up into the air and turned it into a little sun again. "Get back into the tunnel," I told Kol and his father. "Just in case."

Then it was just a matter of waiting—and I hoped that it wouldn't be long because, judging by the stars, it couldn't be long till false dawn.

I'd never seen Serulan in flight before. Not in full flight, that is. It was amazing. He powered along with Brianna at his side, he all silvery blue in the moonlight, she like a phoenix flaming beside him, and my friends hardly noticeable on his back.

Serulan landed with a great show of claws and a gout of flame for good measure. "Where are they?" he demanded as Brianna landed beside him, looking just as impressive as he did, with her wings all fire and flame engulfing the sword in her hand.

Before anyone could look in the tunnel mouth and spot the Trolls huddling inside, I shouted, "*Wait!*"

To my surprise, my voice thundered as if I were a giant, and I felt a brief surge of the magic that had amplified it without my intending any such thing. It was a good thing I had, though, because everyone, even Brianna, froze and stared at me.

"There's a whole lot going on that needs explaining," I said in a more normal tone of voice. "I'll try to make it short."

It didn't take as long as I thought it would to explain everything. Halfway through, with Aurora dozing in my arm, I gestured to the Trolls to come out. They did, with the King keeping his arm protectively around his son, and both of them stood there quietly while I finished the explanation.

"Here," I said, handing Aurora to Brianna. "Can you take her back to the palace and be...diplomatic?"

Brianna had long since let her fires go out and put her sword away. She took Aurora from me; the baby didn't even wake up. "I'll do what I can. It's not as far as I feared. I'll be back." And she lofted into the sky.

That left Serulan, the Companions, and me with the Troll King. He and I looked at each other in silence for a long time. Finally, he spoke. "You remind me a lot of my wife." His strange voice sounded a bit like rocks sliding over one another.

"I hope that's a good thing," I replied.

He chuckled—at least I think that was what the sound was—and rubbed the back of his head with one hand. "You remind me of her when I have been very stupid. And I have been very stupid. Please come with me to a more comfortable chamber before the Daystar rises." Then he hesitated. "Would your fellow warriors like to come as well?"

I turned to them and saw that all of them were showing signs that the night had gone on for *far* too long. Nat and Elle were yawning. "Stay or go?" I asked.

"We *should* stay to back you up," Giles said uncertainly.

"Actually, you *should* go back to guard Aurora in case that Dark Fae the Troll Prince told me about has been watching all this and takes the opportunity to strike again. Your first duty is to her."

"We'll go back," Serulan said firmly, and blew a gout of

flame into the air. "And I will sit on the top of one of the towers to discourage any such notion."

"That's an excellent plan." And I watched them depart before turning back to the Troll King.

"I would be happy to accept your hospitality," I said with great formality.

I was pretty sure that his definition of comfort and mine were a great deal different, but that wasn't what mattered. What mattered was getting all of this well sorted out before King met King and it all became official.

The tunnel—or corridor, as it was much more finished than the tunnel into the palace—was wide enough for two Trolls to pass without brushing shoulders and very dimly lit by metal baskets full of a glowing fungus hung high up near the ceiling. He hadn't taken me far, no more than a hundred feet away, before he opened the door of another chamber just off the corridor and waved at me to precede him inside.

It wasn't what I would have called comfortable, since the furnishings were crude and minimal and completely unpadded, but at least there were stools I could sit down on. My feet were killing me after that long walk. The Troll King sat down across from me and pounded with his fist on the table between us. When another Troll appeared, he said, "Drink...?" and looked at me.

"Water is fine," I said, not knowing what they would drink besides water. But a stone pitcher and two stone cups appeared, and the cold water tasted like it had come from a very deep well. I drank it greedily, and he poured me a second cup while looking at me as if he wanted to start a conversation and didn't quite know how to do so.

"Why did your old home collapse?" I asked. "And did all your people come here?"

"We ate it; we ate at the mountain until the walls that were left could no longer bear the weight of the earth on top of them. We eat rock and goat milk and cheese and sometimes goat meat, and we flavor the rock with wild things we pick in the forest late at night. There was just enough left of the mountain after the collapse to act as a minimal shelter—I suppose it would be like a camp in the forest for you daywalkers. Half of my people are still there, including my wife, the Queen."

"But why come here?"

"First I must explain why we left," he said solemnly. In that moment, I got the impression that Trolls were very deliberate— and literal—about what they said. And *anything* he told me was going to include a lot of explanation before he got to the answer to a question. "We had abandoned this place as unsafe in the before times when my father's father was King. One day some of our goats went missing from the herd so we searched for them and found them penned beside some wooden houses that had sprung up in the valley when we were not looking. We took them back, and daywalkers came spilling out of houses waving torches and weapons."

"I can guess the rest. But why come back when you knew it was dangerous?"

"We can eat only certain kinds of rock." He shrugged. "That kind of rock is here in abundance. And when our mountain fell, the Dark Fae told us how to make the ruler of this place protect us."

I snorted, and he hung his head. "Yes, I know," he said contritely. "I was very stupid."

"Well, I would like to suggest two things immediately. One, that when Lady Brianna returns, you swear to be an ally of the Light Fae and uphold the Fae Compact. And two, that I take you and a *very* few of your retinue to my papa, the King. I will explain about your situation, then you and he should talk until you have made amends and worked out a treaty between you. So tell me more."

It seemed that Trolls liked to tell stories. I heard plenty of them from the "before times." I learned all about why Trolls eat only certain kinds of rock (nothing that contains metal or gemstones) and how they also became goat herders. My impression about Trolls being storytellers was proving to be correct as the Troll King seemed willing to talk forever—and I was willing to listen for as long as it took Lady Brianna to return. In fact, it took her so long that I had a nap in a heap of moss and the Troll King ordered a meal of soft cheese for both of us. He spread his on rocks and ate them while I pulled pieces off with my fingers until Brianna finally appeared with young Kol, who pounced on the remains of the meal and gobbled it up without shame.

"I stayed long enough to summon Domna and Bianca, and left them to calm down your papa," she said. "Let's go."

It was just going dark again when we left, or otherwise we would have had to wait longer because the Trolls obviously couldn't travel by day. The Trolls moved much faster than I had thought they could—at least as fast as our horses. While Brianna flew, I rode on the shoulder of the Troll King at his invitation. Although he was a bit uncomfortable to sit on, it wasn't dull at all. He and

I and Brianna kept up a rather lively conversation off and on for the entire trip.

"My poor friends," I said sadly. "So dissatisfying for them. To have gone all that way in the dark only to hear, 'Oh, everything is all right, you can go home now.'"

"Better that than to find themselves in great peril, King's Daughter," the Troll King said. "You are all young now. You do not think of these things. When you have children of your own, you will."

I didn't contradict him. *I* had certainly thought of those things. In part, that was why I had gone on alone, hoping I could get Aurora out before the Trolls noticed. I hadn't wanted to *lead* my friends into peril, and I also understood why Papa had reacted the way he had.

So I held my tongue and listened carefully while the Troll King and Brianna discussed the best way to approach the palace since we would probably be met by half the fighters in the kingdom regardless of how well Bianca and Domna had done their job of calming Papa down.

I spoke up when there was a lull in the conversation. "The best thing, I think, is to go to the Abbey of Everon. The Abbess will listen to reason, the abbey chapel is big enough to hold Trolls, you'll be out of the sun when it comes up, and you'll be on sacred ground. Not even Papa at his angriest is going to send armed men into a chapel of the Infinite Light."

Brianna almost stopped flying, she was so astonished. But I'd been thinking about it the whole time they'd been talking, and that was the closest thing I could think of to safe, neutral ground for the first meeting. "That's an excellent idea, Miri," she said after a moment. "In fact, I can't think of a better one."

CHAPTER SEVENTEEN

BRIANNA FLEW AHEAD TO CONSULT WITH THE ABBESS. THE abbey was conveniently located outside the city walls, so we could go straight there, and since Papa had no idea that we were going there, we managed to avoid anyone sent to intercept us. I was hoping that he had no idea how fast the Trolls could travel and would be caught off guard by how quickly we got there, and it appeared that my hopes were going to be fulfilled.

The Abbess met us at the gate of the abbey with a smile on her face and wearing her best snow-white habit just as the sky started to lighten with false dawn. Brianna was with her and apparently had arranged everything with a minimum of difficulty. I had been dreading having to make another long explanation and convincing argument, but the Abbess had nothing for us but a greeting.

"Come in, my poor dear," she said to me, looking up at me on the Troll King's shoulder. "Everything is in readiness. Your Majesty, you can set her down; you are all safe in the sanctuary of the Infinite Light." The Troll King examined her but seemed to like what he saw and carefully helped me down off his shoulder. "Come, now, all of you. The dawn will soon be here."

The Trolls and I followed her to the chapel, a large but plainly built structure to the right of the abbey itself. When we got inside, we found that the pews had been cleared to one side to make room for the Trolls, and there was goat cheese and bread and water waiting for us.

I ate and dozed a little in a corner of the chapel on one of the pews and half listened to the Abbess and the Troll King talk while we waited for Papa. But before I fell asleep in spite of my efforts to stay awake, I got a welcome surprise.

Not long after dawn, my friends arrived, led by Sir Delacar! We all picked up a couple of pews and moved them as far from the Trolls and the entranced Abbess as we could to avoid disturbing her. Then we put our heads together for our own conversation.

They wanted to hear everything, of course, and marveled at the six Trolls sitting calmly in the middle of the chapel while they related their history to the fascinated Abbess. She'd had all the windows in the chapel covered, so we all sat in a quiet gloom that was strangely peaceful.

"How badly in trouble are we?" I asked when their curiosity was satisfied.

Sir Delacar shrugged. "I have no idea. Lady Brianna flew in with the baby, the entire palace was thrown into a turmoil, and Aurora's other godmothers arrived and were closeted with the King and Queen while Brianna flew off again. Since I wasn't wanted, I went back to the tunnel entrance—I still hadn't told the King that you were gone. The dragon left the Companions out of sight of the palace, and they slipped back into the palace without being noticed amidst the fuss; Giles figured that I would be at the tunnel and came to get me. Serulan perched on Gerrold's tower, and I suppose that people assumed that Brianna had got him to come. I got the Companions fed in the kitchen, and we waited at the training yard until Lady Brianna returned and told us where you would be." He cast a glance at the enormous Trolls. "I am glad things turned out as they did. I would not like to see any of our men fighting those creatures."

I would have said something about their being surprisingly peaceful, but that was when a ruckus outside heralded the arrival of the King. The Trolls started to stand, but the Abbess motioned them to sit. "You are under my protection now," she said, showing a stern side I hadn't seen before. "Wait here. If I bring in the King, *then* rise."

She was gone for longer than I expected but less than I feared. And when she entered again, it was with Papa and only five guards—exactly as many as the Troll King had. The Trolls all rose to their feet. Papa and his men stopped and stared at them. I couldn't see the knights' faces under their helmets, but Papa's was a stony mask as unreadable as the Troll King's face.

"King Karlson of Tirendell, this is King Grun of Under-Tirendell." But before the Abbess could say anything more, the Troll King went down on one knee and bowed his head to Papa.

"King Karlson, I have been very foolish. The King's Daughter Miriam has told me exactly how foolish I have been. I did a terrible thing, a thing I would not have taken kindly had it been done to me. If you will forgive my people for actions that were only my own, you may order me into the light of the Daystar, where I will die and the Queen and my son will be bound by your wishes. Only let my people return to the mountain where my father's father's fathers once lived and live under Tirendell in peace with your people."

Our jaws dropped. The Abbess was too clever to show her reaction, as was Papa, but I will swear to it that this was not what any of them had expected the Troll King to say and do.

And now Papa was faced with a dilemma. He could have his revenge if he was willing to throw over all his oaths as King and a knight, and destroy someone who had surrendered and was at his mercy.

I saw him waver for a moment, and I didn't blame him one bit. But he would not have been the papa I loved if he had chosen revenge instead of honor.

"And perpetuate a cycle of madness that should have ended centuries ago?" he replied, a little hoarse with emotion. "I think not, Grun. Are you willing to swear to be my vassal, and take me as your liege and High King?"

"If this means you are to be my king as I am king over my people, then yes," Grun replied sensibly. "And we will pay you tribute with the things we cannot eat, the metals and the teeth-breaking stones that the Dwarves love so much."

I hadn't expected that, either, and neither had Papa. He turned around and looked at his men. "Justyn, go back to the palace and tell the Queen that everything is well and that I am going to be here a while." Then he turned to the Abbess. "If I may abuse your hospitality further, could we have a table, some chairs, and a scribe? We're going to need a treaty, I think."

The Abbess smiled like a satisfied cat. "Certainly, Your Majesty," she purred. "I'd be delighted." She glided away, not looking as if she was in a hurry but somehow moving very quickly indeed.

"You have a fine daughter, King," the Troll King rumbled as Papa caught sight of the Companions and me standing at the side. "She is brave, and loyal, and kind. And she is more sensible than I am."

"Than many people, it would seem," Papa murmured, as if to himself although I heard him. "Miri, you and the Companions can go back and get some rest now, I think. Treaties take a long time to draw up, and Brianna and Domna will soon be here to advise me. Your mother needs to see you with her own eyes."

"Yes, sir!" I said promptly and obediently. Truth to tell, I had been out of my depth after scolding the Troll King and I felt as if I was floundering now. I certainly didn't think I could stay awake during a long and boring negotiation, much less be of any use whatsoever in it. I made the proper bow, the Companions and Sir Delacar did the same, and we got ourselves out of there.

At that point, things blurred a bit. I do remember getting back to the palace because we actually got *cheered* by the people waiting for our arrival. One of them was Mama, who was holding Aurora, and while she didn't go all to pieces by crying and carrying on, there was some unroyal hugging and kissing going on, and her eyes glistened wetly. After that, I barely remember taking off my sword and tunic with help from Elle and Anna and nothing at all after that.

I didn't even dream.

*　　*　　*

I came awake all at once, and a servant girl who had evidently been left in my room to wait for me to wake up jumped up off the stool she'd been sitting on and ran off. It was dark outside, but there was plenty of distant noise that let me know that most of the palace was still awake and active.

Elle and Anna came in as I was knuckling the sleep sand out of my eyes. "What's going on?" I asked.

"A big feast to celebrate the treaty with the Trolls," Elle replied promptly. "They agreed to swear to uphold the Fae Compact and to make an alliance with the Light Fae. If you want to come down, we were told to tell you that your place has been set, but if you're too tired…"

"Are the Trolls there?" I asked.

"Yes, and that's why it's being held out in the garden." Anna giggled. "They'd never fit in the Great Hall. The cook is beside himself. He's never had to serve rocks before."

I smiled at that. I could imagine. "I should go down." I paused a moment. "How is the King treating you?"

"As if he'd never been angry at us," said Anna, sighing with relief. "We could have been in *so* much trouble."

"He could have ordered all of you back to your parents' estates and me to mine." My relief was as great as hers. "We'd have effectively been banished. We might just have a lot to thank King Grun for. Although I am not sure he'd understand why I was thanking him." I got out of bed, groaning a little at my sore muscles. I *never* wanted to go on a walk that long again. My feet still ached. "Let's go. Help me pick out something to wear; I'm still a bit muddled, and I can't think about gowns at all."

In the end, they brought out my christening gown, which was probably a good choice given that this was what I'd been wearing when I first defended Aurora. It felt as if I were wearing good luck. They made my hair as tidy as it could be, splashed a little rose water on me, and judged me presentable.

When we got down to the garden, the first thing I noticed was that there were effectively *two* High Tables: the normal one, which had been carried out here, and a second one tall enough to serve the Trolls although they still had to sit on the ground rather than on benches or chairs. The second one was covered in some of the painted canvas banners we hung on the outside of the palace when there were tourneys. The effect was quite festive, especially in the light of torches. The table (without a doubt knocked up out of rough boards as quickly as possible) looked just as nice as the humans' High Table thanks to its decorations.

The three of us came up the aisle between all the other tables that had been set out for the feast and made our bows to Papa and Mama. When I straightened up, I was overjoyed to see Mama looking as if the entire ordeal of the last few days had been nothing more than a nightmare.

But there wasn't a place for me beside them.

"Miriam," Papa said, before I could say anything. "We were hoping you'd join us. Since King Grun and his retinue cannot fit at our table, would you do us the honor of representing Tirendell at his?"

"I would *love* to," I said warmly, and sure enough, there was a human-size space waiting next to Grun.

The arrangements were actually pretty comical. Some of the stairs used for the tournament galleries had been set up around the big table. It was the only way the servers could reach it, and there were bushel baskets of rocks arranged alongside it. Rather than bring me the selections of food one by one, my personal server arranged a plate with what he thought I'd like and brought it to me. I wished they'd do that all the time.

I noticed that the Trolls were looking a bit mournfully at the current selection of fruits, whole chickens, and bread before them. "What's wrong?" I whispered to Grun.

"Too sweet," he whispered back. "Too soft. Makes teeth ache." I blinked for a moment, then realized exactly what was wrong. I caught the attention of my server and gave him orders. Three servers hurried to our table, took everything away but the rocks, and came back with what would otherwise have been an insult—burned bread and bread so old and hard that you could hammer nails with it, unripe fruit and chickens burned black on the outside, the ends of roasts that had gotten charred and anything hard, bitter, or sour. The Trolls tried these "delicacies" dubiously, then their faces lit up, and they stopped picking at their food and set into it with gusto.

Grun and I and the Troll on the other side of me had a lovely feast after that. When the dessert course came, the cook had finally managed to figure out how to make something for them; rocks in vinegar and soured milk with cherry stones. The Trolls were thrilled. I mostly listened while Grun told me more about his people in his slow, deliberate way. I wished that the others could have shared the table with us; it was like having an odd sort of bard with us.

In return, I told him about us. He was utterly horrified when I told him that I was fairly sure that the Dark Fae had assumed that Aurora would die under his care and that this was why the Dark Fae had tricked him into taking her.

"Or if that didn't happen, he'd have probably cursed her himself so you would take the blame if we rescued her," I said.

He nodded, and his voice took on a dark and dangerous quality when he replied. "That may be why we found him lurking about. Troll caves are mazes, though. He never came near her. The third time we found him, we made it clear that the next time he was found, he would be *thrown* out. And that we would not be careful about where we threw him. In less than a night, she had become very dear to us."

I felt a cold chill for a moment when he said that. Another near miss.

But it was also a sign that the blessings of her Fae godmothers were keeping her safe. *You shall give and receive love in equal measure and be beloved and loving for all the days of your life.* And *When all seems darkest, the Infinite Light shall always find thee, friends will appear unlooked for...*

And *that* was when I realized why she was important to the Dark Fae.

She was only a baby and yet look what she had done! She had managed to bring peace between Trolls and the humans of Tirendell! Because of her, the Trolls had sworn to the Fae Compact! If her simply *being* here had brought all that about, what more could we expect when she became an adult?

Grun broke into my astonished thoughts with words that confirmed everything I had just realized. "I wish that it were possible for her to stay with us some of the time. I know that Kol will miss her laugh and her sweet face."

"Well," I said thoughtfully. "We've got a problem that I think we can solve. You cut that tunnel right into our kitchen cellars, and I'm not sure it would be safe to collapse it. But what if you got permission from the King to excavate out *more* space along it and put your embassy there? You'd be the guard on that tunnel for us. You and Kol could make state visits that way. And when she's old enough to walk about on her own, Aurora can visit with you."

I knew exactly what Melalee would think about *that* idea, but it wasn't going to come from me, it would come from Grun by way of Papa. And I was pretty sure that Papa would agree to it. It looked as if King Grun, the three Fae godmothers, and the Abbess had brought him around to looking on the Trolls the way I did: like they were very odd overgrown Dwarves in a way—better, really. The one or two Dwarves I had met were very grumpy sorts and easily angered. Trolls were certainly not the baby-eaters we'd been brought up to think they were.

Great heavens, I wonder what sort of magic Aurora could work on Dwarves.

As I looked at the happy faces around me, I realized that *this* was the sort of christening feast Aurora should have had—not that she was old enough to notice or care, of course, but Papa and Mama certainly were.

That was when I proposed something else to Grun, and he stood up, held up his hogshead of spring water, and instantly commanded silence and attention.

"A toast," he said, in a voice like distant thunder. "To the beautiful little King's Daughter Aurora. Although it be through an avalanche of misfortune, she has brought us together, we love her as you do, and we will serve her until the mountains crumble to dust."

Well, that was a toast everyone could raise a glass to, and Papa looked as if he couldn't be happier.

When the food was cleared away, the entertainment began. It was only the household musicians and Papa's jester, plus several of the courtiers who were decent amateurs, and not the procession of acrobats, dancers, and musicians that had been here for the christening, but it was nice. And at least half of the entertainment came from watching the Trolls, who had never seen anything like this. They laughed at all the jokes, even the ones that were probably from the "before times." They listened attentively to and applauded all the music. They paid such rapturous attention to the young man who had decided to try to flatter both Papa *and* me by writing an epic poem about the christening that I am sure he was convinced of his own genius right there on the spot.

Finally, people started to drift off, beginning with the oldest of the courtiers, who were feeling the effects of rich food and the late hour. I was expecting the Trolls to not understand, since this was their "daytime," but when the Abbess stood up to take her leave, they all rose as well.

"We shall escort the good lady back to her abbey, where we will spend the day, High King," King Grun said politely. "We will remain there until you are satisfied with all the things we must agree on together. I have an idea I wish to propose." Grun glanced at me to let me know what that idea was. "But that can wait until tomorrow."

Papa stood up and gave them a little regal nod. "Go in the

peace you have helped to shape, King Grun. Rest well and we will meet when you send word."

So there went the Trolls, determined to fend off trouble as they followed the highly amused Abbess—as if any trouble they might have encountered down there in the town would have lingered after one look at them!

Once they left, I quickly ran out of energy, and I could see that the rest of the Companions were feeling the same way. They began to drift off too, and when I caught Elle and Anna casting a meaningful glance at me, I decided that this was a good time to say good night.

But I was intercepted by a servant. "The King would like to see you in his chambers before you seek your bed, my lady."

I closed my eyes for a moment. If this was going to be the confrontation I had hoped to avoid—well, there was no avoiding it. He was the King, and I wasn't even a princess. "Very well," I told the servant. "I will be there shortly."

I collected Anna and Elle, and all three of us appropriated big bunches of grapes from the decorations before we left. I was in no hurry to get upstairs, and they were just as tired as I was, if not more so. The palace was still lit up, but not as much as it would have been if there had been a feast going on in the Great Hall. In fact, the Great Hall was dark except for the few night lanterns going.

We walked slowly and ate grapes. Anna and Elle were too tired even to gossip about the squires. But it was a good silence, the kind that falls between friends and makes you feel closer, not more distant, because you know that what they are thinking is probably what you are thinking. That we all did a job we could be proud of. Relief that it all came out as well as it did. Wonder mingled with amusement about the Trolls, who turned out to be friendly after all.

I parted with them at our rooms and left the remains of my bunch of grapes on the nightstand, then headed straight for the Royal Suite.

Papa was waiting for me in his favorite chair, a lamp beside him, and beckoned to me to come into the light. I stood before him silently, my hands clasped behind my back, wondering if an ax was about to fall.

He studied me for a very long time.

"*Technically*, you didn't disobey my orders," he finally said.

I thought about what I was going to say before I said it. "Perhaps. But I *was* with the Companions."

"But you were not with *just* the Companions. You were also with Lady Brianna. You didn't rush off without a plan. You had a Fae warrior with you. You even had a *dragon* with you. You brought Sir Delacar into your plans and got his approval. There was no time to find me or wait while messengers ran after the fighters who had gone haring off in all directions. You made plans, good solid plans, and when circumstances changed, you thought things through and made new ones rather than acting without thought. You are so much like your father. Inside as well as out. He would not have stood by while a child was in danger. He would have done exactly what you did. And he would have been just as deliberate as you were—that's the part that impresses me the most, Miri. Half or more of my knights would simply have snatched up Aurora and tried to fight their way out of there—and the first victim would have been an unarmed child, the Troll Prince. The next victim would have been peace—for the Trolls would certainly have joined the Dark Fae in a war against us. Miri, I do not often admit this, but I was wrong."

A thrill ran up my back at those words and I straightened up, all fatigue forgotten.

"I should not have acted as I did and taken away your responsibilities. You were correct. And I am putting you all back in charge of Aurora's safety again." He smiled at my gasp of happiness. "And I want you to continue to train as Brianna's apprentice—I would like you to learn everything she can teach you about being a warrior as well as a mage. This is clearly something you were born to do. The least I can do is give you everything you need to do it superbly."

He got up and hugged me and kissed my forehead, then he took my shoulders, turned me around, and gave me a little push.

"Go to bed. Get your rest. By morning, all your young friends will know of my decision—and that I expect you all to get right back to work."

Anna and Elle were waiting up for me in my room. "What did he say?" Anna demanded. But Elle had already read the decision in my expression.

"He's letting us be Aurora's Companions again!" she crowed. Then she and Anna jumped off my bed and seized my hands, and the three of us made a happy little circle dance as quietly as possible to avoid arousing the wrath of Melalee.

We sat on the bed and whispered and chortled, and to be frank, we didn't make much sense because we were light-headed from exhaustion and elation. But exhaustion finally took over,

Anna and Elle went to their room to sleep, and I sat on my bed in the moonlight, not thinking for a very long while.

Finally, I got up again and tiptoed into the nursery. Melalee was asleep in her bed. The maid she had taking the night watch started as she saw me come into the room, but a finger to my lips kept her quiet, and I made my way over to the cradle.

"Who's the fairest in the land, hmm?" I whispered to the sleeping baby. "You are, that's who. And I will always protect you."

And I would. I had the feeling that the Dark Fae were done for now. But there would be another time. Certainly on her thirteenth birthday. And her sixteenth. Possibly even her third or her ninth. Her sixteenth would be the most dangerous time of all; that would be when she came of age, and if what I suspected was true—that she would be able to create allies for us out of the unallied creatures who lived in this kingdom—both the Dark Fae and the external enemies of Tirendell would do their best to stop her.

But by her third birthday, the Companions and I would be old enough to be knights with every bit of training and more. By her ninth, we'd be even stronger.

And by her thirteenth? If I had anything to say about it, she'd have been training with us for two years. By her sixteenth...

I smiled a little. There was no reason why my beautiful baby sister could not grow up to be as fierce as she was lovely. In the right cause, of course.

"And I will always protect you," I repeated as she sighed in her sleep. "No matter what."

MERCEDES LACKEY

is the acclaimed author of over fifty novels and many works of short fiction. In her spare time, she is also a professional lyricist and a licensed wild bird rehabilitator. Mercedes lives in Oklahoma with her husband and frequent collaborator, artist Larry Dixon, and their flock of parrots. She invites you to visit her at mercedeslackey.com or on Twitter @mercedeslackey.